THE SQUEEZE

Orange Hat Publishing
www.orangehatpublishing.com - Waukesha, WI

THE SQUEEZE

Paul Schueller

Orange Hat Publishing
www.orangehatpublishing.com - Waukesha, WI

For information, please contact:

Orange Hat Publishing
www.orangehatpublishing.com
603 N Grand Ave, Waukesha, WI 53186

Edited by Christine Woods
Cover design by Tim Kelly

www.orangehatpublishing.com

To my family—the inspirations who drive my life and decisions.

INTRODUCTION

This is a work of fiction but is based partially on first-hand knowledge and unwitting participation by the author in some fraudulent and corrupt activity in early carbon trading markets. This past reality of inadequate market protections is inconsequential assuming mistakes aren't repeated in future markets.

Any unfathomably unlikely profit associated with this work would go to charitable causes. It's cliché, but writing is its own reward . . . and therapy.

1

Lawyers. Tommy wished he had never met any and knew it would have been far easier to never have dated one. Now he found himself surrounded by them . . . his lawyer and on-and-off girlfriend, Susan Hogan, his business partner John DaFallo's representation, along with attorneys from the U.S. District Attorney's office and the Cook County State Attorney's office.

Tommy leaned over to consult with Susan. "Lawyers suck," he whispered.

"We prefer attorneys, and it's not our fault you're in deep shit," she snapped back.

The stately conference room at Young & Erickson allowed sweeping views, both north over The Loop and east to Grant Park and Lake Michigan. The room was reflective of the firm's powerful reputation in Chicago where the biggest firms and their collective egos sought the top floors of the tallest buildings. The expansive views of the sprawling city mirrored the breadth and depth of power that the firm had achieved over more than 100 years in business. Tommy could no longer afford the high-priced help, but past billings from his first successful business and a little prodding from Susan had resulted in pro bono time to guide him through this legal maze. The room, on this late Friday afternoon, had been the setting of Tommy's personal nightmare as he listened to a variety of Federal and State District Attorneys take turns making accusations and threatening prosecution. They all smelled blood in the water and said virtually the same thing: "Mr. Thomas Gardner, your crimes are egregious, and we intend to pursue this case to the fullest extent possible." Tommy's chest tightened, and he dabbed beads of sweat with his cuff as he listened to the seemingly never ending drone.

Tommy noted that all opposing counsel were younger and better dressed than he was with the notable exception of a physically unkempt man in an equally unkempt suit sitting at the far end of the room. Tommy assumed he'd hear something from him soon, but the procession of attorneys mercifully ended. The U.S. District Attorney then slid a single sheet of paper across the table to Tommy's lead counsel, a rotund senior partner and Susan's boss, Sam Meyers. Sam shouldered his way a bit closer to the conference room table like a walrus positioning for prime rock real estate. He appeared to study the paper intently, although Susan and Tommy figured it might be for effect.

"We will get back to you tomorrow on your offer," Sam stated, but to no one in particular.

The lead attorneys requested that they respond by noon, even though it was Saturday. Everyone just wanted this wrapped up quickly.

Tommy's business partner, John DeFallo, wasn't present. He had taken on the brunt of dismantling their business over the two previous days when Tommy refused to deal with it. That had earned John the relative luxury of being second down this painful path with the hope that he would gain some insight from the process. John's attorney had listened intently all day, racking up sizeable fees without lifting a finger.

He spoke for the first time all day. "May I be copied on that offer, please?"

Given that the offer wasn't for his client, the request was met with a collective eye roll and all of the prosecuting attorneys packed up and filed out after a hard day's work, leaving Tommy with his two attorneys. Susan was thirty, fit, and intense with a long blonde ponytail pulled so tightly that her roots might bleed at any moment. She wore glasses for effect,

2

not need, thinking they countered the blonde stereotype. Her thin nose looked no bigger than a fingertip sticking out past thick, dark-rimmed glasses. She wanted to make partner at a younger age than anyone in the long history of the firm, and dating Tommy fit with her plans. He was funny in his own strange, dry way, had a thick muscular body, and was cute for a guy who was ten years older than she was. She liked that their relationship wasn't serious enough to get in the way of her career. She found most guys her age were starting to look for a commitment.

Susan turned to Sam. "How does the offer look?" she asked bluntly.

"Pretty damn good," he responded with a blank stare pasted across his bloated face. "No jail time. No financial penalty. Just a lifetime ban from any commodities market."

"I'm basically broke other than still having my condo, and I need to make a living. I don't deserve a lifetime ban!" Tommy exclaimed.

"Yeah, you do!" Susan shot back. "Your firm put the carbon trading business on its ass. You set the idea of a cap-and-trade system back five or ten years. Everyone wants you served up on a platter! I mean everyone, from environmental groups to hardcore trading firms and anyone in between. You've pissed them all off and that's hard to do. They don't have many common enemies."

"If it's such a great offer, why are they making it?" Tommy asked Susan.

"Because everyone's embarrassed. Representation from the climate exchanges didn't even show up today. They all let the feds take the lead. No one caught the falsified trades on the exchanges or anywhere else, for that matter."

"So, then I have a chance to win," Tommy inquired eagerly.

"No. If you drag everyone through a trial, they'll go out of their way to bury you," Susan snapped back.

Tommy turned and looked desperately to Sam for his opinion. "She's right, and you're a goddamn moron if you don't take this deal."

Tommy realized how hard it had always been for him to get straight answers from the legal profession. They were great at hedging and pointing out "ifs" and "it depends" while racking up billable hours, but not this time. "I get it. I'll take the deal. I assume that you will have some small edits, and I'll sign tomorrow. So, what happens to my partner?" Tommy said, looking at Susan.

"John will likely get a similar offer. Maybe even better, as all the shit pointed to you. And he'll take it. There are too many people who just want to forget you guys ever existed."

Hated from the right to the left, Tommy thought to himself. *How the hell did that happen?* He had always considered himself a pretty good combination of driven and ethical, maybe even socially responsible. Now he had no business and no money. Tommy said his goodbyes to Sam and Susan and begrudgingly pressed the elevator button to go down. After slumping in the corner, the elevator doors opened, and Tommy struggled out onto Wabash Street and into a gloomy late winter day in Chicago. He headed east a couple of blocks to take a walk in Grant Park. The rain fell so lightly that it didn't make a sound. Tommy's chest felt like it was in a vice. Any defiance had been drained from his body by the attorneys' accusations and the pressure of the day. He thought he would take the time alone to figure out how he ended up so screwed. It probably started when his first business had successfully ended just over two years earlier.

2

The Chicago skyline didn't look any better now that he was a newly minted multimillionaire than it did when he was poor, and his hangover certainly didn't hurt less. Tommy Gardner had sold his first business, a PR firm that concentrated on improving the green and clean image of its clients a couple of weeks earlier. He had enough money to be ecstatic, but he never felt worse. Tommy stopped at a street-side newsstand and stared at his picture on the cover of a local business magazine that had done a piece on the sale of his business. He saw a big nose, oversized ears, and a receding hairline. Tommy could always find the worst in himself and others. The reality was a man of about forty with slightly thinning blonde and gray hair, strong, fit and from outward appearances, aging quite well. His blue eyes darted as he reached in his pocket feeling for his Xanax bottle; a couple of pills might help his outlook on the day. The bottle was empty after doubling up on pills since he sold the business, and he slammed it down onto the sidewalk. He glared at the bottle as it rolled into the gutter, then glanced back at the picture in disgust and headed to the pharmacy for a refill.

It didn't help that there was no one with whom to celebrate his new-found wealth. He thought often about how different and better it would have been if his business partner, Paul Smith, was there to celebrate their mutual success. Paul had been a ten percent owner in the business, but he was more of a partner in the success than that ownership indicated, and

5

he was also a friend. He had either drowned or died of hypothermia in the Chicago River in an accident on a very cold winter night just months earlier. It was part of the reason Tommy sold, as the business just wasn't the same for him without Paul there. Paul's stock had transferred to Tommy upon his death. Paul had no family, so Tommy kept the money, but it never felt right.

He loved Chicago, and now with a little time, thought he'd look at it fresh and see if the city could cheer him up. The best way to do that, he thought, was making random L stops and walking around. He spent most of his adult life on the Red and Brown Line trains and thought that maybe he needed to venture out a bit.

Tommy found that not owning a car was liberating. It was great to get around without having to own something that could break, and it certainly didn't hurt the green business image he had cultivated. He had spent a dozen years helping companies figure out ways to reduce their carbon footprint and clean up their image; it was time for something different. He just didn't know what.

Today he was meeting Susan for lunch at a little café just off the Belmont stop. It was the first day of the year they could sit outside to eat. Spring rains had scrubbed the city clean of the dirt and grime of the receding snow.

Sometimes Tommy wondered if he loved Chicago because it was just as bipolar as he was, with the city and its inhabitants caught in a trap of ironic contrasts. Parks seemingly and simultaneously giving birth to trees as well as monoliths of steel and glass. People so poor they would eat the table scraps of people so rich that their left-overs could feed many. Yet they all shared the same streets and space and time with barely a nod to the twists that may have sent their lives in such dramatically different directions.

Susan, who had helped Tommy close the sale of his business, was wide-eyed, cute and full of energy. She was a fitness freak who bounced more than walked. Tommy always felt like her constant highs helped him deal with his lows. That held true for the most part, and was only a problem the few times when he was "up." Then their energy level clashed . . . too many hormones and brain synapses firing to be easily managed.

"Hi, hun. Are you enjoying your new freedom?" she bubbled.

"Surprisingly, not at all. The rest of Chicago is still working, and I've just been wandering from one L stop to another."

"So you really want me to feel sorry for you?" she teased.

"No. I'll roam Chicago for a few more days and then start figuring out what to do next. Maybe I'll try writing," Tommy responded.

"Do you even know how to write?"

"Sure, everyone does."

"I mean, have you ever written anything? Even a short story?"

"Well, no."

"Oh." Susan was unusually terse.

"Sounds like maybe I need to put a bit more thought into this."

Susan didn't respond, hoping her silence would further drive home the point. As they ordered and ate without speaking, Susan saw the flaw in her logic since Tommy was never troubled by awkward silence. Knowing that she would need to propel the conversation, she asked Tommy, "Can I see you tonight?"

"Sure. You want to meet at my place when you're done with work?"

"I'll see you then." Susan stood, having eaten only half of her turkey wrap, pecked Tommy on the cheek, and motored down the sidewalk back toward the Belmont stop for the Red and Brown Line trains. He watched her for half a block picturing the tattoo across her back, precisely at her bra line, where only an intimate partner would ever know it existed. *Carpe quid est cupio*—Latin for *cease what you want*. It still intimidated him at times.

Tommy spent the rest of the afternoon walking south to the Loop, then back north along the lake, through Boys Town, then finally to his condo a few blocks south of Wrigley Field. He thought a lot about Susan on his walk. They had dated for over a year, but if either of them were really busy, they wouldn't see each other for weeks at a time except to hook up for a couple of drinks and sex. Other than their mutual attraction, the only other connection they had was Tommy counting on Susan to help him deal with a world he wanted to, but couldn't always control.

Most people thought Tommy was engaging enough because he could be charismatic if he tried, but even making eye contact was something that didn't come naturally to him. He understood his flaws and could manage them, and he read people well. This hid his near-continuous monitoring of situations and avoidance of settings that would cause stress or an uncomfortable personal interaction. He preferred conversations that led to a decision, direction, or otherwise had utility to them. Small talk was only tolerated with a few people with whom he had a personal relationship.

In work settings, he would do anything short of faking a seizure to get out of some conversations. Tommy had a running list in his head of fictional or real upcoming appointments, meetings, haircuts, and other things to escape from conversations that were a waste of time. If it was about learning, gaining new experience, or helping others, he had all day. If someone wanted to tell him how often they groom their dog and what he eats, he would pull an excuse from his arsenal and move on. Life was too short to waste it on the trivial; however, to others he conveyed serial impatience more than productive urgency.

Tommy also compulsively controlled any need for public speaking— not easy for a guy who had run a public relations business, working with companies to improve their environmental images. He was fine in small groups around a table, but ten or twenty people staring in his direction unnerved him. Even larger groups were only manageable by popping a propranolol or any other beta blockers that he could get his hands on. Just like with conversation time-wasters, he needed a way to bail out of almost any public situation if he wasn't properly medicated. Each day became a minefield to navigate. He felt so relieved to sell the business and move on that the first night as a non-business owner he had been so relaxed, or drunk, that he had wet his bed.

Tommy was already growing bored. Susan's work schedule and his gut feeling that she could only tolerate his presence two or three times a week left him with lots of free time. The writing idea wasn't likely to go anywhere fast. Pretty naive to think that he could just be a writer, but you have to be naive or crazy to do some of the things that Tommy did. He was both.

His magazine picture from his business sale had led to a few calls and voicemails, mostly from financial planners and insurance salesmen along with a couple from people he knew in passing. The only one he decided to call back was a Chicago area business operator whose name everyone recognized. Tommy listened to the message on his cell phone a second time to get the phone number right. "Hi, this is John DeFallo. I saw your picture and business sale announcement. Congratulations. I have an idea about how you and I may be able to help lead the carbon trading business into the future and maybe make some money in the process. You can reach me at Idea Innovations. The number is 312-555-1212." Tommy was flattered that such a high-profile businessman in the city would call. He returned the call, and they agreed to meet at John's office the next day.

When the elevator door opened to the tenth floor lobby of Idea Innovations, it looked more like an Apple Store than an office. The contrast of the old building's exposed brick and modern furniture looked natural. Tommy announced himself to the receptionist. John emerged quickly, his energy level palpable as they moved toward each other. John looked like he did everything urgently, like he could suck the light out of a nearby candle just by inhaling. He had salt-and-pepper hair combed straight back and gelled, looking more Wall Street than anything else, even before noting the custom fit of his dark suit. What little could be seen of his narrow eyes were hazel and focused. Ears tight to his head and the slicked back hair gave him an aerodynamic look that matched a personality designed to cut through life quickly.

At six feet, Tommy was a couple of inches taller and more physically powerful but had less of a presence than John. John commanded the room, the attention, and Tommy's interest. He looked Tommy right in the eye and said, "Thanks for coming. I have a proposition for you today. Let's sit down in the boardroom." Tommy had no idea what a Silicon Valley boardroom looked like, other than it must look like this, minus the view out onto Jackson Street, just west of Michigan. John continued. "We could take hours or days to get to know each other, or I can propose a deal, right here, right now. Then, if you like it, we can go through the personal match dance, or you cannot like it and then, we've both saved a bunch of time. Does that work for you, Tommy?"

Not wanting to slow the train down, Tommy said, "That works."

"Great. I know of you and your reputation—golden boy, friend of the environment first, capitalist a distant second. Hell, I'll bet you were in business just to do the right thing for your clients and making some money just, well, kind of happened. You are the perfect guy to most effectively drive monetizing carbon markets. I am a capitalist first and foremost, but respect what a little green marketing can do."

Tommy had advised clients in his PR business about buying carbon credits to offset or reduce their carbon footprint as part of a larger environmental image strategy. He hadn't participated in these markets directly, but he knew that there were regional carbon exchanges in which customers could buy credits, allowing them to offset their carbon output or just buy and hold the credits to "retire" the carbon pollution altogether. Secondary markets to buy and sell these originally issued credits were also developing.

"I'm listening," Tommy said.

"So, you verify energy savings from projects and create the carbon credits on these regional exchanges. We buy them up. The people doing the project get some extra cash for helping to create the savings, which creates the credit. Then, we have an asset to resell into the carbon exchange markets."

"And we eventually sell them to power plants and other polluters so they can cover their system allowances and go on polluting?" Tommy cynically questioned.

"First of all, I find it funny that you're getting a little judgmental, since that's exactly what you advised your clients to do to clean up their images. But, yes, we would sell some of them. Those firms are putting carbon dioxide into the air, polluting as you call it, either way. It's a voluntary system, and at least these buyers are stepping up and paying someone else not to pollute so they can. No one is holding a gun to their heads to do it at this point."

"I guess," Tommy admitted.

"There will be other buyers, too. Environmental groups and socially responsible self-absorbed businesses that want to buy up the credits to make themselves feel better."

"More than feel better," Tommy argued.

"Whatever. You get my point. So, we help push the popularity and accessibility and eventually sell the carbon credits for more than we paid."

"If the market goes up," Tommy said.

"We will help drive the popularity and the demand. Prices are bound to go up, and if the President or Congress or the EPA or whomever puts a carbon cap-and-trade system in place, voluntary becomes mandatory, and we go from making millions to billions," John explained.

"Billions? Really?" Tommy questioned sarcastically.

"Think big, Tommy," John crooned with arms open wide.

"So, what do we each need to do to make this happen?" Unknowingly, Tommy had asked the exact question that John wanted to hear.

"Rumor has it you made around twenty million selling your PR consultancy. Not bad for a bunch of guys sitting around not making anything. I want you to put it all into the new company, or whatever amount it was after taxes."

"You've got to be kidding," Tommy scoffed. "I worked for a long time to make that happen! I'm not betting the whole thing!"

"If we are going to do this together, you are absolutely going to put it all in, and you'll reap the benefits. You will be running the main business, and I need to know that if things get tough you won't bail. You put in twenty million and I put in forty million. We each own fifty percent. You would make ten million on the first day without doing a damn thing."

Tommy was listening, but not looking at John. He didn't want to give him the satisfaction of seeing the fear and uncertainty in his eyes, so he just stared at the building across the street. John loved this scenario ... a guy's future hanging in the balance, forty million of his own money that might turn into much more, or be gone forever. The adrenaline rush of doing deals was pretty much all he had in his life anymore. His wife had died and they didn't have any children. No hobbies, just work and money. John's social life had revolved around his wife's family and friends. Now that she was gone, he simply didn't know how to connect with people outside of work anymore. He was lonely and filled the void with competition. There was never enough money; there was always someone richer to try and catch.

Finally making eye contact, Tommy spoke. "You have my attention, but how do I know that I would really run the business? How do I know that you'll actually put our future in my hands?"

John was prepared for this response, so he smoothly added, "What if we give one percent to someone we both trust. That person breaks the tie if we can't agree. I believe we have a mutual friend named George."

"You know George Shannon?" Tommy was completely caught off guard.

"Yep. He worked for me for ten years on my first business and cashed a check when I sold it," John said.

"Well, then you obviously know he worked for me, and he just got some money when I sold. He told me he was going to take the few hundred thousand and take some time off to be with his wife and kids."

"My guess is that this venture might entice him to come back. Let's assume, for your decision-making process, that I can make that happen," John offered.

"I don't know . . ."

"Remember, Tommy, you have the chance to turn this into big money. Your name on a building at your alma mater kind of money or, a do-gooder like yourself, you can go change your corner of the world."

"Will you give me a couple of days to think about it?" Tommy asked.

"Two at the most. We've got to move or move on, by noon Friday."

Tommy labored under the weight of the pending decision as he lumbered slowly past the receptionist and toward the oversized glass double doors, scenarios sprinting through his head. He turned and glanced back at John who was already on the phone, poised to tackle whatever came next.

3

Tommy's mind was churning. Do some good and make some money. What's not to like? He shared the opportunity with Susan as they lay on the floor, naked with a sheet and blanket woven around their bodies. "You're nuts. You have all the money you'll ever need. Go work in a soup kitchen if you want to feel good about helping someone. Keep your money." Susan's voice was escalating.

"I knew I could count on you for an opinion." Tommy had expected her response, so he had waited until after he had greeted her, clad only in boxers. Her clothes made a trail from Tommy's front door to the rug just short of the bed that had been the target destination. The physicality of the moment and its accompanying release of sexual tension had been enough for each of them. After the adrenaline ceased, Tommy felt too vulnerable and he had reached for the covers. Both Tommy and Susan started to see a pattern in their visits to each other's homes. Have sex early, before they had time to argue.

"Are you seriously considering this?" Susan asked.

"Yeah. You want to know more about how it works?" Tommy offered and continued without waiting for an answer. "The new business would pay companies to help them complete projects or do more projects that save energy and reduced carbon emissions. In exchange for helping to pay for the project we would keep the value of the carbon credits. The price eventually goes up. There is a positive environmental impact.

14

Everyone wins."

"Sounds like if the value of the credits, or offsets, or whatever goes down, you lose," Susan said.

"Well, true," Tommy responded. "But we'll have sixty million, and as long as we don't get crazy with options, derivatives, or borrowing money, we can ride out any short term drops. We'll be fine in the long run."

"And who is we?" Susan asked.

"John DeFallo. I'm sure you've heard of him. The guy is a legend! He has the background to help pull this off, but he'll be behind the scenes. I'll be running the main business," Tommy explained. "He just takes care of the trading in a sister company."

"Of course I have heard of John and I'm sure then that you have heard he's nearly impossible to work with. Very demanding and uncontrollable. I'm sure that anyone that you ask that knows both of you would tell you this is a bad idea," Susan lectured.

"Probably they would, so I won't ask. I can make this work. I can handle him," Tommy reasoned.

"Even if partners are a good match, I see bankruptcies all the time when people think too big. I still think it's a bad idea," Susan cautioned.

She knew that he had already made the decision by the look in his eyes and the tone of his responses. She knew the possibility of making more money *and* being able to do something positive was going to be something Tommy couldn't pass up.

"I know you're going to do this, so at least let my firm set up the bylaws and get you incorporated," Susan suggested.

"Great!" exclaimed Tommy. "Let's celebrate."

They got up, put on their clothes, opened a bottle of Merlot, and ordered Indian food from a place around the corner.

The next morning Tommy called John and said he was all-in as long as they spent some time getting to know each other and that his attorney could structure the deal. After a week of intense discussions and negotiations they were in business and ready to go with sixty million dollars in the bank and a twenty million line of credit with a promise from banks for more if they needed it. Tommy was confident that he could work with John and excited to take a shot at making something better of his life. He thought John was just the guy to help him pull it off.

John had worked out the details to get George on board, and Tommy hired him as the first employee. They rented an office space so that anyone coming to see them could gaze to the right of the entrance, with comfort, at the Chicago Board of Trade building. Tommy and George would laugh about their office location choice on the corner of Adams and LaSalle. Their business had nothing to do with the old and trusted institution just down the street, but they hoped someday carbon would be traded like other Board of Trade commodities such as corn, soybeans and metals. For now, it would all be through the various, relatively obscure, regional Carbon Trading Exchanges, with the hope that someday there would be more market size and mainstream legitimacy. They thought for now most people wouldn't be any the wiser and perhaps they could garner some comfort level for clients by association with the large pillared institution that was the Chicago Board of Trade building on Jackson.

Tommy and George met once a week with John as they started up, usually in John's office. He was too busy to veer from his schedule. The way John looked at it, he had a great deal of money invested, but even if it tanked, it wouldn't bury him. Besides, he had a lot of ideas about how to help make sure it all went according to plan.

John paced back and forth on the opposite side of the conference room table from where George and Tommy sat. John was bold, colorful, and positive. Tommy thought this contrasted nicely with his own intense but unpretentious style that was accompanied by a somewhat negative outlook on life and pessimistic view of business in general. Being around someone more optimistic, he thought, would be a good thing. For some reason he trusted John. Maybe it was John's confidence. Or maybe it was the challenge of working with a guy many thought was too difficult to manage or who needed fixing.

"We are on the cusp of something huge," John reminded Tommy and George. "With the rep you two have in the environmental community and my ties to commodities, we can create the most powerful firm in what someday will be a huge industry."

"How big? How soon?" George asked.

"A business worth hundreds of millions in two or three years. If we get the right president that mandates this shit, even sooner. Hell, almost overnight then, but we have to be the biggest and the best first." John was caught up in his own rhetoric and continued on. "Right now, there are only millions of dollars of trades a week. If there is a cap-and-trade system, that will turn into billions. This market is only going to get bigger in the meantime."

"How can you be so sure?" Tommy asked.

"Listen. Tree huggers like yourselves, no offense intended, are coming out of the woodwork. Your kind will drive this world. Green this and clean that . . ."

"Our kind?" Tommy interrupted, somewhat offended.

"Yeah. I love you guys. You're creating the opportunity because you need to do the right thing by the environment. Don't take offense; you people will be running the goddamn economy pretty soon if you don't already. Are you against doing the right thing *and* making money? You want your twenty million back right now?"

"No." Tommy said. "Well, maybe some of it."

"Shit, wait until you have a couple hundred million. You can start giving it away if you feel guilty. Bottom line is you need a capitalist slug like me to really make this go." Tommy was thinking and George was dazed, so John continued. "Hey, if it makes you feel better, we can give away ten percent of the profit to whatever swinging . . . do-gooder you want. Plus, it will be good for business and our image anyway."

Tommy smirked. He was way more entertained by John's mannerisms, energy, and word choice than offended. "Fine, but remember in our deal, I am responsible for every aspect of creating carbon credits—engineering, field verifications, quality. You stay out of the day-to-day business."

"You have my word. That sounds boring, anyway," John promised.

"Maybe boring, but we are trying to create millions of dollars of tradable carbon credits virtually out of thin air, so it needs to be done right."

"Well, go ahead, and do it right," John requested. "We're all set. One company you run to create the carbon credits and one that I run to buy them up and resell them on the market. We're in this together, and together we'll make millions."

4

Tommy and George turned all of their attention to setting up the necessary systems and staff to expand from their small startup operation. George wasn't as much a complement to Tommy's skills and abilities as he was an extension of them. He was a decade older than Tommy and an odd combination of engineer and accountant. He was wicked smart and had picked up on everything from marketing to programming during his two previous, separate stints working for John and then more recently for Tommy. George was rail-thin with a full head of surprisingly dark hair parted crisply on the left. He wore larger-than-stylish dark-framed glasses but dressed much more hip than would be expected from someone his age. He had dutifully put three kids through college and now needed to concentrate on his and his wife's financial future. George adored his wife and always thought that she deserved better than he had provided. This was his shot to change that.

Tommy took half of their 10,000 square foot office for his sales team. They worked through contractors to find customers that wanted to do energy projects, or sometimes were doing them anyway and offered them money to own their carbon credits. The way the carbon credits worked was that if someone reduced their energy use, they were deemed to have saved carbon from being belched from a power plant and into the air. They, in essence, had stopped creating some power plant emissions and could sell those "credits" if they were properly documented.

Once a customer project was done, it was turned over to George and his staff in the other half of the office. They collected project invoices, documented savings, inspected projects, and tied a bow around the verification work, sending an electronic file to one of the carbon exchanges. In a few weeks back came verified tradable financial instruments that they could sell right away on the exchange that had certified the credits or hold and sell later. That was the firm's only product for now, but there were also secondary markets developing that they could potentially engage in to make or lose more money. In a matter of months, their firm, Environmental Verifications, was cranking out millions of dollars of carbon offsets a month that were being regularly traded on the exchange that had approved them. Exchanges would only approve projects with real energy and carbon dioxide savings, so Tommy and George were diligent.

Tommy would routinely take projects he had turned over to George and have his team do their own inspections. They always checked out—every light fixture, motor, boiler, wind turbine, or whatever was always in place. The carbon credits were legitimate as were the markets they would help to sustain. When the credits were complete, they were sold roughly at cost plus ten to twenty percent to their sister company that John ran, Carbon Traders, Inc. In turn they were to be resold on an exchange or put in inventory to be sold later, presumably, at higher prices.

Tommy, George, and John sat down to look at the financials for the first six months. It was more a celebration than a meeting. After paying customers for their projects and all of Environmental Verifications' costs, the company was creating credits for about six dollars per ton of carbon emissions and selling them to Carbon Traders for about seven dollars per ton. Tommy always thought that paying seven dollars per ton for a ton of *anything* sounded pretty cheap. Maybe it was, but maybe it wasn't worth more money because electric utilities in the United States were releasing so much carbon pollution—hundreds of millions or even billions of tons. No one really knew what it would be worth in the long run. It was still a small market with huge potential to grow, and maybe someday the price would go up. They were betting their business, and their futures, on it.

John's side of the business, which included two traders and a couple of desks and computers out of his "Ideas" office on Jackson, would take the seven-dollar credit and resell about twenty percent of the inventory at the market price. The market had been moving from about eight dollars to nine dollars per ton. They were holding eighty percent of the inventory at their seven dollars and change cost, waiting for the market to go up more.

"Our inventory of credits is already worth millions," Tommy said. "Why don't we sell more and take some money off the table?"

John shot back, "Do you know what the markets are trading at in Europe? Twenty to thirty dollars per ton. We should wait. This is a gold mine."

"How about ten percent more?" Tommy asked.

"We'd be wasting an opportunity. Besides, remember in our agreement, I have the last say on buying and selling. I'm staying out of your end of the business. You need to stay out of mine," John said.

"It also says we can put anything to a vote. If we split, George has to decide," Tommy said. Tommy and John had placed a lot of trust in George to break a tie but both respected his judgment and found it preferable to a 50/50 situation where nothing would get done if they didn't agree.

They both looked at George to see if they could read which way he was leaning. George gave them nothing to go on, just a stunned stare that said, "Not now. Don't make me decide." There was some irony to that look as George suspected there would come a day when he needed to break a tie, and he was prepared to do so. Neither man had an advantage as George really wasn't that fond of, or obligated to, either of them. Of course he had worked for both for years, but in that time he observed more of their flaws than good qualities. He was working with them again strictly because it was the best opportunity he had to make some real money. Although he would never admit it to anyone, he knew he was smarter than either of them, but it appeared that age, timing, and circumstances wouldn't allow George an opportunity other than in a supporting role. John and Tommy simply didn't see or think that he would be the guy to take the organization further and that giving him one percent of the company, plus a decent salary, was more than fair. Frustrated yet determined to stake his claim, George tolerated both men. At least for the time being.

"Are you forcing this now?" John shouted.

"No, but I'll keep pushing," Tommy warned.

"Okay. I'm guessing that you wanted to gauge where George might land when it comes to breaking a tie," John said and smiled coyly. "To tell you the truth, we do have to sell a bit more of our inventory. We are spending a lot more on the credits in inventory than we are taking in on the ones we are selling into the market so we are burning cash, but we can't sell too much more at this point. If supply outstrips demand the price could implode. I think we can sell ten percent more as you asked, but let's really push this thing and drive up production. Maybe even double it up."

George and Tommy looked at each other and nodded. It was just too enticing. They would try to do just that.

Just saying "double production" didn't make it happen overnight, but it was pretty close. Projects were starting to come in on their own, and Tommy's guys hardly even touched them. They went straight to George. He kept adding staff and cranking out credits. It was almost like printing money, John would say. The firm's notoriety in the market had Tommy attending some environmental conferences and other speaking engagements. He loathed such trips and found himself at the O'Hare Airport much more often than he wanted. Tommy almost always had something with him to do to avoid wasting time, but on this trip he found himself trapped in a plane that wasn't moving with nothing to occupy his mind and no control of his situation. He stared out of the plane window at the seemingly random numbers and letters on the runway signs painted on the tarmac thinking to himself that he would pay a thousand dollars right then and there if the plane would move a single inch, just a nudge. Something to show that the pilot was awake and that there was some hope that eternity would not be spent in that spot. His anxiety flew through the roof but the plane, unfortunately, went nowhere.

Suddenly, Tommy was encouraged by a slight movement of the plane, but it was only the wind. He grew more agitated with the false hope and lack of any communication from the cockpit. Maybe a visit up there was in order, TSA regulations be damned. Tommy felt himself shackled, not seat belted, and treated like a boot camp marine expected to take anything they threw at him. At least the two fourteen-year-old girls that he paid twenty dollars each to stop talking weren't adding to his stress level.

As he bargained in his mind with God, or the FAA, or whoever was out there, it occurred to him that maybe he needed to up the stakes. Perhaps it wasn't about money. He was certainly willing to cut off a finger or two to get out of that plane, and he was probably willing to part with a foot if necessary. Tommy was embarrassed by how his mind worked, how badly he needed to control things and how poorly he handled situations when he was not in control. What was a routine tarmac delay by other people's standards thankfully cleared and another work related trip was underway.

These trips had created a buzz in the market from all the interviews, press releases, and speaking engagements. All of the coverage kept the projects rolling in, month after month. The prices that their second business, Carbon Traders, were selling for weren't going up, but even with all the inventory they were selling into the market, at least they weren't going down. Tommy begrudgingly realized that John was right. The market wasn't big enough if they tried to dump their inventory. Prices would surely fall dramatically.

Tommy knew the value was in the integrity of their firm. He wanted perfection. They checked and rechecked every project his sales guys put through, and every time George's field guys were one hundred percent accurate. At every monthly meeting Tommy reminded George and John how important it was. "We are creating millions of dollars of value pretty much out of thin air. Let's not fuck it up," he would say.

They reviewed the financials every month. The numbers were starting to overwhelm Tommy. They were big; that's about all he knew. The biggest one was "carbon credit inventory," paper now worth more than one hundred million. His twenty million investment was now worth more than fifty million in a little over a year, and if the market doubled . . . he had gone all-in and loved the result. Tommy knew, however, that they needed to be careful because they were at a vulnerable point. They had most of the value of the business wrapped up in the inventory, and they were out of cash and borrowing money.

The good times continued well into the second year as the combination of Environmental Verifications and Carbon Traders, Inc. had become the country's largest carbon credits trading company. Tommy and George now had nearly a hundred sales representatives, engineers, and technicians cranking out credits at an astronomically high rate.

There were now big brokerage firms and others getting into the market and a robust futures trading business developing, all built on a handful of companies creating the credits and driving the market. The appetite among environmental groups and utilities was complemented by that of socially-conscious people and companies that combined to buy up the credits which drove the market.

Tommy, George, and John headed into their monthly meeting for the twenty-second time. The meetings were no longer at John's firm since they now included about ten VPs. The main conference room at Environmental Verifications was big enough to hold the group, although now they had more space on several floors. On the far end of the room in the corner was a life-sized cardboard cutout of Tommy and John from the front cover of the current *Time* magazine.

John clearly wanted to get the meeting over with quickly and he covered the financials wrapping things up in only ten minutes. Tommy and George knew from past experience when John had something additional on his mind, so they remained in the room. Within a minute it was just the three partners and the life-sized caricatures in the room.

Tommy had not seen the final *Time* magazine layout prior to the meeting. The editors had selected a picture of the pair standing back-to-back, looking over their shoulders at the camera. The line under the picture read, *Mean, Clean, and Green: How This Power Pair Are Helping to Drive a New Market.*

Mean, Clean, and Green. Tommy thought it a bit embarrassing, but not John. "I look more handsome, I must admit," John smirked.

"Taller, too. What did you do?" Tommy asked.

"On my tip-toes. Thought us being the same height made for a better picture," John offered.

"Watching out for *Time* magazine's aesthetics. What a guy." Tommy didn't care about that and was generally uncomfortable with the attention. As different as the two of them were in attitude and politics, they didn't really clash over ideology. Neither cared enough about such things to bother, so at least they had that in common. They admired other people's passion for politics but they each loved making money. It was the one thing that connected them and held whatever relationship they had together.

Tommy continued, "All this publicity better make for more sales, or it's not worth it."

"It will be worth it. More sales and more offers for the business," John said.

"Good, because I can't do this forever," Tommy said.

"That's why I ended the meeting early. You, George, and I need to talk. I have been routinely getting offers for our business, but now that they are in the two hundred million range, I thought I should at least make you aware of them."

"That's huge! How come you didn't tell us about the earlier ones?!" Tommy asked excitedly.

"They were insulting. This one's not even that good. If we wait until prices are up a bit, we should be able to get five hundred million, maybe more. I'm not ready to sell."

"What if George and I want to sell?" Tommy pushed.

"You're kidding, right? This thing is still heading up. I can feel it. George? Tommy? You really want to sell?" John asked.

George finally spoke. "What happens if we sell? Do we still have jobs?"

"Well, after an offer is agreed to the buyer comes in with accountants and attorneys and gives us a million-dollar proctology exam," John said. "They will probe and poke at everything. Once we pass, we move on to closing and any individual deals for us."

"What kind of deals?" George asked.

"If you want to stay on, you'll probably have to roll some money back in from your proceeds, negotiate a salary, maybe some options in the new business and then keep working. Personally, I will be gone," John said.

"Me, too," added Tommy.

George just stared at them, looking inappropriately nervous and edgy, hoping the other two didn't notice. "Proctology exam. Sounds uncomfortable."

John pleaded, "Let's wait. I have some ideas. We can buy ourselves a couple of big names to further enhance our profile and create a management succession plan. Buyers willing to pay top dollar will be expecting leaders in place to run the business. You guys could hire that hippie who just left the Department of Energy. A do-gooder like that would enhance our image. We all know that without credibility, carbon offsets are toilet paper."

"You mean Jeremy Irvine, the retiring Secretary of the Department of Energy?" Tommy asked.

"Yeah, that guy. Pay him a million dollars. Heard he's good in both the sandals and wingtips crowds," John continued.

"You said a couple of big names," George interjected.

"Yeah, one on my side, too. The head of the EuroBank commodities trading business, except he would have to really work for a living and make a lot more than your guy. We could be doing more to be a market-maker, commissions on trades, hedging strategies. Plus, with our inventory, we could be doing a better job of managing the market," John said.

He had made little quote signs in the air when he said the word managing. George and Tommy knew that meant manipulate, and they didn't really need the condescension.

Tommy agreed that waiting, bringing in some big names, and getting ready for a sale down the road was probably a good idea. George didn't offer, nor was he asked, to provide input. Tommy put in a call to Jeremy Irvine hoping it would be returned.

5

George left the meeting with Tommy and John even more apprehensive and caught off guard than he hoped it looked to his two partners. He was beyond frustrated, feeling once again disrespected. The idea of selling, and the eventual financial and legal proctology exam, as John had called it, were coming sooner than he had anticipated. George felt John and Tommy should somehow have to pay for not respecting him and his contributions to their businesses over the years.

George was feeling more angry each day knowing that he had been instrumental in achieving the business success that John, and then later Tommy, had both experienced. *And this time around they didn't even give consideration to me running this business,* George thought to himself. *That's the last straw and there is no turning back now.*

The irony of working for John and Tommy again, and them potentially making so much more than him, gnawed at George. He knew the deal that he had made was for one percent of the company, and it didn't cost him a penny to get it, so he didn't fully understand why he was feeling so angry toward his partners. Maybe the tumor he knew was growing in his head was changing him. All he really knew for certain was that he loved his wife, Deb, so much that he would do anything to make the rest of her life better.

The little moves he was making in the market weren't going to be enough and he was running out of time. George needed someone to protect Deb, and he needed a deep-pocketed investor to help. Someone with millions of dollars to pay the fees to borrow millions of carbon credits. Then, if the price went down, they could buy the credits at a lower cost, pay back the originally borrowed credits and make a huge profit. 'Shorting' was a great way to make money if the price of the asset that was shorted actually fell. George was sure that he could help make that happen for a couple of key individuals willing to help him out.

6

Jeremy returned Tommy's call promptly. He was excited about the opportunity and was with Tommy in the Chicago office of Environmental Verifications within a week.

"How was your flight from D.C.?" Tommy asked Jeremy as they shook hands just outside the main conference room.

"Fine. Nice to meet you. I've been doing a little research on your business. Interesting model. Looking forward to our discussion," Jeremy said.

He had evidently read the part of the article in *Time* talking about the company preferring informality. Jeremy was dressed in jeans, a flannel shirt, and ankle-high, well-worn work boots. He had a long jaw line, was thin, tan, and energetic-looking for a man in his early sixties. His hair was gray and thick and looked like it had been dried by a breeze off of the prairie.

John had done some homework and Tommy realized he had made a good pick. Before heading the Department of Energy, Jeremy had run a business manufacturing wind turbines that he sold and decided to give back by getting into politics. He had also been a congressman from South Dakota and had tons of environmental and utility contacts.

"Listen, Tommy. Let's get down to it. You've got a gold mine here but there's more you can do. Heard you're looking at the guy from EuroBank, too. Good idea."

Tommy could see how well John had orchestrated this whole process, but that didn't matter if his ideas were solid. George entered the conference room, introduced himself to Jeremy and sat back to listen.

"So, do you see any problems with our plan?" Tommy asked.

"No, but then again I haven't really looked. Can you give me next week to shadow you two and John so I can get to know the business? If it checks out, and you like me too, I want to be an owner. At least five percent. I'll pay what's fair, but I'm hoping you can do that at a little discount to current market value," Jeremy said but then paused.

"We're listening. Is there more?" Tommy asked.

"Not really. Just don't want to be paid like some figurehead. I don't need a salary. From what I hear, you need someone to run this business after you're ready to sell."

"Would you even consider the paid representative route?" George asked. "I would prefer not to see dilution in my little share."

"Sorry, no, sir," Jeremy answered. "Near as I can tell from the financials that John sent, your business is worth close to two hundred million. I'm ready to write a ten million dollar check if that's what it takes to get five percent of this business."

"Well, I'll talk to John, but looks like he is already good with this. Can you spend a day or two now with us here in Chicago?" Tommy asked.

"Yes, I can. Let's get the basics down this week regarding potential ownership and confidentiality and such," Jeremy suggested. George walked out of the room first, knowing things were moving too quickly and worried about the extra scrutiny. Tommy and Jeremy headed to lunch shortly after George left the room, passing him as he sulked his way down the hallway.

John and Tommy cut very similar preliminary deals with Jeremy and the EuroBank guy. They settled on four percent for each and they were both ready to pay nine million for their shares. Tommy and John would each own forty-five and a half percent, and George would still own one percent. They were pretty proud of themselves. As long as the two agreed, they would drive the business. If they disagreed, either needed two of the other three owners to side with them. Next was a week of Jeremy's due diligence and they could close the deal the week after that.

They continued to avoid considering George as the guy to run the business after the sale or ask what he thought about the deal. John and Tommy both continued to view George as a good soldier but not the leader for the business. There was simply a disconnect between George's view of himself and that of both John and Tommy. Since they continued to make changes without diluting George's one percent, they figured he should be happy. He'd be in line to make a few million dollars down the road, as long as the business continued to do well.

Jeremy was in Tommy's office bright and early the next Monday with a different flannel shirt and jeans, but the same well-worn boots, tan face, and slightly too-bushy prairie hair. Tommy and Jeremy spent most of the morning diagramming how the offset creation and trading worked, including the sales and inventory at the sister company, the opportunities for more income in hedging, future strategies, and the percent of the market they controlled.

"This is amazing," Jeremy exclaimed. "People would kill to own this percentage of any commodity market, and you've done it right under the nose of the big traders and brokerage houses. When you . . . we . . . sell this thing, there will be a bidding war, and my guess is McKinstry will be right in the middle of it with the big boys."

"Why are you so sure?" Tommy asked.

"Other than you guys, they are the only other decent-size presence in the market. They don't want to let the big Wall Street firms or anyone else come in over the top of them. I could be wrong. Hell, it doesn't matter. We just need to get a few buyers salivating."

"First things first," Tommy said.

"Right, diligence. So, are you okay with me spending the next few days with George?"

"Yep. Let's meet here on Thursday morning," Tommy suggested.

Jeremy moved urgently toward George's office. Tommy looked at his schedule for Tuesday and Wednesday and figured he could use some downtime before reconnecting with Jeremy; maybe put in a couple of half days. He called Susan.

"Hey, what are you up to tonight?" Tommy asked.

"Hey, how are you? We haven't spoken in a week. Maybe some pleasantries are in order before you call me out of nowhere just to hook up," Susan snarled.

"Sorry. I didn't say anything about a hookup. I just miss you," he said.

"That's good. I miss you, too, but not tonight. If you want to meet at your place tomorrow night, I'll come by after work. Leaving for court. Gotta run. See you tomorrow," Susan said.

Tommy took Tuesday afternoon off, cleaned his place, got some lasagna from a local Italian place, shoved it into the oven, then buried the boxes in the bottom of his garbage. He tossed a salad and set the table. The place and the food looked like he had made far more effort than the reality.

Susan had caught the security door downstairs as someone was leaving, scurried up the stairs, and knocked eagerly on Tommy's door. She walked in without waiting for an answer knowing it would be unlocked; it was Tommy's way of welcoming her without providing a key. Tommy turned from opening a bottle of wine and noticed that she had changed from her work attire into skin-tight jeans, high heels, and a blousy top that could have hid a slightly-bulging tummy, but there wasn't one to hide. He wondered why she didn't want to be with someone more her physical equal and her age. In his eyes, and in most, she was stunning.

"Thought I might find you in your boxers again," Susan said.

"No chance after our phone call," Tommy replied, looking down toward his shoes.

"Smart man. Can I have some wine?" she waltzed towards him, cozying up around his waist.

"Absolutely." He was suddenly a bit uncomfortable, and tried to make small talk. "What's new?" he asked.

33

"Your partner has been in our office a couple of times in the last few days with some woman."

"What was John doing there?" Tommy asked.

"I thought maybe you knew," she replied.

"Your firm can't be representing him, right?"

"No way we could represent him since we have the honor and privilege of being your counsel. Plus, we have to run everything through the software to check for conflicts."

"You're sure?" Tommy asked.

"I'm sure that we didn't represent John, so I'm almost as sure we represent the woman," Susan confirmed.

"How do you know?" Tommy kept pushing.

"You sure are nosey, almost paranoid."

"I need to be paranoid about people I'm in business with," Tommy said.

"Okay, I know because John was there with the same attorney that represented him in setting up your business, plus my boss, Sam Meyers was involved. For Sam to be there it must have been one of our heavy-hitting clients. Otherwise, he doesn't come out of his office too often. Some attractive older woman in a red dress."

"Okay, I'll let it go then," Tommy said. "But keep an eye open for him. For me, please?"

Now Susan changed the subject. "Anything new with you?"

"Not really," Tommy responded. They sat at the table and talked, split a bottle and a half of wine, and waited for the lasagna to finish baking. When Susan got up to check on the lasagna, Tommy followed her into the kitchen. He gently rested his hands on her hips as she stood in front of the oven, having just closed its door. She did not turn to him, but instead, stared ahead and unbuttoned her blouse. Tommy pulled the blouse off her shoulders, unhooked her bra, and let both fall to the floor. He reached around her thin body and cupped her breasts in his hands and kissed a spot on the side of her neck that he knew pleased her.

Susan unbuckled and snaked out of her own jeans while Tommy stripped off all his own clothes. She turned, and they faced each other. Desire increasing, they kissed passionately. The physical attraction was definitely there for both, and Tommy focused on a primal energy he felt well up in his body. Suddenly, without any suggestion from Tommy, Susan turned away from him again, put her hands near the corners of the oven, and bent slightly at the waist, offering herself, enticing him. Something had changed about her. Tommy could sense it. There was a submissiveness that aroused him further. Roughly, Tommy entered her from behind. Both gasped and moaned with the immediacy of his thrust, and Susan arched her back to accommodate his need. With one hand on her shoulder, and the other on her hip, he looked down at the tattoo across her back. Seeing "cease what you want" this time further excited him instead of being intimidating. All of his focus centered on the release. Susan writhed and he pushed her harder onto the oven, controlling her, pinning her to its surface. In that instant he knew that she wanted and needed more from him than the physical pleasure that he could provide. Tommy surrounded her from behind with his arms, both spent.

The wine and stove had warmed them from inside out. They turned back to each other, kissed and embraced. Somewhat awkwardly, they put on their clothes and returned to the dining room to enjoy dinner and each other's company. Tommy really did like spending time with Susan. The only thing missing was love.

Susan enjoyed the rest of the evening, too, but the rawness and aggressiveness of the sexual encounter had her feeling more used than loved. Susan lay awake half the night in Tommy's bed, frustrated with herself. She didn't need to or want to fall in love with Tommy, but it was happening. Somehow she could see all of his faults from the moment they met, the perfect match for her in that they would never be a match. These feelings were not supposed to happen.

The next morning, Susan and Tommy had breakfast together

before Susan headed off to work, but the enjoyment of the evening had disappeared as both were starting to further grasp the reality of their situation. Susan ate quickly, pecked Tommy on the cheek, and headed out to work as soon as she could.

Tommy took the entire day off since he felt like he was in limbo waiting for Jeremy to finish his diligence but he was back in the office early Thursday morning checking email and ready to go before Jeremy arrived. When he entered, Tommy immediately noticed that Jeremy's typically urgent walk was replaced by a slow shuffle. "What's wrong?" Tommy asked.

"Lots. Glad you're sitting down," Jeremy responded.

7

Things had gone along pretty smoothly for Tommy and John. People who knew them both continued to think they were too different to work together and that the relationship and the company were destined for failure. However, each saw in the other their own weaknesses buffered, not an alliance of people too different to make the business work. The environmentalist and the capitalist, the pragmatist and the innovator; they needed each other, and they were making it work. Their attitude was "fuck the skeptics;" there was too much money to be made to have things *not* work.

Additionally, both men were focused on growth and the competition, particularly with McKinstry, the only carbon trading firm nearly as large as theirs. McKinstry controlled about a quarter of the market and Carbon Traders a bit more. Each firm was equally fixated on beating the other. Carbon Traders was the small startup that got most of the environmental business and a good share from utilities. McKinstry drew on the utility market, too, but courted commodities firms and others looking to exploit a new market. Carbon Traders, the little startup, good guys fighting the big brokerage houses—at least that's how they played it up in the media.

All of the attention, all of the angst, all of the hassles felt like they hung in the balance, waiting for Jeremy to say whatever it was that made him look sick. "So, I followed your trades through from Environmental

Verifications to Carbon Traders all day Tuesday. Everything checked out great," Jeremy confirmed.

Tommy relaxed slightly and said, "Of course they did. I told you we were meticulous."

"However, on Wednesday I worked backwards by randomly selecting approved offsets coming back to Carbon Traders from the exchanges."

"Isn't that like doing the same thing?" Tommy asked.

"No, because the data coming back from the exchanges had more projects than you submitted. There were falsified projects that you have been taking credit for and either selling them into the market or pulling them into your inventory," Jeremy explained.

"That can't be." The agitation in Tommy's voice was palpable.

"George confirmed what I found," Jeremy stated, and as if he was cued, George walked in.

Given the circumstances, Tommy thought he looked oddly calm. George had apparently waited in the hall for Jeremy to deliver the bad news rather than tell Tommy himself. "George, does this mean what I think it means?" Tommy asked.

"If you think it means the business is completely screwed, then yes." George said, staring at Tommy, trying to soak in his every reaction.

Jeremy started to gather his papers as he spoke with authority. "I will be issuing a press release this afternoon acknowledging that I had considered joining your board, but passed on the opportunity. It will be completely ignored by the public as it's inconsequential today, but it will make sense and cover my ass when this shit hits the fan. Good luck, gentlemen."

With that, Jeremy strode out the door without even a backwards glance. The EuroBank guy had a simultaneous and similar conversation with John since Jeremy had tipped him off regarding the mess that was uncovered.

Tommy slumped into a chair in the conference room that had, for nearly two years, been a place to report on their business success. Feeling despondent, he noticed that George now looked nervous. George whispered, "What the hell are you going to do?"

"We are going to get John in here and all the goddamn VPs and figure out what the hell happened. We are locking this place down for the next forty-eight hours. No new volume on the market, only secondary market trading to make sure things stay stable for now."

It took until early afternoon to get everyone together with all of their printouts, computer files, and other ammunition. Environmental Verifications people lined one side of the table, Carbon Traders on the other. Five people stood at the ends of the table; George, Tommy and their CFO on one end, John and his CFO on the other. Battle lines were drawn.

Tommy, glaring across the table, started. "We all know how this is supposed to work. Every day there is a single download of verified credits sent to one of the carbon exchanges. One file, every day, new credits. All are cross-referenced with past volumes to make sure that projects aren't resubmitted." Everyone nodded their heads. No one spoke.

The VPs of the Information Systems group from each company rose in unison. It was apparent that they had decided ahead of time who would deliver the news. With a beard that looked like tufts of bison hair, the newly balding, slightly round, somewhat soft, and pasty skinned gentleman from Environmental Verifications spoke. "It appears that the file that Environmental Verifications sends isn't the same one that the exchange receives."

He stopped to let that sink in before proceeding to the obvious next question, as if it had already been asked. "There is a sophisticated web service data transfer where our original file goes over a firewall between our servers and the exchanges for data security reasons. It seems that each night during the process the file somehow gets automatically expanded to show more projects. It has all the good trades and data, along with projects that seem to be made up. Clearly the firewall must somehow trigger the appearance of the falsified data."

In an instant, everyone in the room who thought that they were going to be millionaires with their stock options were now thinking about their resumes.

"How?! What?!" Tommy furiously spat.

"This is a goddamn outrage!" John thundered. "I'll make sure at least one son of a bitch in this room goes to jail for this!"

Tommy was shaking. He couldn't help but figure it was John. John was probably thinking the same thing about Tommy. It couldn't be George, Tommy thought. Well, technically it could. No one was above suspicion. Maybe either of the CFOs? Hell, none of it made sense since they would all benefit from the business being successful. There was only one thing for sure . . . there was a hell of a computer genius behind this.

John spoke next. "How come no one on the exchanges caught this? They were signing off on fictitious projects. This is their fault."

"They were really busy," Tommy said. "Probably just happy with the volume, and they trusted us. Plus, do you really think they are going to blame themselves?" It was a rhetorical question, and Tommy had the next steps formulated, so he continued to speak. "The information system guys need to figure out who wrote the code to substitute in the bad information. Let's work in pairs, one from each company. Report to me and John every two hours. Nobody talks to anyone outside the company until we can figure this out. None of you should even leave the goddamn building." The room emptied in a matter of seconds. As usual, George, Tommy and John were left, but this time with their CFOs.

"Good idea. Find the computer guy and have him lead us to whomever is behind this mess." John, the powerful, seemingly invincible mastermind, was obviously rattled, and he looked at Tommy.

"Don't you think that person is in this room?" Tommy stared at John somewhat accusingly.

"Well, it's not me, you son of a bitch!" John shouted at Tommy, furious now. They both looked at George.

George put up his hands as if to wave off any blame and said, "Don't look at me. My one percent is down the tubes."

By now, John and Tommy were being held back, more figuratively than literally, by one of George's bony hands on each of their chests. He almost looked amused, knowing it probably wouldn't escalate and pleased that these two were turning on each other.

They both stepped back, turned in frustration, and retreated to their offices to wait for the next update. During that time the impact of the business collapse washed over Tommy in waves. Regardless of how they would try to spin this, his money and reputation could be completely wiped out. John would still have plenty of money. George could get another job, just like the rest. But Tommy knew that was going to be the biggest loser. Two hours to start pitying himself. It went by quickly as he looked up to see others heading to the conference room.

The slightly bald, heavy, soft and white head of the IT department again spoke. "We don't know much more than before, except the falsified data is pretty good—random real businesses with building sizes and projects that make sense. Someone was pulling data from real estate tax records, business directories, and many other sources. Somehow the lines of code were hidden when the file was opened to do the double check. Only good data showed when opened by the QA/QC people on our end. Then, when it gets shipped to the exchanges routing through the firewall, it must trigger the appearance of all the false submittals along with the real ones. This has only been going on for the last six months, but that is when we did a majority of our volume and it looks like about a quarter of that is fraudulent. The exchanges probably saw and checked all those good credits for the first year and a half and just got lazy. Never seen anything like it. Very impressive."

John spoke up, sarcastically. "So, you falling in love with this guy, or can you find him?"

"We have consultants coming in. I'm sure there'll be dead-ends, but we think we can find him, or her, inside a week."

This time, Tommy spoke. "Oh my god. Twenty-five percent. We don't have a week. Find him in two days. Financial teams, how did you miss the disconnect between revenue and project volume?"

Carbon Traders' CFO explained, "We had checked historically but changed our policies about six months ago because everything always matched. We asked the exchanges just to flag anything they didn't approve and figured that would save a lot of time. Plus, with so much of it staying in inventory, I guess that no one ever did the math. Of course, any of us could have caught it." Tommy almost lashed out at the guy not taking responsibility, but Tommy knew he was right, so he moved on.

"I assume the PR groups have already been working on this. We are not losing this company. What do you guys have?"

"How about a plan in two hours?" a voice from the Environmental Verifications' side of the table said.

"Fine," Tommy huffed, and everyone scurried out. It was now after market closing time with all appearing normal. Tommy walked out of the building to get some air and paused to really think for the first time about how to save the business, not lose it. He knew they had less than a week to fix this mess or they would be out of business. Maybe knowing who was benefitting from the market trading activity would help. He called his market desk from his cell phone and asked that Jack, the group supervisor, run a report on all large trade activity for the last six months and have it on his desk as soon as possible. Tommy walked over and over in a two-block circle, grinding through scenarios and ideas, but headed back for the evening update with very little to show for his effort.

"What's the plan?" Tommy asked the room. Everyone knew he meant the PR plan and those VPs stood up. The intensity and immediacy of the moment intimidated them.

"The only way this firm has a chance is if we figure out a way to stabilize the market when the news hits. We did double check the numbers with finance and confirmed that we don't have enough money and borrowing capacity to buy back all the bad paper." Everyone turned towards John.

"Don't look at me. I'm losing enough money. I'm not sending good money after bad," John defensively asserted.

"Why not? You owe us all that," Tommy looked at John in disbelief

"That wasn't the deal. I don't owe you shit! Besides, my money won't be enough to make that work." John said defiantly.

The PR guy continued. "He's right. The only real way to do this is to cover what we can, and bring McKinstry in on it. McKinstry would have the capacity to buy back the bad paper that we couldn't. They would lose some money in the short term, but they would get good assets along with clearing the bad ones from the market and turn those short term losses into market share. We'd each be buying good and bad, but by the time we settle up on this mess, we'd be lucky to still be in business and hold onto five percent of the market."

Tommy knew in the back of his mind that this was the only alternative, but going to McKinstry was the last thing in the world he wanted to do. He set up a meeting for the next morning with Mark Schmidt, the head of McKinstry.

Tommy spent most of the night at the office poring over the reports that Jack, the market desk manager, had provided. There were a normal number of short positions in the market over time but nothing of any significance until the last few business days from a company called Big Mountain Traders. They had shorted small quantities starting six months ago, and the volume seemed to move up at about the same time and rate that the bad credits were going into the market. Those volumes were still relatively small until a massive increase in volume by Big Mountain just in the last couple of days. This was more than coincidence as Tommy was sure that whoever made the short trades knew about what was going on at Environmental Verifications all along, and they were waiting for just the right time to bet big.

The short trades meant that Big Mountain Traders made arrangements to borrow offsets for a fee with the hope that the price would go down. If the market went down enough they could buy credits at that lower price and repay the credits that they had borrowed, making a profit as the market dropped. Big Mountain established thirty times more short positions over a couple of recent trading days than the company had ever done before. Those positions cost Big Mountain several millions of dollars in fees but were set to make about eighty million if the market went down to three dollars per ton. Tommy figured if the news hit that they lost control of the situation, the market could go even lower. Hell, the market could go to pennies, with Big Mountain making even more. He was sure that Jack was already trying to chase down the ownership, so Tommy planned to check with him in the morning. It had to be related to whoever created the false records. It was the only way to turn fraud into big cash.

It was midnight, and Tommy couldn't stand to be at the office anymore. He took a cab home, opened a bottle of Malbec, poured himself a glass, and started to roll the decisions he'd made in last two years through his mind. Why didn't he check things more closely? Why did he trust John? George? Hell, why did he trust anyone? The growth was too good, too big, too fast.

Tommy drank a bottle and a half of wine and took a muscle relaxer. He knew it was the only way sleep would come. Before he knew it, the alarm was ringing obnoxiously. The sun lit up the room and he was still in yesterday's clothes. Reluctantly, he got out of bed and trudged into the kitchen. He threw away the empty wine bottle, corked the remaining bottle, and checked his phone. Two texts and a missed call from Susan. That would have to wait until later. He changed his clothes without showering and headed out of his condo as quickly as possible for his appointment at McKinstry.

Tommy was greeted at McKinstry by a big handshake and hug from Mark Schmidt, even though they had met and talked only once before. Mark was an outgoing man from West Texas who grew up in the oil and natural gas business. He knew all the ins and outs of trading, only now it was carbon instead of fuels. He was a large man with a belly and facial features that fit with his substantial girth. His broad nose and cheeks looked like a roadmap of red vessels and the purple hue of his skin was a permanent reminder of years of whiskey drinking and deal making. He was the only guy in Chicago always wearing a cowboy hat. He hoped Tommy was there to sell, since McKinstry had been trying to court and woo John. Eagerly, he cooed, "What can I do for you, Tommy?"

"I'll get right to the point. We have a little problem that could turn into your problem too." Tommy went on to explain the mess and ask for his help.

"Doesn't seem like a good business opportunity to me. You know we're going to have to pour tens and probably hundreds of millions into buying worthless offsets to stabilize the market," Mark said.

"You're kidding, right?" Tommy couldn't believe what he was hearing.

"Well, no," Mark replied.

"You'll use the money it would have taken to buy our business and basically steal it. Actually, in the long run you'll probably get it all for nothing since you can sell the good inventory later at a profit to make up for the short term losses of the bad paper once the market stabilizes."

"*If* the market stabilizes," Mark said.

"It will. All I need is for you to give me two or three business days next week to get ready. We need to extend our credit lines and raise some emergency capital."

"That leaves me with market info that could get my ass handed to me if I don't report it immediately."

"My guess is that given what you have to gain, you'll live with it," Tommy replied. Mark shrugged but really didn't commit to Tommy's request, and they parted company. Tommy headed back to the office.

8

The next two regular updates to Tommy and John were more of the same. Everyone was still searching for answers. Who was the hacker? Who did they work for? But there were none.

After lunch Tommy finally decided it might be a good idea to check in with Susan. Although he was starting to feel guilty about taking more from the relationship than he was giving, it didn't stop him from wanting her help and comfort with this mess. He called from his cell so that she would know who it was. "So, finally willing to talk?" Susan said without a hello.

"Yeah, sorry. Some pretty ugly things are going on here at work," Tommy said.

As he was about to move past his lame apology and on to possible dinner plans, George burst in through the door saying, "People from Commodities Futures Trading Commission are here to see you, and some climate exchange people are on the phone and want to meet with you this afternoon."

Tommy's shoulders sagged so far they disappeared. The CFTC is not well known to most, but they are the commodities version of the Securities Exchange Commission. Whether it's the CFTC, SEC, or IRS, getting a visit from a government acronym was generally a very bad thing. His guests had followed only steps behind George since they believed their business was urgent enough to demand an immediate audience. The older of the two, the one in the more expensive suit, spoke first. Tommy hung up the phone without saying goodbye to Susan.

"We received a call from McKinstry indicating you might have a bit of a problem with the quality of some of your offsets. They, we, also passed that information along to the carbon exchange markets you trade into. I assume their inquiries will follow ours closely."

"I would guess so," was all Tommy could mumble.

"We need to schedule an immediate audit. The exchange people are going to let us head this up. No reason for you to have to do this two or three more times," Suit Number One said.

"We can have an audit team here tomorrow," Suit Number Two added.

"Great. Thanks for the quick service," Tommy answered sarcastically, then switched his tone. "We will be forthcoming, and yes, there are problems."

"How significant, may I ask?" requested Suit Number One.

"Maybe twenty-five percent of our recent inventory," Tommy replied.

"Oh, my," said Suit Number Two. "If this gets out . . . oh my."

"We will use all of our resources to buy back the bad offsets and support the prices in the market, but we need more time."

"Let's hope you get it," said Suit Number One.

Tommy was dialing Mark before the two were out of the door. "Yeah, this is Tommy. What the hell did you do? I thought we had a deal! You must have called the feds before I even got back to my office!"

"I never said we had a deal, and you put me in a spot where I had to tell them or risk my company and career. Our firm will still be there side by side with you, buying up your crappy offsets to save the market. Only change is the timetable. This shit will probably hit the fan nearly overnight. You guys need to be ready when the market opens on Monday morning."

"What?!" Tommy screamed. He couldn't believe this was happening.

"Deal with it. You set this in motion coming to meet with me," Mark said, and abruptly hung up.

Tommy then realized that earlier he had hung up on Susan. He texted her back, saying he would be in touch in a couple of days. Tommy cancelled the next update and got John and George in his office and laid out the mess for them.

"Hell, why don't we just liquidate our inventory and take whatever cash we have back out of the business?" John suggested.

"If we don't try to save it, they will hunt us. Maybe even go after our personal assets. Besides, it's the right thing to do," Tommy argued.

"It's the right thing to do, particularly if you're feeling guilty," John shot back.

"What are you trying to say?" Tommy asked, defensively raising his eyebrow, and putting his hands on his desk.

"You know what I'm saying."

"More likely you did this than me, asshole!" Tommy cried. He rushed John and shoved him over the table that sat behind his desk guest chairs, sending John headfirst between the table and the wall.

John rose to retaliate but stopped short. As often as he had pushed people to their limit in his career, this was the first time anyone had laid a hand on him. Surprised and somewhat intimidated, he collected himself instead and asked what they needed to do. Tommy settled down quickly, too, not having had a physical altercation since high school and, likewise, not knowing what to do next. "We need to have all our cash available and the line of credit from the bank all set for Monday. They don't know what's up yet. We'll tell them the truth . . . that we are buying up offsets on the market."

"I'm fine with telling them part of the truth," John said.

"Whenever the price starts moving down towards, let's say seven dollars, we need to buy. The market is closing for the week in an hour, so we should be fine until Monday. It depends how quickly word gets out."

"What is McKinstry going to do?" George asked.

"They are going to support by buying at six dollars if things get ugly. They want to see our money out there first, or they'll just let us sink."

Tommy ruefully turned away from his partners, trudged toward the door, leaving them behind. The three partners each headed home, knowing there was nothing they could do except wait for Monday morning.

Tommy didn't self-medicate over the weekend with alcohol and pills; he was hoping to be focused on Monday, and he was sick of always being numb. For some strange reason, he wanted to feel this. He needed to be present. On Sunday night he found himself lying in his bed staring at the ceiling, mind racing. Sleep evaded him, so he finally decided to get up and go in early to make sure everything was ready for the market opening. He was amazed at how many people were on the Brown Line at five in the morning. He got off at Quincy and Wells, his regular stop, and walked a block east to the trendy offices of Environmental Verifications. He realized over the two years in business with John how quickly he'd returned to the commuter grind that he had promised himself to leave behind when he sold his first business.

Tommy was surprised to be the third and last partner in the building at such an early hour. Everything was set for the day. They put in automatic buy orders for 1,000,000 units at seven dollars, even though the market was set to open at $7.75, the previous week's close. The market opened and moved down quickly to $7.50, but trading seemed regular.

The rest of the staff scurried about trying to conduct business as usual. Only a small handful of people worked on tracking the hacker, and Jack was still following the paper trail of Big Mountain Traders ownership. Retribution could wait until after they saved the business. The three partners monitored blogs, websites, and trading activity. No one said a word for more than an hour, each assigned to multiple computers.

"Shit!" Tommy slammed his fists on the table, standing abruptly and knocking over his chair.

"What?" yelled George and John simultaneously.

"Couple of bloggers are saying that Carbon Traders has some problems and is being investigated," Tommy said.

John ran over to Tommy's desk and stared at the computer screen.

"Fuck! Half of the traders and brokers in the market follow these guys!"

"Well, it's having an impact. The market is down toward $7.25," George pointed out.

John countered, "Let's change our buy orders to $7.25 so that this thing doesn't get out of hand before the end of the day. Market makers will think that there is plenty of price support above seven dollars."

"Good idea. It will cost us more than buying as the market drops but maybe this will pass. How about putting in orders for up to 3,500,000 units at $7.25?" Tommy suggested.

The other two nodded and the orders went in. The afternoon passed slowly and all of the orders got filled. They had invested twenty-five million to try to stabilize the market, a small price to pay if it worked. The market closed peacefully for the day.

Knowing that Susan had been right all along, and then to have hung up on her, Tommy went home, too embarrassed to call her back. He set up two computers on an L-shaped desk and opened a beer by each one. He rotated back and forth on his swivel chair, churning through two hours and four beers. Internet chatter increased as time went on. He knew it would be worse by morning. After nearly giving himself whiplash while nodding off looking at computer screens, he moved to the couch and got a couple of hours of restless sleep.

By morning, rumors were at least as bad as the reality. People were expecting an announcement from the trading exchanges. The market opened at seven dollars and they were running through money trying to stop the implosion. They bought all day until they had run through all of their cash and line of credit, well over one hundred million. It was late in the trading day and the market looked like it might be stabilizing at about six dollars but then went into a late-day tailspin. Clearly, McKinstry had moved in and was buying but couldn't or didn't hold off the fall as the concern escalated to panic throughout the day.

At the market close, the regional carbon exchanges made a joint announcement that trading for the following day would be suspended.

Tommy, George, and John stared at the press release wondering what would come next. John spoke first. "Well, we are still in business. If the price stays where it's at, we are still okay."

Tommy started doing the math in his head. "Not really. Remember we held on to most of our inventory and a good chunk of that is worthless, too. Now we own even more, and we know a good portion of that is bad. We can crunch the numbers tonight, but I'm sure we are underwater."

John was more the big picture thinker than the numbers guy, so he asked, "With a little price bump, we can be okay, right?"

"I doubt it," Tommy responded.

As dismal as they all felt, it was a relief to get up in the morning knowing there wouldn't be any trading that day. They had no money to lose, anyway. The three partners had agreed to "sleep in" and meet at seven to review status reports churned out by their staff throughout the night.

Just as Tommy had expected, they were clearly underwater when factoring in the falsified offsets. They had invested over two hundred million, much of it borrowed, and they didn't own enough good inventory to cover their debt. They all stared at the numbers. "That adds up to a big fucking hole and no way to crawl out of this," Tommy admitted.

Optimistically, John said, "If the market doubles, we'll be back in black."

"You're kidding, right? The banks will be crawling up our ass within days. They'll take this thing before we have time. It will take months at the least for the market to bounce back and we have days or maybe even only hours," Tommy said. George got up and walked out without saying a word. Tommy continued, "Maybe if you put in forty or fifty million, we could buy some time." John and Tommy didn't notice George had left. They rarely did. They never gave him enough credit for the things that he did.

"Same answer as before. It would be good money after bad. We still need someone like McKinstry with hundreds of millions available. They can't get us personally. We should just walk away," John said.

"Don't be so sure they won't come after you."

"They can try, but I don't mind paying attorneys for a while until the banks move onto their next disaster. No personal guarantees, no liability. They can't touch me," John was used to getting his way, evading disaster and landing on his feet.

As much as it pissed Tommy off, and while he still thought John was behind the fraud, he might have done the same thing.

John continued, "Time to cut a deal with McKinstry. They can have the whole mess and we don't have to worry about attorneys hounding us for the next few years." The two sat in silence for what seemed like an eternity. Tommy's jaw tightened more each second. He contemplated throwing John across the table again, but that hadn't really helped the first time.

The silence was broken by the receptionist's voice over the intercom. "There's a gentleman from McKinstry here asking to speak to Mr. Gardner or Mr. DeFallo." Tommy stood up and slammed his fist into the drywall. Before the pain from his hand could start radiating through his body, he turned to John. "Cut the deal. He'll want to finalize it before the end of the day so he can stand up with the exchange guys and let everyone know it's all going to be okay. The son of a bitch played us. He let the news leak early so we wouldn't be ready."

Tommy headed down the back hall, knowing he couldn't stand to see the smug look that Mark was bound to be wearing. He walked down the back stairs and through the alley to pop out on Quincy Street like he had hundreds of times before. This time, he did it as a poor man once again, seemingly mocked by the Chicago Board of Trade building. Everything would be fine tomorrow, except for him. He called Susan and waited for her to pick up.

Susan immediately lectured him. "You really should be a little better about getting back to me."

"Well, this time, unfortunately, I have a pretty good excuse. The business completely imploded over the last couple of days. I need your professional help and please, if you don't mind, can you provide it without saying, 'I told you so?'"

"Fine. I can do that. How bad is it?" Susan asked.

"The whole thing is being taken over by McKinstry, with the Federal Commodities people and others in the loop."

"So, what can I do?" Susan asked.

"Keep me out of jail. We threw all our money at this thing and gained some credibility with the Feds, Cook County, and the exchanges. If McKinstry can keep the market from going under through the next couple of days, I'm hoping they will cut us some slack," Tommy reasoned.

"So you need me to interface with all the attorneys I assume," Susan continued.

"Yes, please start by getting in touch with John and his attorney, because they are handling the details with McKinstry. We probably need to wrap all of this up this week. Right now all of the parties want to either sue us or throw us in jail. Can we get that nice conference room of yours on Friday?" Tommy asked.

"Fine, let's assume Friday, here, at Young & Erickson." Susan was definitely annoyed with Tommy, but she found herself wanting to help him.

"Will your fat boss be there?" Tommy asked.

"Yes, Sam will be there. He loves doing work for broke clients. But Tommy, the only way you're going to avoid jail is if everyone's too embarrassed to drag this thing out."

9

The cleanup of the mess was just as swift as the implosion. McKinstry made sure all of the bad paper was bought back and taken off the market. Things stabilized within a couple of days but not until prices were under three dollars per ton. John handled the negotiation with McKinstry over an intense two-day period that basically amounted to handing the business over in hopes that it would lead to a smooth exit for all parties.

The negotiation for a lifetime commodities trading ban that Susan and Sam had helped broker was as good as it was going to get. Tommy met Susan back at Young & Erickson Saturday morning to sign the revised documents that had been presented the previous day. This would keep Tommy out of prison—unless he broke the terms of his probation. Signing the company over to McKinstry had been more difficult since Tommy knew that he had been played by Mark.

"So, Tommy, this should be everything we covered yesterday. The Feds, Cook County, and all of the other entities involved all agree not to pursue any criminal prosecution for securities and commodities-related fraud by either Environmental Verifications or Carbon Traders," Susan said.

"And I admit no personal guilt, right?" Tommy asked.

"Right," Susan replied.

"And George is signing the exact same agreement?"

"Yes, he should be here any minute."

"And is John signing, too?" Tommy asked.

"He's still trying to cut his own deal, but I don't think it will be much different." Susan said.

George walked in and came around the far side of the table to start signing his pile of documents. Tommy stared at George, who looked tired and older than Tommy had ever thought or noticed before. Suddenly, Tommy could see himself down the road of the decade that separated the two, and he sighed with a tired dread.

Tommy turned to George. "Hey, I'm glad you're here. Gives me a chance to say this to you directly. I'm sorry that we got you involved in this disaster."

"Hey, you're the one who lost everything. Yeah, I've got to find another career, but that's life," George said.

"What are you going to do next?" Tommy asked.

"I'm flying out today to do a little late spring skiing in Colorado to clear my head. After that, I have no idea," George said.

"You willing to get back together and try to figure out what happened? Wouldn't you like to know for sure who fucked us over?" Tommy asked.

"What's that going to change?" George said.

"Nothing, but everything," Tommy was worried about George, but more worried about not being able to move on without knowing what happened himself.

"Well, maybe. Probably. Call me in a couple of weeks. Things may have changed," George said.

"What could possibly change?" Tommy asked.

"I don't know. Something. We'll see." George responded.

"Well," Tommy said, looking puzzled by the response. "See you in a couple of weeks, I guess."

10

Tommy and Susan went out in the hallway, leaving George in the room to finish signing his paperwork.

"So, what are you going to do now?" Susan asked Tommy.

"Probably head back to my hometown for a couple of days," Tommy said.

"Going home?" Susan raised an eyebrow. "You've hardly ever even mentioned your home. I mean other than telling me it's a pretty little town; I don't know anything about it."

"I didn't say it was my home, you did. I said my hometown. It's not exactly something I like to talk or think about," Tommy responded. "I kind of blocked it out. Haven't been back in eighteen years."

"What could have been that bad?" Susan asked.

"My dad dying. And losing my friends Jenny and Pat in the process; there was nothing left for me there," Tommy said.

"Are those old girlfriends?" Susan asked. Tommy could tell that she was hurt that he had never shared anything with her about his hometown before this.

"Pat's a guy, and both were just friends."

Susan could tell by his reaction that he was only telling half of the truth. Either Jenny had meant more to him or there was more to the story, so she pushed on with more questions.

"What about your mom?" Susan asked.

"She would visit me here, but eventually she moved to Florida," Tommy said.

"So, looks like you might be going back for your friends. Good luck with that after eighteen years," Susan said aggressively, still pissed that Tommy didn't trust her earlier with this information.

Tommy probably shouldn't have been surprised by Susan's reaction, but he was. After all, she had made it clear she didn't want the baggage of an emotional relationship, and Tommy had always obliged.

Susan pushed through the awkwardness of the conversation and wanted to know more. "How did your dad die?" she asked.

"Suicide by attorney," was Tommy's monotone and emotionless response.

"What?! What does that mean?" Susan was just a bit annoyed . . . again.

"I can't get into it right here, right now. I have to catch a train to Wisconsin," Tommy just wanted to end the conversation at this point.

"That's a pretty big thing to leave hanging out there, don't you think? Especially with me being an attorney . . ." Susan said.

"Well don't take it personally. I never held it against you," Tommy said with a slight grin. "I'll call you from the train to explain."

"Okay," Susan said sadly, more troubled that Tommy never opened up to her than she was concerned about the details.

Tommy was rarely perceptive to emotions, but felt the awkwardness and changed subjects. "Hey, thanks for not saying, 'I told you so.'"

Susan forced a smile and glanced up at Tommy. "What good would that do?"

Tommy smiled back, checked to make sure none of the other attorneys were looking, and softly kissed Susan on the lips before heading to Union Station. Tommy knew it was a strange time to face his hometown but he really didn't have anywhere else to go. He hoped Pat would be supportive. Tommy tracked down his number and texted him. He was hoping to get a ride from Milwaukee, the train's last stop.

Tommy stared out the train window as the northern Chicago suburbs gave way to Wisconsin farm fields. Although Tommy felt like McKinstry stole his firm, he knew this mess was partly his own fault. He should have been more careful. There was so much money flying around, he just got caught up in it all.

They kept identifying projects, paying a portion of the cost and turning them into credits—many of the projects would have gotten done anyway, but this way they created value for themselves. He knew, really, in the back of his mind that even the legitimate projects were a bit of a stretch, but who was he to judge? If someone wants to pay, no harm in that, he thought. That probably would have been fine if someone wasn't faking projects, but who the hell was it? It had been so easy to make money . . . too easy. Tommy thought again about Jack, his old trading desk manager, and left him another voicemail regarding Big Mountain Traders.

Tommy rested his chin on his hand and continued to stare out of the train's window, observing the blurry line between the gray rock track bed and the long strands of yellow, and then just greening grasses that lined the route. He thought about how hard it was going to be to face Jenny and Pat. He had no decent excuse for shutting them out with all the other pain he was trying to leave behind when his dad died eighteen years before.

Certainly there would still be whispers from others around town when he showed up. Even with so much time passing, there would be people ready to gossip about why he had skipped his own father's funeral, never to return. Tommy really didn't care what those people thought then or now, for that matter, but hurting Pat and Jenny haunted him.

After his dad's suicide, he just couldn't bring himself to face anyone. Tommy had said his goodbye to his dad the day before the funeral, but nothing in that moment provided any closure for him. He had taken some of the cremated remains in a margarine container and rowed his kayak a mile out in Lake Michigan. His dad had loved being on the lake as much as Tommy. He spread the ashes on that still and humid August day, watching some clump together and sink and others float off on the flat surface of the water. He wondered then, and still did now, why his dad had been so selfish.

Tommy had been close to his dad; he was the stability in the family that countered his mom's mood swings and erratic behavior. Even at twenty-two years old at the time of his dad's death, Tommy still needed that stability and buffer from his mom. How could his father abandon him without even a word? Without at least a note to him personally? Tommy felt his dad had at least owed him that.

It wasn't that Tommy needed an explanation of the pressures he was under; he certainly understood that. His dad had a successful business manufacturing water filtration systems that were used mostly in remote areas with poor water quality. Tommy was proud of his dad for making something that helped people, and it provided very well for their family. All of that had changed when about 200 or so small children and elderly people got sick due to a strand of bacteria that made its way through some malfunctioning filter systems. His dad was hurt deeply by the news, but was thankful that no one had died. He was committed to put all of the company's resources toward fixing the flawed systems and compensating the families that suffered due to the defect.

That's when Tommy first heard the words that he felt eventually killed his father—class action lawsuit. Instead of going down the path that he had originally planned, Tommy's dad had to spend his days and money on and with attorneys fighting in court. He was going to do the right thing, but the attorneys were drumming up more plaintiffs and burying him in subpoenas and paperwork. The verdict in the case broke the company and his dad. Buried in debt and shame, Tommy's dad saw no other way out.

Tommy put the full blame of his death on the ambulance chasers, as his dad called them. They took a man who wanted to do the right thing, turned him upside down, and shook whatever they could out of him, which in the end was pretty much nothing. Other than attorneys, there were only losers. Although he blamed the class action attorneys for his dad's death, Tommy never fully forgave his dad. He didn't understand why he would take his own life. Why not just walk away from all the hurt and shame and humiliation, like Tommy did?

The one-month trip to Europe that started the day of his dad's funeral turned into eighteen years away from the place where he grew up. Each month that went by made it harder for Tommy to ever go back. Ironically, losing everything himself, like his father had done, was the thing bringing him back home. He wondered what waited for him a mere thirty-minute car ride north of the last train stop.

Tommy was startled when the train was pulling into downtown Milwaukee. The last twenty miles of track and a couple of stops had gone by unnoticed. Tommy shuffled out of the terminal, ready to rent a car, but there was Pat waiting with boyish excitement, a smile, and a big bear hug. Pat finally set Tommy down and spoke first. "Dude, what has it been, like decades?! Finally making the trip home?"

Pat was barrel-chested and solid. His skin was holding everything so tightly, you couldn't tell what was muscle and what was fat. A light brown crew cut was coordinated with a mustache and goatee of the same color and length. His hairline and jubilant eyes had both endured the test of time. He wore jean shorts, a brown T-shirt and sandals, even though it was a cold spring day. "Hey, you're looking . . . solid," was the first thing Tommy could muster.

"Still the diplomat," Pat said sarcastically. His voice was naturally deep in tone but every word came out with a crisp and clear vibrance that matched his personality.

"No, you look good. Happy. I wouldn't have expected anything else." Tommy was truly glad to see his old friend. Really, he and Jenny were his only two true friends from high school and college that he had. Jenny and Pat had stayed close over the years, both living in town with Jenny stopping for dinner or to catch up with Pat and his wife Mary on a regular basis.

"Good to see you! Let's go. You can stay at my house," Pat said.

"Didn't know if you'd be here," Tommy said as they got into the car and headed north.

"Are you kidding? I read about you in the paper. The darling of the environment falls on hard times, then I get your text. Way too interesting to turn down." Pat paused. "Well, you know, I would have come anyway."

"I know. So, how's your family? My mom mostly kept me informed, but I'm sure there's more to tell. You have three kids, right? Tommy asked.

"Yep. Been married eighteen years and have a son who's seventeen and two daughters, sixteen and fourteen."

"Looking forward to seeing Mary. Does she know I'm coming?"

"Of course! She's always had a soft spot for my dark, brooding friend," Pat said.

Thirty minutes of catching up passed quickly as they headed north. Before Tommy knew it they were rolling down a steep hill into town; Lake Michigan was on their right, lit up by the afternoon sun. Pat took a quick left and then another into his driveway. Mary was in the kitchen when they arrived. A pot of soup was on the stove of their early 1900s Victorian. As Pat gave Mary a similar hug to the one Tommy received at the station, he had the perspective of distance and a bit of time to take it in. Pat and Mary hugged and kissed like they hadn't seen each other in days. For a minute, Tommy disappeared to them.

He noticed Pat's "thickness" included solid legs and calves. He had more the look of an immovable nose tackle than the wirery wrestler he first met in high school. His skin was spotted with faded freckles. Mary hadn't changed much, particularly considering three kids and all the years. Dark, thick shoulder-length hair still framed a slightly round face that somehow fought off wrinkles. "Tommy, my tortured-soul brother!" Mary exclaimed. "How are you?"

"I'm still overthinking everything. How are you?"

"Couldn't be better. Have my family and health and a roof. Don't need any more than that," Mary replied.

Pat jumped in. "Tommy's going to be staying for a few days. I think he needs a little time to figure out what's next."

"Stay as long as you like. Dinner is in an hour and one of the girls' bedrooms is ready for you." Pat handed Tommy a beer without asking him if he wanted one. They passed the evening reminiscing. The kids floated in and out, doing homework, watching TV, and listening for embarrassing facts about their parents that they could use to their advantage later. They were perplexed that a man who was a stranger for their entire lives could be someone who their parents knew so well. Somehow, the kids felt like their parents hadn't let them in on this big secret named Tommy. All six headed for bed early not knowing what would come next from Tommy's visit.

11

Hometowns can be comforting or troubling; for Tommy, coming back was looking like both. The place he fled so long ago felt somehow more comfortable and approachable now. He got up and out of the house before anyone else was awake. Tommy walked down to the lake and watched a low foggy mist roll over and through the lighthouse arches. Before, the spring fog was ugly and worsened the depression he struggled with. Today, he had bigger worries than the sun not being out.

A big steepled church on a hill overlooked a downtown that was still. There were more storefronts filled with food and merchandise than he expected given big-box retailers now most assuredly occupied the nearby freeway exits. As he strolled the streets and circled back to the marina, he saw the stark beauty of the place for the first time. Empty boat slips speckled with the last bits of floating ice. Bare trees and rocky shoreline scrubbed clean by the beating waves of winter. A couple of small rotting fish added a gritty, natural ripeness to the scene. He smirked to himself, knowing friends in Chicago traveled to the East Coast to see the very same thing. Then he realized the joke was really on him as he had grown up with this right in front of him. "Dumbass," he said to himself, but loud enough to hear if someone were there.

Self-degradation was one of Tommy's most prominent traits and a significant weakness. He thought it motivated him, kept him hungry and paranoid. That may have been good in business, but not for self-esteem, relationships, or anything else. As with most days, Tommy slipped in and out of daydreams. He was thoroughly convinced that if born later, he would have been diagnosed with ADD and drugged. Instead, he used his weakness to his advantage, creating businesses that thrived on quick decisions and the urgency that they created. The perceived ability to focus quickly on a variety of things was really the inability to focus on anything.

Tommy stumbled up the steps from the boat slips to come face-to-face with his own image in the mirrored glass door of the marina. Tommy wasn't short, but he felt that way if there was anyone taller than him in the room. His dishwater blond hair, turning gray, blended with his scalp to camouflage the thinning. He was built thick and strong with a flat stomach that defied his age. He ate well and exercised regularly, thinking that was a necessary offset to the inner decay caused by bouts with alcohol and pills.

Tommy moved on from the door and his image to his real problems. How could he have been so greedy and stupid? He walked all over town for hours, repeating those words over and over in his head. He returned to the town center; activity had picked up impressively. He entered the same diner he had frequented in his youth. The glossy gray Formica tabletops and orange faux leather-covered chairs had held up quite nicely. He took a table by the window and ordered coffee, oatmeal, and a sandwich. It was late morning and a good time to get in his first two meals of the day.

Tommy sat drinking his coffee and staring out the window when he heard a voice from behind him. "Hey, Tommy, is that you?" Tommy's shoulders slumped slightly before he turned to see the face of one of their old neighbors. He looked to be about seventy, the same age as he looked to Tommy twenty years earlier.

"Yep. It's me. How are you?" Tommy had remembered the face, not his name. It was a neighbor who spent his summers sitting in a lawn chair on his driveway, usually wearing an unflatteringly tight tank top undershirt, too-short shorts, too-high socks, and too-dark shoes. Not an image that Tommy could forget.

"Yeah, seen you in the papers lately. Good thing your dad's not around anymore to see that."

"My dad or my stepdad?" Tommy asked. His mom had remarried a local divorcee a year after his dad died.

"Either one, since they're both dead," The man bluntly said.

"Well, they'd probably be glad that I was at least out there trying, not critiquing and watching the world go by," Tommy shot back.

"What's that supposed to mean?"

"Oh, nothing. Nice seeing you again. Excuse me. I have to use the bathroom," Tommy said, even though he really didn't need to. His plan worked; by the time he returned to the table, his food was there and the man was not.

Tommy finished breakfast and lunch and headed back out on the street. Fortified and enjoying the sun that had melted away the early day fog, he welcomed the mile or two walk to Pat's house. As he walked, he had trouble shaking images of his stepdad. Bill was someone to be tolerated, grudgingly accepted, but not loved.

Bill's only hobbies that Tommy could remember were sarcasm and verbal abuse. As far as Tommy knew, Bill never hit his mom. He was short and slight except for a funny-looking bowling ball-sized beer belly, and wasn't intimidating. His indifference toward his mom was almost worse than if he would have hit her.

Although Tommy could not have cared less what the rest of the town thought, he still felt badly for his mom about not coming back for Bill's funeral. At that point well over ten years had passed since he left, and he couldn't face Jenny, and he didn't know how to deal with a funeral. He still hadn't done either.

Why visit a dead guy? he rationalized. Just reminded him of dying. He thought about that enough on his own, which led to a pretty active case of hypochondria. A couple of times a year growing up, and until about the time Bill died, Tommy would end up in the doctor's office. Sometimes convinced he was having a heart attack, he wove in a variety of other ailments, from a brain tumor to MS to ALS. He was particularly good at conjuring up dying of some of the scariest and most debilitating diseases. Maybe real dying, by comparison, wouldn't seem so bad.

Tommy wasn't sure how he had crossed streets without getting hit, but he was back at Pat's. Everyone was gone. He went up to his room and fell asleep. All of the fresh air and bitterness had taken it out of him as he slept soundly until his own cold, wet drool sandwiched between his cheek and pillow woke him up. He thought maybe he was still sleeping because Jenny was sitting in the corner of the room. "Good morning!" Jenny said sarcastically.

Tommy couldn't have made a worse new first impression as he patted down his hair with one hand and dried his face with the other. "Not quite how I pictured reconnecting," Tommy said.

"Well, at least you were planning to reconnect. It's been, um, quite a while," Jenny said.

Tommy started to regain his composure and focus. He could see that Jenny was still striking. She had gotten up from a creaky, old chair in the corner of the bedroom and moved in a semi-circle around him from the dresser to the window and back. He always loved to watch her move. She flowed more than she walked. Her ears flared slightly at the top, framing her Latin-skinned face. Her nose was as long, narrow and flowing as her body, her lengthy black hair pulled in a ponytail. Jenny's voice was plain and slightly rough in tone, her words meaningful and concise. Jenny's eyes were soulfully deep, dark, and penetrating, sometimes leaving the rest of her face desperate for attention.

Jenny was nearly six feet tall with small breasts that fit with her flat stomach and narrow hips. Her gait was graceful and somehow showed off the subtle curves of her body, but Tommy remembered how that walk and her posture would change with her mood. He instantly felt the old physical draw, but knew she couldn't feel the same, given that he had forgotten to call for nearly two decades.

They had always flirted, but were just friends except for one night at the end of college. They had agreed that was a mistake, but he remembered that to be more her take on things than his. They never spoke of it again, but it had made college graduation and the start of summer awkward before Tommy's dad died and he left for Europe.

"Sorry I haven't been in touch." It felt as lame for Tommy to say as for Jenny to hear.

"You're here now. Come downstairs when you're ready. Pat and Mary want the four of us to go out, you know, to catch up."

"Great." Tommy finally stood up and they shared an awkward, distant friend hug. Tommy listened to the patter of Jenny's flip-flop sandals as she left down the hall, and he smiled. She wore them all of the time in college; she claimed that her feet were too pretty to keep bottled up. Tommy knew it was to avoid wearing heels and appearing taller.

12

Jenny had sat there, in the bedroom of Pat and Mary's house, staring at Tommy as he slept. She fidgeted uncomfortably in the stiff, old wooden chair that may have been there as long as the house. Her mind was racing. Since Pat told her that Tommy was back in town, she didn't know what to think or how to feel.

She smirked to herself for a moment as saliva started to run from the corner of his mouth, but he did not stir. She knew, however, this was no laughing matter. This visit, this time with Tommy finally home was the last chance, even after eighteen years, that they would have.

Jenny realized when she saw him lying there, even drooling and disheveled, that she still might love him. As an independent woman, she lamented the feeling as weak and pathetic. How or why could she still love a guy who walked away? But, as the mother of their son, the son who Tommy knew nothing of, she was comforted that she still cared about him.

It's not like she thought of Tommy constantly over the years, but it was hard not to think of him more lately as their son grew and took on more and more of Tommy's tendencies and mannerisms. He was also starting to ask more about his father, and Jenny had already agreed to introduce them whenever he was ready. She knew that time would be coming soon, but with Tommy here, now, maybe they had one last shot to be together.

Jenny knew that was as far-fetched and naïve as it sounded and doubted Tommy felt much for her. How could he possibly if he hadn't returned for eighteen years? Whatever miniscule chance existed to reconnect, it would have to happen before Tommy knew about their son, or Jenny simply wouldn't let it happen. She had waited this long for Tommy to love her because he wanted to, not because he felt like he needed to.

She knew the window of opportunity would be small since she couldn't wait much longer to tell her son about his father. Jenny knew what it was like for her son. She had been adopted. One look at her rather short and very white parents made that clear. Her creamed-coffee skin and stature didn't come from that gene pool. Unlike her son, she would never know who her parents were.

Jenny continued to fidget. The old chair creaked and popped stirring Tommy slightly. She thought more about how she should react to the uncomfortable initial moments after so many years. Pat had always maintained that he and Jenny shouldn't take it personally, that Tommy leaving was just about his dad's suicide and Tommy not being able to face the desperate act and the circumstances surrounding it. Jenny had a hard time with that, given that she was confident her reaction would have been the opposite, embracing family and friends to help get over the loss. She wanted to forgive Tommy, but really didn't understand his actions. He threw away their friendship just to avoid any shame or embarrassment. Pat had always defended Tommy in their discussions over the years. He was fond of saying Tommy would come back someday as the same misunderstood ass that they used to know. Pat was okay with that and wanted Tommy to have a chance to correct his mistakes and meet his son. Jenny continued to struggle with Tommy's decision. She wondered if she would ever get an explanation that would justify his actions.

Jenny could see Tommy's eyes flutter open slightly, so she rose from the chair and started to pace in front of the bed as Tommy started to fully wake. His skin was pale and gaunt yet still took a turn for the worse when the embarrassment of Jenny seeing him like this spread over his body. Jenny was surprised that she got a perverse bit of pleasure from seeing Tommy so embarrassed.

13

It was early evening when the foursome arrived at a local tavern. It was over sixty degrees, so they decided to be the first patrons of spring on the deck overlooking the marina. The remaining ice chunks from the morning had melted, and the first two charter boats of the year were in their slips. Soon the marina would be alive with half-drunk, half-seasick fishermen watching with excitement as the day's catch was cleaned for them by their charter boat captain. For now, it was still beautifully stark.

Tommy and Pat sat down first. Jenny and Mary had gotten distracted at the bar talking to friends. Tommy started. "There's something different about Jenny."

"How so?" Pat asked.

"She was always pretty, but there's more. Maybe it's how she listens to people, how she holds herself. I don't know what the fuck I'm talking about."

"True, you don't know what the fuck you are talking about. She's not different, nimrod. You just finally opened your eyes. You're so damn dense. You never knew that she loved you, did you?" Pat said.

"In college? No." Tommy offered, dejected.

"Seriously, you always were clueless to signals from women. You didn't know until this very minute. Amazing." Just then, Jenny and Mary joined them. Tommy could see their mouths moving, but couldn't hear them talking over the ringing in his ears. He was further distracted by his stomach spasming.

"What's wrong with him?" Mary asked Pat.

Pat smirked. "I'll tell you later. He should snap out of it soon enough."

They ordered a pitcher of beer and some appetizers. Tommy swallowed hard several times to keep his stomach contents down and for a few more seconds sat still, staring at the horizon, processing the information Pat had shared with him.

"You back?" Pat asked, starting to feel a little guilty.

"Yeah, sorry. Should we order something?" The other three laughed as the pitcher of beer arrived.

Tommy continued to run scenarios through his head. What if he had known? Would they be married? Divorced? Would they have kids? Would he, they, still be living in town?

Mary and Jenny got up to put some money in the jukebox. "Dude, didn't mean to send you over the edge," Pat said. "It was a long time ago. She's over it."

"You sure?" Tommy asked.

Pat rolled his eyes and said, "Yeah, we see Jenny all the time."

"Maybe . . ."

"Maybe what? You can't be in love with her. You've seen her for all of an hour. You're not in love with her."

"Maybe . . ."

"Nice timing. You have to be the slowest son of a bitch on the planet," Pat said.

The women came back. They drank, ate, talked about old times and enjoyed each other's company. Three hours passed. It got cold. No one cared.

Tommy spent several more days strolling around town, eating and drinking with his three friends and relaxing. They talked openly and freely about everything except that one secret that Tommy couldn't know about.

"So, Pat, did you and Mary have a good time before coming out tonight?" Tommy asked.

"Huh, what do you mean?" Pat said and turned knowingly to Mary. "Hey, I didn't say anything to him about this afternoon."

"You didn't need to, you just had that "I just had sex" look on your face. I took a shot," Tommy laughed.

Jenny jumped in. "That's pathetic, you're both pathetic! But I guess it's kind of true. You guys are a little less edgy and competitive afterwards!"

"See, you know what I mean," Tommy said. "Hey, I have an idea. Each woman on the planet should take a guy and screw his brains out every day. We'd be so docile that women would control the world."

Jenny pondered the idea for a moment, glanced at Mary for an unspoken confirmation and then giggled, "Every day? It wouldn't be worth it."

Tommy was surprised he was finding a calm and comfortable place in his mind reconnecting with these special friends that embraced, not judged, him. Maybe he should just move on with his life, forget about who did what with the business. What good could come of it anyway?

The next morning, with nothing to do, Tommy went with Pat making some deliveries for his job. Pat had gotten them lost. After about ten minutes, Tommy grew a little agitated. "Why don't you use the GPS?" Tommy asked. "They build them into these vans for a reason."

"Fine idea. Go for it," Pat replied. Tommy turned it on, then started pushing hard on the screen, trying to get the "home" function to work.

"This goddamn thing isn't working." Tommy said. "Fuck it. I'll use my phone."

"Whoa there, big guy. It's a touch screen, not a smash your finger through the front of the car screen." Pat gently touched the screen in two spots, and they were on their way home. Pat continued, "Man, that was like an anecdote or metaphor or whatever for your life."

"Oh, really?" Tommy huffed. "Enlighten me."

"Think about it. A light touch and observing what you were doing would have gotten you further than trying too hard and pushing too hard. You were clueless with Jenny after college. Too busy plowing ahead, fixating on your career and what to do next."

"Why didn't you tell me if it was so obvious?" Tommy asked.

"Because Jenny asked me not to. She wanted you to stick around because it was your idea, not mine or hers." Pat continued, "So, back to my metaphor or euphemism . . . pushing the shit out of something, like the screen, or in life, isn't going to help."

"Enlighten me even further," Tommy said sarcastically.

"Well, it's like a Zen or Taoist thing. Observe, go with the flow. You can't push or control everything."

"So, how is this supposed to help me now?" Tommy asked.

"You're a control freak. Ease up or die. Oh, yeah, and as it relates to Jenny, don't push her."

"Ah, Master, you are wise beyond your looks."

"Damn right. A regular Dalai Lama," Pat responded.

They drove quietly for a while. Tommy pulled out his cell phone and decided to check his voicemail for the first time in days. There was a call from his old office receptionist who was still doing the same thing, except now for McKinstry. She tearfully informed him that George had died in a skiing accident. The funeral was going to be on Thursday morning at St. Patrick's in Chicago. It was late in the afternoon on Wednesday. Tommy didn't say anything. He closed his eyes lightly and rhythmically tapped the side of his head against the passenger door window. He hadn't attended his old business partner Paul's funeral and had felt guilty for that. Hiding from funerals, and death, wasn't an option this time. He needed to face his fear and convey his respects.

14

John was in Chicago a few days longer than Tommy dealing with the aftermath of their crumbled business. However, after signing his settlement with the legal authorities, like Tommy, he was ready to get out of town. John also retreated home, to Whitefish, Montana. It was the only place he felt really comfortable. He hadn't grown up there, but his wife had. He far preferred it to his childhood home, which had been a rough neighborhood of Philadelphia with a dad who never lived up to his own expectations, and took it out on John and his brother.

John and his wife had met at Northwestern. They visited Whitefish often as college kids and then as struggling, working adults. John always promised her that he would be successful enough to buy one of the big houses on the hill overlooking the town. Shortly before she was diagnosed with pancreatic cancer, they had done just that.

She struggled for a year before dying, with most of that time spent in their big house on the hill, surrounded by family and friends. She often told John during that year that she was grateful for having the place. It let her, "Look out over her life," she would say. She could see the house where she grew up, the school, and the corner store, and from the back, she could see the top of the ski slopes where she and her friends spent most of the winter as kids.

John watched her die with such grace and dignity that he no longer feared death. She gave him that, but he struggled to replace her with anything else positive. Now the big house on the hill was all he really had to remember her by.

In the years since her death, John started to like being the rich guy in the big house. He liked being well-known in a small city better than one of many in a big city like Chicago. Throwing around hundred dollar bills as tips got you noticed and talked about in Whitefish, particularly at the Bierstube, the bar at the base of the mountain.

The Stube was a classic, old, ski hill bar, where locals mixed readily with tourists and where gallons of beer were spilled every year into thousands of cracks in the wood floors. The pungent, slightly sweet odor of evaporating beer would ooze all day and all night long. When John was away, he couldn't remember what the fireplace or the chairs or the tables looked like, but the smell he couldn't forget.

He was early to meet with his friends and walked up to an uncrowded bar. The hill was still open and the spring skiing conditions were excellent. The bar would be busy as soon as the sun moved low in the sky. It was mostly locals left, getting in the last few runs of the year. The bartender was a rugged looking guy that appeared more bouncer than bartender, until one noticed the peaceful soul that rested in his eyes. John ordered a beer and started a conversation. "You manage this place?"

"Nope," said the bartender unapologetically. "I work here just enough to get the free ski pass and beer. Winter is for skiing, not working."

"What do you do in the summer?" John asked.

"Landscape at the golf course. Work enough to get free golf. Summer is for golfing and fishing, not working," he said, and smiled.

"How long have you been at it?" John asked.

"Well, just for one winter, starting fifteen years ago," he answered with a grin. "What do you do?"

"Commodities trading and other things. I live in the old Westermen house," John said.

"You must do pretty well to own that place."

"Yeah, but I'm not having any fun," John said.

"Yeah, but I'm not having any money," the bartender said.

John glanced at the door and saw his friends coming his direction. He headed to a table, but looked back at the bartender, thanked him for the beer and put a hundred dollar bill on the bar. As they moved toward each other, John's friends couldn't help but notice he had put on a few pounds over the winter. They hadn't seen each other in a few months, longer than normal, as John usually made his way home more often.

John's once thick and muscular body was now softened by a fairly uniform, fifteen-pound layer of insulation. His hair was thick. They saw his twitchy and darting eyes were still present. He looked like a dog tracking a squirrel in a tree.

The two men, brothers, had known John since high school in Philly. They had moved to Whitefish partially to hang out and work occasionally for John but more so because of legal problems back home. It was best for them to get a clean start, or as it turned out, a newly corrupted existence. They were only a year apart and looked like twins: thin build, smoking-induced slouching skin, scraggly hair, wide eyes with a psychotic watery shine to them. They were street tough well beyond their weight, strength, and size. They were in and out of foster homes and juvenile facilities growing up, but they always managed to stay together, basically raising each other. Neither had regular jobs now, but they always had cash. Rick, with wrestler ears and a nasty scar on his right cheek, ran book, and Ron, with a scraggy nose and a limp, sold some pot and a little coke. Both had contacts that had them occasionally providing other nefarious services for hire. They each carried small handguns, concealed well enough that only a trained cop might notice.

Rick, a ping pong ball sized Adam's apple wobbling in his throat, spoke first. "Welcome home. Didn't see you skiing all winter. What've you been doing?"

"Working, but that's over for now. Figured I'd lay low for a while. Couple of days skiing, then maybe some fishing. We'll see."

Ron spoke for both. "Call us, man. We always got time."

"Will do. Want a beer?" John asked.

Rick spoke for Ron. "Yep. Make it two each to start."

Ron said, "Say, you're all into financial stuff. Me and Rick had a bit of a payday. Maybe we should invest or something. You're the only guy we know with real money."

"I can help you if you'd like," John answered. "Sure you don't want to just drink and smoke it up?"

"Oh, we'll do some of that, too, but it's a pretty damn good amount of money." Ron said as he glanced up the hill as the last skiers of the day glided around both sides of a densely packed section of trees.

"A good chunk of money you say. What did you boys go and do?" John asked.

"Do you really want us to tell you?" Rick smirked.

"No, I don't!" John said. "Spare me the details."

"All I'll say is that it was a weird job, and those pay the best," Ron said.

John looked down at his phone at a text from his old secretary. It read, "I'm so sorry, John, but George died. Please call me as soon as you can about the funeral." He paused and stared blankly at the phone, then spoke to the brothers without looking up. "Fun is going to have to wait a few days. I'll be back from Chicago over the weekend, but I gotta run now."

15

Tommy caught an early morning train back to the city and made the short walk from Union Station, arriving at the church early. It was very short notice for him to get to the funeral, but evidently George had died almost a week earlier. Tommy figured it must have been his first day on the slopes after the business failed.

Mourners were already starting to enter. He hung back and watched as people gathered, talked, hugged, and went in through the oversized wooden double doors. He didn't recognize a single person. He realized that he couldn't even remember George's wife's name and had to look it up in the funeral program. *Deb, that's right,* he said to himself. It wasn't just his fault. George didn't mix his work and private life. Tommy thought that was the way he wanted it, so he didn't pry.

After fifty or so people entered, Tommy finally recognized someone. It was John. He saw Tommy coming and extended his hand. "Hi, Tommy. Sorry this is the way we get back together. How are you?"

"Broke, but better off than George," Tommy said.

"Yeah, puts things in perspective," John replied, solemnly.

"Speaking of perspective, mine is that I got screwed on this thing worse than you did," Tommy said, realizing that this was an inappropriate time to bring it up, but not caring.

"Really? How do you figure? Remember, I lost twice as much money on the business as you did, and I paid five million extra in fines and penalties to avoid a lifetime ban."

"I get barred and you don't?!" Tommy felt the rage welling up again. He tried to take slow and steady breaths.

"Hey, all the evidence pointed in your direction. Remember, you were responsible for the business that fucked up, and you made it clear it was my job to stay out of your way. You're the one who's lucky you're not in prison. From where I stand, you are the one that fucked me over. It wasn't George and it wasn't me and it wasn't…" John stopped himself and shifted his eyes to the mural on the wall.

"Who?" Tommy asked.

"Mark Schmidt. Who benefited more than McKinstry?" John said. "Or maybe it was you or one of your people." John was about in Tommy's ear at this point, so as not to have to speak too loudly and draw attention away from the front of the church where the service was about to start.

"You really think it was me?" Tommy asked through clenched teeth.

"What am I supposed to think? They trotted out all the same shit for me that you saw." John hit back.

Although the crowd couldn't make out their words, people in the front of the church were starting to turn their attention to the pair. Tommy and John drew a cold, dead, Botox stare from Deb. They had each only met her once. She was tall, spry, and notable with an intensity that cut through the two of them. She had thin and pale facial features and dark brown hair that was impeccably kept.

Tommy and John each moved quickly to pews on the opposite sides of the middle aisle. They both sat patiently, learning all of the things about George and his family and life that they should have known. The solid relationship with his wife and kids, the volunteer work through church, the network of friends, and the fabric of a rich life cut too short. At least Deb and the kids would be taken care of, Tommy thought to himself. The business had a key man life insurance policy on George for ten million with George's family getting half and the business getting the other half. Tommy figured there was no chance of seeing a penny of the business half of the policy. Another win for Mark and McKinstry, as they would lay claim to the other five million since George's death happened after the business transitioned to McKinstry.

Both felt too much like outsiders to greet the family after the service. Tommy slipped out first and started walking with no goal or destination in mind. It was hard not to obsess over who was behind the business falling apart. Obviously, someone at one of the two businesses would have to have been involved. Tommy was also thinking about Jenny and what Pat had said about her. He still thought he should move on, but didn't know if he could. He wandered east a few blocks from the church and ended up very close to their old offices.

Seeing the building once again, Tommy remembered that he had received a message on his phone the other day from McKinstry stating that he was free to use his old key fob to gain access to his office to pick up his personal items. Since he was so close and with nothing else to do, he decided he might as well get that out of the way.

The office was dark and quiet and clearly no longer a place of active business. Paper and boxes were randomly strewn. There were no computers or file cabinets. Everyone had been moved to the McKinstry offices or terminated. Tommy didn't much care which. He opened the door to his office. There was his phone, message light blinking, sitting on the floor with a couple of candy bars and packs of almonds that had been in his desk. The shelves were still there with a few of his pictures and personal books.

He hit "play" for his messages and was greeted by, "You have twelve new messages." He considered deleting them all, but since he had nowhere to go, he sat on the floor next to the phone and listened. "Sorry to hear the business ran into..." Tommy hit delete before the message finished. "Hi, want to have lunch? This is..." delete.

"It's George. Hey, call me soon, please." Tommy listened, hoping for more, but there wasn't anything. He played the message a second time to hear George's voice again and then hit delete.

"Hey, Tommy, it's Jack. You had me researching that company, Big Mountain, that was actively hedging prior to our, uh, problems. I don't know how to say this, but . . . it looks like the business involved John DeFallo."

Tommy scrambled to his knees and stared at the phone for a moment, then he hit delete, knowing full well what he heard and what it meant, and he was sure he never wanted to hear it again. Then he stood up, grabbing the phone as he rose, and hurled it at the window, breaking the inside pane of glass of the big old double-hung. As the phone hit the ground, Tommy pulled out his cell phone and was dialing, rage flushing his face. The redness and frustration intensified as he waited for an answer, the phone warping slightly under the pressure from his grip. Tommy started to calm himself after a few rings, as he needed to sound sane enough to avoid Jack hanging up on him if he was too contentious.

"Hi Jack, this is Tommy. I don't know how long ago you left it, but I got your message."

"Hey, sorry to hear about George. Good guy. Always worked hard for you," Jack said.

"Yeah. Hey, do you have more on John and those trades?" Tommy asked.

"You know, I landed at McKinstry in the shakeup so I could track the trades a bit more easily, but you gotta keep me out of this."

"You got it," Tommy said.

"No, really. I don't want anything to do with this or you or John."

"I said you got it. This is the last time you ever hear from me. Now tell me what the hell you know," Tommy demanded.

"Near as I can tell, he and some partner made eighty million or more on hedges that paid off big when the price tanked. John was a fifty percent partner in Big Mountain with RD Partners, but I haven't been able to track down who owned the RD Partner half," Jack said.

Without saying another word, Tommy hung up his cell phone; his teeth clenched so hard they felt like they could easily grind to powder, the veins in his neck were blue and pulsing. Tommy headed toward the Hilton on Michigan, knowing John's place was nearby and he liked to eat there regularly.

When Tommy arrived at the hotel, he saw John from across the restaurant and he bee-lined for him. Tommy could see he was removing his napkin and readying to stand. As he did, Tommy caught him completely off guard and pinned him against the wall next to the table. Tommy jammed his forearm up against his throat and somehow positioned the chair to hold John's legs against the wall. John was left with no choice but to grab Tommy's forearm with both hands to take some pressure off his windpipe.

Tommy pushed his face up to John's, close enough so that only a few people sitting close could hear. "You made eighty million off of our business going under, you son of a bitch!"

"I only made half of that, and it didn't even cover my losses. I didn't want it going bad. I was approached with an idea and put a little backup plan in place." John struggled for enough air to speak.

"You set the whole thing up to fail. The fictitious trades. You knew that you could cash in if we failed."

"I did suspect that things were going a little too well. You had to see it, too. I was just covering myself. I thought that you were screwing me."

"I wasn't!" Tommy was now loud enough for everyone to hear.

"Still looks like you were to me," John squeaked out.

Tommy's teeth were clenched again, his jaw muscles rippled. It made Tommy realize he was close to doing something that would end with him locked up tonight and maybe forever. He let John down to cough and gasp for air and walked quietly out. Just like when the business fell apart a week earlier, he headed to the train station, calling Pat for a ride.

After the run-in with Tommy, John packed a couple of things and took a cab to O'Hare. He knew word of their encounter would spread quickly in Chicago. No need to stick around for that. He headed back to Whitefish.

16

Tommy rolled over in bed without opening his eyes. He could tell it was morning and the room was annoyingly bright; too bright for his eyelids to keep his brain dark enough to sleep. Still without the energy to open his eyes and with a pounding headache, he pieced together his location by memory. Oh, yeah. Pat picked him up. He had told Pat the whole ugly story about the eighty million and the incident at the hotel. They drank beer; Tommy drank lots of it. He realized he was in a bedroom at Pat's house. He opened his eyes. It was mid-morning on Friday. The house was empty. Everyone was off to normal weekday activities.

He remembered telling Pat why he thought John had screwed him over. He hated John and figured that he was just the worst kind of human being possible. He was all worked up and lashing out figuring he had eighty million, or forty million, reasons to despise John. The exact math didn't matter.

Tommy rummaged through the bathroom until he found ibuprofen. He popped five in his mouth and stumbled around the house, eating and watching TV, not knowing what else to do. It was a cool April day, and just after noon, Tommy heard the back door slam. "Dude, you awake?" It was Pat.

"Yeah, in here." Tommy said, still in long Nike shorts, a T-shirt, and calf-high sports socks.

"You drank pretty fast last night. Talked fast, too," Pat said.

"Yeah, some of it is starting to come back to me," Tommy said.

"Sounded like a pretty nasty day," Pat said.

"I must have shared quite a bit."

"Yep. Good thing this John guy wasn't around. You might have killed him."

"Can you blame me for wanting that?" Tommy asked.

"Yeah, if he didn't do it."

"What do you mean? I told you he made millions and screwed our business," Tommy was yelling.

"He made millions and you think he screwed you. Maybe you should let the police handle it," Pat suggested.

The previous night's conversation kept coming back to Tommy in little pieces. Tommy knew that Pat was entitled to his opinion but thought his tone was too argumentative for the situation. However, knowing that he was going to ask Pat for help, Tommy needed to progressively soften his approach. "You suggested that last night, and you know I can't do that."

"Yeah, you mentioned having some plan in your head that sounded good to you drunk. My guess is today, it doesn't sound so good," Pat said.

"No, it still sounds good and it includes you! Can we talk about it tonight?" Tommy asked.

"I'll meet you at The Pub, but I'm not planning on liking any ideas you have."

"Great, so you'll listen. See you tonight," Tommy said. "Oh hey, before you leave, what's up with your dog? He looks like he's going to die."

"Hey, ixnay ethay ogday yingday alktay," Pat said.

Tommy's mind was slowed by a hangover and struggled for a second with the Pig Latin translation, then said, "Wait, are you serious? You don't want to talk about the dying dog in front of him?!"

"The girls think he understands, and they don't want to upset him."

"You people make me laugh."

"What do you mean, you people?"

"Supportive family types. I might set your dog straight when you're gone. Now, why don't you get back to work so I can get back to lying around your house," Tommy said.

"Do me a favor and get dressed before my daughters get home from school. You look like the pervs I try to warn them about," Pat joked.

"Got it. I'll go for a long walk before meeting you at a back table of the bar. Probably good for me to clear my head before I start drinking again."

"Sounds smart, in a way."

Pat stopped back home later for dinner with his family. He and Mary knew how important that hour each day was, so he texted Tommy that he would meet him after dinner. Tommy left the house early to not interfere with family time, went for that long walk he promised himself and sat down at the back tables with a pitcher of beer and two glasses. The area was elevated a half flight of steps from the rest of the bar and he could see Pat come in the front. There were about twenty people in the bar all dressed for softball. Tommy realized they were "pre-gaming," which seemed like a crazy idea before running around trying to hit and catch a ball. Given how much he'd been drinking lately he wasn't in a position to judge. It took about eight handshakes, back slaps, and hugs for Pat to make it through the bar.

"Do you know everyone in this town?" Tommy asked.

"A fair number. You think that's strange?"

"For me, maybe, but you look pretty damn happy and comfortable. I guess we're just wired differently," Tommy offered.

"Or, part of it is accepting this is who I am and being good with it," Pat said.

"Well, you're happy and I'm envious. I haven't figured it out. Always thought a bunch of money would do the trick. The money didn't last long, but long enough to know that wasn't the answer."

"Hey, at least you're out there trying, taking chances, putting yourself on the line. You're a negative, self-loathing pain in the ass, but I know you want to be a negative, self-loathing pain in the ass who makes a difference," Pat offered.

"Yeah, pretty naïve, huh?" Tommy asked.

"Hey, the longer you can hold onto naïve, thinking you can make a difference, the more likely you actually can." The two exchanged glances for several seconds and then each smirked before Pat continued. "Pretty deep for a townie, don't you think?"

"Good stuff. Perfect for my pitch. So, do *you* want to make a difference?"

"Dude, I already do with my family in my little world."

"Do you want more?" Tommy asked.

Knowing that Tommy was just trying to lead him on, Pat simply said, "No."

Tommy continued, "Have you ever wanted to run your own commodities trading business?"

"Don't even go there! You're barred or banned or whatever. Don't try to use me as your mouthpiece or something. What the hell are you thinking?"

"I need a way to draw John out. He'll eventually figure out I'm involved, and he won't be able to resist trying to get the best of me again."

"Well, so this is just about revenge?"

"Maybe it's more. Maybe George's death wasn't an accident. Maybe John had something to do with it," Tommy offered, somewhat desperately.

"Hold on. Now you just sound crazy and paranoid. Plus, if someone really killed George, do you want to mess with them? Do I?! Your idea is getting way worse," Pat said.

"There's more bad before it gets better. I just need you to pretty much put your life on hold for at least a few months. The business needs to be in Chicago, and you'll need two hundred thousand to really get it going."

"Why me? We haven't spoken in nearly twenty years before this past week."

"Because there's no one else I can trust. We drank and hung out and told each other everything in high school and college. There is no stronger bond for me. There was no pretense back then, no hiding any personal ugliness. You, Jenny, and I shared everything. Plus, you haven't asked me if I did anything wrong. You didn't ask. You didn't judge."

"If I ask now, will you be offended and move on?" Pat asked.

"Too late. Besides, if this works and you make ridiculous money, you can move out of this town. It's so small. It would probably be nice to not worry about one of your kids dating their cousin or something," Tommy deadpanned.

"Great," Pat responded without a hint of enthusiasm and stood up. "We're going to need a lot more beer to drink this into a good idea." Pat returned with the second pitcher of beer and a few questions for Tommy. "So, if I did this, and I'm not saying I am, how would we communicate?"

"You don't have to do anything. Just answer your phone and be observant," Tommy said.

"If we make money, how would we split it?" Pat asked.

"We don't. A dollar of yours can never become a dollar of mine. The Commodity Trading Futures Commission or the IRS would track that down in a heartbeat. This can never come back to me," Tommy explained.

"You should just go to the police. What if I say no? Will you just drop it?"

"I'll go to Jenny or ask someone else," Tommy said.

"You can't do that to Jenny, and you can't trust anyone else," Pat said.

"I will if you don't help me."

"I might do it to protect Jenny, and you, you moron." Pat stared at his beer. "Let me talk to Mary, and I'll let you know by Monday morning. Why don't you just chill here with us for the weekend, but don't bring it up again. I need time to think."

The two talked for a while longer, finished their beers and walked home.

Tommy mostly stayed out of Pat and Mary's way the rest of the weekend but decided he needed to get up with the rest of the family for breakfast on Monday morning. He glanced at Mary and knew from the look on her face that Pat was going to help him. Mary moved toward Tommy and pulled him into the hallway near the kitchen. "You hurt my husband in your little witch hunt and I will kill you. I'm sure you think I'm just talking, but if you ruin a good man, I'll do it. I will hunt you down and kill you in your sleep."

Tommy got the point. "I'm just borrowing your husband for a while. I'll return him better and richer."

"I don't want him better or richer. I just want him back. He's a far better man than you."

"I know that and also know you could have stopped this from happening. Pat loves you more than anything in the world. Why are you letting him do this?" Tommy asked.

"Because I love him just as much, and he really wants to do this. You got through to him at some level I don't understand. If he doesn't take this shot at doing something special for his family, he will always regret it. He thinks that will be harder to live with than failure. It must be some sort of testosterone or ego driven thing I don't get."

"That's good. He is doing it for himself and not for me." Tommy was somewhat relieved.

"Wait a minute, you don't get off the hook that easy. Make no mistake, he is doing this for you, and for Jenny," Mary asserted.

"What do you mean, for Jenny?" Tommy asked.

Mary felt sick, knowing that she meant Pat wanted Tommy to stick around to have a chance with Jenny and their son but knew that she couldn't say that. Mary recovered quickly saying, "You know, you threatened to drag Jenny into this if Pat didn't help, which, by the way was a heartless ploy."

"Yeah, that was pretty low. I guess I can be a bit manipulative," Tommy said, stating the obvious.

"I know that there is more to it with the three of you. High school and college bonds are a crazy thing," Mary said. "I was dating Pat the last couple years of college but was always a bit on the outside with you guys. To tell you the truth I often wondered if there was something sexual there that tied the three of you together."

"Ew, with me and Pat? Sorry, I never thought of your husband that way."

Mary smiled and said "You know what I mean. Either or both of you with Jenny."

"I think that you would need to talk to your husband on that one," Tommy said hesitantly.

"Yeah, I kind of crossed a line there. I think you bring that out in people," Mary said.

"Probably best we move on then. Thank you so much for letting this happen."

"Don't make me regret it," Mary warned and turned away from Tommy to Pat and the kids who were now at the kitchen table.

Pat said to Tommy, "You want some breakfast?"

"No, thanks. I should go."

Pat and Tommy shook hands and stared into each other's eyes for an awkwardly long time. Neither spoke. Tommy turned and mouthed, "I promise" to Mary and headed out the door and back to Chicago.

17

During a couple of recent trips through Union Station, Tommy had noticed the same guy standing in the same place staring at him as he left the station. Normally, he would not have noticed a single face among the masses pouring in and out of the station, but this guy made a point of being painfully conspicuous. The same frumpy-looking man with ill-fitting clothes stared at him from the same spot near where a street saxophonist often played.

Tommy tried to avoid eye contact as was the habit of almost everyone on big city streets, but this guy had forced Tommy to take note. This trip, it appeared the man had run out of patience thinking Tommy would be intrigued enough to stop and talk to him. When the man saw Tommy pass again, the stranger grabbed Tommy's elbow from behind. "You don't remember me, do you?" the stranger said.

"Sure. You're the guy who stares at me half the time I come out of this station. What do you want?" Tommy said.

"My name is Doug McClellan . . . Detective Doug McClellan. I'd like you to come with me to talk about the murder of George Shannon."

Tommy didn't look or act surprised at all. He knew the timing of George's death was suspicious, and he had just said as much to Pat recently. Maybe George found out what John had done or possibly he was in on it from the beginning. Either way it didn't shock Tommy. "I thought it was an accident. Why do you want to talk to me?" Tommy asked, maintaining his composure.

"'Cause I think you did it. Need a lawyer? I understand if you're not going to talk to me," McClellan said.

Tommy suddenly recognized him. "You son of a bitch! You were at the law office when I had my ass handed to me. You were the only poor fitting suit in a room full of suits. Wait, what the hell? George was alive then. This isn't making any sense."

"I was there to make sure that you didn't crawl out from any non-financial criminal activity, past or present. Got to admit, I didn't expect a murder case to come out of it so quickly."

"Arrest me or go away," Tommy said as he turned, and his head started to swell with angst and fear.

"All right, get more attorneys involved, asshole," Doug said. He had looked into Tommy's past and knew the history with his dad's business and attorneys. Doug was banking on the fact that Tommy might be pathological in his dislike of attorneys and had called that correctly.

"You've got a half an hour. Then, charge me or I'll leave." Tommy was pretty convinced he could get more information than he gave, since he didn't know anything. They walked to Doug's car and then drove to the precinct in silence. When on foot, Tommy set the pace. Doug, four inches shorter and thirty pounds heavier, struggled to keep up. At the precinct entrance Tommy gave way to Doug who escorted him to a second-floor interrogation room. There were two cameras in the corners of the wall that Tommy faced; he knew it would be standard procedure to record this interaction. "What can I do for you, detective?" Tommy said.

"Well, since you are going to tell me you don't know anything about George dying, I'll tell you some of what I know. First, there's the incriminating voicemail on your work phone. You want to tell me about that?"

Tommy's heart revved and it felt heavy in his chest. His eyes darted about the room. He didn't expect to be caught this off guard. He remembered that he had not finished checking messages on his work phone after getting word that John had made millions off of the company's misfortune. *What the hell was on his voicemail,* he thought. "I didn't get a voicemail," Tommy answered.

"The system shows that you checked your messages. You must know what I'm talking about," Doug said.

"I didn't get any messages that you would care about." Tommy was in survival mode now and never gave getting an attorney another thought. Doug had one thing he wanted—a truthful answer to a question that he knew the answer to. Doug knew from the McKinstry phone system that eight messages had never been checked. There was an incriminating message, but Tommy really didn't know what it said. Doug planned to let him worry about that for a while. Tommy continued, "Wait. If you took the time and effort to get a subpoena and checked my messages, then you must be looking at John because he made forty million dollars, maybe more, off of our company tanking. That kind of money could lead to a reason to kill someone," Tommy said.

Now it was Doug's turn to look confused. The phone system didn't save the messages Tommy had deleted, including the one from Jack about RD Partners and John owning Big Mountain Traders. Tommy could see in Doug's eyes the advantage that he now had and he continued to speak. "So that's it? A phone message I didn't listen to?"

Doug had to give Tommy more to keep him interested. He got in Tommy's face so much so that the booze on his breath assaulted Tommy. It was a nauseatingly sweet Southern Comfort kind of smell that made Tommy convulse slightly and flash back to a college party. "There was also some incriminating evidence on his body and at the ski hill in Montana," Doug said, exaggerating at this point, just trying to see if he could get Tommy rattled or talking. It worked. Tommy assumed that there must have been a thorough investigation and autopsy.

"Montana? He told me he was going to Colorado," Tommy said.

"Nope. Ended up near Whitefish, Montana," Doug replied.

"You mean a few miles from where John lives?" Tommy asked.

"Of course we know that, but we discounted it. Who would go out of their way to kill someone in their own backyard, so to speak?" Doug reasoned.

"Someone as cunning as John, knowing you'd jump to the conclusion it wasn't him," Tommy said.

"Or someone trying to frame John," Doug shot back.

"Hell, maybe so, but that doesn't mean it's me. You've got some work to do. You've been so busy assuming I did this; you haven't even looked at shit that stinks right under your nose. So, is there more? Otherwise, I'm walking," Tommy said.

Doug was so convinced it was Tommy who killed George that he had hoped to coerce a confession, but now knew he had to spend more time eliminating other suspects. He watched Tommy walk past him without saying a word. Tommy saw the indecision on Doug's face and turned around when he reached the door. "You really haven't given even a thought to John doing this, have you? Incredible. You really fucked this up, and your boss isn't going to like it."

As Tommy turned again to leave, Doug took one last shot. "You knew John lived out there. It was the perfect place for you to plan the murder."

Tommy laughed and said, "Yeah, maybe if you have a couple more drinks, you'll really believe that." And with that, Tommy stormed out. Doug slumped alone in a chair at the table where he thought he was going to get a big confession.

Tommy walked north from the police station, figuring the very long walk home would help to clear his head. Was George really murdered? If he was, who could it be other than John? What evidence did McClellan have, and what the hell was on those phone messages? Tommy tried to remotely access the rest of his office phone messages from his cell phone, but the code no longer worked. He knew McClellan didn't have any obligation to tell him more and probably wouldn't, particularly after Tommy had embarrassed him in front of whoever was behind the cameras and glass. The hour long walk did absolutely nothing to clear his head, but it was enough time to have missed a call from Doug. The voicemail message asked that he come back to the precinct again tomorrow.

18

Doug sat at his brown metal desk in the middle of the bustling precinct office, dejected over how his interrogation of Tommy had gone. Outdated fluorescent lights created a strobe effect on the open case files strewn about his desk. The pit, as the detectives called it, wasn't a great place to concentrate, but Doug did his best to comb through the materials. He thought if he could just close a case or two more his boss would get off his back. Tommy had been right about that part of Doug's situation and his relationship with his boss; he was in trouble.

Doug pretty much just had work in his life which allowed time for a growing obsession with Tommy that started when Doug first investigated Paul Smith's death. Doug had tracked Tommy's career and knew that he had sold his business just a few months after Paul's death. Even at that point, he didn't know how much it sold for and didn't have anything else to go on. However, when he heard and read about the implosion of Tommy's second business he called in some favors. He got himself invited to the Friday meeting where all the attorneys went after Tommy. Doug used the connection to Paul's death as justification to represent the city to ensure their jurisdiction in any local crimes wasn't compromised. He enjoyed watching Tommy squirm all day and then gained significant credibility with the city and county when George died just days later. That put Doug into full conspiracy mode and it certainly helped make his case that Tommy might tie back to Paul Smith's death. It was enough for the ADA to seek and attain a subpoena for Tommy's phone records.

He looked down again trying to focus; an after-bar shooting with no witnesses didn't hold much promise, nor did the jewelry store murder of a security guard. Doug came right back to two files, one with the name George Shannon and the other Paul Smith. Ironically, they weren't even murder investigation files, but obviously for Doug, Tommy Gardner was the suspect who tied these two deaths together. There was nothing simple about these cases. Only the Paul Smith file was really his case, and it was still classified as an accidental drowning death. George's death was still Montana's jurisdiction, but Doug liked Tommy for both.

Doug found Tommy totally unlikeable, even from a distance, and an arrogant ass who looked capable of murder, along with circumstances that surely indicated the same. This was all assessed just by being in the room with Tommy a couple of times, but never having spoken to him directly until the previous day's interrogation. After that conversation he was even more convinced Tommy was capable of murder.

Doug periodically glanced up to see the pitying looks from passing detectives and officers. He had the worst murder case close rate of all active homicide detectives in the city, but he vowed, again, to make something out of this mess. His other cases were stone cold anyway, and solving two murders this complicated might give him enough breathing room to get all the way to retirement. It appeared to Doug and his colleagues that his boss was letting him run with his intuition about Tommy, knowing it might lead to either a big win or Doug's termination. His boss saw an upside either way. No matter how you looked at it, Doug had been persistent, clever, and manipulative enough to at least have a shot at turning two accidental deaths into murder cases, and ultimately convictions.

Even though it had been a couple of years, Doug remembered talking to George when he briefly investigated Paul's death. Although George and Paul worked together, Doug had been more interested in the main owner of the business, Tommy Gardner. The only motive Doug could find at the time was the fact that Paul's stock options reverted back to Tommy upon Paul's death. At the time, all of the company stock was held by Tommy, the business wasn't for sale, and Doug viewed it as a small PR firm that couldn't have been worth much. Since the value of the options was pure speculation, it made a motive pretty difficult to prove. The only slightly incriminating evidence was a cell call from Tommy to Paul minutes before he drowned. Paul had been walking along the Chicago River when he received the call. However, there were several witnesses who confirmed that Paul was very drunk when he left a downtown bar, and based on where they found his body, he likely had fallen in the river and drowned walking home. Doug had agreed at the time with the decision to list it as an accidental death. He didn't mind avoiding another open murder case on his record, but he never let go of his suspicions.

For Doug, George's death just a couple of days after the plea had changed everything. Two accidental deaths were way more than Doug could chalk up to coincidence, so he spent the days after seeing George's obituary digging back into his old Paul Smith case file and researching everything he could on Tommy. Paul's stock options were for ten percent of Tommy's business, and it turned out that if he had lived he would have made about two million when Tommy sold his company.

Doug continued to fidget in his chair and page through the file, thinking through the information he had collected and where he could go with it next. His boss's glare unnerved Doug slightly before replaying in his mind what he had learned when he contacted the Whitefish Police Department the previous week. The local Whitefish police, led by Officer Murphy, hadn't seen any reason to view a fifty-something-year-old guy hitting a tree while skiing as anything other than an accident. Doug remembered exaggerating the extent of the tie to the Paul Smith case to soften Officer Murphy into sharing more information. The officer sent over the autopsy report and pictures from the scene. The Whitefish Police Department view was that this was clearly an accidental death and would stay that way unless Doug found enough evidence to make them think otherwise. They would be happy to help, but were not planning to drive an investigation. Doug had even gone as far as to contact George's widow, Deb, just a few days after his death to ask if George's personal belongings could be sent to him, for administrative reasons. To his surprise, Deb had agreed.

Doug was happy to at least have an autopsy report, some pictures from the scene, and George's personal effects and computer to go on. An autopsy due to any death at a ski resort was standard procedure because there was plenty of lawsuit potential with such situations. Doug noted that the death resulted from blunt force trauma to the brain. He had passed the report on to the Chicago Coroner's Office for their review.

The warrant that Doug received was only for cell and office phone records, not Tommy's home. That turned out to be enough to further fuel Doug's interest. There was a message from George on Tommy's work phone from the day he died informing Tommy that he had "fixed the problem" they had discussed earlier. If that wasn't incriminating enough, there were also three short calls from a payphone in Whitefish to Tommy's cell. The first was only ten seconds, the second a bit longer, and the third nearly a minute. Those calls were the day before George's death. Doug didn't want to share too much of this information with Tommy too soon, and planned to dole it out slowly to keep Tommy talking.

That added up to a lot of coincidence . . . but very little proof. Doug knew that without a weapon, a crime scene that was never treated like one, and little, if any, admissible evidence, he would never get an arrest warrant, much less a conviction. Doug's only hope was to go after Tommy and get him to confess. He didn't have any other choice. It had clearly backfired the first time, but it wouldn't stop Doug from trying again.

19

By morning, the sunny spring weather had given way to a blanket of fog so dense that water accumulated on anything that tried to cut through it. The dreariness matched Tommy's mood as he willed himself up the police station steps for the second day in a row. He was ushered to the same room as the previous day. Doug was already waiting. "Thanks for coming back," Doug said.

"Well, since I haven't done anything, I figured why not? You already know I hate attorneys," Tommy said, "and I need to get you guys pointed in a different direction."

"A different direction or the right direction?"

"You know what I mean. Or do you really still think I did this?" Tommy asked.

"I still know you did this," Doug offered. "Only reason we're here again today is because my bosses think maybe I was a bit premature in wanting to arrest you."

"You were going to arrest me yesterday?"

"Still thinking about doing it today," Doug shot back.

"That's bullshit. A Chicago cop arresting me for a Montana case. If you're that delusional, then I should get an attorney. You mind if I make a call?" Tommy asked.

"Go ahead, but if you wait a couple of minutes here you might get some more information by cooperating," Doug said.

Tommy paused, still believing he couldn't say anything incriminating, then said, "Fine. Five minutes, tops."

"Kind of a coincidence, don't you think, the timing of George's death?"

"Yeah, a fuck'n terrible coincidence for me. He was my only hope to get my name cleared." Tommy was feeling picked on again, and he sounded like it. He was whiny.

"You already made a deal on all of the trading related charges. You were banned from any commodity business for life. Remember, I was there."

"If you were sober enough to have read all the documents, you would also know the ban only holds if I can't prove it was someone else," Tommy said.

"Seems like getting rid of someone who could prove you did it would be half the battle."

"That's your motive?" Tommy asked.

"Yeah. You get rid of George and try to point all the shit you did back to him. A dead man don't defend himself," Doug said.

"Weak," Tommy muttered.

"You made it better yesterday, pointing out that it was in John's backyard. That way, if it ever did come out that it wasn't an accident, we would look at John."

"Yeah, see how that worked out for me?" Tommy said.

"Don't you get it? You were the reason I was there in the negotiations. Cook County and the City of Chicago didn't want some white collar criminal getting away with another blue collar crime."

"So the city of Chicago put their best detective on a crime that hadn't happened yet? Sounds to me like they were just trying to keep you busy." Tommy was under Doug's skin again.

"Listen, you son of a bitch. I knew you were scum from the moment I got this case."

"Yes, the case that hadn't happened yet."

"No, the reason I got assigned to this is that I investigated a suspicious death of one of your employees at your first company. Turns out that Paul Smith would have gotten at least a couple of million dollars in the sale of your first business if he had lived a little longer."

Tommy started to get a little scared and confused again. Had McClellan been watching him on and off for more than two years? Paul had fallen in the river and drowned.

Doug continued. "Over two million dollars sounds like a good motive to me."

"How come I never heard anything about the investigation?" Tommy asked.

"Wasn't enough evidence at the time that it was you. This whole thing with the stock options reverting back to you . . . I discounted it at the time because it was only ten percent of some PR business. I thought, "what could that be worth?" But with George's death, I took another look and realized it was big money, and now it looks like we have a pattern."

"I'm starting to get it. You got yourself assigned to my settlement because you spent the last couple of years looking to pin something on me. No wonder you didn't look at John; I'm your pet project."

"Sure, I kept my eye on you and wanted to make sure the settlement was only on the financial stuff, but now that looks pretty smart given another accidental death and all."

"Not smart, just obsessive," Tommy said. "So, you got right on a plane to Montana to prove an accident was my fault."

"Well, yeah, the local guys thought it was an accident. No reason, without a motive to think it was anything other than a guy running into a tree."

"So, big Chicago cop comes to save the day," Tommy said.

"They were happy to share information with me," Doug reasoned.

"Sure they were. What kind of evidence did you make up for that exchange?"

"Didn't have to make any up. Just needed to get the autopsy report back to Chicago and start piecing this together."

"What did you find out?" Tommy asked.

"Wouldn't you like to know?" Doug snorted.

"Listen. I'm back here because your bosses think you're as overzealous and vindictive as I do. You've had this case for maybe a week and already honed in just on me. Did you ever give a serious look at any other suspects? I need to know what you have on me and what the hell is in that phone message."

Doug paused, looked at the camera, and then said, "The whole thing looked like an accident if that's what you wanted to see on the mountain, but the body said something else."

"I'm listening."

"Well, first of all, it looks like a tree hit him not that he hit a tree."

"What?"

"Smacked in the side of the head, we think, with some type of bark-covered tree club. Had to be standing up because the other side of his head wasn't caved in."

"So that sounds like he ran into a tree to me."

"Except when you look at his body, his ribs and pelvis were crushed in the front and the back, like he was hit lying down," Doug explained.

"That's it? Somehow that points at me?"

"Well, it points at murder."

"Yeah, and I know a ton of criminal types to help with this in Montana," Tommy said.

"Listen. George is the second guy you've known to have a deadly accident with so much at stake. Seems like too much of a coincidence," Doug said.

Tommy could see his point and wanted to shift gears. "So, what's in this phone message?"

"First, you need to tell me about John or anyone else who might want George dead." The list of George's enemies was pretty short, actually near non-existent, so Tommy started with John.

"Well, maybe John put George up to the fraud. He knew he needed someone on my side of the business to pull this off. Then, once the business imploded, he would need to get rid of George, or risk losing millions. Or, maybe it was someone at McKinstry. They're going to make a lot of money, hundreds of millions, probably even billions over time."

"Tell me more about the forty million John made," McClellan asked.

"He basically bet against his own business, our business. Kind of a massive hedge strategy. He shorted carbon credits, which means he agreed to borrow them for a fee. If the price of carbon tanked, he was protected because he could buy them at a much lower price to cover the credits that he borrowed. If they didn't go down, he was out a couple million for the fees for the short sales, but then our business would have been a big success. The guys at McKinstry can get you more details."

"Anything illegal about what John did with the hedging, assuming he didn't commit fraud within the business?"

"Well, I don't know. Maybe not, but it's sure unethical."

"So, he killed George to hide his unethical behavior?" Doug asked.

"Maybe George was John's partner because someone else made forty million, too. I think the name of the other business was RD Partners. Figure it out. Follow the money for God's sake! Who knows, maybe George figured out it was John messing with our business and he killed George to avoid being exposed." Tommy explained.

"But there's no evidence that George did anything, right?"

"Not that I know of," admitted Tommy. "But someone did, and they had to have access. It had to be someone inside the company."

"Could John have simply been covering his ass financially with his hedging positions and not have been involved in fraud at the company or any murder?" Doug asked.

"I guess, but not likely from where I sit." Tommy said.

"I think where you sit is messed up. Looks like his strategy wouldn't have paid off if the company was successful, so he wasn't going to win twice," Doug said.

"Maybe not win twice, but it sure stopped him from losing," Tommy said.

"So, that's it?" McClellan asked.

"Uhh, yeah."

"Anyone else come to mind?"

"Well, no."

Doug got up and offered Tommy a handshake. "So, thanks for your time."

"What about the voice message?" Tommy asked.

"I don't think I want to share that today," Doug said. "Maybe if you have some more tangible information later. This is an ongoing investigation."

"You promised," Tommy said.

"You asked. I didn't promise. And by the way, you are still a person of interest in the death of George Shannon. Please don't try to leave the country." In a matter of seconds, Tommy found himself on the precinct steps for the second time in less than twenty-four hours wondering what had happened.

20

Doug knew that he needed to find more evidence tying Tommy to the murder. He needed this case, and he needed it soon. His job was probably in jeopardy. He headed back to meet with the coroner who had received the autopsy report.

The coroner assigned to work with Doug on the case was Shirley Callahan, a bright doctor with a promising career married to another bright doctor with a promising career. Given that she wanted kids and had the right equipment, along with a more realistic ego than her husband, Shirley had settled into a less glamorous career, but one with manageable hours.

During his previous visits, he observed that scrubs and tennis shoes weren't enough to hide an appealing figure. Natural red hair and fingernails to match had Doug enamored. Doug was doughy, had a face marred by alcohol and was only mildly interesting in conversation, none of which got in the way of believing that he was a sought-after commodity. "So, what new information do you have for me?" Doug said as he walked in on Shirley's autopsy work.

Shirley recognized him, but it took her a moment since they had only worked together on this single case. "I didn't call you, and I'm a bit busy," Shirley said as she pulled a bullet from the rather large ass of a heavily tattooed Caucasian corpse.

Doug got that she wasn't amused and changed his tone and demeanor.

"Sorry. Do you have a minute to discuss my case?"

"Our case," she corrected him, and she was actually interested. Over nearly ten years, Shirley had developed quite a reputation as a skilled coroner and got more than her share of interesting cases. This was turning into one of them, and although she found Doug repulsive, she interrupted the autopsy to talk to him. The fact that her patient could wait was part of the beauty of the job and her schedule. Shirley continued, "You and I have been over this before, but since you're back, I'm assuming things aren't going well."

"You could say that," Doug admitted.

"Let's see," Shirley said pulling out the file. "The coroner in Montana did a decent job on this report. Separate blows to the head and the body. The body blows could have been done when the body was lying on the ground, causing fractures to the front and back of the ribs and pelvis."

"What do you mean, could have?" Doug asked.

"Just that—it could have been done on the ground, but it also could have happened when the guy planted the side of his face into a tree and had the front and back body injuries occur as his body tumbled after initial head impact."

"I thought you said it was murder."

"No, that's when I used the word 'could' as in it *could* be murder. Do you always have this much trouble hearing what people say? Plus, it's all in the report," Shirley stated.

"Yeah, the report," Doug mumbled.

"You haven't read it, have you?" Shirley asked incredulously.

"Figured I could go on what you told me," Doug explained.

"That might have worked if you had listened to what I said."

Doug thought about the couple of drinks he had at lunch that day, paused, then continued, "Do you have anything else for me to go on?" Doug asked.

"Blow to the head killed him within a few minutes. The broken ribs and pelvis and ruptured spleen wouldn't have done it . . . at least not quickly. No sign of hypothermia, which confirms it was a quick death."

"Thought the ribs and pelvis were crushed when the body was on the ground," Doug asserted.

"No. Broke . . . cracked. Crushed is your word, not the report's or mine."

"So that means no murder?" Doug frowned.

"No. You need to figure out what he hit, or what hit him."

"So, if it's murder, I need a murder weapon?" Doug asked.

"Kind of, yeah. The history this Tommy fellow had with the other suspicious death and the other information you shared about the phone records makes this intriguing, but I think that you need to get to the scene. I need more information. Maybe blood and guts splatter from the tree. There was significant tissue mass missing from his ear and the right side of his face. It still might be out there. I'm not sure what I need. Why don't you go be a detective?"

"I guess I should do that since I already brought Tommy in and threatened to arrest him," Doug said.

"You did what?! I didn't even rule this a murder, nor did they in Whitefish," Shirley said. "As of now, this is still an accidental death. You don't have a warrant or even clear jurisdiction for that matter."

"Hey, I can arrest someone without a warrant, but yeah, I got a bit ahead of myself on that one," Doug said.

"You think?" Shirley questioned, her tone escalating.

"Great. The local cops will be glad to see the guy who took their closed accidental death case and tried to turn it into a murder investigation. Instead, why don't you do some fancy image or simulation thing from the photographs to show the bark pattern and test the shit the Whitefish coroner pulled off of him, then tell me what hit him and how fast he was going?"

"I can tell you all of the stuff that was in the report that you should have read. That it was a Douglas fir, and the bark pattern and angle makes it look like he hit a branch, not the trunk."

"Is that everything?" Doug asked.

"He had liver cancer that had metastasized to his brain. Probably had it for more than a year but doesn't look like he even knew it. I checked. He hadn't been to his family doctor in almost two years and no sign of treatment or any records. He only had a few months, even with aggressive treatment."

"Ironic, murdering a guy that was going to die anyway," Doug offered.

"Murder. Again, your words, not mine. The death certificate still says accidental death and will until you get me more. You need to go to Montana, or let it go."

It took Doug a couple of days to convince his bosses that he should go to Montana and to schedule a meeting with the local law enforcement and ski patrol staff who had handled the investigation. Doug had previously led Tommy to believe that he had already been out to Montana and even tried to make him believe that he had a warrant, but that was still far from the truth.

Doug hadn't run into the reluctance yet from the local law enforcement that he had anticipated. A lot of cops get territorial, but the main concern he heard over the phone was taking up their time with a useless trek up a mountain. He convinced the deputy, Officer Murphy, who had originally handled the case and who he had spoken to previously, to meet him at the bar at the base of the hill with the lead ski patrol guy. The Bierstube was the same bar that John and his friends liked to frequent.

As Doug pulled into the parking lot, he could still see plenty of snow on the mountain and lift chairs that looked abandoned for years, not a week. The gravel parking lot was as big as a football field, but was nearly empty, not a surprise for early afternoon after the close of the mountain. He walked into a building that felt and smelled as tired as it looked. If a building could need a rest, this one did. The bartender and waitresses didn't even give Doug a glance as he entered. He strolled past the main bar and peered into the back room, immediately spotting the two he was set to meet.

As Doug moved toward the pair at the far wall, he started to see this place might be a good reason to take up skiing. Everything was wood, nicely worn, and a fireplace still sooty and full of ashes. The walls were noisy with beer signs and food specials. The only one that stood out to Doug was the small *Pabst Blue Ribbon* club sign, presumably a good way for the locals to buy beer cheap, leaving the tourists to overpay for more sophisticated brands. He was accustomed to using his finely honed detective skills to find cheap alcohol.

The Whitefish Police Department officer was in full uniform: wide brim hat on the table, brown, properly adorned shirt with the name 'Murphy' on the pocket, tan pants, and a gun belt stocked with pepper spray, club, flashlight, radio, and every other accoutrement, looking way too heavy to be wearing if he really had to chase someone.

The second man looked like he could have been Officer Murphy's brother, both being in their early thirties, clean-shaven with similar thin noses, shallow-set pale eyes, and light complexions. Dressed in jeans, a sweatshirt, and hiking boots he introduced himself first, reaching out a hand to shake. "Hi. You must be the detective from Chicago. I'm Brett Kelly, the ski patrol supervisor. This is Ryan Murphy, the officer assigned to your case."

"I am. Thanks for meeting me here. Hey, can I buy either of you a PBR?" Doug said and watched as Brett signaled the waitress to bring two beers, since Ryan was on duty, and the three men sat down. Doug wasn't much for small talk, getting right to it. "So, what happened the day George died?"

"We got a call well after dark that a skier didn't show up for dinner with a friend. Didn't think too much of it. We get at least a few calls like that each season. People are usually just somewhere having fun and drinking or whatnot and by morning, they are back where they belong," Brett said.

"Who called it in?" Doug asked.

Murphy spoke up. "Some guy. Only said his name was Joe. He left a cell phone number that turned out to be a pay-as-you-go phone. We tried to track it down once we found out the missing guy was dead."

"Didn't that look suspicious to you?"

"Well, the call went to the ski patrol, not 911," Murphy offered. We only had their caller ID to go on and yes, maybe a little suspicious."

"Then what happened?" Doug asked.

Brett spoke again. "We waited until morning. If a skier is down on or near a run, the ski patrol or the groomers will find them. If they're in the woods, we wouldn't have a prayer in the dark anyway."

"What happened next?"

"Early the next morning, he was still missing, or so we thought since the original caller couldn't be reached," Brett said. "We were trying to decide what resources to dedicate to looking for our mystery man when all hell broke loose."

"What do you mean?" asked Doug.

"This guy must have been connected. All of a sudden, we had a helicopter and a group of locals organized and searching. Found the body in an hour. Guy was pretty frozen. Clearly died the day before. These accidents happen every few years. He fit the profile. Guys in their forties or fifties out to prove to themselves or whomever that they're still young, but the reality is they don't have the reaction time that they use to anymore," Brett explained.

"You said accident," Doug reminded him.

Murphy jumped in again. "Besides fitting the profile, the scene looked like an accident. No helmet and a good chunk of blood and guts were on a tree at what looked to be the right height for him to have hit it on his own."

"Was it the tree trunk or a branch? What kind of tree? Where was it?" Doug asked with no time for answers.

"Let's go take a look," Murphy said, and then pointed up the mountain.

After an ATV ride up the mountain, they arrived at a steep wooded area that separated two runs. It was about 100 yards across and extended about 300 yards down the mountain. A route was clearly discernible, but spring rain and melting snow masked any other activity. The entrance was partially blocked by a stumpy evergreen that didn't know if it was a tree or a bush. There was a slight mound within the trees that, along with small evergreens, would have blocked anyone who happened to pass by from seeing what happened.

"Mostly locals use this kind of path through the woods. We just thought he came in hot and didn't know what hit him," Murphy offered.

"Yeah, if you come in too fast, you need to bail out down the mountain into these small firs. You try to stay on-line and you can hit the big Douglas, which he did. Left part of his face right here," Kelly pointed to a spot about eight feet up the twelve-inch diameter of the trunk.

"That seems pretty high. Has that much snowpack melted?" Doug asked.

Murphy answered quickly. "Yes. That mark was about six feet off the top of the snow the night of the accident."

"How come the branches are cut up from the ground? Seems like a strange place to be tree-trimming," Doug said.

Kelly handled this question. "Some of the locals plan routes in the summer and trim them in. This is all Flathead National Forest land, but as long as you aren't spending a half a day with a chainsaw, no one's going to catch you."

"Would George have been in here without help from some local skiers?" Doug asked.

"We figured if he was with locals, he wouldn't be dead. We thought he followed someone in trying to keep up and didn't know what he was doing."

"How fast could he have been going?"

"If you were crazy, you could probably hit the opening at about twenty-five miles per hour. There really isn't time or space to build up more speed before you enter, and obviously you wouldn't want to. By the damage, it looked to us like he was going as fast as he could."

Spring rains had removed most everything from the tree, but Doug collected and bagged what he could. He took what looked like tissue, some tree bark samples, and more pictures in between taking notes. He looked for anything that resembled a club or branch that could have been used as a murder weapon, but after scouring a fifty-foot perimeter, he felt going further was a useless exercise. He returned to the bar to look at his evidence and have a couple more PBRs. His return flight wasn't until morning. He would get everything to Shirley and see what she could do.

21

A few days after returning from Montana, Doug received a message from Shirley asking him to stop by the morgue when he had a chance. Doug, of course, thought she was interested in him because they could likely just talk over the phone, but she wanted him there. An inflated ego, a semi-constant stupor, and a propensity to sleep with married women had him again hoping for the most.

When Doug arrived, scrubs and tennis shoes had been replaced by a black skirt, teal blouse, and heels, all of which he thought were for his benefit. Shirley, however, had other plans. "I have to be in court to testify in twenty minutes. I have five for you."

"That's all it will take," Doug said and smiled slyly.

"Yeah, well, your guy hit a Douglas fir, or the Douglas fir hit him, whichever way you want to look at it," Shirley said.

"Kind of already knew that from the last time around."

"Good. You remembered something. What I really meant is the tree with blood and guts on it is a Douglas fir and so is the one that hit his face."

"Great," Doug said. "So, my murder weapon is a tree. Do you have anything I can use?"

"What's left of the splatter pattern on the pictures looks a little small, but that may be because of the rain."

"Anything else?"

"A colleague of mine looked at the facial injuries from the original photos and thinks he needed to be going at least 40 mph to do that kind of damage."

"Can you testify to that?" Doug asked. "Because the local guys said he couldn't be going more than 25."

"Sure, but under cross, we'll probably get killed because we didn't do the original autopsy, and it's an inexact science to begin with. Given the bark patterns on his face are perpendicular to a normal tree trunk, I assumed that he hit a branch. Maybe thought he could get under it, or whatever. Now that I see he hit a trunk, he would have almost had to be parallel to the ground to leave the imprint on the side of his head that it did, so yes…"

"So, you think he was murdered but can't prove it?"

"I think someone hit him with a club made from a hunk of Douglas fir, then hit the tree to transfer splatter to the tree," Shirley continued. "Then smashed his ribs and pelvis when he was laying on the ground."

"What do I do now?"

"Get me more, or find other evidence that a killer was there. You can win cases with good circumstantial evidence or good physical evidence, but it's difficult with neither. Find more, please." With that, Shirley turned and headed down the hall. Doug lusted in her direction until she turned the corner.

22.

For early May in Chicago, the air was alarmingly thick and even a touch oppressive. Tommy thought it felt more like Beale Street than Belmont as he waited in line for coffee a few blocks from his condo. The floor was dried-orange-soda-sticky as Tommy pried loose his shoes for each painfully slow step while the man in front of him overpowered the smell of coffee with his ripeness. Tommy let out a pathetic sigh, loud beyond warranted, that he somehow thought could be heard by baristas over the din of espresso machines and conversation. Tommy knew in his mind that everyone was inconvenienced by lines and waiting but was convinced in his heart that no one suffered more than him under their weight. There were no texts or emails to return or calls to make, so Tommy was forced to look inward to think about what he always thought about. *Why? Why do I do the stupid things that I do?*

When his coffee was finally served, he sat down, not having any idea what to do next, although he assumed finding a job someday would be in order. For today he decided he would again turn to wandering Chicago's public transportation system trying to decide what to do, but now it was without money or a future. As usual he turned to Susan, this time with a text.

He typed, "*I'm back in town. Can we meet tonight?*"
"*Are you thinking wine and sex at your place?*"
"*Sure.*"

"Not what I was thinking. Not by a longshot. Goodbye Tommy. We're done. You were just too selfish too often, and to think by the end of our relationship I actually loved you. My mistake."

Tommy stared at the text, emotionless. He didn't call Susan in an attempt to get closure. He really didn't love her, and Susan knew that love wasn't supposed to be part of their relationship. He had kept his end of the bargain by not getting too attached. Tommy was sure that he would have felt worse about the breakup, and even fought to win Susan back, if it weren't for the hope of working things out with Jenny. Instead of riding the L as he planned, Tommy walked the Lake Michigan shore from the north side, walking south towards downtown. The wind off the cold lake water made it feel comfortable compared to the rest of the city, but that went unnoticed by Tommy. Without money, a career, or a girlfriend, he was too busy feeling sorry for himself.

He thought maybe, with some time passing after talking to Doug, he would calm down and come to grips with his situation and move on. However, the more he thought about John living his life in Montana, the worse it got. John was going to get away with it, whatever *it* was, unless Tommy did something.

He was convinced that getting Pat involved to draw John in was the only thing that he could do, but knew that he owed Jenny an explanation. He also knew from his last conversation with Pat and Mary that Jenny was in Chicago with friends for a couple of nights. Tommy called her and asked if they could meet. Jenny was staying with a friend who lived near the Hilton on Michigan, so she suggested meeting there. He hoped that no one would remember him from his last visit. Tommy was only a short cab ride from the hotel, so he asked Jenny if they could meet right away.

Jenny entered the lobby of the hotel and scanned it for Tommy. She had recently gotten back from a run in Grant Park. No makeup, hair pulled tight in a ponytail, black, calf-length leggings, and a T-shirt that fell straight down from her breasts. Jenny wasn't a woman who caught most men's eye at first glance but did for those smart enough to look twice. Tommy was in the bar, and she spotted him first, then headed in his direction. "Sorry. I'm not exactly dressed for this place. Can we talk in the coffee shop?" Jenny asked.

Without hesitation, Tommy moved to the waitress station and poured his drink into a paper cup, and they headed across the lobby to the coffee shop. "Is that a gimlet? You still drink those? You were the only one who did when we were in college, and you're still the only one."

"If I drank something that tasted better, I would drink more."

"Also, mid-afternoon is a bit early for you," Jenny said as she glanced at her phone, noticing the time.

"It's been a rough week. I have a cop who is convinced that I killed my business partner, George. He has a hard-on for me and won't stop short of a restraining order."

"Why does he think it's you? Because of evidence?"

"Well, yeah, some, I'm sure, but I don't know exactly what."

"Why don't you ask him?" Jenny suggested.

"Doesn't really work that way, but I'll keep trying. I gave him good reason to look elsewhere, so my guess is he will be tied up for a while. I really need to get some information to Pat. Can you do that for me?" Tommy asked.

"Just talk to him yourself. You're a big boy."

"I can't just call him anytime I want until this whole thing is done."

"What whole thing? What are you talking about?" Jenny asked.

"That's why I wanted to talk to you. Pat's willing to start a little business to help me out. Maybe even find George's killer in the process, but it's a securities business and I'm . . ."

"Barred, yes, for life. I get it. You want me to be an illegal go-between so there's no connection between you and Pat. No!"

"I need you to do this for me."

"Why? So you can go after someone? Who? This John guy?"

"Yes, please."

"You said this cop was stalking you. Don't you think he saw you and

Pat together already?"

"Maybe, but I think he stayed in Chicago. I always used cash when we were together. I think I'll be okay."

"Oh, or do you think *WE* will be okay?"

"Yeah, that's what I meant," Tommy offered. "We."

"I'm not doing it. Figure something else out." Jenny's contorted face revealed an orange-red tone that blazed through her richly pigmented skin. Tommy thought she still looked beautiful and had trouble staying on track.

"Okay then. Now that I think about it, I don't need you to do anything so much as I need you to know this was happening, although I might ask for your help if Pat and I really get in a bind," Tommy offered.

"Well, I guess by avoiding telling me details and not making me an accomplice, yet, to whatever is going on is kind of nice, in a way," Jenny said.

"See, yes, it's because I care about you and Pat, and I want to give you a chance to talk him out of it. That's really what I want, but sometimes the words don't come out right," Tommy explained.

"Don't worry. I'll give that my best shot."

"I'm counting on it. If you need more information to motivate you, he has to remortgage his house and take loans against his retirement accounts to pay for the start up," Tommy said.

"What?!" Jenny yelled. "That's insane. I'll definitely talk him out of it!"

"Well, if you don't, please let him know I will be in touch in a few days," Tommy said.

"And you're not going to use me as some kind of a bag lady?"

Tommy smirked. "Right. I'll keep you out of this, if I can."

"You should have ended that sentence three words earlier."

"I get it. So, will I see you around Chicago?"

"Not sure if you'll see me, but I'll be here some this summer. Once school is out, I like to spend a little time in the city. Lots to do here in the summer."

"Great. See you then," Tommy said.

Jenny didn't answer, smiled slightly, got up, and headed out of the hotel.

Consumed by what had transpired over the last few weeks and without women he was interested in, interested in him, he had only one place to turn. He knew that he could make Pat successful in the carbon trading business. Like other commodities and stocks, it had become an impersonal, detached, electronically-executed business. All he thought he needed to do to be successful was obsess over it like he obsessed over other things until patterns developed that he could exploit.

For days, Tommy sat in his condo popping Modafinil and watched trades stream across his screen. The effect of the drug flung open the windows of the dark, musty attic of his mind. They infused him, pushing Tommy beyond his own wishes to do more. He could feel weary and tired in the background, but only if he really went out of his way to pay attention. He logged and tracked everything, looking for trends. He didn't shower for days. A reddish mold started to grow on the dishes in the sink. He couldn't figure out or see anything . . . no patterns, no tells— nothing. It was too volatile and didn't seem to be tied to publicly available market news and long-term conditions. There weren't even predictable daily trends and runs like a day trader could utilize.

Carbon trading was still relatively new, and volumes so low, that the market responded more to short-term supply and demand of credits than it did to general market conditions. Tommy thought that might be the case going in, but he needed to prove it to himself. He had hoped to be wrong so he could just sit at his computer having discovered the secret to how and why this market moved. This wasn't a market for day traders mining trends and making thousands of dollars, and it wasn't about big firms relying on their speed of trading in large volumes to make millions. This was about short-term supply and demand of newly issued offsets and the opportunity to make millions of dollars, but information was key and wins and losses would play out over days and weeks for each cycle.

He had hoped to avoid this option but it was now the most logical one, and the only one. He would have to clean himself up and get out of his cave and talk to people at McKinstry as well as other buyers and sellers. He preferred the company of his computer screen, but he had no choice. He spent Friday afternoon setting up appointments for the following week. That gave him the weekend to mentally prepare to engage again with people beyond those in restaurant delivery uniforms.

On Saturday morning, Tommy left his condo for the first time in a week. It was mid-May and the weather in Chicago had varied from strangely oppressive, to cold, and then lastly to ideal during Tommy's hibernation. It seemed as though there couldn't be anyone in the city left inside. Tommy hopped on the Brown Line and found himself downtown in minutes. He returned to a familiar block on LaSalle Street overlooking the Chicago Board of Trade building. Why not have Pat's business settle in the same area? These buildings would always stand for stability and would always be there, built by the hands and on the backs of those long since forgotten.

Tommy wrote down the address and phone number in block letters for a small second-floor space for rent, then wrote, "Rent this," on the paper. He addressed the envelope to Pat and dropped it in the mail.

He felt dirty and cheap. The carbon trading business had nothing to do with the venerable, old buildings. He was just playing on an image again, but in a way was probably just doing as the building architects had done on this very street about 150 years earlier— creating an image of stability where risk existed. Commodities and other markets had evolved beyond substantial old structures and face-to-face trading. Now it was a mysterious electronic process that involved upstanding banks, brokers, market-makers, and clearing agents all playing by important rules, processes, and procedures so that every transaction was beyond reproach. Well, except for the ones involving John and Tommy's old company.

For the most part, there weren't people in colored vests dealing with each other anymore, just information flowing between computers. The system had taken some of the ugliness out of making and losing money. This was cool and quiet. No one could hear the screams of anguish from those who were losing millions. It was sterile, separating losers and winners. It was easier that way, better for business.

What had started as a method to help ensure fair pricing of commodities and a way to hedge legitimate risks had degraded into legalized gambling facilitated by those making commissions. Each new commodity that came to the market over the years offered another chance to create a never-ending revenue stream. Many of these commodities also offered a relatively brief window for fabulously risky and large gains, as well as horrific losses. Low volumes and big egos could collide in a thinly-traded market where a few people could, or thought they could, control pricing. It was carbon's turn to be that commodity, a showdown of large dreams and money. A fight fairly officiated by rules, regulations, and computers. Surely there would once again be big winners and losers.

Tommy spent all day Saturday and Sunday walking, reading, and most notably sober. He bought a prepaid phone with cash on Sunday night, and he dialed Pat's number. Pat immediately picked up and said, "Yeah, Tommy, what's up, man?"

"How did you know it was me?" questioned Tommy.

"You're the only guy who would call me from a local area code number that doesn't come up on my phone. Besides, Jenny talked to me and I knew you would be calling sooner or later."

"Yeah, well, when I call in the future, don't use my name, and the calls will be brief. Sooner or later, McClellan will stumble upon you, tap your phone or whatever," Tommy said.

"Wiretaps and burner phones. This is some real clandestine shit," Pat said.

"Come on, this is serious," Tommy insisted.

"Really, I'm putting all of my money and my way of life on the line for you and you need to tell me this is serious?"

Mary and Jenny thought Pat was crazy, but Pat really wanted to help his old friend. Plus, what Tommy had said in the bar when he first brought up the idea was weighing on Pat. Pat did start feeling like he needed to take at least one shot at doing something big, something that could change his life and his kids' lives forever.

"Sorry. So, you're still in, then? Jenny couldn't talk you out of it?"

"No, but I told her I would try one last time to talk you out of it," Pat said.

"Go for it."

"Seems like, from what you've told me, some of this is your fault."

"Yeah, so?"

"So, why are you blaming John?"

"Because it's *more* his fault. I'm mad as hell. I need to find out what happened to the business and to George. I can't let it go. You know how I am—how hard it is for me to let go of my mistakes. This one will never go away unless I do something."

"Come on, you're exaggerating."

"Really? Remember when we were in college, road-tripping through the Nevada desert? I was convinced I knew where to go and got us lost for three hours," Tommy said.

"No. Well, wait. I remember getting lost."

"Well, it was my fault and there were so many clues that we were going in the wrong direction. It was so stupid. I replayed that for weeks, even months, easily a thousand times in my head until the next dumb thing came along. Take that little mistake, think about the massive mistakes I have made, and then, picture my life."

"Dude, you need to get some help," Pat offered.

"Yeah, I've got more disorders than you can count, and I've had more prescriptions than I can remember. I can't work or think straight when I take them, so I quit."

"Sounds like you might be better off not thinking straight."

"Maybe true, but not this time, and I can't move on until I try to fix things."

"How can you fix this? Does revenge fix it?"

"It's all I have."

"There are other more important things that you can have." Pat was hoping that Tommy would think of Jenny.

"Not until I put this behind me. I need to hold someone accountable for this mess," Tommy said.

"Why not hold yourself accountable and move on?" Pat suggested.

"I hold myself accountable every day. Don't you get it? Shit is always my fault. I can't sleep. I can't eat knowing that I fucked up my life. I had all the money I would ever need and I tossed it all away. The only things I do now are drink and feel sorry for myself, and I was already an expert in both. I don't know what else to do." Tommy was getting exhausted by the sound of his own voice.

"So, now you want me to put all of my money on the line. If that works, how do you know I won't go down the same path of not knowing when enough is enough?" Pat asked.

"You don't have millions, and you don't need them to be happy."

"Are you saying I'm too lazy to be rich?" Pat said.

"No. You're not stupid enough to chase money or ghosts."

"You're telling me you're too stupid to stop yourself, so then, maybe if I don't do this, maybe I can stop you."

"You know I'll find another and even worse way to try," Tommy offered. "We've been over this before."

Pat paused. "That is the main reason I'm going to do this. You can't stop yourself, even if it kills you."

"Right. I'll call you back soon with specifics on how to set up and operate the business, but you won't hear much from me directly much after that."

"Well, make it soon. I'm quitting my job tomorrow."

23

A few days after Pat and Tommy's phone conversation, Pat's phone rang again. It was the same number that Tommy had previously used to call him. Pat answered, "Hey, shouldn't you be throwing these phones away?"

"Not each time. You have plans? Or do you have a few minutes?" Tommy asked.

"A deuce is the only thing in my short-term plan. Mary and the kids are all out. Okay, it's clear that I'm stupid enough to do this. Now what?"

"Did you find an office?" Tommy asked.

"Yes. Rented. A lead just popped up. Private bathroom is nice. I'll add a futon in the back room and call it home," Pat said sarcastically, knowing that the cryptic mail about the rental space had come from Tommy.

"A guy will be by to set up your office, help get you incorporated, make sure you are licensed. That's going to take a couple of weeks of intense training and a test."

"A test . . . um, no. I haven't taken one since I froze at my last college final. Almost didn't graduate. I was told there would be no test."

"Don't worry. This visitor will take care of everything."

"What will all of this cost?"

"Nothing. He owes me," Tommy said.

"He must owe you a lot."

"You have to remember; I've helped make a few millionaires along the way. I'm just not one of them. This is the only guy in Chicago I would trust, and there's no way this blows back on us. Just don't ask him any questions or look at him too closely, and you'll be fine."

"So, he's going to cover everything? Including how to trade, or hedge, or whatever the hell I'm going to be doing? And you're kidding about the 'not looking' at him thing, right?"

"Yes to all of your questions."

"And this is all going to result in making millions of dollars?!"

"Maybe tens of millions. Or of course, you might end up broke. Here's the deal. In Europe they have a more robust carbon trading system for connecting buyers and sellers with more diverse financial instruments so it will likely grow here," Tommy explained.

"So this is the same type of market that was already set up previously in the U.S., and you and your partners almost single-handedly fucked it up, right?" Pat asked in a concerned tone.

"Well, kind of. I'd like to say that we tested the system and capitalism fixed it. You don't need the details, but you can't do the types of projects we were doing anymore. Abuse and fix, that's how capitalism works."

"But you're telling me you figured out another way to abuse the system." Pat was moving from sarcastic to worried.

"This is legal. The trading in the U.S. is small and still voluntary. All we plan to do is take advantage of a small, volatile, thinly-traded market."

"I'm no genius, but for us to make money there has to be some sorry fuck on the other end losing it. Sounds like I could end up being that guy. Jesus, let's get this conversation over with before I change my mind. Besides, now I'm crowning. I gotta go."

"I'll protect you. This will work. You won't have any access to insider information or insider trading concerns."

"Well, I didn't have insider trading concerns until now. Thanks," Pat said.

"Remember, just be observant. In a few months, you'll be a carbon trading savant."

"Right. Are we done?"

"Yes. Go take care of business," Tommy said.

"See you on the other side of this mess, I hope."

"I hope so, too."

24

It was a clear, crisp Monday morning, both outside and in Tommy's head. He was drug free, sober, and ready to face the grind of information gathering. His breakfast meeting at a little café near the north end of Millennium Park had gone well. He met with one of the younger partners at McKinstry who was surprisingly forthcoming with information about their clients and the large increase in credits that they anticipated needing to buy for a big client late in the month. Tommy got those details by simply asking how things were going.

It puzzled Tommy until he realized that people might consider him as someone who couldn't do anything with the information. After all, everyone knew he had been banned from commodity markets. Maybe he could keep positioning to be an advisor, a sounding board, their would-be psychologist. He didn't care, as long as the information flowed.

With his spirits up, the weather good, and a few extra minutes before his next appointment in the Intercontinental lobby, he started walking north on Michigan. A Loyola University van sparked memories of college when his steps were cut by the van as he tried to cross the street. He flashed to an economics professor who taught him that if anyone has an information advantage, they can profit from short-term market directional changes. Not minute's worth in the trends that day traders see, but days of an advantage. The better the information and the smaller the market, the bigger the advantage. The professor made it clear that no one can control the eventual price, and the ultimate mistake would be to think anything different.

Tommy was confident that on most given days or weeks, he'd be able to figure if there was more buy or sell pressure on the market and play the direction. The key was not to be too greedy or hold onto positions too long. He couldn't afford to get Pat on the wrong side of a long-term trend.

Tommy's second appointment arrived right on time. This time the appointment was with a developer who had credit approvals on a massive project delayed. Many players in the market were planning to buy these offsets, and soon they would be finding out that they would have to look elsewhere.

The combination of the two meetings indicating that demand would be up and supply down, which forced Tommy to act more quickly with Pat than he anticipated. He was sure the market would head up. He pulled out his second pay-as-you-go phone and called Pat. "Hi, this is Pat at MAAP Commodities. How can I help you?"

"Wow. You're ready to go. MAAP . . . Mary, Aaron, Abby, Paula. I get it."

"Yep, my favorite four people in the world. I figured it was you, so I thought I'd try out my work voice. What do you think?" Pat beamed.

"Excellent. I would certainly trust you with my money, if I had any," Tommy joked.

"I would certainly like the opportunity to help you map out your investment future . . . get it?!" Pat crooned, and Tommy could almost see Pat's smile over the phone.

"Are you serious with that one?" Tommy asked.

"No, just having a little fun. Why are you calling already?" Pat asked.

"You need to buy 100,000 credits at market."

"I thought they were offsets."

"Credits and offsets are different terms for the same thing," Tommy responded.

"Hold on. The market is at about eight dollars, so that's like 800 grand, and I'm not set up yet. Besides, you know I only have 200 grand, and I'm not licensed."

"Run it through my friend who helped you get set up. He'll handle the trade and let you do it on margin. Figure it out. Sell at ten dollars, or in one week, whichever happens sooner."

"What if the market goes from eight to seven dollars?" Pat asked.

"Well, if I'm doing my math right, you'd lose a hundred thousand dollars. Come on, hasn't my friend taught you anything yet?"

"It was kind of rhetorical, dumbass," Pat said.

"Okay then. And by the way, if the market goes to ten dollars, sell the credits. Then if it stays there for a couple of days, short 100,000 credits."

"Short?"

"Short."

"Oh, of course. I'll do that."

"If this detective asshole starts snooping around, these calls will get less frequent, or won't happen at all. So. . ."

Pat interrupted. "Keep my eyes open. I know."

"See you around. Actually, no, but you know what I mean," Tommy said, and hung up.

It only took about six trading days for the market to cycle up and down as Tommy had anticipated. Pat followed directions well and timed it right, so the two positions he was already in and out of had him sitting on five hundred thousand, plus his original two hundred thousand.

Tommy continued for weeks, grunting through meetings and getting trade advice to Pat through the rest of May and well into June. Pat had run early trades through Tommy's friend, but now had his business fully set up. In fact, to Tommy's surprise, Pat had fully embraced his new job and role.

However, he figured that Pat still hadn't found time to connect with industry people in more social settings, so Tommy headed to an after-work event for carbon traders on the rooftop deck of the Civic Opera Building. Social events didn't normally interest Tommy, but saving the time and effort of tracking down all of these people did. Tommy came off of the elevator actually looking forward to the event and maybe even his first drink in nearly a month.

When Tommy got off of the elevator and turned the corner, he saw Pat was at the bar doing his old cascading beer trick from college. Who would have thought beer falling from one glass into another and into another until all four beers were in his belly could still draw a crowd? No one saw Tommy, so he slipped back around the corner and got back in the elevator.

Tommy was proud of himself for fighting off the urge to stop for a drink alone after ducking out of the event. He rolled a prescription bottle around and through his fingers in his pocket as he walked east and then caught the L back to his condo. Both temptations were conquered, at least for then.

He got as good a night's sleep as he ever got anymore and headed to the early morning Amtrak to Wisconsin. His small roller bag clunked and tipped as he navigated the manholes, uneven sidewalks, metal grates, and other urban obstacles between the L and Union Station. He caught the train, planning to rent a car in Milwaukee and surprise Jenny.

Things had progressed faster than Tommy had anticipated. Pat was now up over two million. Tommy had heard through Jenny that Mary and the kids were going to be down in Chicago for the next couple of weekends. He had worked hard, and things were going in the right direction. Maybe he could spend some time with Jenny. School had ended, so he hoped she would have some time for him.

Staying at Pat's was no longer an option regardless of whether or not they were in town, so he checked into a hotel by the Interstate, cleaned up a bit, and headed to Jenny's house. It was a small, red brick bungalow with flower boxes hanging from the front windows and an inviting leaded glass front door. During his previous couple of visits to town he had been with Pat to drop Jenny off or pick her up but was never inside. Tommy knocked at the front door and simultaneously turned the door knob. When it opened, he slowly peeked his head in. "Jenny, you home? It's Tommy."

Jenny yelled from the kitchen. "I know who it is, but why aren't you outside, waiting for someone to answer the door?"

"I guess I just thought it was okay," Tommy answered.

"To open the door or to just drop by?"

"Both, I guess. I . . . just happened to be in the neighborhood?" Tommy said with a smile.

Jenny peeked into her son's bedroom in the back of the house, saw that he had on headphones, so she closed his door and then moved quickly to meet Tommy in the foyer. "You seem a bit curious, like you're looking for something. Maybe my boyfriend? So, I guess why don't you come in and meet him."

As they walked toward the kitchen, Tommy wished he hadn't been so nosy. This would be awkward at best, and humiliating at the worst. He felt ashamed that he didn't know much about what was going on in Jenny's life. "Tommy, do you remember my dad?" Jenny said. She could see the relief on Tommy's face.

"Yes, of course. Nice to see you again. How are you?" Tommy asked.

"Shitty," he shot back. "Dying isn't any fun." Jenny's dad, James, never Jim or Jimmy, tended to enjoy the awkward silence he created with such announcements. With the dull ache of cancer simmering in his body, awkward personal interactions were the least of his worries. He was perfectly comfortable making Tommy uncomfortable. Jenny knew it was one of her father's perverse little pleasures, and he had few, so she let Tommy suffer. Besides, she wanted to teach him a little lesson.

After a considerable delay, Tommy finally spoke. "I'm very sorry to hear that."

"Not as sorry as I am to be dying," James said.

Sensing that was enough, Jenny tried to break the tension. "Come on, Daddy, you remember Tommy. We hung out in high school and college all the time."

"Of course I do," James said. "He's the ass that took off on you and his other friends. Welcome back."

Tommy started to regain his composure, but felt ridiculous for having forced himself into this situation. "Thanks. I'm glad to be back, and I am an ass."

"Actually, you're worse than that, but I'm trying to be a decent guest in my daughter's home."

"Can we settle on inconsiderate ass and move on?" Tommy suggested.

James finally smirked a little and said, "Yes, that sounds appropriate," and then continued, "I'll leave you two to talk." He shuffled out of the room with the aid of a walker. It was hard for Tommy to watch as he knew that James was only about sixty-five, and Tommy pictured the vibrant man of twenty years earlier who had always intimidated Tommy a bit.

"Happy you just stopped by?" Jenny asked.

"I get it. I was wrong. No more drop by visits. I'll come when invited . . . if invited . . . but as long as I'm here can we hang out for a bit?" Tommy asked.

"Tommy, I know you're trying, but you really need help learning how to develop a relationship."

"What do you mean? I'm here. I'm reaching out to you. I'm trying."

"I guess, but it seems like you're trying when it's convenient for you. Is this how your relationships go?"

"No, not really," Tommy said unconvincingly. "This was just our first chance to connect without Pat and Mary supervising."

"So, you're thinking like a real date?" Jenny asked.

"Yes, I would like that."

"Are you asking me out?"

"Yes. Would you take a walk with me to get coffee?"

"Not today, but I will tomorrow. I want to check with my boyfriend first," Jenny said, and smiled.

"I get it. I've been a touch self-absorbed."

"A touch? That's not the guy I remember. You were always introspective but not self-absorbed. What happened?" Jenny asked.

"That's a long story that can wait. Let's talk about you." Tommy said.

"Ahh, at least you're a quick learner. Let's talk about both of us tomorrow. I can clear the whole day if you have the time. How about meeting for coffee at ten tomorrow morning and see where it goes?" Jenny asked.

"Perfect. See you tomorrow." Tommy wasn't happy he wouldn't see Jenny that day, but he knew that his surprise visit had thrown her off. He spent the rest of the day planning his date with Jenny. With each passing hour the butterflies of anticipation built. He was puzzled but pleased by the warm and bright feelings slowly overtaking the darkness that usually cluttered his mind. The only dark corner left for now was Jenny's reaction to his surprise visit. She seemed much more stressed and tense from his presence than he expected. Maybe she did have a boyfriend.

25

Tommy was anxious to see how the day would play out, so he arrived at the coffee shop early and positioned himself where he would be able to see Jenny come in. She wore attractively tight-fitting olive green capris, a perfectly snug white tee that flattered her breasts and ironing board stomach, and her customary flat sandals. Tommy wore khaki shorts, a tight blue polo shirt that showed off muscular arms and Velcro sandals. Both had light jackets and looked prepared for the seventy-degree early summer day that it was.

"Nice to see you, Tommy. What do you want to do today?"

"Well, after coffee, I have made a few plans, but whether we do them will be up to you," Tommy responded. As they waited in line to buy coffee, Tommy noticed that a table of four teenage boys were regularly glancing over at Jenny, as if to catch her eye. Jenny must have sensed it as she grabbed Tommy's arm after they had their coffee and steered him toward the boys' table.

Jenny said, "Hello, guys! Are you enjoying the start of your summer?"

The response, in unison, was, "Yes, Ms. Landimere."

"Good! And who has started their college applications?" They all looked down at their mugs. "Yeah, I thought as much. Remember, when we get back to school in September, I'll schedule appointments with each one of you. You should be ready to start submitting applications early in the semester. Be prepared, please. And remember, don't do drugs," Jenny said light heartedly but with their best interest in mind.

Again in unison, each with a little grin, "Yes, Ms. Landimere."

The tallest and pimpliest of the group said, "Who's your friend?"

Jenny said, "Sorry, this is Mr. Gardner."

"Is he your boyfriend?" the pimply kid asked.

"He wishes!" Jenny replied and smiled. The boys laughed as Jenny and Tommy turned to find a table.

"So, now I know what you do," Tommy said.

"Yep. High school counselor," Jenny replied.

"I'm sorry I didn't word that well, again. I knew what you did. I just mean I didn't know you were so good at it. Those boys like you. No, they respect you. No, it's both, I can tell," Tommy fumbled.

"They are the easy ones who know what they want to do. The challenging ones are in my office after school, asking if they really have to go home because they're worried their dad is going to hit them or they just have no idea what to do with their lives."

"Do they all look at you like those four did?" Tommy asked.

"No, but I try."

"It shows. I can tell just from that little interaction," Tommy noticed that he was making her uncomfortable, so he changed the subject. "Does the fact that your dad is sick scare you?" Tommy inquired.

"Uh, yes, I guess," Jenny muttered, caught off guard, with Tommy turning one uncomfortable moment into another.

"Is he a good dad?"

"Absolutely. Even though I knew I was adopted and my sisters were his biological daughters, I always felt like I was one of them. I remember so many times that he was there for whatever we needed, whenever we needed it. I like that I can be here for him now," Jenny's love for her family and her father were obvious.

"Is he always with you now? Not your sisters?" Tommy asked.

"Yes, because dad wants to be here, and they don't live in town anymore and have families of their own. They come regularly on the weekends, so I can get a little break," Jenny explained.

"Is it hard on you?"

"It's hard on him. His body is letting him down. He doesn't want his daughters to see him like this. I'm sure it is the hardest thing that he has ever had to do."

"That's depressing. The hardest thing that he ever has to do will ultimately be rewarded with death." Tommy muttered.

"It's the price that sometimes has to be paid, knowing that you are breaking down and dying," Jenny said.

"I can't even imagine, especially when you see someone going through it. How are you all managing?" Tommy's brow furrowed with concern.

"My guess is that if we have done enough, loved enough, given enough, it will be okay."

"Do you think that your dad did enough of those things for it to actually be okay?"

"I think so . . . I hope so." Jenny looked away, wishing that she had a crystal ball to see into both her dad's future . . . and even her own.

"Maybe you ought to tell him you think he did a great job, and that he was a good dad." Tommy couldn't help but wonder what might have been different if he would have said these words to his own father.

Jenny paused, smiled, and said, "I think I'll do that. Thanks." Jenny then hesitated knowing that a reciprocal question might be tough on Tommy, but decided to ask anyway. "What about your parents?"

"My dad was well on his way to a great life until all the lawsuits. But when you kill yourself . . ." Tommy slowed, trying to keep his composure. "I can tell you he was a great dad, and I was a proud son, although I didn't show it by running out before the funeral."

"I'm sure your dad knew." Jenny tried to sound reassuring but she knew this was a sore subject for Tommy.

"And he was a good husband. My mom really needed him. She needed someone. She just kind of latched on to the first guy that came along after my dad died. My stepdad and her together . . . they were not so good." Tommy said.

"What do you mean?"

"Let me give you an example of a conversation they had while visiting me in Chicago. My mom said, 'Did you see our old neighbor Bob died? You remember him, had some spinal problem. Looked like the hunchback of Notre Dame.' Then my stepdad said, 'Yeah. Didn't his wife lose a foot to diabetes? She can't be in very good shape either.'"

"That's it?" Jenny said.

"It wasn't the words; it was what came next. They both looked at each other with kind of smug looks on their faces. Like God had a quota for healthy people in town and seeing someone suffer just improved their life by comparison. Or maybe it was simply taking pleasure in someone worse off than themselves. Regardless it was pretty sad." Tommy said.

"So, that's the extent of your view of your mom and stepdad together?"

"Well of course there's more, but that sums it up," Tommy said.

"You don't paint a very positive picture. It sounds like it impacted you," Jenny offered.

"I was in my early twenties before any of this happened, so I don't want to blame my parents or make excuses for what I am. *Me* is my fault, not theirs," Tommy stood as a way of politely ending the conversation. He was in a rare good mood and didn't want to lose that feeling. Almost a bit formally, for comedic effect, he asked with arm extended, "Are you ready to move onto the next portion of our date?"

"What might that be?" Jenny asked with anticipation.

"A walk on the beach with a picnic lunch. Then some shopping and a movie, followed by dinner. Are you interested in the entire package?" Tommy asked.

"Let's take it a step at a time, but most likely I am. Thank you," Jenny replied.

As the day progressed, everywhere they went, they ran into people Jenny knew. Parents, students, friends, and acquaintances of all sorts.

Each person looked sincerely happy to see her. It astounded and slightly unnerved Tommy.

After Jenny hugged the hostess at the restaurant, Tommy and Jenny were seated in the back corner. Exposed 150-year-old brick walls served as the backdrop for the rugged hewn, two-person table that contrasted pleasantly with trendy modern place settings. Tommy asked, "Do you know everyone in town? You couldn't have swung a dead cat today without hitting someone you knew."

"Good thing I'm not a cat person, and no, I obviously don't know everyone," Jenny said.

"Well, you know more people here than I do in all of Chicago."

"This is my hometown. I'm part of the fabric of the place and I like it."

"Doesn't it bother you that there's always someone, I don't know, watching you?" Tommy raised an eyebrow disbelievingly.

"It doesn't feel that way. It's a support structure. The people you know…they are all there for each other. You don't get that, do you?"

"Not completely, no."

"Well, let's say someone you love dies."

"OK, I guess."

"What would happen to you? How would you feel?" Jenny knew that this was dangerous territory, but she needed to know the answers.

"I would be sad and deal with it, and I can tell you that I wouldn't go to the funeral. George's was my first and, other than mine, my last."

"That just seems so . . . alone. Here, you would be sad and supported and consoled and people would follow-up with you and you would get over it together. You have a community to share things with, good and bad. Plus, a good funeral every once in a while, helps one appreciate life. A reminder that it is fleeting."

"Well, I could have that in a big city." Tommy was feeling a bit defensive.

"Absolutely. People build their community of friends and family all the time, no matter how big or small their circles may be."

"Then, you're saying it's *me*? My problem?"

"It's you, yes, but it's only a problem if you think it is."

"Well, it hasn't been. I don't need all this," Tommy said. "It's just that what you have; what you do here is more noticeable than in the big city."

"I guess," said Jenny. "I'm also guessing some people think that doing this in their own hometown is sort of a cop-out or failure."

"I didn't say that," said Tommy, not wanting to ruin what had thus far been an exceptional day.

"But you thought it, didn't you?" Jenny asked.

Sensing from her body language that it was OK, Tommy said, "Yes, I guess at times."

Jenny asked, "Do you think I'm a failure? Or that I gave up or could have done more?"

"No. I believe you are part of this place and you are making a difference here."

"Are you just being nice because you want things to go somewhere tonight?" Jenny asked.

"Surprisingly, no. I may not be overly-perceptive, but somehow it was very clear that we weren't going to be sleeping together tonight," Tommy said.

"Glad you picked up on that," Jenny said. "My guess is that what I have here, this life, isn't what you want."

"It certainly hasn't been what I want, but I need to rethink everything."

"Don't think too much. Feel it," Jenny said.

"Easier said than done." They finished dinner and Tommy drove Jenny home, walked her to the door, kissed her softly on the lips, turned and left.

The next day Tommy called Jenny, but only asked her to dinner, which she accepted. He knew she had a life, unlike him, and that he needed to respect that. It couldn't be all about what he wanted, even though to him, it still was.

It was a cool, brilliantly sunny and viciously windy day and Tommy was once again walking, thinking, and biding his time until dinner with Jenny. He had just bought a coffee and wanted to get out of the wind, so he ventured out onto the random looking but strategically placed yellowish boulders that made up the inner harbor. He knew the wind from the northwest would be blocked and the sun would be in his face. As Tommy navigated the boulders, he thought maybe he could find his favorite quiet spot. In high school and college, he would walk out to a sofa-sized and shaped rock, sitting for hours looking at the waves slapping up against the lighthouse.

As he navigated from one boulder to the next, the head of a young man popped up from about twenty feet farther down the breakwater. It was a boy that Tommy had seen with Pat's kids. He was wispy thin with elbow joints bigger than his biceps, puffy black hair that blew in the wind and baggy pants that defied gravity. The boy slouched and shuffled forward a couple of steps under the weight of acne and self-doubt. But as Tommy got closer he could see the intensity in his eyes that clearly indicated he would outlast awkward and emerge stronger for it. He looked half-startled by someone being out there and half like he was caught doing something wrong. Tommy was equally startled, minus the guilty look. It was Sunday morning, and perhaps he was supposed to be at church. Tommy had remembered this spot was his church at the time. It was as close as he ever got to God.

Tommy considered talking to him, but instead, nodded a hello and continued past the boy who nodded in return. The boy, coincidently, was occupying the spot Tommy had remembered, so he continued past him another 100 yards to create enough separation and found an equally pleasing view of the lighthouse. He leaned back, enjoying the view and his coffee, thinking about Jenny and trying to let thoughts of Pat, John, and the rest of his troubles go, but that didn't work out as he hoped.

Tommy not only wrestled with the utter destruction of his finances at his own hand but now he was starting to replay the *what-ifs* of a life with Jenny that could have, and maybe should have happened. He started to rock gently back and forth with his legs pulled into his chest and his knees near his face. This position was all too familiar to Tommy, and he knew that it often led to escalating rage that would not subside until he hit or pounded on something or took a pill. Given there were only very hard surfaces available and no pills, he pulled himself out of it and onto his feet.

As he walked back past the young man, Tommy regained his composure enough for a second nod. He knew that he had to be careful as he was fully off of antidepressants and mood enhancers for the first time in years. He was down to only using alcohol to manage and control his emotions. He worried that Jenny might not like this version of him. But it was a tradeoff he felt a need to make since he would be sharper and more focused on providing good trade advice to Pat.

Tommy walked the mile and a half along a bike path back to his hotel. The trees had filled in since his spring walks in the same area and now blocked the view but not the sound from a creek that led back down to the lake. He passed several people he didn't know, or only vaguely recognized from many years before. He enjoyed the relative solitude and thought about how much different it would be for Jenny, who would have to stop at least a few times to exchange meaningless pleasantries. He figured maybe he could get used to it. Maybe it would be okay being Mr. Jenny Landimere. He was embarrassed to even think it was possible, given how he had left things after college.

Tommy realized that whenever he spent time with Jenny, his senses seemed to heighten. It must have been a combination of being with her and the clarity of being prescription-drug free. He recalled the previous night's dinner and he could re-experience her perfume and wine mixing near her face, the combination of French fries and stale beer rolling out onto the sidewalk from the bar that they strolled by and the odd mix of other scents along the way including wet grass, roasting lamb, burgers, and newly poured asphalt. For some reason, with this particular encounter, every scent came to mind more than the things he saw. He couldn't wait until the evening to see what he experienced next with Jenny.

As Tommy got out of the car he noticed Jenny approach through a sullen, rain soaked evening. As she got closer, he wondered how much information she could handle without being scared away. The drugs, the drinking, his dark sometimes unrelenting thoughts . . . and there was something deeper, too. Something between them that needed to be said, but he didn't know what it was. It was a haunting, sick, and remorseful ache stirring in his mind. A buried fact that needed to be discovered. It was screaming at his conscious brain but only his gut was listening. He felt like the ache would stay until the inner scream was heard, until whatever was unsaid between him and Jenny finally got out.

Jenny reached Tommy, kissed him on the cheek, and asked where they were headed. He was startled by the greeting, but still, it felt comfortable. "We are headed to The Shores, if that's okay with you," Tommy said.

"I didn't picture you as a supper club guy," Jenny's expression completely lightened.

"Come on! They are *in*! Everything comes around. I think mullets are going to be cool again someday," Tommy joked.

"Hey, there are still a few around town. They have always been cool," Jenny said, playing along.

When they arrived at the restaurant, the hostess told Tommy that the table would be ready in fifteen minutes, but when she saw Jenny, a table suddenly became available.

They placed a drink order and when the waitress left, Tommy said, "You have a lot of pull in this town for a guidance counselor."

"Oh, that. I helped her kids when they were still in high school when she lost her husband, their father."

"To divorce?" Tommy asked.

"No, to cancer," Jenny replied. They sat in silence for a minute, both staring at their menus. Finally, Jenny looked over at Tommy and asked, "What are you thinking about?"

Tommy was thinking about what Pat had told him the first time he was in town; that Jenny had actually loved him all those years ago. Tommy responded. "Nothing. Uh, just thinking about you and whether this, us, can go anywhere."

"What do you mean?" Jenny prodded.

"Well, I kind of hurt you when I left," Tommy admitted.

"My God, don't flatter yourself. Do you really think I've been waiting around for you? Sitting here pining away for my one lost true love?" she gasped. Then continued, even more defensively than before, "Sure, it hurt for a while, but I haven't given it a moment's thought until you dragged your sorry ass back into town."

"Fine. Then we are starting over, no baggage. That's great," he said.

"Works for me," Jenny said.

That little exchange created a guarded awkwardness to the rest of the evening unlike the comfortable and natural nature of the previous day, when they had talked and laughed like old friends should. They ended again at Jenny's front door. Their lips met for a brief and slightly uncomfortable kiss.

Tommy had to head back to Chicago and Jenny was going to be there with friends in two weeks. They decided to meet on a Saturday at the ground-floor restaurant of the Intercontinental, where Jenny would be staying. Tommy dropped off the rental car in the morning and took the train back into Chicago wondering if their relationship might be headed in the wrong direction.

26

As Tommy and Pat continued to make millions more over the weeks, Doug struggled to put any reasonable case together against Tommy. He had been forced to spend some time looking into John and some of the top guys at McKinstry as suspects, but it was more to appease his boss than actually believing that they did anything wrong. It was hard for Doug to look past the first "accidental" death that Tommy benefitted from. How could the two be a coincidence? And there was the voicemail message from George and the three short calls to Tommy from Whitefish . . . it had been enough for his boss to keep Doug on the case.

So, Doug knew that Tommy had a motive for murder but no clear opportunity to have pulled off such a thing in Montana. Meanwhile, John had an opportunity, since he lived almost within view of the crime scene, but didn't appear to have a motive. Then there was Mark at McKinstry who had the means and opportunity but no direct motive, although his company had benefited greatly from what had happened. Lastly, Doug needed to find out who RD Partners was that had made millions as John's partner in Big Mountain Traders. Doug knew sorting through a labyrinth of shell companies and dead ends was beyond his capabilities. He needed to get the federal commodities people interested enough to help. The case was going nowhere fast, and his boss told him he had two more weeks to make progress, or he would be reassigned.

Doug decided he would sit on Tommy and try to pressure him into a mistake. Doug still had access to Tommy's credit card information from the subpoena and checked his transactions to see that he had bought a round trip Chicago to Milwaukee Amtrak ticket on Friday. Doug thought he'd take a chance that he could catch him coming back to Chicago on the late morning Monday train.

How fortunate for Doug if they again could run into each other. He hurried out of the precinct and positioned himself at the entrance to the Brown Line stop a short walk from Union Station that Tommy would likely take home. Doug was smart enough to know by now that Tommy would be using different exits out of Union Station to avoid the possibility of seeing him. As Tommy walked into the Brown Line stop, he made eye contact with Doug, was stunned a bit, but kept walking.

Doug ran after him as if desperately sprinting after much needed answers. "Hold on there," Doug panted. "You just going to ignore me? I made a lot of effort to run into you today."

"You spend a lot of your time doing that," Tommy said.

"Well, remember I have access to a great deal of information on you, including credit card transactions. Maybe I'll even get a warrant to search your place. Lots of ways I can make your life difficult," Doug warned.

"Is that what you're here to do? Threaten me?"

"No. Just letting you know I'll be watching. Waiting for you to make a mistake."

"At least until you lose your job, right?" Tommy smirked.

"Don't worry about my job. I'll be fine," Doug said.

"So will I. Now leave me alone, or I'll get a restraining order," Tommy yelled.

"You're a goddamn suspect. You ain't gettin' no restraining order. You watch too much TV." Doug was starting to show signs of worry and seemed to be losing his cool.

"Well, if you don't have anything else, I'll be going," Tommy said.

"Go on your way, but I'll be around," Doug said. That was the last thing Tommy needed. He had to be more careful than ever when communicating with Pat. Since he figured it would only get worse, he called Pat right away from yet another cell phone.

Pat answered on the first ring. "Hey, it's Pat."

"What, no company name, or 'how can I help you?' You're slipping," Tommy said.

"Hey, I'm not slipping. In fact, I think I'm kind of getting the hang of this business. If you really think about it, buying low and selling high is all you really need to know."

"Well, there's a bit more to it than that."

"Oh, I get it. All I'm trying to say is that all these guys I thought were so smart probably aren't really all that smart, and some of them make stupid money."

"You're making stupid money," Tommy reminded him.

"Well someday if we get out I will have. Until then, it's pretend money," Pat replied.

"Who's making real money?" Tommy asked.

"Well, I heard a rumor that Mark cut a deal to own ten percent of all of McKinstry if he hits certain profit targets in carbon commodities."

"That can't be. First of all, he'd be worth like close to a billion dollars, and they aren't just going to give him that kind of ownership," Tommy rationalized.

"Heard he's running some other business unit too that is making big dollars and he cut this deal right before your business imploded. He told me himself that it might make him very rich if things fell into place. He was particularly excited that it might make his CEO, Barbara something or other, look bad with the board for recommending they agree to the deal. Refers to her as his CEB and you can guess what that stands for. Dude has some woman issues. The McKinstry board knew that he would have to get the carbon business up to nine figures in profits for the ownership deal to go through, so they figured it would never happen but be good for everyone if it did. It's almost like he knew that he would get a break like this."

"I hope that's not true," Tommy said incredulously, but he had an uneasy feeling it was true. It would mean that Mark had somehow set him and John up to steal their imploding business before the day Tommy walked into Mark's office looking for help. It would mean he was somehow connected to the fraudulent trades. Tommy felt sick and abused.

"Well, I've got my sources, and I've heard it more than once," Pat informed him.

"I can't see that happening, but now with their market share? Who knows."

"Regardless, I'm sure he makes lots of money now," commented Pat.

"True, and hopefully you do, too."

"Fingers crossed. What's up today?" Pat asked. "We need to move this conversation along. It always feels like when we talk we have ten pounds of shit to shovel through a five- minute window of opportunity."

"Ah . . . you know you're mixing weight and time measurements there, right?" corrected Tommy.

"God, you are a literal son of a bitch. Let's move along since I am totally ready to call it a career any time now," Pat cautioned.

"Not yet. We have to turn up the heat. The market is going to go up, and you're going to help force it. I want you to take all the money, leverage it as much as the banks will let you, and keep buying everything you can until the money runs out. You need to do it all in two days. You'll know when to sell."

"How?"

"When you think you've made enough money. Sell it all at once. Make a big splash. Then, talk it up with all your new-found industry buddies. Throw some money around town."

"Calling it a career sounded better to me," Pat frowned on the other side of the phone.

"Do me another favor. Stay away from the Intercontinental the weekend when Jenny is down. I don't need to be bumping into you."

"Why?"

"Don't ask," Tommy said.

"Ugh. Crap."

"And pay your taxes," Tommy continued.

"I'm not an idiot."

"And never use my name."

"Again, not an idiot." Pat was getting perturbed.

"Just making sure. This is going to get uglier."

"Since I can't be near you or Jenny, I kind of figured what to do and what not to do on my own. Just because I'm from your little old hometown and haven't been in this business before doesn't mean you can treat me like your bitch," Pat said.

"I get it, but please, just do what I asked."

Pat was not too interested in seeing more of this side of Tommy. "Hopefully, I don't hear from you for a while," Pat growled, and hung up.

Tommy knew that Pat was one of the nicest, most engaging, and genuinely fun people to be around. Everyone liked and could relate to Pat, and here Tommy was turning him into something else.

Tommy headed for home and planned to just go about his business for the next two weeks until Jenny was in town. The timing looked like it would work out perfectly for him. Pat would be busy, and Tommy could make a little money working with his old environmental and public relations contacts . . . a little consulting work to stop him from losing the condo and starving. He almost hoped that Doug would be wasting his time watching him.

27

A week went by and Tommy went about his routine of doing freelance consulting. He spotted Doug twice, waved, and smiled. Tommy wasn't sure if Doug wanted to be seen to somehow intimidate him or if Doug was just bad at surveillance. It didn't matter to Tommy. He figured if he could just wait him out, Doug's bosses were bound to give up on this.

On Saturday morning, Tommy was hanging out at his favorite neighborhood coffee shop. It was crowded, but Tommy really didn't mind being near people. He just generally didn't like being with them. He was getting work done, making some money, and this glimpse of a normal life had his spirits up. He sat uncomfortably close to the person occupying his preferred corner table until they left, hiding under cover of the background noise, only occasionally looking up to see people laughing, smiling, interacting, and clearly living fuller and more interesting lives than his.

The caffeine kicked in, and he was frantically writing notes about all of the things that he wanted to do with his life. The garbled grumbling of the espresso machine, the music, and conversations seemingly escalating to be heard over each other allowed Tommy shelter. There was just clarity and focus.

He was so engrossed in his own thoughts that he didn't even notice Doug grab the chair and sit down across from him. Doug waited patiently for Tommy to notice. Finally, Tommy looked up, and of course, Doug gained perverse pleasure from the sheer level of disappointment etched on Tommy's face upon seeing him. Tommy had been happy, if only for a few minutes.

"What the hell do you want now?" Tommy said. "Haven't you got kicked off this case yet?"

"Funny you should ask. I have to admit, it might have been getting close, but then we received an anonymous call that you might be connected to commodities trading through a Mr. Pat Marcum. Would you like to comment on that?"

"Anonymous, my ass. John called you," Tommy said, somewhat nervously.

"I can neither confirm nor deny that," Doug said smugly and continued, "So, I'll be getting some help on this from the SEC, but just to save some time, would you like to comment on your association with Mr. Marcum?"

"Well, first of all, I'm sure you'll actually be getting help from the Commodities Futures Trading Commission since this is a commodity issue, not a stock exchange issue," Tommy said.

"Yeah, them," Doug responded, "but the SEC sounds more impressive."

"Whatever. So, I'm sure you already know that Pat and I were friends in high school and college," Tommy said.

"Roommates actually, right?" Doug replied "Probably still pretty tight."

"I kind of moved on. We have been out of touch for nearly twenty years."

"Okay, sure. Well, *I'll* be in touch," Doug said and started to get up.

"You know, he's still playing you," Tommy offered.

"What are you talking about?"

"John. He's feeding you things to keep the stink off of him, and you're buying it."

"Well, you're trying to do the same thing to him, except he's more believable. I'm not going away," Doug said, and he walked out into the midmorning sun.

Tommy looked down at his pad of paper. He read his words from just a few minutes earlier: visit all the national parks, save a life, help businesses realize their environmental vision. It was trite, shallow, naïve, and idealistic crap. He felt like a fool. Only one thing really mattered now.

Tommy had hoped to get John's attention with Pat's success and grandstanding, and this was certainly an indication that he had accomplished that. He hadn't, however, expected John to go to the police. It really didn't change his plan. It was just going to make it more difficult. Tommy was edgy and nervous now. For the first time in more than a month, he reached into his bag and popped a couple Klonopin into his mouth. Tommy had originally gotten a prescription as a treatment for a panic disorder, but he abused it in larger quantities as a tranquilizer. There was nothing he was going to do about Pat until after Jenny was in town the next weekend. He just needed to relax and keep going, like nothing was wrong, biding his time until next Saturday. He couldn't believe how often he was thinking about Jenny. Nice, he thought, to obsess over something pleasant for once.

28

Tommy feared that the week might never end, but Saturday morning finally arrived. He was to meet Jenny in the Intercontinental lobby. She had come down the night before to go to dinner with friends. Tommy and Jenny had planned to spend a few hours on Saturday at Navy Pier and walk on the lakefront.

Tommy was anxious and arrived at the hotel a bit early. He was generally late for things, other than for Jenny, and wanted to start the day off right. He scanned the coffee shop area for a place to sit and was pleasantly surprised to see Jenny. She was talking to someone who had his back to Tommy, and at first Jenny didn't see him coming. Jenny then looked up, smiled brightly, rose quickly, and met him halfway. She gave him a warm, comfortable hug and said she missed him. Tommy was locked in on her eyes and equally as glad, or more, to see her, but as he hugged her, he looked down to see Jenny's coffee guest, who had turned. It was John.

Tommy grabbed Jenny by the shoulders and steered her to the side and then faced John, who was still sitting. "What the fuck are you doing here?" Tommy roared.

John smirked at Tommy, knowing that he had obviously rattled him. "Having coffee with this lovely woman. You two obviously know each other. Small world."

"Small world, my ass," Tommy said. "Stay the hell away from me and from her and from Pat."

Jenny butted in. "Tommy, stop being so rude!"

John spoke next. "Well, looks like you two have some things to work out, so it's probably best if I go. Tommy, maybe I'll see you around town. There's been a lot of interesting market activity, so I thought I'd check it out first-hand."

"Doubt you'll run into me," Tommy said.

"Right. Should be interesting. Jenny, nice meeting you last night and thanks for the coffee," John turned and left for the elevators around the corner.

Tommy waited a few seconds until he knew John was gone and turned back to Jenny. "That was John. *The* John."

"Yeah, I gathered that, but how was I supposed to know?"

"Did you go out with him? Did you sleep with him?" Tommy huffed, unable to control his emotions wondering how much was jealousy and how much had to do with hating John.

"What?!"

"Well, you met last night, at a hotel, and here you are in the morning . . ." Tommy said, obviously hurt and still trying to sort through his own reaction. He was confused, not really even knowing what it was like to feel jealous.

"You're insane."

"What am I supposed to think?" Tommy yelled.

"I don't owe you an explanation, but here it is. He talked to me and my friends last night. He was nice. He asked us all if we wanted to have coffee in the morning, and we said yes. The others just left to take a walk, and I was waiting for you," Jenny said.

"And you think that was a coincidence?" Tommy pushed.

"Obviously, now that I know who he is, no," Jenny said.

"Good, then you won't see him again. Let's get out of here."

"You're kidding, right? I'm not going anywhere with you today, and you certainly won't decide who I see. I don't want any part of you today," Jenny said.

"Ah, come on, please?" Tommy begged.

"No. I'll be catching up with my friends for the day." Jenny was fuming and offended. She dialed her cell phone and walked out onto the street without saying another word or even looking back at Tommy. He slumped down at the table that John, Jenny, and her friends had used. He could still smell her for a few moments before the memory was overpowered by coffee. He sat there, finishing Jenny's coffee, knowing that was as close as he would get to her today. In an instant, he had thrown away all that he looked forward to for two weeks.

Then, John strolled back up to Tommy, confident and smug. "Looks like things didn't work out for you and Jenny today. Too bad, and she told me how much she was looking forward to today."

"Leave me alone," Tommy said.

"See, I can't do that because I know that you're behind this Marcum character. He's all over town spending money. Everyone's buddy, from what I've been hearing. Makes me sick," John said.

Tommy's eyes had been dead, but lit up slightly. "That sounds a little bitter. Is he spending money that had been yours?" Tommy asked.

"No, I didn't say that," John said defensively.

"Your body did. Now I get it. Sore loser." Tommy felt the need to ridicule John. To hurt him.

"I won't be losing for long. Speaking of losers, it's you today, man. Hard to have a beautiful woman walk out on you. Can't imagine there are that many even interested."

"Jenny and I will be fine," Tommy said.

"Maybe. We'll see. Remember, I'll be around. Might even go over and talk to Detective McClellan, see if I can help him out," John said.

"You do that," Tommy said. "I know your angle."

"If by my 'angle' you mean trying to catch George's killer, if there is one, then yes," John replied.

"Don't give me that. You just don't want him looking at you."

"Really, Tommy, you have this all figured out. I feel sorry for you."

"What do you mean?"

"I didn't do anything to George either, but you think the world's picking on you. It's not. McClellan has evidence. You still don't know what's on that phone message or anything else he has, do you?"

"No. Do you?" Tommy was curious to know what John seemed to know.

"There was one message from me, so that's why I know about them. They had some questions about it."

"What was the message?" Tommy asked.

"Why don't you ask McClellan? I'm not in the mood to help you out," John said.

"I hope Pat keeps kicking your ass," Tommy said with a smile, he and got up, heading out into the July morning sun in the opposite direction from where Jenny had gone.

29

Tommy, still fuming, walked a few blocks south on Michigan before calling Pat.

"What?" is all Pat said when he answered his phone.

"Not much of a greeting," Tommy snorted.

"Well, these days when you call my stress level usually goes through the roof, and you were a complete ass the last time we spoke."

"Yeah, sorry. I guess I can be just a touch overbearing, but are things working out each time?" Tommy asked.

"A touch overbearing? You're an ass beyond normal comprehension, but yes, things are going well. It's been a couple of months of full time trading and we are up more millions than I could have ever expected. Let's just put a couple of million aside, please," Pat urged.

"No. We got him right where I wanted, sooner than I thought possible. We can't let up now. Sell any inventory you have and buy short positions. I think it's heading way down. Use all the money," Tommy said.

"Are you kidding me?! All the money on short position fees? So you want me to spend all the money to borrow way more credits than I could ever buy with the cash? If the market goes up enough that I have to start buying credits to pay for the borrowed ones, this could get ugly in a hurry. Shit. This is the big squeeze your buddy taught me about when I started, except I could be on the wrong end of it. I might be forced to buy credits to pay back the borrowed credits as the market is going up when it's going up partially because I keep buying!" Pat's frustration and fear were pushing an all-time high, testing Pat beyond any reasonable limits of a friendship.

"You learned well. That would be the definition of getting squeezed out. Paying fees to gain short positions instead of having to pay for the entire credit is the ultimate leverage play, so when the price drops you can make ridiculous amounts of money. Risk and reward baby," Tommy said.

"If the price drops," Pat said dejectedly and he paused, but Tommy did not speak, so Pat continued. "This is our big move then?" Pat asked.

"Yeah, one of them."

"Why push so hard if you have him where you want him, as you said?" Pat asked.

"Well, the bad news is this could get a bit stickier. Don't be surprised if the CFTC comes calling."

"Yeah, I can guess why they'd be contacting me," Pat said.

"Yep, to ask about me," Tommy responded. "Just tell them that your success is magic."

"They better not put this together or I'll roll over like a dog," Pat warned.

"No you won't."

"We'll see. I don't want to, but cops make me nervous."

"It won't get to that. There's no trail. Thanks for doing this."

"Yeah, but let's be done already," Pat suggested.

"That's what I'm trying to do. Picking up the pace. I know that you are reaching the end of your rope. No one has ever done anything like this for me before nor will they ever again. I need you to come out of this in a good place. I'll never able to thank you enough."

"Let's hope that I need to thank you, too!" Pat said.

Tommy kept the phone until he could smash it and chuck it in a dumpster off the Red line miles from his house. Dangerous to keep it, even for a brief period each time, but he thought he'd be more likely to get caught dumping it right away if Doug was watching.

Tommy walked back to his apartment with nothing to do but lament his conversations with Jenny and John. Did he really ask Jenny if she slept with John? Just seeing him with her made him snap. He thought maybe Jenny would give him a chance to apologize. He guessed that she would check out of the hotel as late as possible before heading home, so he planned to be hanging out in the lobby the next morning.

The long walk back to his apartment from the hotel was filled with more fresh air and time outside than he had experienced during the past two weeks that he had spent in Chicago. Although he had been doing the PR consulting work, almost everything was via email and the phone, so there was no need to venture out. Whenever he did have spare time, he spent it studying the market and looking for trading opportunities.

He was still mad as hell at himself for blowing it with Jenny, but his head was clear after the walk. That made him more aware of his surroundings as he entered his place. His home now smelled like his grandparents' house. He always thought that stink was mothballs, but he really didn't know what mothballs smelled like. Perhaps this smell, his variety of the stench, was the combination of standing water in the sink, crusted dishes, take-out food containers, and liquefied bananas that oozed from their blackened peels and onto the counter.

He ventured back to the two bedrooms where the kitchen odor was replaced by the odorous assault of unwashed skin and clothes. Ah, that was his grandparents' house smell. Sun pried through the blinds, highlighting the dust on every surface and in the air stirred by Tommy's presence. He hardly recognized it as his own. He spent his Saturday evening taking down his three computer screens, charts, and graphs, turning his trading research room back to a guest room. He cleaned and dusted every surface, did laundry, and planned what he wanted to say to Jenny.

30

Doug had followed Tommy from his apartment to the Intercontinental on Saturday and then watched the exchange between John, Jenny, and Tommy from the lobby just outside the coffee shop area. All the hours and days of painstaking surveillance looked to be paying off. He took pictures, mostly of Jenny so he could try to figure out who she was. Doug figured that Tommy was so incensed and preoccupied after the exchange that he would never notice, so he followed Tommy as he talked on his cell phone. He saw Tommy smash and dump the phone, and Doug picked it up immediately. Knowing how little Tommy left his home, Doug knew that he would likely kill the rest of his Saturday waiting there for nothing. Besides, the five-mile walk was a month of exercise for Doug so he was exhausted and didn't have a car to wait in. He decided to catch a cab back to the Intercontinental to see if John or Jenny would return.

Doug waited patiently all afternoon, reading newspapers, and wandering the lobby. No need to hide in a corner since the woman didn't know him; he guessed Tommy wouldn't be back, and he didn't care if John saw him. That might even be good, as John could help Doug fill in some of the gaps. It was early evening before Jenny and her friends came through the lobby. He noticed one woman stopped at the coffee shop in the lobby before heading to the elevators. Doug opened the door for her as she left the coffee shop.

"Thank you, sir," she said.

"You're welcome. Say, that taller woman you were with, she looked really familiar to me. Does she live around here?" Doug asked.

"No, she doesn't," the woman said and quickly started to head to the elevator as that question, out of the blue, coming from a guy like Doug made her uncomfortable.

Doug sensed her apprehension and pulled out his Chicago PD badge. "Are you sure she doesn't live nearby? I'm looking for a local woman who fits her description."

"No, sir. I can tell you for a fact that Jenny doesn't live in the city so she can't be the person you're looking for. She lives in a little town north of Milwaukee."

"Well, I guess not, then. Thanks for your time." The woman seemed relieved to help Jenny avoid any mistaken identity and headed up the elevator.

Doug was pleased with himself. He had discovered that Jenny and Pat were from the same area as Tommy, and he had picked up the burner phone that Tommy dumped. He figured this woman was the key to finding the connection between Pat and Tommy. He would get Jenny's last name figured out on Monday and now he had enough evidence of a potential tie to keep the feds interested in any commodity trading improprieties. It wasn't direct help on the murder investigation, but Doug figured two people looking for evidence was better than one, and he certainly wasn't going to get any additional resources from his department.

That was plenty of quality work for one Saturday, Doug thought. Hell, for the whole weekend. He headed to the corner bar, a half block down from his near-west-side apartment, where he'd spend the majority of the remainder of the weekend. He anticipated having a really nasty Monday morning hangover.

31

Sunday morning was slow coming for Tommy. Cold air from a clattering air conditioning unit tumbled over the floor and snuck under the covers. He rolled himself in a blanket cocoon, too tired to get up, too restless and troubled to sleep.

Tommy was back at the Intercontinental in the morning, ordering coffee and positioning himself at a table where he could see people coming and going from the elevators. He sipped coffee and read the news from his iPad for a while before Jenny, pulling her luggage, emerged from the elevators. No makeup, hair still damp from being washed . . . Tommy thought she looked adorable.

Tommy rose and moved quickly toward her, anxious to read her reaction. She saw him and there was none. "What do you want, Tommy?" Jenny said, blankly staring through him.

"To apologize. I'm so sorry that I reacted the way I did. I had no right to do that to you, but John, he's the one person in the world . . . I just lost it."

"The first half of that sounded like an apology and the second half sounded like an excuse. Which is it?" Jenny asked, crossing her arms.

"It's an apology. I'm sorry. It doesn't matter how much I hate John. It's not your fault, and I can't drag you into it."

"I don't want to be presumptuous, but I'm wondering if there was a little jealousy woven in there," Jenny said playfully.

Tommy looked at her sheepishly and responded, "So that's what that was. It's still new to me."

Interested, Jenny wanted to know more, but there wasn't time to delve too deep. Knowing that Tommy had learned his lesson and that John had clearly manipulated the situation, she was more than ready to move on. "I do understand now how tough a setting that was for you."

Tommy was startled by the speed of her opening up but quickly grasped the opportunity, "Great. Can we start over? Can you join me for coffee?"

"I would like to, but I can't. I really need to get home to check on my dad," Jenny said.

Tommy knew it was a good time to be patient. "I understand. When can I see you next?"

"I'm teaching a seminar on counseling troubled teens this week, but I'm free next weekend. Chicago or home?"

"I'll call you during the week and we can decide. Does that work?"

"That would be great," Jenny said. She moved toward Tommy to give him a hug. She cradled his neck in her right hand and whispered into his right ear, "You, we, could have had so much fun this weekend. I was ready for anything. Anything. Maybe next weekend, but we'll see." Tommy's flushed all over, and Jenny walked away.

32

Doug stumbled into work Monday morning, having predicted the extent of his hangover. What he had forgotten, though, was the voicemail message he left for the federal field agent on Saturday about the potential tie between Tommy and Pat. That had increased the interest level of Kyle Bremer, the field agent assigned to all matters related to McKinstry, along with Tommy and John's former businesses. Pat's new business was now deemed potentially related and also assigned to him.

Kyle was a young accountant who was newly introduced to forensic accounting, which he found far more interesting than the standard audit work he had been doing for the previous five years out of college. He had closely-shaved, dark brown hair on the sides of his head and an only slightly longer tuft on the top. Kyle's eye color nearly matched the black of his pupils with thick eyebrows and a tea colored hue to his skin. He wore tight-fitting and stylish clothes. One would guess him to be straight off of fraternity row, but he was past beer drinking and goofing around, anxious to make a name for himself.

Doug and Kyle had not previously met, but Doug's boss had given him Kyle's phone number, instructing him not to bother Kyle unless there was a reasonable amount of evidence that Tommy was involved in illegal market activity. Doug considered that Tommy, Pat, and Jenny being from the same place created enough of a tie. Being intrigued, but slightly confused by Doug's half-drunk voicemail, Kyle called Doug back on Monday morning and arranged to meet for lunch just one block from Kyle's office. Doug filled Kyle in on what he knew of the potential tie between Pat and Tommy.

"So, the only thing you really have is this Jenny person being from the same town? My boss isn't going to be too happy you pulled me into this," Kyle said.

"Hold on before you overreact. I have a voicemail message that you need to hear, plus just give me thirty minutes of your time, and I'm sure you—we—can find a tie. You young SEC guys must be wizzes with database stuff," Doug continued.

"I work for the Commodities Futures Trading Commission. The CFTC is for commodities, and the SEC is for stocks," Kyle explained.

"Oh yeah, kind of like a poor man's SEC?" Doug smirked.

"Funny. Do you really want my time or not?" Kyle asked.

"Yes. I'm sorry. I didn't mean to be rude. Can you help me out?"

"Only because I'll show you I'm smarter than any SEC yahoo. Let's go back to my office. It won't even take thirty minutes if there are connections between the three," Kyle stated.

Kyle tracked down Jenny's last name and quickly matched up addresses, college transcripts and job histories. It was easy to see the overlap in their early adult lives. Just as clearly, they could see that Tommy had separated from the other two, so making a tie to Pat's business wasn't that apparent, but Kyle thought the cell phone was interesting enough to keep talking.

"Have you looked at other potential suspects?" Kyle asked.

Doug answered the question with a question. "For murder or market charges?"

"Either, I guess. One case is yours and one is mine," Kyle stated.

"John made back forty million of the money he lost in the main business from some hedging strategy that Tommy and McKinstry have both tried to explain to me," Doug responded.

"Not cool, from Tommy's perspective but not illegal so it doesn't sound like a motive for murder and he's not banned from commodities trading, so nothing there," Kyle concluded. "Anything else?" he then asked.

"John's hedge partner also made forty million, so maybe there's something there. It's a company called RD something, I think, but there were too many shell companies for me to chase. I still don't think that they did anything illegal, so it hasn't been a priority," Doug said.

"So, I should get on that when I have time," Kyle said, stating the obvious.

"Better you than me, and you can show me how much smarter you are than an SEC guy," Doug said, hoping to motivate Kyle.

They kicked around next steps, including talking to John, Jenny, or Pat, but Doug, as usual, gravitated to leaning on Tommy, even though that hadn't really been fruitful in the past. He was determined to get the upper hand with Tommy. Kyle was just excited to be part of any potential interrogation. Police work, particularly the interrogation, fascinated Kyle so the best strategy mattered little to him. They planned to visit Tommy at his home the next morning. Kyle went about his other business for the afternoon. Doug did some paperwork and called it a day by midafternoon.

The next morning, Doug and Kyle rang the buzzer at Tommy's building. When Tommy heard who it was, he rested his head for a moment on the inside of the door, sighed deeply, and then buzzed them into the building. When they arrived at the door Tommy said, "What do you want now?"

"Nice to see you again, Tommy. This is Kyle Bremer from the CTFS or the CTFT . . . or something like that. Anyway, we'd like you to come with us down to my office for a discussion."

"To tell you the truth, I was kind of getting tired of the false accusations regarding George's death. Since you have your sidekick here, from the CFTC, I can only assume that now you're looking at some market related charges," Tommy stated.

"That's right," was Doug's simple reply.

Feeling smug and superior to Doug, Tommy saw very little risk each time that they interacted. "As crazy as it sounds, I will go with you again. Let me tell you, this is going to be like the first time we met, Doug, where I will be doing the listening. That didn't work out that well for you then. This is also my last time without you having an arrest warrant."

For the third time, Tommy was ushered into the same room. He was getting more comfortable but kept reminding himself not to get *too* comfortable. Tommy actually caught Kyle and Doug off guard and started. "So, you must have some revelation about me being connected to Pat's business. I'm anxious to hear it."

"As a matter of fact, we do," Doug said.

"Well, I figured as much with this young man here. Kyle, you said?" Tommy asked.

Kyle replied with authority, "Yes."

Doug continued. "We see you've met with Jenny Landimere. How long do you think it will take us to connect you with Pat?"

Tommy was slightly surprised and worried about getting Jenny pulled further into the mess, but he maintained his composure. "Well, I have seen Jenny, so I might be running across Pat too, but that doesn't mean you can connect me to his business."

"We'll see about that. Shouldn't be too hard," Doug said. "These young guys like Kyle, they're so damn tech-savvy. Cell phone records, website browser data, emails, text messages, credit cards, security camera footage, whatever. I'll put my money on him." Doug nodded toward Kyle.

Tommy looked at Kyle and said, "Good luck."

Kyle took Tommy's smugness as a challenge and said, "I won't need luck."

"So, just another warning that you are doubling up the effort to crawl up my ass?" Tommy said. "This is getting old."

Doug shifted gears. "No, there's more. Did you have George working on any special projects before he died?"

"No, nothing," Tommy replied.

"Well, then, it may be hard to explain this call that George made from Whitefish shortly before he died," Doug said. "Listen to this."

Finally, Tommy thought. *The phone message.* It was George's voice. "Hey, Tommy, it's George. I took care of those special project records you wanted handled. They should be just fine."

Doug appeared pretty happy with himself, and Kyle was watching like it was a movie. Tommy was clearly baffled by the message, but he jumped in quickly. "I have no idea what that message is about, but it just sounds like normal business to me."

"Funny, it was just as the business was shutting down, so to me, it sounds like he was letting you know that he was covering your tracks for the falsified projects that appeared in the database run from Environmental Verifications through the exchanges and back to Carbon Traders. Do I have that right, Kyle?" Doug said.

Kyle responded, "Yes, and it sounds like that to me, too."

Defensive, Tommy spat, "That's not what I hear. Besides, we already settled the potential fraud issues just a day or two before that message."

Doug jumped in. "You're getting a little confused, Tommy. I get that this isn't about trades. From my perspective, this is about a motive for murder. Your agreement doesn't cover that. I think that motive is somewhere in here. Sounds like George knew about and took care of something for you. Maybe something you didn't want him talking to anyone about."

"And if I may," Kyle said, looking at Doug, "From my point of view, this actually is about market activity, too. If we can find any current activity that breached the original agreement, your protections are gone on the original fraud charges. And this cell phone that Doug found might be of interest."

Doug laid a plastic bag with a damaged phone in it on the desk and said, "Maybe we'll find something on this cell phone that I saw you dump this weekend. My guess is that you called Pat, but that will take a bit to figure that out."

Tommy looked helplessly at the cell phone, his burner phone, lying on the table in an evidence bag. "I guess it's time for me to get an attorney. I'm done talking to you guys."

Doug said, "That might be best. Sounds like you have some things to work out."

Kyle gained confidence, his adrenaline soared. He had never experienced anything like this. The thrill was intoxicating. "While you're talking to your attorney, I'll get going on more connections between you and Pat."

Doug added, "And I have enough to keep working on the murder case. We aren't arresting you today, but don't plan on leaving town without checking with me."

"So, I guess we all have plenty to do," Tommy said, and stood up to leave. "And I'll pass on that ride home."

Tommy dejectedly walked out of the building knowing that he underestimated Doug and Kyle and that it was time to make a very uncomfortable call. He sighed, anticipating a cold reception and punched numbers into his phone. The voice on the other end said, "Hi, this is Susan Hogan."

"Hi Susan, it's Tommy," he said, tentatively.

"What do you want, Tommy?" Susan asked, irritated.

"I'm up to eyeballs in shit, and I don't know where else to turn." Tommy hoped that she still cared enough about him to help.

"There are thousands of attorneys in Chicago. There are plenty of other people who can help you," Susan said.

"But you and your firm are the best, and to tell you the truth, I can't afford the best right now unless you do me a favor."

"We already worked for free keeping you out of jail when your business shut down." Susan replied.

"Can you do it again?"

"You have a lot of nerve asking, given that we haven't spoken since our breakup text.'"

"Wait, you broke up with me."

"True, but I had to. You don't love me, but I know that you really don't get this relationship stuff. Anyway, how bad is it?" Susan asked.

"No charges yet, but I have the Chicago police investigating me for murder and the feds are checking into me violating my securities ban," Tommy said sheepishly.

"What?! Are you kidding me, Tommy?"

"Wish I was," is all Tommy could manage.

"To tell you the truth, I'm not so sure I should bother. I need to think about it, and I have to ask Sam. Can't imagine he will be excited about the idea. You have to wait. We'll see." Susan didn't wait for a response or an excuse from Tommy; she simply hung up.

33

Tommy knew that he had to level with Jenny to some extent about what was going on, at least the part about Kyle trying to identify a tie between Tommy and Pat's business. Jenny had decided that Chicago was a better place to meet for the weekend. After spending the week training counselors and taking care of her dad, she wanted to get out of town; however, Tommy worried that Chicago was the wrong place for him right now. Tommy knew he would be happy wherever Jenny wanted to be, and they agreed that meeting anywhere other than the Intercontinental, where they had seen John, would be a good start. Jenny booked a room at the Swissotel near the river east of Michigan Street and made plans to meet Tommy in the lobby for drinks on Saturday evening. When Jenny was away from home on weekends, one of her sisters would come into town to watch their dad. James insisted that Jenny stay at nice hotels, and he would pay. It was his way of saying thanks for all of the time Jenny spent caring for him.

Tommy spent the days leading up to Jenny's visit finishing up some consulting deliverables and got paid, so he was set for the next few weeks. He kept his place clean, even exercised a couple of times, ate right, and was down to just his laptop when it came to watching and analyzing carbon markets. He tried to have a normal guy's week, even though he never really felt normal to begin with, and his current circumstances certainly weren't.

Tommy was waiting in the hotel lobby for Jenny before they were scheduled to meet. For nearly half an hour he watched every single person coming off of the elevator, each time anticipating it was Jenny, until she finally arrived. It was worth the wait; he loved to watch her walk. Tommy rose and smiled, but waited a split second for Jenny to initiate the greeting. This time she grabbed his hand and gave him a peck on the cheek.

"Glad to see you!" Tommy said. "How was your week?"

"Long, busy. Happy to be in Chicago," Jenny said. "How about you?"

"Productive. Manageable. Cleared my calendar and my head for your visit," Tommy said.

"It would be nice to get off to a little better start than last weekend. I don't have my friends to hang out with as a backup plan this time," Jenny said and smiled.

"No need for a backup plan. How about some symphony music in the park instead of the hotel bar? Too nice to sit inside on an evening like this. Is that okay?"

"Sounds great. Let's walk over." Jenny beamed as she agreed. Tommy's heart melted.

Tommy was right; it was too nice to be inside. It was a perfect summer Saturday evening. Mosquitoes had not descended, or had been eradicated by the city, and the grass of the amphitheater area of Millennium Park was lush, the ground still damp and soft. Massive metal tubes sprouting from the ground arched gracefully over the park and joined in a webbed structure overhead. Tommy had brought a bottle of red wine, two glasses, and a blanket. Jenny wondered what else he had in the backpack. The pinot noir was delicious, and a couple of sips helped both relax even more. Bright sun shone on the south face of nearby buildings, reflecting into the park and creating an iridescent glow even though the park was in the shadows of those same buildings.

Time passed effortlessly for both. The air started to chill, but Tommy was prepared with a fleece for Jenny and a second bottle of wine as backup.

They continued listening, talking, drinking. Nearly two hours passed. Jenny looked over at Tommy and smiled, interested in hearing what was running through his mind. She missed the hundreds of thoughtful and thought-provoking conversations they had in their younger days. She could tell from the familiar look on his face that he was lost in his own thoughts. "What are you thinking about?" she asked.

"What do you mean? Nothing," he replied a bit defensively.

"It's no big deal. I could tell that your mind was wandering a bit, but this time it was like most people do; it wasn't like you to be completely checked out. I know what that looks like, too. Please just tell me."

Tommy's heart softened a little when she brought up their past together. She knew him well, and it felt good. "I was thinking about what comes next, after this mess is behind us. Where will I live, what will I do?"

"Now, that wasn't that difficult. Just like always, thinking about the future instead of living where you are now," Jenny said.

"Other than you, 'now' sucks, so why not?"

"Because I'm right here, right now. Why not just enjoy each other's company?"

"That's what I was doing, really. In fact, I was enjoying it so much I started thinking about you and me, and our future," Tommy revealed with a little hesitation.

"Well, that's flattering, but I'm concerned for you; you're always worried or planning or thinking so much. I wonder if you'll ever just be happy," Jenny said.

"I think those things helped me be successful before, and I will be again. If you don't worry and plan and think and sacrifice, how can you accomplish anything? Or do you think I need to finally give up on my naïve, idealistic college views because they really haven't resulted in much?"

"No, don't give up. They're some of your best qualities, but then maybe if it's important, why don't you move forward now instead of going after John?"

"I can't get myself to move on without dealing with this. I'm trapped."

"Okay, well, you can't do anything about it tonight, so let it go. Enjoy who you are with right now! Not every moment can be spent on analysis or you'll end up in analysis," Jenny said.

"Ha, too late," Tommy laughed.

Jenny didn't know if he was kidding and decided not to ask. Instead, she simply asked, "Are *we* okay?"

He looked into her eyes, and the rest of the whole mess fell to the wayside. All at once, he realized just how good he could have it with Jenny. How lucky he would be. "Actually, I'm only happy when you're around. You're all that I have," Tommy whispered. Knowing how desperate and pathetic that sounded, he quickly tried to clean up his mess. "No, you're not all I have. You're all I've got tonight."

Jenny smiled. "Funny. I remember when one of us would sing that song to the other whenever the night ended with just the two of us together. Was that The Cars?"

"Yeah, if I could do that over . . ."

"You can't, so don't think too much!" Jenny said.

"Yeah, I'm getting it—just really slowly."

The concert ended as the conversation did, and they packed up and walked back the few blocks north to the hotel. They held hands briefly and sporadically as they walked, which was completely new for them, but comfortable.

When they got back to the hotel, Jenny said she wanted to change clothes before they headed to dinner, so she went into the bathroom. A little buzzed, Tommy was enjoying himself for the first time in a long time, so he poured the remainder of the second bottle of wine from the park.

He figured it might be a while, so he took off his sandals and settled into an overstuffed chair that he had turned toward the window to enjoy the beautiful view of the darkening lake. It was purple over the water, melting to black, as the sun had already set behind him. He was comfortable and looking forward to the evening.

Suddenly, Jenny came up from behind him and kissed him on the neck. Tommy froze, startled, excited, scared. Jenny walked around to the front of the chair and grabbed his hands so that he would stand up. She wore only a hotel robe. Her lean legs showed from mid-thigh. Tommy was amazed at how good she looked, but was still moving and reacting slowly, as if in shock.

They met face-to-face, but did not kiss. Jenny slowly unbuttoned Tommy's shirt and pulled it off his shoulders, tossing it aside. She then unbuttoned his shorts which fell to the ground under their own weight. Their chemistry undeniable, he couldn't believe that after so long, she still made him feel so excited, so hopeful. In her eyes he saw his future, and in her arms he felt whole. This was more than either of them had ever expected, and even though they had been together all those years ago, something about standing there now, with each other, totally vulnerable, was new. Tommy took her face in his hands, and kissed her. It was slow and passionate. He needed her desperately, but he was trying to hold back as best he could to make sure it was right for her. His hands dropped to her shoulders, and he stripped the robe off so that it fell to the ground. The kiss was gentle, and deeply reciprocated. The warmth, smell, and taste of the wine mixed, cultivating a whole new blend of pleasure for them both.

Tommy was starting to regain some awareness. He turned them and eased her down into the chair. Their kissing intensified, and Jenny's leg straddled Tommy's body. He kissed her neck, her shoulder, her breast. Her head arched back meshing perfectly into the soft, rounded top of the chair. Jenny had initiated the encounter, so she thought somehow she would be able to better control her passion. That idea was gone as she gave in fully to the intensity of the moment.

Tommy had never felt this; completely vulnerable, unguarded and intensely focused on pleasing his partner more than himself. He was acutely watchful for any signals from Jenny. He wanted to be fully submissive, hoping Jenny would recognize his commitment went far beyond this encounter.

Jenny gently put her hand on his head, subtly suggesting he move lower. Without hesitation, Tommy took the cue. As he did, Jenny moved her body up, putting one foot on each of the chair's overstuffed arms, arching her back across the top of the chair. As Tommy sunk lower, Jenny alternated between arching back with her eyes closed and looking forward to the Navy Pier Ferris wheel and the dark Lake Michigan abyss, never looking down toward Tommy, but clearly pleased by his actions.

Tommy started moving back up her body. As he did, she effortlessly traded places with Tommy, removed his boxers and then straddled him from the top. They did not kiss. Instead, Jenny eased him inside of her. There was no violent thrusting and heaving, but a slow, rhythmic motion controlled by Jenny. Then, she arched back, further than Tommy thought possible, and clearly found a euphoric spot to dwell on that pleased her. He was equally thrilled, but at times physically uncomfortable accommodating Jenny's lead. It was if years of pent up passion were released in those moments. Tommy had clearly only had sex before. This was much different.

They climaxed simultaneously and came to rest with Jenny's face buried in Tommy's neck. He stared at the ceiling, surprised by an experience unlike any he had ever had and baffled by how much he loved this woman. They laid, intertwined until Jenny had to move as her arm had fallen asleep pinned between the chair and Tommy's torso. She turned her head and tenderly kissed his neck, grabbed her robe, and headed into the bathroom to get ready for dinner. Tommy put his shorts on and sunk back into his new favorite chair.

Tommy took a quick shower after Jenny was done in the bathroom and put on worn clothes. He wasn't dressed for anything fancy, and they were both famished, so they settled on a pizza place within walking distance of the hotel. They enjoyed each other's company and talked comfortably and openly for hours. Some additional wine, the heavy

Chicago style pizza, and the emotional and physical nature of their evening caught up with them all at once. They settled their tab, and Tommy walked Jenny back to the hotel and kissed her goodnight in front of the elevators, turned and started to walk away. Jenny said, "Do you want to sleep over?" It was quite endearing and sweet. Like they were kids again.

Tommy turned and smiled. "Do you mean stay over?"

"No, I mean *sleep* over. I'm exhausted," Jenny said.

"Actually, so am I. Do you like Sports Center?" Tommy asked.

"Not really. My room, I get the remote."

"Fair enough." Jenny laced her arm through Tommy's, and they headed up in the elevator. They fell asleep in each other's arms before the first commercial.

They slept comfortably until the sun was high enough in the eastern sky to peek through the curtain and shine a sliver of light onto Jenny's face. She woke first, showered, and brushed her teeth. When Tommy woke, he was uncomfortable that Jenny, with her hair pulled in a ponytail and a light dusting of makeup, looked far too stunning to see him so disheveled. He strolled past her and headed to the bathroom where he splashed cold water on his face, matted his hair to something resembling normal, and brushed his teeth. Trying to make up for his brusque departure into the bathroom, Tommy returned overly cheerful. "So, what do you want to do today?"

"Maybe I can meet up with Pat. Mary and the kids are down for the weekend. Maybe Navy Pier? The kids would like that. I'm guessing that with whatever you have going on with the police and all, it wouldn't work for you to go," Jenny said.

Tommy knew that he needed to tell Jenny about Kyle trying to use her to tie Tommy to Pat's business, but letting all that spill out just then didn't seem like the right thing to do. "I was hoping maybe just the two of us could spend the day together," Tommy said, figuring he could ease into that conversation later.

"That sounds nice, too, but I don't want to be rude," Jenny reasoned.

"They have each other. They'll be fine. I really need you." The words hung out there again, temporarily stunning both Jenny and Tommy. Tommy felt sick. It sounded pathetic just like the night before. 'I love you' would have been far less awkward. Tommy thought to himself, *that doesn't sound like me—or does it?* On one drug, then another, then off, then drinking, then not; it was hard for Tommy to say anymore what normal looked like. Neither of them verbally acknowledged the remark, and they moved on; Jenny folded some clothes, and Tommy grabbed the TV remote.

Tommy thought about what he had said, and realized it was true. He desperately wanted and needed Jenny. He turned the TV back off and moved toward her, slowly. Each day he saw Jenny, every feature of her face and body became more interesting, more intoxicating for him. Tommy gently turned her around, and they faced each other. Tommy ran his hands up and down Jenny's arms; they were thin and strong. He looked her in the eye. "I. Need. You."

"How do you mean?" Jenny asked.

"In every way possible." Tommy couldn't believe that he felt this way, let alone that he was saying it.

Jenny was startled by the intensity in his voice and in his eyes. She let him guide her to the bed, where they stood and unbuttoned and took off each other's clothes. They kissed, and Jenny let her hands linger on his chest. Tommy rested his hands on his favorite part of a woman's body, the curve at the top of the hip. Jenny's were athletic and subtle. Tommy fell backwards onto the bed, pulling Jenny with him. She straddled Tommy's body.

They intertwined their fingers on both hands, and then Tommy lifted their hands above them, raising Jenny's breasts to his mouth. She moved up and down and side to side, allowing Tommy's mouth to land where she wanted. As if choreographed, they rolled together until Jenny was on the bottom. She wrapped her legs around his body and locked them at her ankles as they came together.

The intensity of the moment thrusted Tommy's hand on each side of Jenny's head and arched his body backward, and without really knowing it he had raised them off of the bed and into a push-up. Jenny hung on with her legs and arms, lifted off the bed, freed to control the movement from the bottom. Again they reached a simultaneous peak before Tommy lost the strength to hold them both up and came down a bit hard.

"Whoa, you could have knocked the wind out of me there," Jenny gasped.

"Sorry about that. I'll have to work out more if we want to do that again," Tommy said.

"How did we do that?" Jenny said, still breathing heavily. "I guess the core training is good for some things!"

They laid together for several minutes in comfortable silence, then Jenny decided to provide direction to a conversation knowing that she wasn't ready to deal with the 'I need you' yet. "Are you okay if I meet up with Pat and Mary?"

"Yes, absolutely. It's the right thing to do. But before you go, we need to talk," Tommy said.

"About what?"

"This whole mess with John is getting more complicated, and I don't want to drag you into it. This isn't a good 'naked conversation.' Let's get dressed first and grab some breakfast."

"Sounds good," Jenny said, and they got up and ready for the day.

Near the corner of Randolph and Michigan, they found a cafeteria-style restaurant where there wasn't a wait. They picked a table in the corner by the window. The restaurant was loud, so in a way, private. Cocooned in a layer of hustle and bustle, Tommy explained the whole situation with Kyle, and how he was trying to find a trading tie between Tommy and Pat's business and that he saw Jenny as the link. Jenny listened intently, seemingly devoid of emotion. Tommy finished and waited for her reaction.

"So, why didn't you tell me all this when we first got together yesterday?" Jenny asked.

"You're concerned about the timing, not the ramifications?" Tommy asked.

"We can get to the ramifications, which, by the way, I think are totally manageable. But the timing is more important to me right now." Jenny frowned, still a bit disappointed that he didn't trust her with this information earlier

"I was waiting for the right time," Tommy said.

"You mean *after* we had sex? I put myself out there, and you weren't even honest with me." Jenny's accusation cut him.

"That was much more than sex for me, and I didn't even know that was going to happen. Oh, and you think *you* put yourself out there? I basically told you that I loved you," Tommy said.

"You said 'need.' I didn't hear 'love.' Do you love me?" Jenny asked, tentatively.

Tommy again stared into her eyes and decided that this was, one hundred percent, worth the risk. "Yes."

She smiled, but still interrogated him. "Okay, then all the more reason to be respectful."

"I'm so confused! You also told me last night to live in the moment, enjoy who I was with and what I was doing, and then, you initiated things in the hotel room . . ."

"Yes, but you knew that telling me might change the whole weekend," Jenny said.

"Exactly, and I had already screwed up last weekend."

"But you didn't do the right thing. The right thing would have been to tell me so we could deal with it and move on," Jenny said.

"We did. I did. We are. I think we had a wonderful time. I get that I didn't do the right thing, but are you sure I didn't do the better thing?" Tommy rationalized.

Jenny thought for a second, looked sheepish, and then smiled again.

"Well, I'm pretty sure. Okay, I get your point."

"This relationship thing is new to me. It's hard," Tommy admitted.

"Yes, it is, but haven't you been through this before?" Jenny asked.

"Not really. Guess I have always been in situations where we just used each other to get what we wanted," Tommy said.

"I understand. It's always been you and your ideals and your businesses. That doesn't change overnight," Jenny said.

"Are you willing to work with me?"

"Probably, but sounds like we have some law enforcement logistics to overcome," Jenny said.

"Yeah, about that," Tommy replied.

Jenny interrupted. "It doesn't seem that difficult. This Kyle person can't control who you or I talk to. He should only be concerned with what we talk about."

Tommy agreed, "Good point, but he will keep looking. What happens if he gets enough for a search warrant? Are there any emails out there? Notes? And if they find enough for an arrest warrant, what would you say in an interrogation?"

"Okay, okay. Well, first, let's call it an interview," Jenny said.

"You may have to deal with this even sooner. I wouldn't be surprised if either Doug or Kyle approached you, particularly when you're in Chicago."

"I'll be fine. I really don't know much. But Pat? That could get pretty ugly," Jenny said.

"Yeah, Pat needs to know more about Kyle. He knew it could happen. Now he needs to know some specifics," Tommy said.

Jenny thought about it and said, "I'll talk to him, but then, that's it. I'm not coming back to Chicago until this is over."

"Can I come to see you at home, because . . ." Tommy's voice tapered off.

Jenny finished his thought. "Because we are in a relationship?"

"Yes, I think that you get my level of interest," Tommy smirked.

"Hard to miss the 'I need you and I love you' parts." Jenny was obviously having a good time with this.

"So, do you want to deal with all that right now?" Tommy asked.

"I need some time to absorb it, but I'll give you this; we are *definitely* in a relationship, and I *definitely* really like it. I believe you need me, but I'm not so sure on the last one," Jenny said.

"I do love you," Tommy said.

"Oh, really? Because you've been in love before? I doubt it." Jenny pointed out the obvious, and it hurt Tommy a little bit.

"Yeah, with you nearly twenty years ago," Tommy said. Jenny was sad and mad and confused. Nothing came out of her mouth.

"So, are you just going to leave me hanging here?" Tommy pleaded with her.

"Yes . . . I am going to let you hang for a while." Jenny wanted to say she loved him, too, but knew she couldn't. She had waited this long, and she really needed to know that this was real, not just an old fling that had resurfaced and could just as quickly disappear again. There was too much riding on it.

"Really, I put myself out there," Tommy said.

Jenny reached across the narrow table and put her hand on his cheek and said, "You have, and I'm sorry, but you have so much going on right now. It still sounds like you just need me."

"I do, but can't it be both?" Tommy asked.

"It could, but I can't be sure. When this is over and some time has passed, if you still feel the same, let me know. If not, you can just walk away," Jenny offered.

"I'm not walking away."

"We'll see," Jenny replied.

Knowing there was nothing he could do at that moment to convince her, he had to move on. "So, when can I come to see you?" Tommy asked.

"I need a couple of weeks to take care of some things, and give me a little notice this time," Jenny said.

"I learned my lesson," Tommy replied. They kissed and hugged goodbye, and Jenny headed out to meet Pat and his family. Tommy waved to her one last time as she passed outside in front of the window where he still sat.

Tommy planned to go back to the hotel and purchase his new favorite chair. If there was one thing that he had learned from John, it was that everything is for sale if you are willing to pay. Before heading to the hotel, he thought about the conversation with Jenny as he finished his coffee. She was right about a lot of things, among them the fact that he could talk to Pat. There was nothing illegal about that. It might even be easier and safer than the cell phone conversations. What if they were tapping Pat's phone? They had already recovered one of his burner phones.

There's no way, he thought, that they could have tapped the early conversations with Pat. They would have arrested both by now. Tommy thought about his visits home. It would be hard to detect what he did unless Doug followed him all that way there. He usually left his personal cell phone on and in Chicago. He didn't use his credit card in town, but he had used it to buy the train tickets, and that could have been to see Jenny. He thought he was okay.

Tommy concluded that the biggest risk for trouble was Pat being interrogated, but there was also the murder, and now things with Jenny. It was suddenly too much. Tommy loved to be in control, and he wasn't on so many fronts. The one thing that he could control was what he put in his body. It was the weakest of rationalizations for popping a couple of pills while he waited at the L stop. He wasn't exactly sure what they were. He ended his weekend alone in a stupor courtesy of whatever it was that he had swallowed.

34

Tommy forced his eyes open on Monday morning, but he couldn't even complete a thought in his head, much less a sentence, until almost noon when the effects of the pills had mostly passed. He headed to the Loop knowing that Jenny had talked to Pat on Sunday, so Tommy was sure Pat would be more alert and ready for new modes of communication. Tommy set himself and his computer at the cafeteria-style bakery and restaurant on the block between Pat's office and that of McKinstry. There was a decent chance that he would catch Pat or run into some traders and collect some market intelligence. If nothing else, he would have time to lament about how stupid it was to take whatever combination of pills he had the previous night. Unfortunately, things continued badly when John was the first person he recognized.

"Thought maybe you would head back to Montana," Tommy said as John walked past with his order to go.

"I'll be here for a while. I want to stay close. Not that you would have anything to do with it, but there's a lot going on in the market," John insinuated.

"I know. I can still read about it," Tommy said.

"And follow it on your computer, I see," John added.

"Yeah, so?"

"Didn't mean anything by it. You take care and be careful."

"Is that some kind of threat? Who tells a guy to be careful?" Tommy demanded.

"No physical threat from me. You just need to be careful to not end up in prison over this by messing around in the market." John's tone was warning, nonetheless.

"Thanks, but you have more to worry about than me," Tommy threw back at John, who simply turned away and headed down the street that led to the McKinstry office.

Tommy knew that John's attorney's office was in that direction, too. He thought about following John, recalling the woman in the office who Susan had previously mentioned. Tommy knew John was working with someone, and maybe she was the partner who made the other half of the eighty million, but he decided to stay put. Shortly thereafter, Pat strolled through the door. Tommy rose to greet Pat before he could react and gave him a big hug, like they hadn't seen each other in twenty years. "Pat! How are you?" Tommy pretty much yelled.

Pat looked only mildly startled and said, "Great. How are you?"

"Do you have a minute? Can we talk?" Tommy asked.

"Uh, actually, I'm just picking up a sandwich and I have to get back to the office. Maybe we could schedule something," Pat suggested.

"Yeah, great," Tommy said. "Do you have a card? I'll call you about meeting later this week."

"Sure. See you then," Pat said.

Pat paid for his food and got out of there as quickly as he could. The conversation was painful, awkward, and inappropriately loud. As he walked back to his office, he pulled his phone out of the pocket of his light fleece, having felt a slight tug as Tommy hugged him. There was a post-it note clinging randomly to the phone which contained a letter and number combination: CASB800LT6SMT8. Pat stared at the message for a moment and then realized it meant to close all short positions out and buy 800,000 units at less than six dollars each and sell at more than eight dollars each. He headed back and placed the orders immediately.

Tommy sat at the same table, refilling his coffee, supplemented by periodic muffin and scone purchases through early afternoon. He had several more conversations with old acquaintances who were now at McKinstry, plus a couple of other competitors and industry attorneys. More than enough for Doug and Kyle to try to sort through.

Tommy walked out of the restaurant and stopped to zip up his windbreaker. It was misting out, and the wind was starting to whip between buildings. The light spray of rain coalesced into much larger drops and fell from the elevated train as he jaywalked across the street. As he reached the other side, he noticed Doug and reactively waived in his direction, but Doug pretended not to see Tommy.

Tommy headed home, feeling like he had just put in a sixteen-hour day. The social part of work was that exhausting for him. Six conversations that probably lasted a total of an hour over a three-hour period, and he was ready for a nap. The extra pressure of the circumstances was getting to him, but Tommy was always drained by such interactions. He envied past co-workers who were energized by the interaction. More than ever, this kind of communication was a near-debilitating chore. Tommy slowed to a sloth-like pace as he thought about the next couple of weeks. No Jenny, a lot of stress, and way too many conversations with people he *had* to talk to, not ones he wanted to talk to.

Without really knowing why or where he was going, Tommy had schlepped himself down to Michigan Avenue, the home of the Magnificent Mile, an unadulterated testament to capitalism. Retail businesses, the kind where you could spend thousands of dollars on a watch or a dress or almost anything, were everywhere. The retailers seemed to serve as both the economic and structural foundation for the offices, businesses, and homes that rose hundreds of feet above them. Tommy marveled that all of these people found all of these things to buy, and it all kept churning along.

It wasn't that Tommy was naïve to the ways of the economy. After all, he had made millions addressing environmental concerns and exploiting commodities markets, one of the most basic and cruelly-competitive institutions of the economy. He understood how things worked and had taken advantage of it, but in the end he didn't know when enough was enough. He got capitalism, but capitalism also had gotten him.

It didn't bother Tommy that he couldn't buy all the nice things in the windows, but it did make him feel badly that he could hardly afford to help the guy right outside those windows asking for sandwich money. He felt the ropes of his depression tugging at him again. If it wasn't with him, depression was always nearby, like a fly buzzing in and out of range of hearing and not knowing whether it was gone or sitting on him.

Even before his dad died, Tommy remembered his mom being depressed, sometimes completely immobile. He knew that she had a pack of adult diapers in the closet, and he guessed that she must have used them to avoid having to get out of bed at all. Tommy was a teenager when she got like that, and he had wanted so badly to be able to help her. When he asked what he could do, all she would say was, "Can you make me younger? Can you let me redo the things that I did wrong?" Although she never said it, Tommy thought that he was one of those things.

The few times that Tommy had seen his mom over the last ten years, she increasingly didn't like being around anyone she considered 'young.' But it wasn't the normal 'youth is wasted on the young' sentiment. It was a true, hostile jealousy, a parasite that consumed every inch of her heart. Tommy hoped that Florida was good for his mom and liked to think that she was getting better, but somewhere inside of himself Tommy knew that he was just hoping for a happy ending.

35

Doug and Kyle started to meet or talk daily about their respective cases. Kyle considered Doug an old-school bore and a drunk, but loved the idea of more interrogations and action that he knew Doug could stir up. Doug thought Kyle to be nothing more than a young punk, but one who understood markets, computers, and had some good hacking skills. Doug's own department wasn't going to dedicate extra people, so Kyle was his only resource . . . a match made out of need, not out of respect or friendship.

They met in the second floor precinct breakroom at a pale yellow, linoleum-covered table surrounded by four unmatched, molded plastic chairs. Every surface in the room was easy to clean, but looked like it hadn't been for years. Doug covered the six meetings Tommy had, including surveillance photos from each one. As interesting as the idea of surveillance photos was to Kyle, he had the more exciting news.

"Even prior to your call about Jenny, I was assigned to this case," Kyle reminded Doug.

"Yeah, I know. So?" Doug was annoyed.

"Well, I was trying everything that I could think of to trace the source of the ghost files that appeared in the transfer between John and Tommy's two companies and the climate exchanges."

"Well?"

"They actually trace back to George, or at least to his laptop. I can't believe that you got his wife to turn that over. Otherwise, I don't think that I would ever have figured it out. If he was doing something wrong, she certainly didn't seem to know anything about it, or she never would have voluntarily handed it over," Kyle said.

"Can you tell who he was working with?" Doug asked.

"No. I went through some emails, but I'm not likely to find anything. It took us weeks just to trace this back to him. He was very good, very thorough. In fact, he was so good that it seems strange that he forgot to delete one encrypted path that incriminated him. It's almost like he wanted us to eventually find it," Kyle said.

"He had to be working with Tommy," Doug said, trying to rationalize that he had been onto something all along.

"Well, there's hundreds, if not thousands, of emails to both John and Tommy on his work computer. Nothing on the laptop. You're welcome to them, but I'm not looking through them. It's a dead end."

"And you know this based on your years of police work?" Doug asked sarcastically.

"No. Based on the fact that this guy is, was, really smart. You are not going to find anything unless he wants you to find it," Kyle said.

"Send them my way," Doug said.

After a few clicks on his laptop, Kyle said, "Done. What do we do now?"

"George likely didn't get killed because he was an innocent victim. Maybe he double-crossed John or Tommy or Mark. Remember, Mark's company benefitted more than anyone from the trading scandal," Doug said. "Or maybe someone was just worried he would eventually talk."

"This is the first time I've heard you include John and Mark as suspects," Kyle said.

"Still hope it was Tommy, but as I've been snooping around these guys, it gets a little more complicated," Doug admitted.

"How so?" Kyle asked.

Doug pulled out some more pictures and tossed them one by one across the table toward Kyle. "Hell, all I need to do is hang out at the couple of coffee shops and restaurants around LaSalle near the Chicago Board of Trade or whatever hotel Tommy or John frequent. Here's another picture of John and Tommy from yesterday. After seeing them together, I followed John because I knew that Tommy was either going to stay at the restaurant or sulk home. John met with Mark, which makes no sense to me since the only thing that John and Tommy agree on is that Mark screwed them out of any chance of saving their old business. Then, he met with some woman at the same firm where Susan Hogan works," Doug offered.

"Who's Susan Hogan?" Kyle asked, thoroughly intrigued.

"Tommy's ex-girlfriend. Well, I'm guessing the 'ex' part as she has been out of the picture for a while as far as I can tell," Doug said.

"This is kind of complicated and interesting to my case but probably not much help to you building a murder case," Kyle said.

"All this fucking time I was convinced that Tommy was behind everything—market manipulating, George's murder, killing his old partner, all of it. I was so sure."

Doug's hands shook uncontrollably like he was having alcohol withdrawals. It was out of frustration with himself, but it manifested the only way that his body knew how.

"Why aren't you sure anymore?" Kyle asked with a calm that contrasted with Doug's agitated state.

"It's not adding up. The evidence should be apparent by now, but evidence is pointing all over. I think every one of these assholes is guilty of something. I can't explain it. Now when I take more time to really think about it, Tommy didn't act guilty from the very beginning. The way he reacted to me telling him that George was murdered . . . he didn't act surprised so I took that as guilty, like he must have known. But usually guilty guys play dumb, lie, or get defensive. He didn't do any of that. He was interested and attentive to what might have happened. Not only that, but the dumb bastard just kept right on talking to me, God knows how many different times. Either he is innocent or one arrogant son of a bitch," Doug said.

"Are you sure you aren't still right about him?" Kyle asked.

"Hell, I don't know anymore, but I am convinced someone killed George, so I don't think it will hurt to shake things up a bit. I don't think the man hit himself with a tree," Doug said.

"Pardon?" Kyle said.

"Nothing. Forget it."

"So, you need some help on the murder case? Maybe known associates of Tommy, John, and Mark? You know, any overlap or shady characters in their past. I'll make a list," Kyle offered.

"A list of who from where?" Doug asked.

"Phone records, surveillance cameras, parking tickets, credit cards . . . like you told Tommy, I might be able to figure out if one of these guys was in the wrong place at the wrong time. I'll find out if they even passed each other on the tollway."

"I'm usually not a stickler for the rules, but that doesn't sound very legal to me," Doug said.

"Do you want legal or do you want fast? Besides, you don't have enough evidence on Mark or John to ever get a warrant," Kyle said.

"So, I will take fast then," Doug said.

"I have some unique services and skills and a bit of a network that might surprise you, but I only offer them in fairly desperate settings. You look desperate enough to me," Kyle said.

"That I am," Doug said as his hand tremors started to fade and the tightness in his left shoulder eased.

Kyle was still primarily interested in the tampering charges, as that was his case. He thought the pictures might help so he asked Doug, "Mind if I keep these photos?"

"Hoped you would. If you find anything out that helps me, you'll let me know?" Doug asked.

"Of course, and good luck with those emails. I gotta run," Kyle said.

"See you back here tomorrow, same time," Doug said as he pulled up his laptop and started to read George's emails. Doug preferred the breakroom to stay close to the coffee and out of his bosses' sight. Regardless of what Doug now thought about the murder, Kyle thought that with the burner phone and what he could dig up on other ties between Tommy and Pat that he would have enough to get a warrant and arrest Tommy on the market charges. They needed to do something soon, even if it was the wrong thing.

36

For two weeks, Tommy felt like anywhere he went he was being followed or watched. He guessed that Doug and Kyle had split up surveillance duties. His suspicions were confirmed when he caught Doug and Kyle on back to back days watching from a car outside a coffee shop that a lot of people in the carbon trading business frequented. Then it dawned on Tommy that they probably weren't really following him anymore. Maybe they were just waiting for people to show up and were finally expanding their list of suspects. Tommy realized that another meeting with Pat could happen and might be worth the risk. Tommy waited outside Pat's office before lunch and started walking toward him. As they passed, all Tommy said was, "Big swings at six." Pat didn't acknowledge anything and kept walking.

At six o'clock that evening, Pat walked up behind Tommy in the park that was sandwiched between Lakeshore Drive and Lake Michigan on the near north side. He was sitting on a park bench watching the trapeze training sessions going on. In a big city, there are lessons for everything. It was an early August and suffocatingly hot and humid day where the wind picked up moisture from the lake and dropped it in their laps. "Were you followed?" Tommy asked.

"Hey, Tommy how are you? Nice to see you," Pat looked annoyed.

"Yeah, sorry. How are you, and were you followed?"

"I was pretty careful. I took the train and got on and off a couple of extra times and didn't see anyone. We should be fine," Pat said.

"Good idea. You're getting pretty good at this."

"About that, Tommy. This cloak-and-dagger shit is getting old. We have, I have, more money than I ever imagined. This needs to be over."

"Soon," Tommy said.

"No. 'Soon' can drag out a long time. I'll give you one month at the most. At that point, I'm closing down and going home. All the money in the world isn't worth losing my wife and kids," Pat said.

"You're being overly-dramatic. Mary's not going to leave you over this."

"Maybe not, but I'm not willing to put her through this any longer." Pat was genuinely worried, which worried Tommy.

"That means we're going to need to force John's hand. He knows I'm behind this, and he wants to teach me a lesson."

"This is crazy. We can walk away with millions now. Why risk it? What will it prove? You want to lose it all again?" Pat demanded.

"I'm not going to lose. Besides, I can't lose. I'm playing with your money," Tommy said.

"Right. So, I have some leverage here. Not one month. Two weeks." Pat looked serious for one of the very few times Tommy had ever seen.

"I get it. Two weeks then. That will be enough time. It has to be," Tommy said.

"And another thing, you have to tell me more than 'buy this' and 'sell that.' I'm not your bitch. I'm your friend."

"That's exactly why I'm not telling you more. You find notes, messages, put two and two together, whatever. You're safer knowing less," Tommy argued.

"That's crap. Regardless of what you're saying, I am completely screwed, going to prison screwed if this goes bad," Pat said.

"You're still better off not knowing more," Tommy said.

"Bullshit. Share. This is probably our last time to talk about this," Pat said.

Tommy thought for a couple of seconds, and realized that Pat was the only real friend he had, and he deserved to know more. "Okay. I think John has been on the losing side of most of your wins. I don't think it bothers him that much to lose some money here or there, so I think he's trying to set us up for the right time to bet really big. It's going to happen soon, I can feel it, and he's only going move if he's sure he can win."

"How is he going to be sure?" Pat asked.

"I don't know, but he'll have something big. Maybe some news will break that he figures will move the market in his direction."

"How am I going to know?"

"You'll hear something in the wind or maybe from me," Tommy said.

"That all sounds too fuzzy." With an arched eyebrow, Pat struggled to wrap his brain around how all of this would work.

"It won't be," Tommy said.

"Okay. I assume it will be more funky communication about what you want me to do," Pat said, his face still contorted with confusion.

"Yeah, but I may not always be able to reach out. You might get to the point where you just need to do what you think is right," Tommy said, figuring the pressure from Doug and Kyle might get to the point where communication will be nearly impossible.

"Count on that being selling. I much prefer holding money to some digits on my computer screen that represent carbon credits," Pat said.

"It might not be that simple," Tommy said. "But I'll try to stay in touch. We really shouldn't worry as much about seeing each other. They know the connection through Jenny. Besides, we run in the same circles now."

"We're bound to run into each other, right?" Pat said.

"Yeah, just small talk, though."

"Speaking of small talk, saw you out with some guys from McKinstry the other night. Looked like you were all pretty loaded."

"I wasn't. Maybe I acted like it a little, but I have to be alert, or I won't get the info we need."

"How you swinging that? You have special liver function or something?" Pat asked.

"No, I talk to the bartender ahead of time and tip him or her big to make sure I get the virgin variety of whatever we're drinking."

"Do you play that trick on me?" Pat asked.

"Hell, no. I love to drink. I just save my liver for my friends," Tommy said.

"As pathetic as that sounds, it might be the nicest thing you ever said to me." Pat smirked and appreciated the break in tension.

"You're welcome," Tommy shot back and smiled. "Thanks for everything. I will get you out of this mess. I promise."

"Well, let's hope so because I can't handle much more," Pat said.

One look at Pat's face, and Tommy knew that was true. His eyes were glassy and sagged on the outside edges. It looked like tears were pooling in the corners, ready to flood the bags under his eyes. Tommy turned and walked north. Pat headed south. Neither looked back at the other. As Tommy walked, he dialed his cell phone and when the person picked up, he said, "Hey, Susan, can you help me? I couldn't tell from our conversation a few days ago since you kind of hung up on me."

"Well, that should have been a clue. I really can't help or care anymore what happens," Susan said. "It's too hard to get through, too hard to watch. You know why I can't do this anymore. You know I fell in love with you. Trust me, I didn't want to, and never thought I would, but I did." Susan was obviously hurt.

"You made it clear that love was off limits," Tommy reminded her.

"I did, but then I thought maybe you loved me, too, and were only holding back because of this history with your dad and attorneys. But that's not it, is it?'

"Of course not. Do you really think that I'm that shallow? I do have to admit that when we first met, your profession was a little insurance policy against me getting too serious," Tommy quipped, but then knew, even over the phone, that that his effort to lighten the mood fell flat.

Tommy continued, "I'm sorry. I really didn't know until your breakup text, and then I just didn't know what to do."

"Well, now I know you don't love me, and I need to move on." Dejected, Susan just wanted to hang up.

"All right, then don't help me, but can you help a friend of mine who I got messed up in this? His name is Pat Marcum. That's it then. Closure, I promise."

"I can assure you that you will not want to cross paths with me again. Ever." Her tone scared Tommy a little, and he wasn't sure whether or not he should feel threatened.

"Now, what can I do for Pat?" Susan asked.

"Help him be ready for whatever the police and feds throw at him."

"How can I do that?"

"You know people at Ross & Associates; they're his attorneys. Maybe just call them up and have them prep Pat. If nothing else, have them remind him to never say anything without counsel."

"Good advice that seems to have escaped you, over and over again," Susan said.

"So, can you help me, uh, Pat?"

"It's one call, and I have an idea for them, too. Yes, I'll do it."

"Thanks, and I won't bother you again."

"Just let me know how it all turns out for you," Susan sighed. They both lingered on the phone for a second or two. Then, Susan hung up.

A couple of days after his conversation with Susan, Tommy was sitting at his kitchen table in the middle of the afternoon, thinking about her again, and what he had inadvertently done to her. If Jenny wanted nothing to do with him, would he be bitter and resentful? Tommy hoped not, but wasn't the most mature guy around and was certainly capable of such a reaction. Suddenly the intercom buzzer sounded, startling Tommy out of his daydream. He very rarely had visitors, other than food delivery people and Doug. He considered ignoring it, but answered anyway. "Yeah, who is it?"

The voice shot back crisply and professionally. "This is Jake Olemeyer. I'm one of Pat Marcum's attorneys at Ross & Associates. Can I come up?"

"Yes, please do," Tommy said and buzzed Jake into the building. Tommy was puzzled by why an attorney would show up at his door unannounced, but when Jake got to Tommy's unit it was clear that this was an unusual circumstance. There was no small talk, just the nervous energy of a young associate way out of his element.

Jake started. "Mr. Gardner, it's highly unusual that I would be here talking about our firm's client, but I have been instructed to show you something."

"Instructed by whom?" Tommy asked.

"By my boss. I don't know exactly what's going on here. All I can figure is that my career is the most expendable. Can I just show you a video clip and leave? Please?" Jake asked, obviously stressed.

"Yes, go ahead."

Jake opened his laptop and had a clip cued up. It was Pat connected to a polygraph, sitting in a conference room that Tommy assumed was at Ross & Associates. Pat looked nervous and fidgety. No one else could be seen in the video. After a few seconds, an individual off-camera started to ask questions. "Mr. Marcum, can you state your full name, please?"

Pat said, "Pat Marcum…Patrick Marcum…Patrick Hilliard Marcum."

"Hilliard?!" Tommy said and smirked.

"What day were you born?" the voice asked.

"January tenth," Pat said.

"What year?"

"Is that important?" Pat asked.

"Sir, do you know Mr. Thomas Gardner?"

"No, well, yes, a little," Pat said.

"Have you seen or talked to him recently?" the voice asked.

"No, well, yes, a little," Pat said.

"Have you talked to him about your commodity trading business?"

"No," Pat answered.

Jake shut off the video, closed his laptop and started packing up to leave. "There's more, but I think you get a feel for things."

"That's it?" Tommy said. "Well, did he pass the lie detector?"

"He flunked with flying colors."

"So, the polygraph showed he was lying regarding the last question?" Tommy asked.

"It showed he was lying about that question and every single one we asked him. His name, birthday, kids' names, and wife's name. He got so worked up that the test showed that he's lying about everything."

Tommy smirked. "So, he kind of passed, then?"

"Not how I would look at it," Jake said. "The guy is a twitchy mess."

"Just making light of the situation," Tommy said.

"Can I go now please? I would like to avoid being disbarred."

"Go. Thanks," Tommy said as his joking to make light of a bad situation faded and the reality of his and Pat's problems started to resonate. The urgency to escalate things rose up in him again like a combination of caffeine and adrenaline. Pat might not hold up much longer, and Tommy needed to find a way to draw John out.

37

Tommy followed up the news about Pat with a day of meetings throughout Chicago with key commodities market players, not just carbon traders. He knew that for Pat's sake, he really needed to move quickly. He didn't care what Kyle or Doug saw. In fact, the more they saw the better, since most of the meetings were helpful to Tommy about historical lessons learned from other commodities, but meaningless to an investigation. He desperately wanted to understand what happened in the past with other commodities when markets were small and a significant event occurred. He needed to be prepared.

Tommy was getting messages to Pat on an almost daily basis; an email from a hotel computer to Pat's website contact email with just a sequence of letters and numbers, an occasional burner phone call, and a variety of other clever ways to communicate. They kept right on making money, and Tommy assumed that more often than not, John wasn't. The thought still lingered that John was somehow trying to set them up.

Pat had become a decent-sized player in a thinly-traded market, with McKinstry and now John as the other most active participants. The carbon markets were being manipulated just like sugar, copper, silver, and others before them, still too small to avoid such abuse. The price of capitalism, some would rationalize. Tommy had enough information to take advantage of inter-day trends, but it would take one additional big move now to separate winners from losers.

Just the day before Tommy had noticed there had been an unusually large level of short selling of carbon credits which had continued into the morning. Now short positions were reaching record levels. It looked to Tommy like John and probably others were setting up, assuming a big downturn was coming. Tommy went for a run hoping that might create some clarity regarding what to do next. It was a sunny Friday, and the streets were filled with locals. He stopped for some fruits and vegetables at an open-air market that he stumbled upon at the end of his run.

Tommy went home and opened all of the windows. The fresh air invigorated him. The distant rumble of the Red Line trains was comforting. The taste of fresh vegetables fortified his pill and alcohol ravaged body. The numbers crossing his computer screen were intriguing. Tommy felt energized and aware beyond what he'd ever experienced. Steady short selling continued throughout the day, ending with a new record number of shorts, putting downward pressure on the market, but the price of carbon held at the Friday close.

With so many short positions in the market, there had to be many people who could easily get squeezed into a financial mess if prices dramatically turned one way or the other. People who shorted credits had borrowed them thinking that the price would go down and that they could repay the borrowed credits by buying at a lower price. However, if the price started to go up, they might be forced to buy credits to pay back the borrowed ones and manage their losses; otherwise, the more that prices went up, the more they would lose. Every time that people want to buy in a market that is already going up it puts more pressure on the price to go up even further. Someone in this spot could get squeezed out of the market and out of money. Or, if prices went down, the same person could make big money.

Tommy needed to help get Pat on the right side of such a market, and John wanted to do the same thing for himself. They were taking opposite positions, with John likely borrowing credits thinking that the market would go down and Pat as a buyer assuming the market would be stable or going up. Something big was about to happen, but Tommy hadn't figured out what would trigger it. He took the L to Quincy and Wells, and then walked over to Union Station to catch the Amtrak train north. Whatever was going to happen, it wouldn't be over the weekend.

38

There was a stretch of Chicago city streets that pushed up against the railroad tracks and the two traveled north together. The cars were stuck in traffic but the train shuffled along giving Tommy this strange feeling he was making up for lost time. Tommy walked out of the train station in Milwaukee to a wall of humidity as the automatic doors opened, but it was pleasant compared to the overly air-conditioned terminal. The sun was low in the late-summer sky and blinded him as he turned to his left, reacting to a beeping horn. Shading his eyes, he could see a sleek, feminine figure leaning against the front door of a less than sleek Ford Taurus. It was Jenny. "Hey," Tommy yelled. "You here for me?"

"Well, I guess so. Thought you would want to see a friendly face," Jenny responded.

"None better than yours," Tommy said, dropping his bag and initiating a warm embrace instead of waiting for Jenny's lead.

"Yikes! Any tighter, and I'll break," Jenny squealed.

Overwhelmed with sincere happiness, Tommy couldn't help but apologize for his enthusiasm. "Sorry. Just glad to see you." He hugged her again, and didn't care if it was too tight. He loved this woman deeply.

"Good to see you, too. Let's get you home, checked into a hotel, and go out for some dinner," Jenny suggested.

"Great idea." Tommy hadn't felt anywhere near this good in weeks. They drove back mostly in silence. The music was good, the traffic light, and they would have plenty of time to talk. Tommy felt like a different person around Jenny. She made him feel like a better and stronger version of himself. Just days earlier he was drinking and drugging himself to sleep. Now that seemed like months ago.

Tommy was always anxious, ready to be successful, whatever that meant. At work, he longed to be on an adventurous vacation. On vacation he wondered what he was missing at work and worried about falling behind. Now, he wasn't working and not really caring, too much, that he didn't have money. For the first time, he understood what Jenny and Pat each had. They were winning; he had been losing . . . his whole life. The uneven pavement of the off-ramp jostled Tommy from his thoughts. "Where are you staying?" Jenny asked. "I'd offer you a place to sleep, but with my dad . . ."

"No worries. I'll stay at the little hotel down by the water. You know I like it there anyway," Tommy said.

"I do know. You would stare at that lake for hours. I think it was one of the main reasons the rest of our class thought you were strange."

"Not dark and mysterious?" Tommy asked.

"Sorry, just strange," Jenny responded, giving him a sly smile.

"Well, why don't you let me show you what I saw?" Tommy suggested.

"Okay, then. Show me." They parked, checked Tommy in, and threw his bag in his room. Both grabbed a beer-sized plastic cup full of cheap red wine from the manager's reception and walked out on the breakwater to Tommy's favorite rock couch. The summer sun had just dropped below the horizon, and a flock of starlings flying in tight formation crossed paths with the random chaos of bats beginning their evening feeding. The starlings didn't break ranks as they flew through the chaos of bats and then out of sight. The bats bounced around in a big circle, like electrons in an atom, coming closer until their search for small insects engulfed Tommy and Jenny. There was a charge in the air that raised the hair on their arms and then passed as the bats did. The pair marveled that the bats didn't collide with them or each other, or the starlings earlier, for that matter.

The last charter boats slowly waded into the harbor, filled with semi-loud, half-drunk guests happy with the day's catch. The fresh breeze off the lake died without the sun's energy and Lake Michigan's breath turned slightly foul, fishy. Tommy and Jenny melded into the rock like it was a comfortable, low-slung deck chair and took in the tremendous stillness. The water was black, sucking up the light, unwilling to give back anything or anyone that might fall into its grasp.

Jenny finally broke the silence. "Okay, I kind of get it," Jenny said. "What did you think about out here?"

"Anything and everything; this was my church and sanctuary and escape. I thought . . . too much."

"Our classmates were right. You were a strange dude," Jenny said.

"Still am," Tommy acknowledged.

"So, what have you been thinking about tonight, standing out here again?" Jenny asked.

Tommy pointed to a small, silver, dead fish in the water and said, "I was thinking I'd like to make it through the next couple of weeks and not end up looking like that."

"Is it really that bad? That dangerous? This John guy can't be that bad," Jenny reasoned.

"Remember, someone is dead already," Tommy reminded her.

"Well, I hope you're just thinking too much again," Jenny said.

"Yeah, wine usually gets me thinking too much just before it gets me thinking too little," Tommy said. They wandered back off of the rocky breakwater and onto the concrete pier that led to a classic, white, tall lighthouse, continuing to talk, looking more often at their feet than each other to avoid falling.

"While you're still thinking too much, what else is in that head of yours?" Jenny asked.

"Oh, just repetitive, relentless, negative thoughts. Sometimes I'll fixate for days, months, hell, even years about something stupid I did.

This last one, blowing a lifetime supply of money, might take a lifetime for me to get over."

Jenny was happy that Tommy trusted her, but she was still hesitant. She knew there was more to him. More baggage. "So, there are meds for that kind of thing, right?"

"The good ones are good because they leave you in a fog. You still know the problem is there, but you just don't care. If I take that now I would also need to take something else to increase my focus," Tommy said. "It's a vicious circle."

"Are you on anything right now?" Jenny asked.

"There may be some residual effects, but mostly I am on a big glass of wine," Tommy quipped.

"Is there more to share?" Jenny asked hesitantly.

Tommy wondered how much she could absorb, but this was his one chance to get everything out there. Tommy said, "Unfortunately there's more. I feel like sometimes I'm only a split second away from losing control of my body, my life, everything. Is it those brief moments that result in murders and suicides, or getting hit by a train or a bus? One second at the wrong second?"

"Do you really feel like you're living on the edge of disaster?" Jenny asked.

"Not always, but I do now. I have myself and Pat in a pretty tight spot. The wrong thought or action at the wrong time, and he'll never financially recover," Tommy said.

"Sounds like you better not fuck it up!" Jenny offered, trying to break the seriousness of the moment.

"I appreciate the insight, and thanks for not freaking out over my multiple layers of crazy." Tommy hesitated, but then continued, "And there might be one more thing."

"Spit it out Tommy. No time like the present," Jenny said.

"I really can't. I don't know what it is. It seems like there is something more that I am supposed to tell you, some unspoken baggage that still exists. It feels like we need closure, but I can't put my finger on it."

Jenny turned pale, but she hoped that it was dark enough that Tommy didn't notice. She nearly panicked wondering if he somehow was sensing the real thing that was hidden between them was her fault, and it was their son. She spoke quickly and dismissively. "I wouldn't worry about it. You have plenty of other things to think about."

"Yeah, you're right," Tommy said and was ready to change the subject.

"I'm glad you shared with me, although it's mostly things I suspected or knew," Jenny said and grinned.

"Funny. Is it that obvious?" Tommy asked.

"To me and Pat it is. We had the time to see through that and get to the good stuff, and the good is still there . . . you've just hidden it well."

"Thanks, I think. I kind of hid it all away for the last twenty years trying to focus on what I wanted to accomplish. I really didn't have anyone to talk to and just wanted to push it all down," Tommy said.

"Can you see how that's going to all come off as crazy and self-centered? You've got to learn that you can't get away with being an ass in a small town as easy as you can in a big city," Jenny said.

"Yeah, I get it, but there's more to it. When I was growing up, I saw this town suck the life out of too many people. My mom and stepdad, their friends; they settled when they could have done more. They got stuck in a lifestyle where they needed the jobs and couldn't get out. My stepdad and mom, they just went through the motions, waiting to die."

"That's what you think of them?" Jenny asked.

"Yep. I'd rather die trying to make a difference than live waiting for the end."

Jenny paused, and then said, "Is that what you think of me, too?"

Tommy felt sick and jumped quickly to speak. "No. You have a huge impact right here, where you are. I see the way kids look at you. You're getting many of these kids through school and figure out what they want to do with their lives."

"You mean out of this dead-end town?" Jenny asked.

"No, I get it now. This town is only a dead-end if you let it be. I just always thought it *had* to be," Tommy said.

"And Pat?" Jenny asked.

"Pat's fine. He has a family he cares for. That's where my family went bad. They just didn't care enough, didn't love enough. What I don't understand is that if you say a person's priorities are God, family, and friends, they're off the hook. At a funeral, they're golden. Well, except for the whole being dead part. Everyone thinks that they must have led a good life. Some people need to be held accountable for more." Tommy was rambling on in a desperate need for her to understand.

"So, you're saying Pat should do more?"

"Well, I think this is his chance if he can do it without fucking up the other stuff," Tommy said. "I get that he has God, love, family and friends. That's his priority; anything else is gravy," Tommy said.

"Until now," Jenny said. "Remember, if you hurt him or his family . . ."

"I know, but you would have to get in line to kill me. I won't, I can't. If I screw things up for a man as good as Pat . . . it will all be over soon," Tommy said. By this time, they had made their way back from the lighthouse, their glasses of wine empty. Without asking each other, they quietly walked toward the main street of town, each wondering about the enormity of the impact that this situation could have on Pat, Mary, and their family.

39

Jenny and Tommy's stroll back toward the downtown area was interrupted when Jenny noticed a hulking mass of a tattoo and gold-garnished man in a nice suit coat with an open-neck dress shirt coming toward them. He looked out of place, but she was never one to judge quickly and wasn't alarmed until he stopped right in front of Tommy, like a roadblock to the rest of his life.

The stranger spoke in a low mumbling voice. "Say Tommy, do you have a minute for me?"

"Who are you?" Tommy asked hesitantly.

"Why don't we talk without your lovely friend," the stranger suggested.

Sensing something ominous, Jenny insisted, "Let's just speak with me here."

The stranger looked at Tommy with palpable intensity and said, "This conversation really will end much better if just the two of us talk."

"Jenny, go ahead," Tommy said, knowing the encounter had something to do with George's death and wanting to do anything to keep Jenny out of harm's way. "I'll meet you at the bar in a couple of minutes."

Jenny stared at Tommy, who reassured her with a calming glance that it would be best. She looked back several times until she turned the corner onto the main street. Tommy and the stranger watched until she was out of sight, at which point the stranger grabbed Tommy by the neck and forced him into the alley and up against the brick wall of an apartment building opposite a windowless back entrance to a business on the main street.

"Listen, it would be good for your health if you let go of this idea that George's death was anything but an accident. And feeding the cops information . . . that has got to stop. Do you get me?"

The stranger's grip had the intense pressure of a vice. Tommy could barely get enough air to force out a few words. "I'm not helping them; they suspect me of murder."

The man looked slightly puzzled, and then a second later Tommy felt the pain of a meaty fist thrust up beneath his rib cage. As he dropped to the ground, he could no longer smell the sickly sweet mix of booze infused vomit that moments earlier had made him wince. He longed for it if it meant he could breathe again.

"Well, just make sure you don't because I don't want to have to come back to this little shithole of a town."

"I haven't" was all that Tommy could squeak out as the stranger disappeared, leaving Tommy still gasping for air. He finally relaxed enough to let some air back into his lungs, and his senses started to return. He could hear someone coming toward him and thought it was the stranger wanting to deliver more of a message and maybe in an even worse mood. He grabbed a 2x4 off a construction pile in the alley and steadied himself at the corner of the building, ready to strike back.

He could tell the person was only steps away when he recognized the patter of Jenny's flip flops. He dropped the board before seeing her and turned the corner, falling almost gracefully into her arms.

"What the hell happened?" Jenny screamed.

"Actually, not as much as I thought would happen. I knew I would eventually piss someone off. This was just a message that I should leave whatever happened to George alone."

"Then do that," Jenny said.

"I'm not helping the police."

"Doesn't it bother you that someone who had something to do with George's death is after you?"

"Not too happy that they came here, but it's good to know, in a way, that something really did happen to George. This way there actually is someone for the police to go after. There has to be some evidence, at some point, that it wasn't me. Can't you see it? If it was all some bizarre accident, the police might never get turned in a different direction on this. I could be the guy that they always want to catch. I don't think he will be back. I think that he knew when he looked into my eyes that I was too afraid to lie, and I knew looking into his that he was completely surprised that I wasn't working with the police. I could see how someone might think that I was helping them since I've talked to them often enough without an attorney."

"So, you want to head back to the hotel? Or to the doctor?" Jenny asked.

"You know, I'm a little shaken up, but I'll be fine. Whoever that was, and whoever they might represent, doesn't have anything to fear from me."

As strange as it felt to both, they decided to continue on with the evening. Tommy looked no worse for the experience, although he would be plenty sore the next day. Jenny sat Tommy on a bar stool so he could rest and regroup, and she went to buy a couple of shots of tequila thinking that may offer them each some support.

The pair drank their tequila, made small talk, and each had a beer and a bison burger. Tommy hardly ate anything since his gut still felt upended. They sat contently until Jenny suddenly sprang up, looked at her watch, and said, "We've got to go! Pat and Mary asked me to help with their kids since they are in Chicago. I told them I would pick them up after the summer play at the high school. With all the commotion I completely forgot!"

They hurried to the car and were in front of the high school in no time. Jenny spotted Pat and Mary's three kids talking to a slender, bushy-haired boy who Tommy thought might be the kid who he saw on the pier and another boy that was strongly built with dark brooding features. She hesitated and then asked Tommy to wait in the car. He watched Jenny walking down the sidewalk away from him and noticed some of the boys leaving the auditorium gave her a glance and a wave, but then, an extra look as she passed.

When Jenny arrived next to the five teenagers, she pointed at Tommy in the car and waved. Tommy politely waved back, but then turned toward the gym, thinking back to those not-so-glory days. Within a minute, Jenny got back into the driver's seat. "Don't they need a ride?" Tommy asked.

"No, their friend Jim will give them a ride home," Jenny said.

"Can you trust him?" Tommy asked.

"Yes, he's a good kid. Look at you, getting all paternal!"

"Whatever. Hey, I think some of those other boys that you walked by thought you looked a bit on the hot side," Tommy said with a sly smile.

"That's disgusting. No, they don't. Are you trying to cheapen the work that I do?" Jenny asked.

"God, no! Just suggesting you should use all of the tools at your disposal."

"You're a tool! And a pig!" Jenny scolded, but she didn't really mean it.

Tommy knew that Jenny didn't have a clue how beautiful she actually was, and that was one of her many charms.

Without asking him, Jenny drove them back to the hotel parking lot, which really didn't imply an end to the night, or anything else, since it was the same parking lot they always used to stop at one of the two local bars that they had frequented before.

"What do you want to do?" Tommy asked with a sheepish grin.

"I believe the same thing as you. So now, in your room, or not at all," she said playfully. "The kids promised to be home in two hours, and I want to check on them."

They went upstairs and enjoyed their time together talking, making love, and doing both things over again. After that, Jenny slipped on her clothes and eased out the door as Tommy faded off to sleep.

Tommy woke in the middle of the night and felt behind him in the bed, almost certain Jenny wouldn't be there, but hoping nonetheless. He tossed, turned, and struggled to sleep until early in the morning when the pain in his stomach made it too difficult to stay lying down any longer. He had surprised himself the night before with his reaction to a message that was very much meant to intimidate him. The only two things that he was sure of were that someone killed George, and now, whoever did, knew he wasn't a threat. He thought about it some more and realized that John probably wouldn't have sent anyone because he knew that Tommy wasn't working with the police. Then again, maybe John was just playing him.

Tommy checked his phone and was happy to see that there was already a text waiting for him from Jenny. It read, *Do you want to take me to breakfast? I can meet you at the diner.* Tommy responded *Yes* immediately and readied himself for the day.

Tommy arrived first but didn't even open the menu. He knew only the prices had changed since college. Jenny bustled in right on time, greeted Tommy with a kiss on the check from behind, then sat and stared tentatively at the menu. Tommy watched Jenny and thought about how he had been immediately attracted to her from the moment he saw her again, and it had only deepened. The way she handled herself, the impact her life was having. Tommy had impulsively said the words before, but he said them again with deep and thoughtful conviction. "I loved you then, I love you now."

Jenny seemed unfazed, but she paused before answering. "I loved you then, and I'm still not sure about now." Tommy felt sick as he waited those few seconds for Jenny's answer, but actually then felt relieved. Jenny reached across the table, grabbed his hand and looked him in the eye. "We'll see. Like we talked about in Chicago, I'm still not sure you know how to do that."

They spent almost all of their waking hours together the rest of the weekend, except for a few times when Jenny went to check on her dad.

No drugs, drinking, or sex. Just a real effort on both of their parts to get to know each other better. Tommy headed back to Chicago on Sunday evening feeling good, maybe better than he had, ever. He had clarity as to what needed to be done, and the market was in the right spot to make it happen.

40

Pat spent the weekend in Chicago with Mary, and it was just as enjoyable as the one Tommy and Jenny had. They splurged on high-end dinners and a show, living like they were millionaires because, at least for now, they were. Pat had learned over his three months in Chicago to appreciate what it had to offer—the skyline, the energy, and the choices regarding just about anything that could be eaten, drank, or purchased.

Pat walked Mary over to Union Station on Monday morning and then headed south and east wherever he could catch a walk light until he was at his office. He walked past the elevator and took the stairs at the end of a long hallway since his office was only up one flight.

Tommy arrived at the building less than a minute after Pat did, and as he strolled toward the stairs he was hit by a unique and all too familiar odor wafting from the open elevator. It was Doug's signature mixture of booze, cigarettes, and coffee with a spearmint gum cover-up. Tommy sprinted down the long first floor hallway and up the stairs, getting to Pat as he unlocked his office door which was just around the corner from the long second floor hallway that led back to the elevators.

"What are you doing here?" Pat asked, a bit surprised by both Tommy's presence and breathless demeanor.

"Just came by to say hello to an old friend and see how you're doing," Tommy said as he reached out his hand to shake Pat's. As they released their handshake, Doug rushed around the corner and said, "Thomas

Gardner, you are under arrest on charges of commodity market tampering. Under authorization of the federal government, I will be delivering you to the Federal District Courthouse for processing and arraignment."

Pat was stunned, but Tommy looked confidently into Pat's eyes as Doug handcuffed him, pulled him away, and escorted him down the stairs. Pat went into his office and watched from his window as Tommy was loaded into the back seat of Doug's unmarked police car.

As he turned from the window, Pat unfolded the paper that Tommy had passed to him during their handshake. It read, "Cover shorts, buy, go all in, including margin. The squeeze is on!" Pat quickly got on the line with a couple of market-makers, brokers, and his banker, giving them instructions to be carried out until he said stop or until the banks ran out of money that they were willing to loan him. He sensed a need for urgency, and he was right. As he finished up his last call and sat thinking of Tommy, there was a knock at his office door. He opened it to find Kyle, who was accompanied by another federal agent. "Mr. Patrick Marcum?" Kyle asked.

"Yes, that's me," Pat answered.

Kyle and the other agent displayed their credentials and asked, "Would you accompany us to our offices for some questions?"

"Regarding what, if I may ask?"

"Just some questions about your firm's trading activity," Kyle said.

"Am I under arrest?" Pat asked.

"No sir, but we really would appreciate your cooperation." Kyle enjoyed his authority, which annoyed Pat.

"Well, let's go then, but I won't be talking to you without my attorney present. So, will you please give me a minute to call him?" Pat was demanding. Not asking.

With an eyebrow raised and a smirk on his face, Kyle responded, "Of course."

Pat didn't reach his attorney, but he left a message with his assistant who assured Pat that they would meet at the Federal District Court Building a few blocks away.

Pat and Tommy were taken to the same building and put in interrogation rooms across the hall from each other. The plan had been for Tommy and Pat to be taken in simultaneously, but Kyle got caught up waiting for an officer to be available. Pat surmised that Tommy was somewhere in the building.

By the time Kyle arrived with Pat, Tommy had been sitting alone after processing and mugshots. Tommy, although repeatedly warned off by Susan, took one last desperate shot at getting her help by leaving a message saying, "If you can't help me, can you please call another attorney? Anyone you know will do."

Doug entered the room, followed closely by Kyle. Tommy had grown accustomed to this routine, but now it was in a Federal District Court building with actual federal securities charges pressed against him, not a Chicago precinct.

Again, Tommy spoke first. "I will not be talking to you today without legal representation. I've learned my lesson."

"As you wish," Doug said. "Your friend Pat feels the same way. He's just down the hall."

Any sign of smugness or control quickly drained out of Tommy's face and body. He could deal with this, but wasn't sure about Pat. He thought about the lie detector dry run that Pat's attorney had done with him. Tommy assumed that Pat was picked up immediately after he was escorted out of the building. "Ah, did you arrest him, too?" Tommy asked.

Doug shifted his weight on the table, poised to pounce. "None of your business. You should be worried about yourself. Things are a little different this time. Did they treat you well in booking?"

"Yes, they did," Tommy admitted.

Doug strolled over to Tommy's side of the table, getting closer and closer with each cocky step. "You up for talking?"

Tommy leaned back a bit uncomfortably in his chair. Doug was getting so close that Tommy wanted to get as far away from Doug's natural stench as possible. "As I said, not this time. I already placed my call, but if you want to talk to me, that's okay," Tommy said, hoping to find out what was up with Pat. He was planning on keeping his mouth shut for once.

"Well, since we shouldn't talk about charges that are pending, let's talk about the other charges we considered filing. Thought we might arrest you for the murder of Paul Smith or George Shannon or both!" Doug knew that he was getting under Tommy's skin. Tommy was squirming in his chair.

Defeated, Tommy could only hope that there had to be a way out of this mess. "You should just put me in a cell until I'm arraigned," he said.

"Well, if you had just been a little more patient and let nature take its course, you could have avoided this whole messy murder situation." Doug didn't want Tommy to shut down, so he figured that he'd throw him something to think about.

"What the hell are you talking about?" Tommy asked, agitated, and tapping his fingers on the tabletop.

"Turns out George had stage four or five cancer. Whatever terminal is," Doug replied.

"I didn't know that," Tommy said softly, staring into the corner of the room.

"Apparently, neither did he," Doug said.

"So, why are you telling me this?" The gravity of this new information weighed heavily on Tommy. He had considered George his friend.

"Thought you might be interested and thought it might tie into the voicemail message and the three calls from Whitefish," Doug added slyly to keep Tommy engaged.

"Yeah, I know about the call to my office phone before George's murder. You already told me about it, but that sounded like some work-related thing to me," Tommy said.

"How do you explain the other three calls from Whitefish?" Doug asked.

"I never heard about them until now," Tommy said, annoyed.

"Three calls, each longer than the previous call, totaling over a minute," Doug informed Tommy.

"Wait, now I remember . . . what area code was that?" Tommy asked.

"406," Doug said.

"Yeah, I got a recording and hung up after a few seconds. Then when I got the call back, I tried to get through to a human being; I figured that otherwise the calls would keep coming. I got called a third time and just kept getting more frustrated and eventually hung up. The calls stopped, and I never gave it another thought," Tommy explained.

"Well, it wasn't a recording. Turns out there's at least one public phone left in this country," Doug said calmly, a smirk on his face, knowing that Tommy would choke a bit on that information.

Tommy's eyes started to dart around the room. Sweat coated his upper lip and his voice puttered as he spoke. "What? Supposedly I arranged a hit in all of three calls lasting a total of a single minute? Obviously I was being set up. And, besides, why are we talking about murder again? I was arrested by the feds on commodity charges. Why the hell are you even here?"

"Well, we also have physical evidence that George was murdered. We have a cold case in which someone else died, too, when they were between you and money, and we have the incriminating voicemail and other phone activity." Doug was eager to see what kind of impact his words had on Tommy. Enjoying this little game more and more, Doug's adrenaline rushed through his veins. Tommy, on the other hand, was ready to run out of the room.

"You don't have shit. You aren't even charging me for murder."

Kyle had been fidgeting and waiting for his opportunity to speak. He saw the nod of approval from Doug and proceeded with his meticulously planned out comments. "We have the market interference charges and the evidence to prove that you have broken your commodities trading ban," Kyle said.

"I'm not talking," Tommy said, folding his arms.

Kyle continued anyway. "As you know, we have a phone that you dropped in a dumpster a few weeks ago and even though you smashed it, we know that only two numbers were dialed: the sushi place just around the corner from your condo and Pat's cell phone," Kyle said. "Turns out that same day, Pat was involved in some substantial transactions."

Tommy just stared, and, for once, didn't say anything.

"What if we have more than that, like a recording?" Kyle asked, trying to bluff Tommy.

"You don't," Tommy said, and focused on Kyle's eyes until he quickly looked away and Tommy spoke again. "No, you don't have a recording, but nice try, young man."

"Well, we do have a pattern of you meeting up with Pat several times, followed quickly by high trading activity at his firm. In addition, it doesn't look good using a throw-away phone for a call to a friend. Looks more like you're hiding something." As Kyle spoke, he slowly laid pictures of Tommy and Pat having several conversations at hotels, coffee shops, and restaurants.

"Please send in my attorney. I assume he or she is here by now; I'm looking forward to meeting them," Tommy said.

Kyle smiled a little and then continued. "Oh, and by the way, there are some really interesting trading levels developing today, but never mind, you're not active in the market, so that shouldn't worry you."

Doug interrupted, "Say, Kyle, we can't talk to Tommy anymore, but you and I can talk. I'm guessing it will take nearly forty-eight hours to get him arraigned on the market fraud charges. Does that sound right?"

"About that long," Kyle replied.

"Maybe we should see if we can get jurisdiction changed on the murder charges while we're waiting. It's still technically a Montana case, but maybe the charges could be federal given the interstate calls and activity across state lines and that it did happen on federal lands," Doug reasoned.

"You son of a bitch, you can't do that!" Tommy blurted out and stood quickly, sending his chair rocketing straight backward into the wall, startling both Doug and Kyle.

"Excuse me, we weren't talking to you," Doug said to Tommy.

Tommy picked up his chair, flopped back down in it, folded his arms, and looked down and away to avoid eye contact with Kyle and Doug as they walked out, both quite pleased with themselves. It took every ounce of effort Tommy had to regain his composure as the pair had pushed every button he had. Market charges and possible murder charges? Plus, Tommy knew that Doug and Kyle were about to head down the hall to talk to Pat. Things were only going to get worse. Tommy assumed that Pat couldn't put in any trade orders before he got picked up and didn't know how long he would be held.

As Kyle and Doug walked between the interrogations rooms, Doug grabbed Kyle by the arm and said, "Where the hell were you this morning? Why did it take so long to pick up Pat?"

"Got caught up waiting for an officer. Sorry, but I called you, and you should have waited," Kyle shot back.

"I couldn't wait. I was following Tommy. How the hell was I supposed to know he would head to Pat's office?! Well, I actually did figure it out just before arriving at the building and thought I would get to Pat first. Somehow Tommy slipped past me and got to Pat's office just before me. I couldn't let the two of them talk, so I arrested Tommy because we actually had a warrant for him," Doug explained, and then went on, "Well, how late were you?"

"According to your radio dispatch on Tommy's arrest that I heard, maybe twenty minutes," Kyle reasoned. "Enough time to put some orders in, I guess, but that only matters if those two had a chance to talk," Kyle said.

"We grabbed Tommy as soon as those two met," Doug said.

"We should be fine, then," Kyle said. "Let's have Pat sit for a while before we head in there. Let the nerves fray a bit more." Later, Kyle knocked on the door as he entered, followed closely by Doug. "Hello, again," Kyle said.

"Not very nice of you to keep me waiting. I've got business to attend to," Pat said.

"Sorry about that, but it's your business that *we* need to attend to," Kyle warned.

"Okay, talk," Pat said, trying to stay calm. "My attorney still hasn't arrived anyway."

"Well, you see, we have all of this interaction between you and Tommy." Kyle spoke as he again laid out the same pictures he had shown Tommy. "You do realize that Tommy has a commodities trading ban?"

"Yes, he told me, but we're just old friends reconnecting," Pat said, proud of himself for staying composed.

Doug had been standing behind Pat, his frustration with this case growing. His hands were shaking again, and he reached over Pat's shoulder and slammed his open hand on the table. "You expect us to believe that you just happened to wander into this business by accident? With no experience and make tons of money? And there's no connection to Tommy? Do you think we're morons?"

Doug came around the table and sat down next to Kyle so he could look Pat in the eye if he answered. Pat knew with every fiber of his being that he shouldn't talk, but a strange and unexpected calmness and clarity washed over him. He realized that if he chose his words well he might be out in minutes, not hours or days. Pat proceeded slowly. "It does seem like a pretty big coincidence, I have to admit, but yes, that is what I expect you to believe."

"Is it the truth?" Doug asked, very loudly and leaning close enough to spray spit on Pat.

"It's what I expect you to believe," Pat said calmly, his confidence building.

Most people who meet Doug think that they can outsmart him, but it's harder than it looks, and Pat was playing with fire.

"What the hell kind of answer is that?" Doug said. Given that it was a rhetorical question and Kyle didn't know what to do, the three sat in silence. Pat knew that he shouldn't be talking at all in this negotiation-like situation, so he wasn't about to be the next to speak. The three exchanged glances. Doug rose from the table and turned to leave, but turned back to Pat. "We know you've gotten burner cell phone calls from Tommy. When we subpoena your phone records, I'm pretty sure we're going to see a whole bunch of those calls, and we'll tie you to Tommy."

Pat thought for a moment before answering, and then words again came out slowly and with scrutiny. "I do get a lot of calls, and some are from Tommy, but unless you have been following him around as he drops phones all over town . . . or you have recordings of these conversations . . ." Pat paused, thought further, and decided to continue. "I have also been interfacing with Mark Schmidt and numerous others in the industry. It's what we do. I may even have a selfie of me and Mark at an industry event on my phone that you might want to check out."

"What?!" Doug yelled.

"You know. A picture with me and him that I took," Pat replied.

"I know what a fucking selfie is, you dick," Doug screamed, obviously shaken by Pat's brazen attitude.

Doug turned to Kyle and said, "You can deal with him. He's not my concern. I have a guy in the next room who I'm thinking of charging with murder, but regardless of that decision, he's going to be tied up here for quite a while." Doug turned toward Pat to gauge his reaction.

Pat fidgeted slightly, but so slight Doug thought it might have been his own shakes. He needed a drink. As Doug opened the door to leave Pat and Kyle, Susan was coming out of the room where Tommy was being held. She had told herself she was only coming to watch out for Pat, but was generally curious to find out how much trouble Tommy was in. She glanced through the open door and it looked like Pat didn't have an attorney with him. She recognized him from the mock interview video, and instinctively grabbed the door before it could close. "He is my client now. Unless you are going to charge Mr. Marcum, we will be leaving."

"Wait!" Kyle yelled. "There is no way that you can represent Tommy *and* Pat. It's the same damn case."

"I am not sure that you are right as they could be co-defendants without adverse impacts, but we don't need to get technical since I am not Mr. Gardner's attorney. He asked for my continued services, but I refused and arranged other counsel for him," Susan said.

"No, we won't be charging him, but we would like to ask him a few more questions," Kyle replied.

"Really?" Susan said incredulously. "No, that won't be happening."

Pat spoke next but more to himself than anyone as the reality of the risk that he had taken started to wash over him. "Yes! Someone here to stop me from talking any more. What the hell was I doing?"

"Suit yourself. We don't really want to chase after Pat. We all know who should really be going to prison for this," Kyle said. "Perhaps your client can stay out of trouble by cooperating."

"May I have some time alone with my client?" Susan asked.

"Take all the time you need," Kyle said, and walked out.

Once the door closed and they were alone, Pat asked Susan, "Who are you?"

"Susan Hogan, your attorney," Susan said.

"The Susan who used to sleep with Tommy? What were you thinking?" Pat asked.

"When I slept with Tommy or when I decided I was representing you?"

"Both, I guess," Pat answered.

"I have no idea on the first question, and because I think Tommy was actually more worried about you than himself, for once," Susan said.

"Well, things are moving kinda fast. I really should have waited for my attorney to get here, but strangely enough I felt that I could handle the conversation. Now all I know is they said I can go, so I'm getting out of here."

"That makes sense. Go," Susan said. "I'm going to stick around here for a couple of minutes."

"About that. No offense, but you representing me and knowing Tommy seems like a bit of a conflict of interest, don't you think?" Pat asked. "Plus, I have an attorney already; he's just not very prompt."

"Well, I'm not representing Tommy anymore, but yes, I still get your point," Susan answered.

"So, I guess I'm firing you, but thanks for your service," Pat quipped, trying to make light of a difficult and stressful situation.

"My pleasure, but wait for your attorney next time! And be careful. I don't know what Tommy has you messed up in," Susan said.

"But I'm not messed up with Tommy," Pat said.

"Oh, yeah, right, and attorney-client privilege doesn't end with my termination as your counsel," Susan said. She then fidgeted uncomfortably in her chair and looked only at the table, her sentence trailing off to a whisper, and she didn't get up to leave.

"I don't have anything else to say to you . . . but do you have something for me?" Pat pushed.

Susan looked at him, hesitated and said, "Tommy wanted me to, but I can't. I don't have anything, but good luck."

"Well, guess I'll need to figure this out on my own," Pat said.

"It will probably be a while before Tommy gets out of here. Looks like they may jerk him around considering a second set of charges. It could take a couple days."

"In that case, if you talk to Tommy, can you please let him know that I was able to get twenty minutes of work done before I was brought in? Can you please tell him exactly that? He'll sleep better, and I don't see that breaking any rules, but I'm no lawyer."

"Okay, I guess," Susan said, hesitantly.

"Thanks for the help. See you around," Pat said. They walked out of the room together. Susan waited until Pat slowly sulked around the corner and then she went back into the room with Tommy.

As soon at Tommy saw Susan, he asked, "Did you tell him? Did you tell him he can't sell? He needs to just keep buying?"

"No, I didn't tell him! Susan yelled. "I told you I wouldn't."

"You could have just said you were his attorney and then told him," Tommy pleaded.

"I actually was his attorney, for about a minute, but he fired me, as he should. Besides, aiding and abetting a felony isn't covered by attorney-client privilege," Susan said.

"Whatever," Tommy protested childishly. "Is he at least out?"

"Yes, he's out and he asked me to tell you he got in twenty minutes of work before he was brought in," Susan said. "And you are still an absolute jerk. You know you asked me to put my whole career at risk, don't you?"

"Yes, I know. But it's important." Tommy looked at her, pleadingly, hoping that she still cared enough about him to help.

"Yeah, important to you . . ." Susan said, almost feeling sorry for Tommy.

"And to Pat," Tommy said.

"I thought you were more worried about Pat than yourself for once, but now I can't tell. You clearly aren't worried about what happens to me," Susan said, obviously disappointed.

Tommy hesitated and gave her statement some thought before speaking. "Say, actually I'm more worried about Pat, but that doesn't mean we can't work on getting me out of here. Where is your high-priced criminal attorney?" Tommy asked.

"You know damn well he isn't coming, and you know that I referred you to another firm. They must be on their way by now. But what the hell is with you?"

"Oh yeah, sorry. Residual drug impacts, maybe," Tommy offered weakly, but the reality was he hoped she would change her mind and help him yet again.

"Even though I'm not your attorney, I can tell you there is no way you're getting out of here in the next forty-eight hours if they don't want you to. One more thing, even if you were still a client, I would have dumped you when I saw Pat in there without an attorney. I couldn't have very well represented Pat, even for the few minutes that I was his counsel, without letting the cops know I was no longer yours."

"Either way, this worked out nicely for you, getting rid of me," Tommy said.

"And for Pat. Who knows what would have happened in there," Susan said.

Tommy slumped. "Forty-eight hours. By then, it will be over. John's going to get away with everything."

"Maybe so," Susan said. "Somewhere in this whole mess there's still a lesson or two for you to learn, whether it's me teaching you or someone else."

"What's with all the threats and hostility lately? Seems like you've taken our split a little too personally," Tommy said.

"God, you are an insensitive ass," Susan had turned towards the door but swung back around, defiantly looking down her nose at Tommy. "You'd think that being in the same awkward spot with Jenny that I was in with you, a little more sensitivity might have developed."

Stunned, Tommy couldn't utter a word.

Susan continued, "Well, your reaction answered my hunch about you two."

As Susan walked out, Tommy was still speechless, trying to wrap his mind around how Susan even knew enough about him and Jenny to pose the question. He thought maybe it was as simple as Pat sharing information with her in the other room or as disturbing as Susan stalking him. The way she was acting lately? Well, he wouldn't put it past her.

41

After leaving the police station, Pat headed back to his office. He stared down the street to the spot where Tommy had been loaded into the back of a police car a few hours earlier. Tension radiated from his shoulders and up through his neck; his ear drums were pounding, and his head throbbed painfully.

He was mad at Tommy. Mad for being put in this spot where everything, tens of millions of dollars and his family's well-being, might all be at risk, and for a guy he hardly knew anymore. If he just sold now, he would walk away with more money than he ever dreamed of. If he waited, positions on margin could eventually bury him if the market turned the wrong way. He would be the one squeezed out, not John.

His family was only 100 miles away, but even if they were in the next room, he would be all alone to decide what to do next. He continued to stare at that spot on the street until a knock at his office door startled him. Remembering what happened earlier in the day when he answered the door, he hesitated, but slowly opened it. Pat didn't recognize the man, but quickly noted the pulsing muscles near the back of his jaw. He would have hated to be this man's teeth. "May I help you?" Pat said reluctantly.

"Why, yes, you may. I wanted to meet the hotshot of the carbon market. My name is John DeFallo." Pat recognized the name, and as he did, his body slumped, losing a couple of inches in height. The day that couldn't get any worse, just did.

Reluctantly, Pat moved to the side. "Come in, I guess."

"We haven't met before, but you sure don't seem to be very happy to see me." Knowing that he had Pat between a rock and a hard place, John sauntered into the room, oozing confidence and control.

"Well, it hasn't been a very good day." Finding a nearby chair, Pat sat and leaned forward with his elbows on his knees.

"Might that have something to do with your friend being arrested?"

"How do you know about that?" Pat's surprise just confirmed to John that he was ahead of the game.

Strolling around the room, John picked up items from Pat's table and desk. One by one he examined them and then returned them without a second thought back to their original positions. "I'm just trying to be a good citizen, you know, helping the police out where I can. Sounds like Tommy might be out of circulation for a while. Looks like it might be just you and me."

"I don't know what you mean," Pat said, but without much conviction.

"I think you do." John smirked, knowing that he got under Pat's skin. That was the goal. That was the game. He didn't need any more from this exchange. "Nice meeting you," John said and walked out of the office. Pat turned, and without hesitation, dialed the phone.

"Hey Jenny, it's me. Any chance you could come down to Chicago for a couple of days? I could really use your help." Pat was audibly shaken.

"Is Tommy putting you up to this? I told him to leave me out of this mess," Jenny stated.

"No, this is coming from me and if you can make it, please don't tell Mary," Pat pleaded.

"So, it's that bad?" Jenny asked.

"It's not good."

"For you, not Tommy, I'll be there."

"Thanks, and you probably won't have to worry about seeing him. I'll explain when you get here."

"I'll meet you for dinner tonight," Jenny said, and hung up.

After stressing about his next move for hours, and still not coming to any conclusive decision by evening, Pat left his office and hailed a cab. The market was closed now, but Pat had watched as the purchases continued to pile up. He had gone through his cash and expected people to keep selling, so his buy orders would keep getting filled. Except now he would be borrowing money from the bank to do it. This was a whole new level of risk, and he needed Jenny's help to think it through.

As he got in the cab, clouds had engulfed the city, and the tops of towering buildings disappeared into a grayish haze. It misted more than it rained as his cab headed east into heavier-than-normal traffic. After watching the stoplights on Clark turn green twice without moving, Pat threw ten dollars on the front seat of the taxi for the five-dollar football field length ride and without a word, got out and started to walk. He could hear the cabbie yelling in a language he didn't recognize. The mist had turned to a steady rain. It all felt good compared to being stuck in traffic. He felt edgy, caged, trapped—and wondered if this was how Tommy always felt.

He trudged on, eventually reaching the lobby of the Hilton on Michigan Avenue. Jenny had texted Pat where and when to meet her, and she was sitting in the hotel restaurant when he arrived. Jenny offered Pat a smile and a napkin as he walked up. "Sorry. No hug. You're a bit damp for that, and no offense, you look terrible," Jenny said.

He took the napkin, which was more than adequate to dry his face and close-cropped hair. "Thanks. I feel terrible." Pat proceeded to give Jenny all of the details of the last ten hours, including the meeting with John. As he finished, John walked up to the table.

"Well, isn't this my lucky day? Two of Tommy's favorite people, probably lamenting his fate," John smirked.

"What are you doing here?" Pat asked, annoyed.

"Following you. So, I see you called in reinforcements," John said as he extended his hand and leered in Jenny's direction. Pat and Jenny just stared up at him. John continued, "I can see you two want to be alone to strategize, so I'll be on my way." John took a few steps away from the table as Jenny and Pat sighed with relief, but then he turned. "Oh, I almost forgot. Pat, are you coming to the Carbon Trader Association lunch tomorrow or are you too busy going on your silly buying spree?"

"I'm going to the lunch, I guess," Pat admitted.

"Please do, and maybe you want to bring a guest. It should be quite interesting," John said, and left for real this time.

"What the hell was that about?" Jenny turned to Pat, incredulously.

"I'm not sure. He's certainly trying to play me. Wants me to keep buying, I think, or stop. Hell, I don't know. I do know that Tommy wants me to keep buying."

"Do you trust Tommy enough to keep buying?"

"I guess," Pat answered. "He's truly brilliant when it comes to this stuff."

"Then keep buying," Jenny said.

"You do realize that brilliance comes with a price. You've gotta realize the guy's on the spectrum."

Jenny paused, then understood what had always been in the back of her mind. "Oh, I guess that makes sense, but in the big picture aren't we all somewhere on the spectrum?"

"Sure, that's profound and all, but we aren't on the spectrum like Tommy is."

"But if he's going to be right then keep buying," Jenny offered again.

"Even if Tommy wants me to do it for the wrong reasons?"

"I think so."

"I don't know what the hell to do." Pat said staring at his menu and dreading what tomorrow might bring.

42

Doug and Kyle continued to search for evidence even though Doug's interest in Tommy for murder had waned. Clearly they both thought that there was something to the market charges but they weren't above using a murder investigation to further pressure the situation. They could be much more effective with Tommy in custody and not chasing him around. They searched Pat's phone records, looking for a pattern of contacts prior to big trades or activity. They isolated a handful of short calls from non-local area codes and traced them to several cell phones.

Unfortunately, some of the calls they thought might have been from Tommy actually originated in various cities around the country including Whitefish, Montana. This case had way too many unexplained and confusing ties to Whitefish and this was yet another. They also noted several calls from McKinstry, although that could have just been normal business, Kyle reasoned. Plus, Pat had acknowledged being in touch with Mark. They put the list aside, deciding to take a quick look at everything else and then they would prioritize their next steps.

Doug pulled out the box of evidence from George's murder case, hoping that going through it again might produce a different result. Doug had obtained George's personal effects from George's wife, Deb, shortly after his death. She had even provided George's laptop, which had been requested but not expected. The other items that he had with him when his body was found included a set of rental car keys, a money clip, some change, a cell phone, lip balm, and a pack of gum. He rolled the items around on his desk before picking up the money clip. He took the credit cards out. Nothing unusual. Even though he had looked at a report showing the call log several times before, he turned on the phone and started scrolling through it. There were outgoing calls to several Whitefish numbers, but they had checked out as restaurants, ski hills, and work-related calls. Suddenly, one of the incoming numbers that hadn't registered before jumped off of the screen. It matched the incoming number that Doug had just seen in Pat's phone records. Who the hell would have called both George before he died and Pat after other than Tommy? Doug pulled up his desk phone and dialed the number. The pleasant voice on the other end said, "You have reached Mark Schmidt. Please leave a message." Without responding, Doug slammed down the receiver and shoved the phone across his desk and crashing to the floor.

"What the hell?" Kyle said.

"Things aren't adding up, and I need a drink," Doug said. "You coming?"

It was almost quitting time, so Doug and Kyle went around the corner from the precinct to a lower level bar and they each ordered a tap beer. The bar was lined on one side with opaque windows with bright fluorescent lights behind them to make patrons feel like they weren't in a basement. The bartender was young, plain, and aggressively upbeat.

Doug purposefully struggled to find his wallet, so Kyle turned over his credit card and told the bartender to open a tab. Doug explained the complicating factors of the new information and the extra work that it was going to take to track it down. Mark could have done business with George before he died, and with Pat later, but it seemed like a pretty big coincidence.

"I would have bet that would tie back to Tommy, not Mark," Kyle responded, "But it doesn't mean that Tommy's not guilty of at least the market related charges."

"I know, but it casts doubt and eats up time," Doug said. "What the hell was Mark doing calling George? And there were a couple of calls in Whitefish that weren't commercial businesses. We're going to have to track those down, too. Maybe George was in on this with Mark, or even John. Maybe one of them killed George. All these goddamn calls and numbers will probably track back to John, Tommy, Mark and who knows who else. Pretty soon we'll have too many suspects, and everyone will keep looking guiltier."

"Well, let's keep tracking down what we need that pertains to Tommy on my market related charges case while he's still in custody and let the other stuff slide a little longer," Kyle offered. "John and Mark aren't going anywhere, and if you help me with my market case, I'll spend nights and weekends trying to find the right ties for you on the murder."

Buying the logic, Doug continued, "Good point. Anything that we can find to sweat Tommy should still be our highest priority. Plus, with what's going on in the market, he's got to be worried that he can't help Pat. Maybe he'll give us something, something big, so he can get out before whatever he's planning implodes."

"Well, we've only had him in custody since this morning so the earliest he'll be released is sometime late tomorrow, assuming someone posts bail for him," Kyle said.

"We threatened Tommy with this already, but what if we actually try to get a petition for a change of jurisdiction on the murder charges based on the interstate calls and George's murder being on federal land? That could probably delay his release until maybe Thursday."

"That would be enough time to drive him crazy," Kyle offered. "He's not real patient, and something is definitely going on. I can feel it," Kyle said.

"What do you mean?"

"John DeFallo is in town again, or still, for all I know. There are McKinstry guys and other firms crawling all over. There are big, really big, positions out there . . ."

"Say it straight," Doug requested.

"There are a record number of short positions betting on the carbon market tanking, but those shorts are getting covered, and there is also some support for the price stabilizing. There's a big trade association lunch meeting tomorrow. There will be lots of talk," Kyle said.

"You going?" Doug asked.

"Yeah, you want to come?" Kyle asked.

"No, thanks. Too many pretentious suits for me. Besides, I better keep on-task tracking down leads," Doug said.

"Not if you have too many of those," Kyle said as he pointed to Doug's second beer.

"Buy me one more, and I promise to go straight home and be back at the office by five in the morning."

"Deal," Kyle said. "And I will check with our attorneys about changing jurisdiction on the murder charge."

43

Tuesday morning brought clear blue skies and a dry wind from the northwest. The welcome air bullied unpleasant moisture out of town. It was a normal workday for most of Chicago, but the drama continued for those very few that paid attention to, or cared about, one relatively obscure commodities market. It was very clear to Pat and John that they were on the opposite ends of an escalating bet about the market's direction, and Pat's firm continued to counter the short positions that John was taking. Either of the two could easily get in big trouble if the market turned dramatically one way or the other, squeezed out of the market under the pressure of their own actions. Prices were inching down. People saw the building short positions and were waiting for something to happen. The market was like a stretched rubber band, ready to break.

That afternoon, men in dark suits and a few women in comparatively brightly-colored professional attire started to gather on the top floor of a downtown skyscraper. It was an impressive room with the outdoor brightness pouring in through the three-windowed sides of the large meeting room. The setting was very high end, a private club where, on most days, men gathered doing nothing more than being rich together.

Pat stood far away from the entrance staring out of the window, looking south over Grant Park. He could see Soldier Field and possibly all the way to Indiana, the sky was so clear. He took deep breaths and exhaled slowly, trying to calm himself. He had made many friends and acquaintances over the last several months. He had become well-known in this quirky business, both for his success and his anti-establishment look and attitude.

He knew it would only be a matter of time before someone recognized his stocky frame and ill-fitting suit from behind. He wasn't going to turn from the window and the view and the solitude until forced. He hoped it would be Jenny. Pat was concerned that he was starting to think and act more like Tommy every single day, but he had started to understand it was the pressure that Tommy always put himself under that masked many of his good qualities. Only a few close friends could push through the façade and get to the good stuff. That same pressure was now impacting Pat. He needed this to end. He wanted his old life back and didn't care if it came with a single dollar.

The room was buzzing with rumors as the 200 people in attendance bustled about. This month's association meeting drew a much larger crowd than normal since many members were looking for information and an understanding of what was going on in the market. Pat could feel the energy and finally decided to turn from the window. He noticed a group of people huddled in the opposite corner of the room. That had to be Mark. He always drew a crowd and he could see the top of a cowboy hat. Pat then saw Jenny appear at the entrance. She had a dress that looked perfectly tailored to her body, but had actually been bought off the rack by Pat and Jenny on Michigan Avenue the previous night, five minutes before the store closed. Pat made his way over to Jenny. They both looked happy to see one another. They hugged, which was normal, but Pat's hand lingered on Jenny's as they started to talk.

"So, you seem a little affectionate today. Are you hitting on me?" Jenny said, trying to lighten the mood.

"No, but you are smokin', and I don't mind if the people in this room think we're together," Pat said.

"Oh, I see! Looking to use me to enhance your rep," Jenny smiled playfully at Pat, fitting into the role.

"Oh, that's perfect, and go ahead and give that old 'you've got it bad for me' look if you wouldn't mind."

"Anything to help, but let's get through this next hour," Jenny said, still smiling and appearing to flirt with Pat.

"I hear you. Everything is normal so far," Pat said.

"Not for long. You may want to turn around."

Pat whirled to see John taking a seat at the table on the stage, facing twenty or so round tables. People were quickly taking their seats, ready for salad and half of some small bird. Pat escorted Jenny to a table in the back and sat where they could see the stage without having to turn. He noticed Kyle at the next table, who smiled and nodded in his direction.

As the Carbon Trader Association's executive director stepped to the podium and tapped his finger on the microphone, the attendees ended conversations quickly and scurried to their seats as if they were playing musical chairs and someone would be "out." Pat was surprised that such an independent, aggressive, and entrepreneurial group could move in such precise unison.

The group half-heartedly listened. "Thanks for coming, blah, blah nice day, blah blah. We'd like to thank our sponsors, blah, blah." Then came more information on the organization and finally the words, "Let's welcome John DeFallo as our guest speaker." That got Jenny and Pat's attention.

John was a commanding speaker. He understood timing and had a presence at the podium. Without saying a word, he entranced them all. His charisma was infectious. Even the light clinking of silverware on china as people nibbled and cut through their bird halves, asparagus, and boiled potatoes stopped when John was speaking. John knew that all eyes were on him, and he savored their attention. "Friends, the commodity trading business can't survive unless we all have the utmost integrity and respect for our roles in the process. This is our business, and we can all make good money, but we have to be careful."

Pat and Jenny looked at each other and Jenny couldn't help but note how Pat's face had gone so pale it almost matched his shirt. She worried he might pass out.

John continued. "Over the years, we have had our problems in commodities. It started long ago and includes the Hunt brothers in 1980 trying to corner the silver market and a firm I was unfortunately part of that caused significant problems in the carbon markets. It must end today with people manipulating carbon markets paying the ultimate price for their wrongdoing. I have it on good authority that the CFTC has a current situation under control, and I commend them for protecting the integrity of our business."

John paused for effect and to allow for the whispers and subtle pointing and head-nodding to ensue. He continued on with more thoughts on integrity and current market conditions. He may have just as well been reading the phone book. No one would have noticed after the subtle, but effective, accusation that someone was tampering with the market and had gotten caught. He finished and sat down.

Next, the group's CFO rose to give the financial report and run through some other business. With each passing PowerPoint slide, a few more guests, not so discreetly, headed for the exits and their cell phones.

Pat buried his head in his thick hands and fingers and rubbed his face, trying to scrub away what had just happened. Kyle waited until the meeting was over, then got on his cell phone to call his boss and then planned to call Doug. Mark sat in the corner of the room taking it all in. John stood on the podium stage answering questions from those that lingered looking for more information. He didn't associate the name Tommy Gardner with the current alleged wrongdoing; he didn't have to . . . people would find out soon enough.

Not even two hours later, word spread quickly that Tommy Gardner had been arrested on market tampering charges, and people started to sell.

44

The late Tuesday afternoon sunlight sparkled off of the lake, and a cool early September breeze danced through the streets of Chicago. The atmosphere in Pat's office was much different, though. It was thick with tension as he nervously watched the computer screen, and Jenny anxiously watched him. She wanted to be there to help, but she didn't quite know what to do, so she watched and listened. As Pat stared at his monitor, Jenny would occasionally hear a muffled, "Fuck, fuck, fuck," chant. Each time she would ask what was wrong. Each time, Pat said, "It just keeps going down."

After the third time, Jenny asked, "How far can it go down?"

"In one day?" Pat answered, "I think it's twenty percent before trading is suspended, and that's where it's headed. It will be over for the day soon. Then we can figure out what to do next."

"We?" Jenny asked.

"Yeah, you and me . . . oh, there we go. Trading is locked out for the day and won't resume until noon tomorrow. Good, I guess, because now we have time."

"So, what do you want to do?" Jenny asked.

"I want to sell. I think it's going into a freefall. When Tommy's name gets fully tied to this, it will be even worse. Today everyone in the know was just looking out for themselves and their biggest clients. Tomorrow is bound to be an even bigger free-for-all when word spreads to smaller investors.

"But Tommy wants you to keep buying and covering shorts, right? Do you have any money left?" Jenny asked.

"Real money? No, but I haven't used that much of the line of credit. I can probably invest, or throw away, whatever, another twenty million when the market opens," Pat reasoned.

"So, are you going to listen to him?" Jenny asked.

"I don't know. I ran the math, and even selling into a falling market I can still probably pay off the line of credit we used so far and walk away with a few million dollars," Pat said.

"If you don't sell everything, what happens?" Jenny asked.

"If I keep borrowing money and it goes down let's say another fifteen percent I'll be well underwater. The banks will eventually require that I start selling, which will put even more downward pressure on the price. It will get uglier and uglier, and I won't even be able to cover the loans. I'll be done, squeezed out by John."

"Shit! And you want my help with this?" Jenny said. "No way. Your call. Good luck!"

"Come on. Give me something," Pat begged. "I'll tell you what . . . I'll give you half of whatever is left if you convince me to sell!"

"You'd really give me half if you sold!?" Jenny said, smiled and continued. "No, don't answer that. I know you would actually do it."

"Yes, I would. Now, please, give me something," Pat said.

"Fine. Do you think Tommy is driven more by logic and experience or by vengeance at this point?" Jenny asked.

"That's easy—vengeance," Pat said.

"Then you should sell and get out. It's your money, not his," Jenny said.

"But I'd be letting him down."

"But you'd be saving yourself," Jenny argued.

"So, I shouldn't go big? I should just go home?"

"Well, what is the upside if you go big and it works out?" Jenny asked.

"Who knows? Could easily be fifty to a one hundred million," Pat said.

"Shut up! How could it be that much?"

"Well, with all the cash we had made, plus borrowing way more than that and throw in a bunch short sales and futures contracts . . . this is pretty damned leveraged. House of cards. It's whether ours falls first or someone else's does."

"You mean John's?" Jenny knew where this was going.

"There are way more people out there on each side of this bet than me and John, but probably not any as far out on a limb as we are. There will probably be a billion dollars trading hands here in the next couple of days, and I have until noon tomorrow to decide how we play this out."

"Sounds like we should drink a little on this," Jenny said.

"Good idea. Let's find a bar that John would be too uptight to frequent. I couldn't stand running into him again," Pat suggested.

"It's a big city. We won't see him."

"Unless he wants us to see him." They walked out onto the street packed with people moving purposefully toward their lives outside of work.

45

While Pat and Jenny were drinking away their Tuesday evening, Kyle was with Doug giving him the update on the meeting and the market activity. They quickly turned their attention back to Tommy and their plan.

Doug got them on track. "What did your attorneys say about the jurisdiction issue?"

"They said that we didn't have a prayer of turning it into Chicago jurisdiction, and the feds aren't interested in taking it over. They asked what the real goal here was, and I told them we wanted his help until the end of the day on Wednesday," Kyle answered.

"We picked him up on Monday. Does that still work for whatever due process laws you guys have on federal charges?" Doug asked.

"I guess I should have known this but I'm new to this law and order stuff. We have up to seventy-two hours, so holding him until the end of the workday on Wednesday isn't a problem," Kyle said.

"Did you see Tommy today? Were you there to tell him when he was likely to get out?"

"Yep."

"And his reaction?" Doug asked.

"Strange enough, he just smiled, but I don't think that meant anything. He's just trying to mess with us. Technically we could hold him until Thursday morning, but we plan on releasing him after the market closes tomorrow."

"Please make sure he knows he can talk to us if he wants to speed up the wheels of justice," Doug said.

"He does, but I don't see him talking. He knows we have a shit case and he seems strangely calm about whatever is going on in the market . . . like he knows what's going to happen," Kyle said.

With Tommy in custody and no other leads to follow on the market case, Kyle turned his Tuesday evening attention back to helping Doug look for connections between Tommy, Mark, John, George, and John's co-owner in Big Mountain, RD Partners. Doug wasn't able to track down ownership through the maze of shell companies but figured Kyle could. Kyle had put some of the pieces together over the previous couple of days, but he now worked through the night. By morning there was more dirt than he knew what to do with. Kyle called Doug first thing in the morning, having not slept a single minute that night.

"Hey, can you meet me at my office?" Kyle said, exhausted, to Doug.

"You usually come to the precinct. What's the deal?" Doug asked.

"I've got the computers and files here that we may want to access," Kyle said. "I have some interesting information on known associates for your murder case."

"I'll be there in thirty." Doug hung up, not waiting for a response.

Their offices were only blocks away from each other, but architecturally they couldn't have been more different. Plus, Kyle's office was all granite, glass, and chrome instead of Formica, plastic, and steel. Cubes were still cubes as Kyle guided Doug back to his.

"We have some interesting overlap in people coming in and out of these guys' lives. For example, two brothers, small time criminals who grew up with John. One of them was with Mark in Whitefish. To top it off, it was shortly before George died," Kyle said.

"What?! That's huge. Wait. How the hell did you piece that together?"

"Well, we started by creating a database for each of them with all of their known contacts and cross referenced them," Kyle said.

"I'm sure that created a pretty significant overlap."

"Yes, it did. There were 252 overlapping contacts between John and Tommy, 157 between John and Mark, and 193 between Tommy and Mark along with 50 that were in all three files," Kyle said.

"How did you narrow that down?"

"Of course we checked how they came in contact looking for outliers," Kyle said.

"Why, of course," Doug stated.

"There are a lot of sources that we are talking about here. We used facial recognition software from pictures on social media sites and internet searches to find any overlaps. We also used more mundane sources like conference attendee lists, newspaper articles, internet searches, and collected information anytime they were in touch with another person. There were thousands of entries for each guy," Kyle explained.

"We?" is all that Doug said, trying not to look impressed with the speed, thoroughness, or intrusiveness of the process.

"I had some help. I mentioned previously my little network of guys that help each other out with this kind of thing. They have been working on this since I first brought it up the other day. Of course some sources—okay, most—were things where a warrant would have been in order. You did say that fast was important, right?" Kyle asked.

"So, great. All very impressive, but let's get back to the guys who John grew up with. Isn't that the critical overlap here?" Doug asked.

"Probably, but Deb, Susan, Sam Meyers and Mark's boss, Barbara came up as common contacts across all three guys. Does that seem strange to you?" Kyle asked.

"I don't know, maybe, but I could think of reasons for all of them. If you pushed me I'd say Deb being in contact with Mark and this Barbara person being in contact with George seem the most distant, but they are all in the same business, so what the fuck do I know?" Doug wasn't that interested in his own question.

Kyle sensed he needed to move on and started to push pictures across the table toward Doug, saying "Yeah. So, these two brothers . . . one of them ended up in a car in Whitefish with Mark, as I mentioned. They were caught on a traffic camera running a red light. You can only see his legs, but my guess is the other brother is in the back seat."

"Nice work!" Doug said with as much inflection as Kyle had ever heard from Doug.

"There's more. One of the brothers talked to John on his cell two weeks before the murder, and the two brothers were on the ski hill the day George died. Well, at least their season passes were scanned that day," Kyle said.

"No offense, but it would have been nice to have all of this information a lot sooner. We wouldn't have gone after Tommy so hard about what happened to George and spent it looking at these other guys for the murder," Doug said.

"Sure, but remember we didn't have enough to even get a warrant for anyone other than Tommy. Plus, all you really have is a bunch of information that will get thrown out in court. There is no way that this goes anywhere without a confession," Kyle said.

"True enough."

"So, are you going to go after the brothers or Mark first on this?" Kyle asked.

"Well, actually it will be the Whitefish PD's call. As much as I want to confront Mark, because he's here and looks guilty as hell, my guess is that the brothers might be easier because we can work one against the other. Mark can't possibly have a logical explanation for this, but he probably will anyway, and he'll figure out that the information wasn't obtained legally," Doug said.

"So, you flying to Montana?"

"Not sure my bosses will be too comfortable with another trip. I'll try to talk the Whitefish cops into interrogating the brothers first. Hopefully they let us participate online," Doug said.

As they were wrapping up, Kyle's cell phone rang, and he answered. Kyle's side of the conversation amounted to a series of yes and no answers.

"What was that?" Doug asked.

"It appears you and I have plans at eleven this morning. We'll be issuing a joint statement, followed by questions from any media people who care," Kyle said.

"I get to be on TV?" Doug said, feigning interest.

"Maybe we should make sure Tommy finds out. He should really get nervous."

"Sounds like you need to write something up for us to read."

"Why me?" Kyle objected.

"Because we both know you'll do it better and I care less than you if it gets done well, or at all, for that matter."

"I'll email you the draft in an hour so we can each get our boss's approval."

"I'll change into my best suit."

Although exhausted, the words came quickly to Kyle as did the approvals, and they were ready to go at eleven. Kyle was excited about his first chance on a big case. Doug and Kyle were flanked by PR specialists from each of their departments. Their big stage was a table and a microphone in a conference room off the lobby in the federal courthouse. Kyle started to speak to the five or so newspaper and local TV people who had nothing better to do this day than to show up. His voice was steady and self-assured.

"Mr. Thomas Gardner has been arrested on charges related to commodity market tampering. He has not been charged, but is also a person of interest regarding an ongoing murder investigation revolving around the death of George Shannon. We believe these cases to be related. Mr. Gardner has a commodity market history that led to his lifetime ban from those markets. We believe the people's case will be strong, and the CFTC, Cook County and the City of Chicago intend to prosecute these cases to the fullest extent of the law. Are there any questions?"

Kyle and Doug sat stoically, trying not to look guilty of exaggerating the truth, as both knew the chances that Tommy had anything to do with

George's death were remote and the reference to the City of Chicago wasn't relevant given the issue of jurisdiction.

An attractive female reporter with a Channel 7 microphone asked the first question. "Are there any other firms involved with Mr. Gardner in the alleged market tampering?"

Kyle answered. "We have our suspicions, and they are focusing on one firm."

A handsome but surprisingly thin looking male reporter with a Channel 32 microphone asked the next question. "Our research indicates Mr. Shannon, the alleged murder victim, died in Montana. Why is this a Chicago case?"

Doug gathered himself and cleared his throat. "Well, jurisdiction in this case is complicated. There was a death a few years back, before Mr. Shannon's, in Chicago that may be related, so we are working closely with Montana authorities and sharing information. There is also the potential that the alleged murder, which took place on federal land, could become a federal case instead of a Montana case. Regardless, local Chicago involvement made sense."

Suddenly a voice from the back of the room burst through rather forcefully. "Good morning. Jennifer from the, ahh People's Free Press. So, you're saying that you are going to arrest Mr. Gardner on a charge where you don't have jurisdiction?"

Doug stumbled. "Well, no. It's complicated. We didn't arrest him on a murder charge. He is a person of interest in that case."

Jenny interrupted. "Well, let me ask a simple question of the young gentleman with you. Do you have evidence of a trading tie between Mr. Gardner and the firm you mentioned?"

Everyone turned to Kyle. "We have a known personal association and phone conversations that . . ."

Jenny again interrupted. "Do you have known associations between Mr. Gardner and let's say, oh, a hundred or more other marketers, brokers, and people working in the commodities market?"

Kyle said, "Yes, but not with the history . . ."

At this point, both of the PR handlers for Kyle and Doug were ready to jump in simultaneously. After sharing a quick glance, the Chicago Police Department spokesperson took control. "Clearly, we aren't here to try our case in the media. There is substantial evidence to proceed on the securities fraud charges and we will share more information when the time is right. Thank you for your time today."

Jenny was proud of herself for interjecting and expected the real reporters would want to speak to her, but instead, they all packed up their things and moved passed her without even making eye contact. Jenny left, disappointed that her questions hadn't created more of a stir.

46

Jenny stopped by Pat's office and relayed her actions and the reactions to him. She then asked him, "The market is just about to reopened, right? What are we going to do?"

"I still don't know, but I'm about to get on the phone with brokers and bankers. I may have to flip a coin.

"Okay, then." Jenny sounded startled.

Pat continued. "You realize that with John behind this, if I walk away, actually probably even if I don't, John will make tens, or even hundreds of millions of dollars if the market tanks."

"Oh," is all Jenny said.

"Yeah. If I walk away, John will make millions and beat Tommy."

Jenny went for a walk to try and clear her head. It seemed like there was nothing she could do anymore for Tommy or Pat. She rubbed the back of her neck as she walked and took long deep breaths. That didn't stop the anguish and frustration from welling up into tears.

When trading reopened, it wasn't like people started running around in colored vests yelling to each other like the old days of trading. Instead, magically, the trading websites awoke, on time. Trading data started scrolling across computer screens. Pat finally decided to commit brokers to keep buying, and then he watched nervously from his office. John watched on a laptop from his apartment. Mark was in his office at McKinstry. Tommy sat in jail, wondering what was happening. He considered asking for Kyle or Doug and admitting to anything they wanted, to everything he did or didn't do, just to get out to see what was happening.

Each computer screen showed the same trend as the previous day: carbon credits down $0.62, then, $0.78, then, $1.08. Each trade was lower. By midafternoon the market was down nearly fifteen percent. There didn't appear to be any support. Pat couldn't buy any more. There was no money to be invested and no more to be borrowed.

Pat had barely borrowed the money to make the trades and his bankers were already calling to let him know that if the market ended down fifteen percent or more for the day that they would need to talk. The banks would want to start discussing the timing of a margin call. If that happened, Pat would need to start selling into what, by then, could be a freefall market. He had borrowed as much as he used in cash and was further leveraged by futures contracts. It wouldn't take much more of a downturn to bury him. If he reversed course and started selling now, it wouldn't help. It was already too late unless the market rebounded, but there was no sign that would happen.

The office was quiet. It was mid-afternoon and Pat hadn't seen or heard from Jenny since she went for a walk. Pat sat back like the granite Abe Lincoln on his monument, paralyzed by fear. Jenny pounded on the glass door to his office, startling him. He opened it, and she smiled. "How's it going?" Jenny asked.

"It's a nightmare," Pat answered. He looked shrunken, defeated.

"How bad?"

"If the market falls twenty percent again today and they shut down trading, who knows where it will stop? It won't matter because I'll be wiped out," Pat offered.

"Maybe financially out, but you'll bounce back." Jenny could feel that her words rang hollow.

"Well, you want to spend the next hour with me watching a computer screen?" Pat offered. They sat down and watched as the market inched closer to another automatic shutdown. Pat hoped that time on the trading day would run out fast. Finally, however, there was a blip, or more accurately, things stopped going down. For thirty minutes, the price didn't move. Then, finally up twenty cents, then a little more. The market closed down ten percent for the day. Pat blurted out, "Hey, I'm not dead yet!"

"So, I'm pretty new to this," Jenny said, "but someone must have been buying, right?"

"Someone's always buying and selling, but you're right. There were finally enough buyers to stop the fall."

"Say, we should probably get down to the courthouse. Someone needs to pay Tommy's bail," Jenny said.

"Funny. I don't have a penny to help post bail. You?" Pat asked.

"No," Jenny said.

"Well, even if I had money, I couldn't help. That wouldn't have looked too good," Pat said.

Jenny smirked at her own absent-mindedness. "Oh, yeah. Good point," then added, "Well, what should we do?"

"Head down there, and see what happens, I guess. Maybe they will release him on his own recognizance or he can pay his own bail," Pat said.

They left quickly for the federal court release office, walking as fast as the midweek rush hour traffic would have allowed by cab. As they hustled, sweaty and puffing, towards the entrance, Tommy and Susan were walking out.

Glaring at Jenny, Susan spoke in a matter of fact and emotionless tone, like she was too tired to care. "Well, give me one minute and then you can have him." She turned and guided Tommy a couple of steps away from where Jenny and Pat waited so that they couldn't hear the rest of the conversation.

Once separated, Susan's tone sharpened and the urgency and fire in her voice rose with each word. "Look here Tommy. Look into my eyes as

I say this to you. The only reason that I posted your bail is that you finally didn't ask for my help. I helped Pat because you asked for something for someone else not yourself. That's progress, but this needs to be it as I warned you before. Stay away from me. Even if you just see me from across the street, walk away like your life depended on it. I can't see you anymore. Do you hear me?"

Tommy was stunned by the intensity in her eyes and said, "Yes, I hear you, and thank you for everything you did to get me out of this mess alive, so far."

"Goodbye, Tommy." Susan gracefully walked down the steps and hailed a cab. Tommy was shaken by her intensity and thinking that would be the last time he would ever see her.

Tommy realized there wasn't much good that could come from being seen with Pat, but there were bigger negatives coming if he didn't find out what was going on. The three agreed to split up and meet near the softball fields. It was a spot in Grant Park that each knew from past visits with Tommy. Even if Kyle or Doug were watching, he hoped they wouldn't know what they talked about.

Soon thereafter, they found their way to the meeting spot. They stood near a small berm and talked with Pat explaining where the market was and all that had transpired over three days, including the interaction with John. "So, things are good then," Tommy said, holding a magazine over his mouth like an NFL coach, looking to avoid lip readers.

Pat followed suit, rubbing his nose as he spoke. "What? Going good? If the market goes down even five or ten percent tomorrow, it all falls apart."

"But you said it went up at the end of the day, right?" Tommy said.

"Yeah, like four percent in the last hour. That doesn't mean shit," Pat argued.

"Well, maybe McKinstry is out there saying enough is enough. They don't want to see this market tank further, or with another black eye. My guess is they are buyers," Tommy said.

Jenny jumped in. "You're guessing?"

"Yes, but it's an educated guess," Tommy said. "Mark did this before to save the market when John, George and I fucked it up. He needs this market to succeed. They are making too much money to let it go down further. You'll be fine . . . if it's them, and if they keep buying."

"Multiple 'ifs' don't make me feel better," Pat said.

"Well, you don't have any choice now," Tommy offered.

"Sure I do. Start selling if the market keeps going up. Then, I still might be able to get some money out," Pat said. "Or get back to zero. I'd like to avoid bankruptcy if you wouldn't mind."

Tommy looked at his friend and realized the last three days were harder on Pat than on him. Pat's eyes were sunken with bluish-hued bags under each eye. His face looked puffy, and his right hand was trembling. Tommy proceeded more cautiously. "Please, Pat, no. If it's McKinstry supporting the market and they see you selling, that will put more downward price pressure on the market and they will have to buy even more units to stabilize prices. Eventually, Mark might say, *'Fuck it, let them rot. It's too expensive.'* The way I look at it, he knows we have way too many long positions and John has way too many short positions to cover. He can probably squeeze one of the two of us into oblivion if he wants. Burying us costs him the market he needs to protect, and burying John doesn't. This is just a business decision for him as long as we don't make it personal."

"So, you have this all figured out from your jail cell?" Pat said.

"Well, I did have lots of time to think about it, and the two of you. Please stick with it just a day or two longer."

"You're right about one thing. I really don't have much choice," Pat said.

Jenny continued to look on, kicking occasionally at the ground, not wanting to choose a side. As Tommy and Pat were ready to go their separate ways, Jenny realized that they were both probably expecting her to leave with them. Pat turned to go west and Tommy north, and they both looked back at her. She plopped herself down and said, "Don't make me choose."

Her words lingered for a moment, but before either could speak, the tension was suspended by a loud "hey" from just to their south. It was John, looking smug even from fifty yards away. He had on a baseball hat, sunglasses, a T-shirt, and cargo shorts. Unfortunately for the trio of friends, the tourist clothing ensemble was completed by a long lens and camera. John yelled, "I'll copy you on the pictures that I'm sending to Kyle and Doug!"

Tommy and Pat turned dejectedly and went their separate ways, leaving Jenny on the berm by herself. She stretched out her legs and arms, looked straight up, and sighed deeply. As Jenny was rolling her head trying to relieve the tension that had built up in her neck and back, she caught a glimpse of John coming in her direction. She jumped to her feet and started to walk quickly down the sidewalk away from him. John hastened his pace and cut across the softball field to intercept her.

"Come on, don't take this personally. It's just business," John said.

Jenny turned on a dime, and they came face-to-face, Jenny peering down at him slightly. "Not personal? You morons are trying to bury each other."

"No, we're not. We're trying to make big money. That's all," John said. "It's not personal for me, and that's why I'm going to come out on top."

"So, you think you have this all figured out?" Jenny asked.

"I think I do. People are spooked by Tommy's involvement, plus I'm not all emotional about it like your two friends. They're going to mess this up unless I give them a break," John said.

"And you would do that, what, for me?"

John was infatuated with Jenny from the moment he saw her with her friends at the hotel restaurant the first night they met. He really did want her approval in some strange sort of way. In addition, there was pragmatism to the idea. He knew this market still had a chance to bury him.

"Yes, if you will do something for me." John took a long, greedy stare at Jenny, but then his cell phone rang.

"You're a pig," Jenny blurted as John's cell phone continued to ring.

"Hold that thought. Really, I have to grab this," John said. Jenny had her chance to escape, but for some reason lingered, perhaps wondering about the urgency of the call. She kicked at the ground a bit again, folded her arms, and walked away a few feet. John turned away from her as he started to speak, but she heard him say, "Yes, yes, yes, I know," and, "I'll start to cover before it gets there."

John turned back to Jenny and said, "My apologies, but where were we . . . oh, yes, you were calling me a pig."

"Yes. Do you really think you have any chance with me?" Jenny said.

"Well, I guess not, but I thought you might want to try to help your friends."

"What do you mean?"

"One of us doesn't have to lose everything. If the price of carbon settles in at about the right price, I could offer them a way out."

"So, you'll tell me when that time comes?" Jenny asked.

"Possibly, yes. Well, yes. All you need to do is keep an open mind about me," John said.

"That's it?"

"Well, and meet me for a drink tonight at the Hilton. I'll explain it further, and you'll see I'm not evil and not what Tommy thinks I am. I have a solution to this mess, and I know that Tommy won't listen to me," John offered.

"It appears that you have adequately stalked me to know I am staying at the Hilton."

"I have, and I hope to see you there. A little flexibility could be worth millions of dollars to you and your friends. Sure, I'll make a lot more, but they won't lose everything," John said and headed south, while Jenny walked directly west back toward the hotel. She felt sick at the thought of spending any time or doing anything with John, but why not if Pat

256

comes out of this without losing everything and instead, is set for life? Jenny knew it wasn't as simple as one drink, but she knew Pat would do almost anything for her. Jenny headed for the drug store around the corner to pick up some things that she thought she would need and then left a message on John's cell phone to meet her at a bar near the hotel so they wouldn't run into Pat or Tommy. She could do this, she *would* do this, for Pat and Mary and the kids.

47

Pat and Tommy both spent Wednesday night obsessing about what would happen the next day and knowing they shouldn't talk to each other. Tommy was back at his condo. He tried calling Jenny's cell phone and her hotel room several times. He figured she was pretty mad at him and he knew that Pat needed her more than he did to get through this. He stared for an hour at a full bottle of vodka and his assortment of prescriptions on the table. He walked around them, occasionally pushing at the pill bottles and rolling them across the table. Finally, knowing he wouldn't see or talk to Jenny, he poured four pills into his palm and slammed them into his mouth. He reached for a glass of water, but sent it spilling over the table and around the vodka bottle. Frustrated, he grabbed the vodka. As he struggled with the seal on the cap the pills started to dissolve, becoming bitter in his mouth. Finally, he spat them out over the table and watched them dissolve in the spilled water. He placed the still-unopened bottle of vodka in the middle of the mess and went to bed.

Meanwhile, Pat stopped at the first bar that he saw after the three parted company, but after a couple of beers he realized that getting drunk wouldn't solve anything. Pat swung the bar door open into the unseasonably cold and still night air. His stocky silhouette in the pool table light made him look as if he was made of building blocks. As he took two steps out onto the sidewalk, the door closed with a thud behind him.

The fluorescent outdoor bar sign twitched on and off, making the turn of his head look like an old projector recording. He scanned the streets and parked cars before proceeding. Now he always thought someone was watching. His time in Chicago had changed him. He swung his arms in a graceful arc clearing his own girth and plodded, bull legged, down the street.

Pat tried Jenny's cell phone and hotel room phone as he walked. Frustrated, he went to the Hilton and knocked on her door. When no one answered, he convinced the manager to open the door, claiming that Jenny was epileptic and might be having a seizure. He half expected to find her there with Tommy. When the room was empty, he was a bit jealous, assuming Tommy and Jenny were off somewhere else together.

He felt like he was back in college when he had to watch their bond and sexual tension play out. He had Mary now, and the kids, and felt ashamed at his reaction. He called Mary and talked to her the entire walk home. He told Mary everything, and she assured him no matter what happened she would be waiting for him to come home. Their bond had survived the years based on complete honesty. Mary even knew that Pat had a bit of a thing for Jenny for a while back in college but neither ever let Jenny or Tommy know. Pat always told Mary it was ancient history, although she still wondered from time to time.

Once back, he hung up his cell phone, grabbed a beer, and sat in an overstuffed chair. He took a few sips and drifted off to sleep. Mentally and emotionally spent, Pat didn't move a muscle until first thing in the morning when an incoming call seemingly vibrated both the table next to him where the phone laid and the chair he sat on. It was an assistant to Mark at McKinstry, asking that he join Mark for lunch at his office. John and Tommy didn't answer their phones but received similar early Thursday morning voicemail messages. After Mark confirmed with his assistant that the calls to Pat, John, and Tommy had been placed, and that a sit-down lunch was set to take place in the main conference room, he turned his attention to the morning's trading activity.

Mark had his hedge manager and trading manager with him in his office, and they set up laptops at small tables on each side of the room. No one else entered the room, and buy and sell orders would go out only from the two managers. The entire firm knew what a big day this was; there were millions of dollars of potential bonuses hanging in the balance. People at the firm would be watching their screens like it was the Super Bowl and they had a chance to win a big pool.

Trading opened Thursday with many sellers. Rumors of Tommy's involvement continued to spread. Now brokers were starting to take care of their less important customers after getting their own needs and their higher profile customers taken care of previously. Mark didn't flinch. "Buy. Fill orders fast. I want people thinking there are plenty of buyers out there." The pressure from sellers was relentless for the first two hours of trading. The price held nearly flat only because McKinstry put over three hundred million of firm and client money into the market.

Late in the morning, prices moved up nearly five percent as McKinstry continued to buy. Each time one of the two managers suggested pulling back, Mark groused at the thought and just yelled "buy" louder.

Finally, to no one in particular, Mark said, "Where the hell is John? He must not be covering his short positions by buying. That son of a bitch thinks he can outlast me."

The bulky hedge manager with large pores and gelled comb-over hair jumped in. "Maybe John can outlast us. We are through most of our reserves and soon we'll start using our lending capacity. We can't support the prices in the market by buying for much longer."

"Well, we have to keep buying. That piece of shit has to cover those short positions pretty soon. His bankers have to be all over his ass. He's got to be buying." It was almost time for the lunch meeting, so Mark put his suit coat on and headed to the conference room. Just before he got to the door, he turned to his managers. "Buy only what you have to in order to keep the price from falling. There has to be support out there somewhere . . . I can feel it, I know it. We are too damn close to

260

grabbing the market share I . . . ah . . . we need to really be successful in this business." Mark was so close to owning ten percent of McKinstry he could taste it. He'd have so much "fuck you" money he could say fuck you to his boss Barbara, whenever he wanted.

Mark headed to the conference room to find Pat and Tommy with five impeccably displayed place settings waiting along with pork fillets, boiled potatoes, and steamed carrots. Mark's philosophy during touchy business meetings was always to class it up enough to stop people from brawling in the gutter. It didn't always work, but he figured it helped. Mark had expected four settings but seeing five quickly figured that Barbara had invited herself. He wasn't surprised as there was a lot of money at stake and she didn't fully trust him.

Mark joined Pat on the far side of the table opposite of the door and Tommy. Before they could even sit down Barbara entered and introduced herself to Tommy and Pat and sat at the end of the table. She was an open and engaging person with striking gray hair and an infectious smile. Neither was surprised by her presence, given what they knew of Mark's stock deal, but were caught off guard by the difference between the first impression she made and the image that Mark had conveyed.

All that was missing was John until he pushed anxiously into the room a few minutes later. The four instinctively stood as a reaction to John's urgent demeanor. Clearly he hadn't seen a razor or a brush since yesterday, and he looked like he had a bad hangover. "Sorry I'm late. I, uh, overslept, I guess."

Mark spoke next. "So, you haven't seen what's happened in the market today?"

"No. I wasn't awake ten minutes ago. Thought I would have better access to information and trades here, so I came straight over. What the hell is going on?"

Tommy couldn't control himself. He had to tell John. "The market is up over five percent for the day."

"No fucking way. There was too much bad news out there, unless you guys bought everything in sight," John said, staring at Mark.

Mark responded quickly. "Of course I can't answer that, but it does appear there aren't many sellers left out there, at least at the current price."

John started to panic. The other three men were surprised to see him looking so disheveled. John said, "Well, then you guys need to sell to me. It's probably pretty obvious that I need to cover some short positions."

Pat spoke up. "I'm not really in a position to sell. That might spook the market and besides, I think there's some upside now."

"Right, asshole. That upside will be me driving up the market, having to buy to cover my shorts," John said, now sweating and near hyperventilation.

"If you say so," Pat offered somewhat cautiously while glancing at the floor, not knowing how far John could be pushed before losing control.

John fired viciously at Tommy. "I know you're behind this whole thing. Pat's just your puppet."

"Not true, but even if it was, who'd blame me? You screwed over our business. I was just trying to do the right thing. Build a business that made a difference, but you had to fuck with it." Tommy was matching John's intensity.

"Do the right thing? Make a difference?" John yelled. "Listen to yourself. Always a do-gooder. Always better than the rest of us."

"That's not what I said or thought," Tommy shot back aggressively.

"You're lying to yourself, you arrogant piece of shit. You had to know something was wrong back then. You had to see the volumes. Look at the money we were making. At some level you had to know, but if you did the wrong things for the right reason, then it was okay."

Tommy and John continually moved closer together as the conversation escalated, while Pat and Mark looked on anxiously a step back from where they started even though they had the table for protection. Barbara stood her ground risking becoming collateral damage if they went after each other.

Tommy was speechless. This verbal punch in the gut rocked him as if it were physical. He could barely breathe. There was some truth to John's comments, and Tommy knew it. Pat stared at Tommy with his arms crossed knowing the same thing. Pat clearly understood in that moment that Tommy had abused their friendship more than he previously could have known.

John continued, almost desperate. "And now, look at you. Manipulating Pat and brokers, marketers, and fund managers. And why? To get back at me? You think we are all money and power whores and now you're worse than any of us. Congratulations."

"I'm not making a penny on this. I can't," Tommy was trying to stand up for himself, but he was still shaken to the core.

"So that's how you rationalize it? You can be a vengeful, righteous ass as long as you don't make money doing it?"

"I didn't do anything!" Tommy was starting to get his footing again, and wasn't about to keep taking all of these accusations without a fight.

"Not officially, but we all know . . . and you know what's funny, I didn't do a damn thing. I didn't fix trades and I sure as hell didn't kill George!"

"You made eighty million dollars watching our business flame out," Tommy glared at John, hating him for everything that had happened. Hating himself for trusting John.

John was equally mad and thinking of Tommy as nothing more than a self-righteous asshole. He spitefully corrected Tommy, "It was forty million and I was approached by someone who needed cash to put a hedge strategy in place. So we shorted a shitload of carbon that protected my original investment in our company. That was just smart business. Hell, I thought you were the one cheating me! And did if ever occur to you that maybe George dying really was just an accident?"

"Bullshit. Somebody killed him!" Tommy knew it in his gut and had it confirmed by the thug that had roughed him up. He was pissed that no one else would acknowledge that truth.

"You don't know that for sure, and you still don't even know who made the other forty million in Big Mountain Traders do you?"

Tommy grew sheepish again. His confidence waned. "Who?"

"I don't have time for this anymore. I've got to try to save my ass. I need a phone and a quiet room," John said.

"By all means," offered Mark. "Help yourself to the conference room across the hall. John put on a headset, starting kneading a stress ball he carried in his suit coat pocket and started dialing. Pat, Tommy, and Mark stared at him through the two glass walls of the hallway separating the two conference rooms. No distance could have been greater.

No one ate a single bite of food. Pat and Tommy said their goodbyes to Mark and Barbara and headed out together into the thick heat of the afternoon. Nothing either of them could do to help or hurt John at this point. If Pat sold, Mark could, and probably would, flood the market and crater the price just to spite Tommy and Pat. They needed to let Mark and others in the market determine John's fate.

John would likely be scrambling until the market closing and again Friday morning, trying to climb out of a huge hole. If the market price kept climbing, Tommy figured that John might be broke before the market closed on Friday. It didn't feel as good, nor did it provide the closure Tommy had anticipated. He was more interested now, anyway, in seeing Jenny than worrying about John.

Pat and Tommy received the same message from Jenny at the same time when they turned on their phones. She texted, "Hey, I went back home this morning. Please don't bother calling until you guys come home. I did everything that I possibly could to help. I can't watch this anymore."

Tommy looked over at Pat and said, "Did you see the message from Jenny?"

Pat said, "What? Yes. Did you say something to her last night to piss her off?"

"I didn't see her last night," Tommy clarified. "I figured she was with you."

"No. She must be tired of both of us, but she wasn't in her room last night," Pat said.

"How do you know?" Tommy asked.

"Don't ask," Pat said. "I wonder where the hell she was."

"You don't think . . ." Tommy paused, "that she had something to do with John oversleeping, do you?"

"Well somebody must have done something to him. Nobody oversleeps with this kind of money at stake," Pat said.

"She couldn't have, no way she would do that for us, I hope," Tommy said, starting to feel sick at the thought of pushing Jenny to such an extreme.

"She could and would," Pat stated flatty, knowing she was such a good friend to Tommy and Pat she'd do almost anything.

"If she did, it could ruin us. It could ruin her. I can't think about that now. What are you going to do?" Tommy asked. "We could watch carbon prices until the market closes."

"Haven't you—haven't *we*—done that enough? Besides, there is nothing we can do or change," Pat said.

"Good point. So, you want to get a beer? Some place outside?"

"Together?" Pat asked.

"Eh, what the hell. It will give Kyle and Doug something to do. Do you see either of them?" Both men looked up and down the street and peered into a small restaurant next door, not seeing either of the two men who had occupied the periphery of their lives for months.

"Maybe they're giving up on us," Pat said, somewhat hopefully, but knowing full well that wasn't reality.

"I doubt that, but who knows? Besides, we won't be talking about trading," Tommy said.

The two friends walked less than a block, sat down at the first outdoor table they saw and ordered a beer. They sat there for hours, talking about family, friends, and college. Reminiscing about their youth reinvigorated their bond, and somewhere inside each of them, they realized that loyalty, friendship, and history outweighed all of the recent events. But still, somewhere even deeper within them, they each thought about Jenny and what might have happened with John. But they didn't talk about it. Neither gave a thought to Mark or carbon markets. That could wait until tomorrow.

48

Tommy's wait for sleep and for Friday seemed interminable. He went for a run and sat down in his kitchen for the breakfast that he picked up at the corner coffee shop. Trading had opened shortly before he fired up his laptop and Tommy noted the market ended up eight percent for Thursday and was already up in Friday's early day trading.

Tommy thought about John. He must be out of his mind and maybe just hours away from losing all or most of his money. Tommy wasn't getting nearly the pleasure from this knowledge that he expected. In fact, he just felt bad. Tommy had spent so much time hating and blaming John that he never fully accepted his responsibility for the mess. He was greedy and selfish. Seeing how badly the relationship with John ended reminded Tommy of him and his step dad. Tommy had originally thought that he could fix him too, just like John. Tommy had let things go to hell before his stepdad died without ever making things right. Maybe he didn't need to do that with John, too.

Today was a new day, he thought, and he needed to change, or he would never have a chance with Jenny. She deserved and would demand better than the bitter person Tommy was becoming. Maybe he could convince Mark to somehow ease the pressure off by working out a deal to let Pat sell to John at a discount to the market so John could walk away other than broke. Mark had made his point, the market was stabilizing, and he had won. There was no reason to completely bury John.

Tommy picked up the phone and dialed. The voice on the other end was clear and professional. "Good morning. This is Mark Schmidt's office. May I help you?"

"Yes, this is Tommy Gardner. Can I speak with Mark?"

"No, he's not available. You can leave a message . . . wait, I see he can now take your call via his cell phone. Please hold. I will connect you."

Mark picked up immediately. "Surprised you are calling, but I have something to cover with you, too."

"Yeah, I've been thinking a lot, and I would like to talk, but not over the phone. Can you meet me in the next hour? It's urgent."

"Well, I can meet you, but at the University of Chicago Hospital. Evidently there's been an accident. It's John," Mark said.

"What happened?" Tommy asked.

"I'll find out and tell you when you get here. They just reached John's brother now. They had contacted me first because they found my business card in his pocket. It was last night. I just arrived at the hospital," Mark said.

"I'll meet you there," Tommy said and hung up. He felt sick. His first thought was suicide. Had he driven John that far? Regardless, it had to be his fault. He went into the bathroom, threw up his breakfast, got dressed, and took a cab to the hospital.

As he exited the cab, he was hopelessly disoriented. The hospital buildings appeared to be shoehorned in one addition after another. After two false starts at reception desks in other buildings, Tommy found the right waiting room. John had been transferred from emergency to ICU. He scanned the waiting room to see Mark in the corner, facing him, and talking to a woman.

Tommy approached, catching Mark's eye, and he and the woman both turned to him. Tommy was shocked to see it was George's widow, Deb. Tommy said, "Oh, hey, uh, I'm surprised to see you here. How are you doing?"

Deb said, "Mark called me. He knew that I wanted to talk to John. I was just waiting for the right time. Now I'm worried that I won't get that chance."

Tommy turned to Mark, confused by Deb's comments. "Is it that bad?"

Mark said, "It appears so. There was a car accident, and his body was crushed. We'll know soon from what I have been told." As Mark finished his sentence, Deb turned and slowly shuffled away to stare at the snack vending machine. She was waiting around for something, but Tommy couldn't tell what.

"So . . . I wasn't aware that you even knew Deb," Tommy said.

"I've been communicating with her a bit since George's death. I met her a couple of times through George," Mark explained.

"Oh, um, that's nice of you," Tommy said, still slightly confused by the relationship.

Deb returned with a very hard and dry granola bar and asked Mark if he'd take a walk, but in a tone that didn't sound much like a question. He obliged, leaving Tommy alone. Since he hadn't even talked to a doctor or nurse, he didn't know exactly what he was waiting for, but he waited, and waited, and waited until Deb and Mark finally returned.

Deb, Mark, and Tommy didn't speak at first. They each stared mindlessly at their phones, moving about the waiting room, avoiding conversation and each other. Finally, an individual who looked surprisingly young for the name tag, "Dr. Montgomery—Surgery" came up to Mark. Clearly, they had spoken previously. The doctor spoke first. "John's brother won't be in town until tonight, and he authorized me to be able to share with you any relevant medical information. He wasn't close to John and figures that you people are."

"Well, what can you tell us?" Mark asked.

"Well, I'm afraid to tell you that the timing of his brother's arrival really won't matter much. Mr. DeFallo's injuries are too severe. To tell you the truth I have no idea how his heart is still beating. Pretty much other than his heart and lungs, his organs are mush. He will die soon." Mark, Deb, and Tommy were startled by his candor, and they hoped that his bedside manner improved before John's brother arrived.

"Can we see him?" Deb asked.

"It's a bit unusual because the family isn't here, but his brother did send a release, so it clearly shouldn't be an issue," the doctor said. "I'll have a nurse escort you."

The three entered cautiously. John was unconscious, but looked to be resting comfortably. That is, if comfortable could occur with tubes up one's nose and mouth and wires extending from all parts. The sucking and clunking of the breathing machine went unnoticed.

Deb went around the far side of the bed. Mark and Tommy watched her attentively from the side nearest the door. The nurse had barely given them a look before moving on. The sun rushed in through the window, making John and Mark look old under the glare and Deb look younger, as the glow from behind her was ethereal. It also drowned out details, including any emotion on her face.

She started to talk to John, keeping her arms folded in front of her. "Well, it looks like I won't be able to follow through fully on a request George made, but at least one of the two of you will get this message." She glanced at Tommy as she ended her sentence, including him in on what was to come next. Deb continued, "George wanted me to relay a simple sentence to you both. He said I would know when the time was right. I'm guessing that time was coming very soon, probably even today from what Mark has told me." She appeared calm, and she continued, "A couple of days after George died I received a note in the mail in his handwriting. Among other instructions, he said that he loved me and our children, and he would do anything for us. I never showed the police, and if you push me, I will deny that I ever received it."

Tommy's heart was pounding, but he didn't understand why. Tommy couldn't wait any longer to speak. "I assume there was also a message for me and John . . ."

"Yes," Deb said. "The message to both of you was simple, 'I went to a doctor. I knew.'"

Tommy stepped back from the bed. His eyes darted around the room. Mark watched him calmly, closely. Deb looked somewhat satisfied by the confusion on Tommy's face, then nodded to Mark indicating that she was going to leave the room, and for that matter, the hospital. Tommy didn't even see Deb leave. He was still trying to process that short statement. Tommy remembered hearing from Doug that George had terminal cancer, but everyone had assumed that George didn't know. Mark closed the door and took up Deb's spot on the opposite side of John's bed from Tommy.

It took only those few more seconds for words to start pouring out of Tommy's mouth, much more for himself than for Mark. "George went to the doctor . . . so he knew he was dying . . . he wanted to take care of his family . . . my god, the business had a ten-million-dollar policy on George. The business got half and Deb got half. So, George killed himself or had himself killed?! That doesn't make sense. He could have just waited and gotten the money for his family when he died if he was that sick." Tommy paused as he continued to process things. "But of course, if we sold before he died, the policy would have ended. And if we did try to sell, he must have known this whole mess would have been uncovered before the sale closed, and he wouldn't have gotten a dime. Jesus, not only must he have been behind the falsified trades, he set me and John up to go after each other. My god, once he knew we were selling, it was the only way he was going to get any money for his family ..." Mark continued to watch Tommy try to make sense of it. "But you can't throw yourself into a tree . . ." Tommy finally looked up at Mark. "You helped him, didn't you? You killed him!"

Mark was still very calm. He had the benefit of time to think this exchange through. "George asked me for a couple of favors, and I obliged. I set up and attended a meeting, but it's not what you think," Mark said.

"You had him killed!" Tommy screamed.

"I didn't say that, and I didn't do that. I facilitated an introduction or two as a favor to George. Then I get an anonymous call that there is evidence that my facilitation ended up with George being killed, so now I'm an accessory to murder if this thing ever comes to light. Oh, and by the way, if you don't keep it together, this conversation will end sooner than I'm guessing you want it to."

"Okay, so he was going to die a slow and painful death. He also most likely would have died when the insurance policy expired, so you helped him kill himself," Tommy said.

"Not knowingly," Mark said.

"But why put me and John in the middle of this? The incriminating voicemail message to me? Doing it right in John's backyard? We took good care of him," Tommy offered. "That part must have been your idea. You wanted me and John out of your hair. You knew what George had done to our business and set this whole thing up! You knew that we would have to come crawling to you when we found out about the falsified trades. And with the deal you cut for McKinstry stock . . . that will be worth hundreds of millions, you son of a bitch!" Tommy was enraged, but somehow restraining himself. He knew one more blow-up and Mark would just walk out, and then Tommy might never learn more about what happened.

The two men spoke quietly, but intensely, like nothing else in the world existed for those few minutes. Neither thought anything about how strange it might appear to be talking over John's mangled body.

"George and Deb felt like neither of you ever treated him as your partner. You moved him around, tossing him a few hundred grand each time one of the two of you made tens of millions. He thought it could happen again unless he did something about it. I did figure George was up to something, so I put things in place to own a good chunk of McKinstry if my hunch was right but I didn't know exactly what he was doing. What he did was his business and his idea, not mine," Mark said.

"Even if that's true you still screwed me and John out of our business."

"George screwed you out of your business. I was just around to benefit," Mark responded coldly.

If what Mark said was true, Tommy could start to see more of the vindictive genius in George's plan. He knew given Paul Smith's death that a second accident would result in Tommy being a suspect. Maybe George was even in on framing Mark. It would be good to have a guy with that kind of power on your side and in a position to clean up any loose ends. George probably wanted that to make sure Deb could hang onto the insurance money.

"So, was George John's partner in Big Mountain? Was he RD Partners? Did he take this thing that far to pit John and me against each other?!" Tommy asked.

"No. It had to be someone else. George couldn't afford to have that money trace back to him or Deb. The insurance money was all that he could get, but he was clearly behind the falsified trades. Maybe this whole thing was the brain cancer messing with his thinking. I just don't know," Mark offered.

"You helped a guy kill himself. You're a felon, and you should go to prison."

"Oh, and you're not?" Mark shot back.

"Murder and finance are two different things," Tommy reasoned.

"There is more going on here than you can handle. Don't you get it? With what just happened to John, things have escalated."

"Is that supposed to scare me away?"

"If you were smart, it would."

"If I go away now, then you are one of the winners in all this," Tommy said.

"Well, financially, but someone knows that I helped George and I could have an accessory to murder hanging over my head forever," Mark explained.

"Who knows?" Tommy asked.

"Who do you think?"

"RD Partners? Tell me who that is," Tommy demanded.

"Whoever it is was willing to kill John. Do you think they'll stop short of taking you or me down? Probably the only reason I'm still alive is that I need to clean up this mess, and they have me over a barrel," Mark said.

"Or you are playing me."

"Do you want to take that chance?" Mark asked.

"Listen, you son of a bitch. You're not going to get away with this," Tommy was growing more animated.

"Do you really want to do this again? Go down this path of revenge? Best case scenario is you prove it was suicide, and then the insurance company takes the money away from Deb and her kids. Or if it gets pointed toward me or RD Partners . . ." Mark paused and glared at Tommy. "Might be time for you to let go and move on."

"I don't think so. You'll be hearing from me," Tommy growled through clenched teeth and stormed towards the door.

"Suit yourself, but that girlfriend of yours isn't going to wait forever for you to get your head out of your ass. Plus, next time, it might be you or me in this bed," Mark said.

"Keep with the threats. That will only get me more motivated to follow through."

"When it turns out that John's car was tampered with, or that someone ran him off the road, it will be one more strange event in an already bizarre situation. Do you really feel safe? You need to listen to me very closely. I'm sure I can help make this murder thing go away for you and the securities fraud charges too, but you and Pat need to do the right thing to make that happen. Otherwise, it seems like people close to all of this can end up with some bad luck," Mark said.

"That sounded like a favor, and another threat," Tommy said.

"I can see you taking it both ways," Mark said.

"How can you make this go away, and why should I trust you?"

"I do have a lot to gain financially if this market holds together, and I would like to stay out of prison, too. There are enough guilty looking parties to go around. Some well-placed calls or information leaks could have evidence pointing all over the place. An attorney looking for reasonable doubt could find an unreasonable level of doubt for their client, whoever that client happens to be. Besides, what's your alternative?"

Tommy glared at Mark for a second, then looked at John and gently closed the door behind him.

49

Doug really didn't have much of a life outside of work. Like many police officers and investigators before him, the job ate away a lot of who he was, leaving an empty spot Doug chose to fill with beer and more work. He had gotten divorced, and his kids grew up and moved out to the suburbs. Now the job that had cost him so much was the only thing he had left.

The night of John's car crash, Doug was sitting at his kitchen table with a beer, staring at an array of notes, pictures, and timelines. The pictures of George and of Paul Smith kept getting his attention. He had tried so hard to prove that there was a connection, but now he realized it didn't likely exist. Thanks to Kyle, he had other suspects. Mark and the two brothers from John's past had to be involved. If John was still tight with those brothers, how could he not know? Then there was John's mystery business partners with the forty million dollars and many other reasons to remain anonymous. He needed, somehow, to sort it out quickly; progress on the cases had bought him some extra time, but his job was still on the line. Doug turned up his police radio as he thought and stared and drank.

It took until the third mention of John DeFallo being transported to the hospital for it to register with Doug. The voice over the radio instructed the accident investigation team to treat it like a death-related accident. That obviously told Doug that John was in really bad shape.

Another dead body showing up was more than Doug could chalk up to coincidence.

Although it was after midnight, Doug picked up his cell and dialed Kyle. "Yeah, it's me. You want to go to an accident scene that I think is about to turn into a crime scene?"

"Yes. You want me to pick you up? My guess is you've had a couple," Kyle said.

"Just a couple, but that would probably be best," Doug said.

"Who got in an accident and where?" Kyle asked.

"John DeFallo, on Lakeshore drive, south of the loop," Doug said.

"I'll be there in ten minutes," Kyle said.

John was long gone to the hospital when they arrived, but four police cars and yellow tape had the area secure for investigators. Doug looked around, quickly spotted the lead investigator and approached.

"Good evening," Doug said. "Can I ask how it's going?"

"You can ask, but I'm not inclined to answer," the thin, tall lead investigator said.

Doug flashed his badge and stretched the truth saying, "This guy was a suspect in a murder investigation."

"Sounds pretty coincidental that he would get in an accident."

Doug extended a business card to the man. "Can you keep me in the loop, please?"

"Yeah, will do. I can tell you something right away. This is no ordinary accident. The car is pretty messed up, and I'm guessing from what I heard that we find paint from another car or his brakes were tampered with or maybe even his seat belt was compromised. He was thrown from the vehicle."

"So, what do you see?" Doug asked.

"It's not really what I see so far, it's what he heard." The investigator's eyes darted over to his left as he spoke. "You need to talk to the first cop on the scene. He's over there and you won't believe what he has to say." The investigator pointed to a young, clean cut Chicago city officer leaning against the hood of his patrol car.

"How is the crash victim doing?" Doug asked.

"Can't be doing well if they got me out here. Paramedics told the initial cops on the scene that it was bad."

"Thanks," Doug said, and he and Kyle turned away from the yellow tape, walking back toward the patrol car.

Doug flashed his badge and gave the young officer the same story that he told the accident investigator. The officer looked like he was barely out of high school, with short brown hair and a dazed look on his baby face.

"So, what can you tell me young man?" Doug asked.

"I've never seen a guy that knew he was dying before, so I don't know how one is supposed to act. But this was strange," the officer said.

"You talked to him?" Doug asked, totally surprised.

"More listened than talked. I was the first one here. Looked like the bottom half of his torso was flattened. He was pinned under his own car but still alert, at least for a minute."

"What did he say?"

"Well, first off he was freakishly calm. I was ready to shit myself, and dying didn't seem to scare him in the least."

"Yeah, well, what did he say?" Doug asked.

"He mumbled something about at least getting to see his wife again, then he paused and asked if I thought people that were murdered usually knew before they died."

"And?!" Doug said.

"And, that was it. I asked him if someone was trying to kill him and who it was, but he just stared at me and then passed out. I'm not sure he would have answered or knew."

"Jeez. Okay. Thanks for your time, and I wouldn't worry about seeing something like that again. You could be a cop for a hundred lifetimes and not have that happen." Doug turned to Kyle, motioning that they should leave.

"That's it?" Kyle said.

"Yeah, unless you know something about accident reconstruction. One thing I've learned about car accidents and fires . . . I don't know shit," Doug said.

"So, who do you think did this?" Kyle said.

"Take your pick. Mark. Tommy. RD Partners. I don't fucking know anymore. What do you think? Doug asked.

"I think I need to find out who RD is. That's been hanging out there too long now. Why didn't you make that a higher priority?" Kyle asked.

"Why didn't *you*? I told you that I couldn't figure it out," Doug insisted and then continued. "You'll know when you try to track it down, it's not easy. Plus, until John's accident there was never a decent tie to a crime."

Could be a falling out. A fight over money. That's enough money to cause some problems," Kyle said.

"Well, you chase that down then. I'm going to the hospital," Doug said, then hesitated. "Well, I'll go in the morning. John's not going anywhere."

"I'll take you home and head to the office," Kyle said.

"It's the middle of the night."

"I have to track down this other owner, and I won't be able to sleep until I do."

"Suit yourself. My bet is it's a dead end."

After dropping Doug back off at his apartment, Kyle pored over his files and the state business incorporation database. The path back to John DeFallo was easy to find as he had before, but the other owner eventually always circled back to the company name, RD Partners. There was one shell company after another incorporated in different states, all with post office boxes, until Kyle finally found an address for the law office of Young & Erickson.

It was six in the morning, and Doug would probably be getting up soon, Kyle thought. After six rings, Doug whined. "What the hell do you want?"

"Hey, I've been up all night. Don't get testy with me. Does the law firm of Young & Erickson mean anything to you?" Kyle asked.

"Young & Erickson is where Tommy's ex-girlfriend works. You met her the other day when we had Tommy and Pat in. They represented Tommy when this whole mess started," Doug said.

"Well, the firm represents RD Partners. We need to find out who RD is."

"Yeah, no shit. We find out who and we may have our killer. You want to pick me up at eight and we can head over to the law office?" Doug asked.

"We should do that. I suppose you think RD is short for Tommy Gardner," Kyle said sarcastically.

"Hilarious. Maybe because it's early in the morning, but I don't know what to think anymore."

Kyle and Doug were escorted to a conference room at Young & Erickson. It was the same room that Tommy had spent many hours in, squirming and fighting to stay out of jail just four months earlier. Susan rushed in, skirt and blouse tightly cut, her ponytail typically securely bound. "What can I do for you gentlemen? I'm assuming it might have something to do with Tommy Gardner," she said.

"Yes, how'd you know?" Kyle said.

Susan hesitated, thinking she should just let the dumb question go unanswered, but instead, she said, "I don't have many clients, actually former clients in this case, that attract police interest and only one who attracts the police and securities' people. What can I do for you?"

"Are you familiar with, or did you set up a corporate entity, RD Partners?" Doug asked.

"No, never heard of it," Susan said.

"That's surprising, since your firm set up a series of shell companies, one of which owned one-half of an entity with John DeFallo."

Susan immediately grasped the potential ramifications implied in that statement and became much more engaged in the conversation.

"I'm sure we didn't represent Mr. DeFallo. That would have been a clear conflict with our representation of Mr. Gardner when they set up their business," Susan offered.

"Why don't you try really hard to help us out here, because even representing RD, whoever that is, opposite Mr. DeFallo looks a little problematic given his relationship and history with Mr. Gardner," Doug said, and added, "and now Mr. DeFallo is lying in a hospital."

Doug was surprised how little the whole conversation phased Susan as she started to speak again. "I do remember John being in here a couple of times, and I even mentioned it to Tommy once."

"Can you remember anything else?" Kyle asked.

"Normal work comings and goings. Wait, there was a woman. Really well-dressed, always in red," Susan said.

"Might RD be red dress?" Doug asked.

Without answering, Susan opened her laptop and typed RD Partners into the firm's client cross-check software. Although Susan actually knew what would come up, she had to go through the motions. RD Partners was a client of her boss, Sam Meyers, Young & Erickson's managing partner. "Ah, gentlemen, I can't share anymore with you. I have to go," Susan said.

"Wait a minute. You can't just go. Is Tommy behind this?" Doug asked.

"All I can tell you is that Tommy has nothing to do with RD Partners, and you need to talk to our managing partner, Sam Meyers, if you want to continue this discussion."

"Is he in?" Doug asked.

"I'll check, but I doubt it. Good luck to you, gentlemen," Susan said and disappeared.

With one brief interaction, RD was confirmed as a prime suspect for John's murder, if it turned out to be that, and Doug and Kyle were also thinking quite possibly George's. They stared at each other, too exhausted to discuss the possible scenarios running through their heads. They walked out knowing that Doug had more legwork and Kyle had more research to do. They had a follow up scheduled for later in the day and would talk then.

Doug headed over to the hospital where John was in ICU. It was late morning Friday after the accident the previous night. Doug figured if nothing else, he might run into family or friends of John's and start digging a little. He knew that would be risky since this was still an accident, but he just had a feeling it would be worth the trip.

As Doug entered the ICU waiting room, he passed Deb as she was leaving after her brief conversation with Mark and Tommy. Doug knew she looked familiar but couldn't place her until the picture of George's wife from his file flashed into his head. He was puzzled by her presence there, but had more pressing things on his mind.

Doug got more than he expected when he came around the corner and saw Tommy and Mark through the ICU room window, talking right over John's body like he wasn't even there. He thought he heard Tommy say something about murder, but didn't know for sure. Doug thought about going in, but he stood by the closed door and listened. The men started to talk more quietly, so he couldn't make out another word. There was nothing he could do at that moment because he preferred to separate Tommy and Mark for his questions. It was a nice day, and Doug had recently taken up smoking again, so he figured he'd grab a cigarette and wait outside for Tommy or Mark. Soon after Doug lit his smoke and took a drag, Tommy blew out the door, still reeling from the info from Deb and confrontation with Mark.

"Hey, Tommy, what's the hurry?" Doug asked.

Tommy's hair looked like he had grabbed fists of it and tried to pull it out. He focused on the ground five feet in front of him, totally unaware of his surroundings. Clearly something had gone on in the hospital, and Doug knew it. "My God, what now?" Tommy said.

"Do you really need to ask what now? Another dead body—well, near dead body—in your wake."

"Come on, I have nothing to do with this," Tommy said.

"Not so sure about that. They all start out as accidents with you. My guess is this one ends up as something else, just like George and the guy before him."

Tommy had to admit from Doug's perspective, this was looking pretty bad. "Listen, if you knew what I knew, you wouldn't be looking at me for George, or this, or anything else," Tommy said.

"Really. Enlighten me, then," Doug said sarcastically.

"I can't. I won't . . . I don't really know for sure. Why don't you talk to Mark or George's wife or John's business partner?" Tommy offered.

"Where the hell did that all come from?" Doug asked, trying to look surprised, but knowing he was struggling with the same questions.

"Oh, I don't know, maybe finally take the advice I gave from the beginning, and follow the money! I'm out of here since I assume you're not taking me in again."

"No, you're free to go," Doug said. "I'll wait until after the accident investigation guys tell me that it was no accident."

"You do that. Then, I'll tell you again where to go . . . looking," Tommy said and turned, nearly running down the sidewalk. There was nothing left for him to do at the hospital. He headed home broke, exhausted, and confused about all he had learned at the hospital. He knew now that George had been behind the false trades, too. Tommy wouldn't believe it—he couldn't believe it—but in the back of his mind, it made everything else make sense.

50

Tommy sat down the next morning with a large cup of coffee at his favorite table at the little coffee shop a block from his apartment. The smell and sound was the same as every other coffee house in the city, but this one looked more like someone's grandmother's house with old worn fabric furniture, thin spindled tables, and framed chairs with stuffed fabric seats. Tommy adjusted the time of day that he came throughout the year to match the one precious hour a day where the sun rose over the building across the street and snuck in under the canvas window canopy.

Tommy sat down to read a book. A novel of fiction, no less. He had to do something besides drinking and pills to take his mind off his troubles. He never read without purpose. Enjoyment wasn't purpose. He was bored within minutes and looked up to see Doug, yet again. This time he saw something different as Doug approached. Instead of plopping himself down uninvited, he walked up, and then stood by Tommy's table for a moment.

"May I join you please?" Doug asked.

"Yeah. I guess," Tommy answered.

"Thank you. I thought that it would be a good idea for us to talk outside the precinct and in a more civilized manner for once. What do you think?" Doug asked.

"Given how those conversations have gone, I guess it can't hurt,"

Tommy said. "But I have to tell you, congenial looks pretty creepy on you. What changed since yesterday?"

"You know, Tommy, I have never talked to a potential felon on a case I was working as often as I have talked to you. I just wanted you to know that this is—you are—a personal record for me."

"Uh, okay . . . thanks?" Tommy muttered, still surprised by the dynamic of the conversation.

"Well, I have been trying to figure out why a guy would do that as often as you have without an attorney. For a while I knew that your issues with attorneys because of your dad's death would keep you coming back, but that doesn't explain all of your actions. Either you are guilty and ridiculously arrogant, or you don't have anything to hide."

"I'd like to believe that I am in the second category, but what do you think?"

"See, therein lies the problem. I might not be the best detective in the world but I can read people pretty well, and it seems like you are innocent, arrogant, *and* guilty," Doug said.

Tommy thought for a few seconds before speaking again, noting Doug's demeanor and the fact that Kyle wasn't with him. He decided to take a bit of a chance. "Well maybe I am a little of all of those things. I can tell you that I didn't kill anyone or have anything to do with anyone dying."

"Why do I get the arrogant and guilty vibes, too?" Doug asked.

"I am not saying I'm guilty, but on the securities side, maybe, just maybe, you are picking something up there."

"I'll let Kyle worry about that, but I am rethinking the murder side of things and solving the murder is my primary concern," Doug offered.

"About fucking time!" Tommy exclaimed.

"Don't get ahead of yourself. You are still a person of interest, just not of much interest," Doug said, and he rose and headed for the door.

Doug hoped that the conversation would get Tommy more in the mood to help with the murder investigations. He also knew that it would likely shut down Tommy's willingness to cooperate on the market charges, but that wasn't his case or problem. He headed back to the precinct to catch the live video feed of the interrogation in Whitefish of the brothers with ties to Mark and John.

A Chicago PD IT guy had rigged up an interrogation room with two laptops, each paired with a speaker phone. The laptops each showed two camera views. In one room, Rick was on one side of the table with his attorney and officer Murphy on the other. The second laptop showed Ron in another room waiting alone at a table across from an empty chair. Doug was informed that the attorney was very well-known locally and well compensated; someone way out of the brother's price range, but who would be representing both men. The attorney's presence made it evident that this ran deeper than the two brothers. The instructions were simple . . . only have one mic open at a time. Green light, mic is on. Red light, mic is off. Doug didn't appreciate the condescending tone of the young IT person who probably figured that Doug barely knew how to turn on a cell phone. Activity on camera started before Doug could vent his frustration.

"Please state your full name and why you think you are here," Officer Murphy said.

"Richard Sparks, and I have been asked to come in because I was skiing the same day that this George guy, whatever his last name was, died, or was killed," Rick said.

"George Shannon," Officer Murphy added.

"Yeah, him. Seemed like a nice enough guy," Rick said.

Officer Murphy was surprised by the response, but quickly countered, "You admit to knowing George Shannon?"

"Yes. Well, I met him that day. Ran into him on the slopes. I can only assume that you would have figured that out sooner or later. There are quite a few cameras out there," Rick said, glancing at his attorney for approval.

"Where, exactly, on the property did you meet him?" Murphy asked.

"I don't recall. Wasn't a big deal at the time." Rick was quickly getting comfortable but stayed alert for cues from his attorney.

"And do you know Mark Schmidt?"

"Um, I'm not sure," Rick answered.

"Well, I have a traffic cam picture of you two," Murphy said as he slipped the picture in front of Rick and his attorney, who both looked slightly uncomfortable.

"Oh him, yes, Mark, right. Didn't remember his last name. He was checking up on John about some business deal. Wanted to make sure John was on the up and up."

"And was Ron with you in the back seat?" Murphy asked.

Rick hesitated, looking at his attorney, who seemed to move his head ever so slightly sideways, then Rick said. "I don't recall."

"So, you're trying to tell me that Mark came all the way out to Whitefish to do a reference check with you? Seems like that would be a pretty unusual thing and that you would remember who was there at the time," Murphy asked, feeling that he had Rick on the ropes.

"You would have to ask Mark why he was there and . . ."

Rick's attorney jumped in ". . . and Mr. Sparks has already told you that he doesn't recall if his brother was with him."

"Fine," Murphy said turning back toward Rick. "Do you know John DeFallo?"

"Of course. We go way back. High school," Rick said.

"When did you see him or talk to him last?" Murphy asked.

"This spring, toward the end of the ski season. I've been told it was a few days or so after this George fella died," Rick said.

Doug jumped in, sensing an opportunity and proceeding in his normal bulldog-like fashion. "Did you see or talk to John just prior to the murder? Did you talk about killing George?"

Rick was startled by the voice coming over the phone and then glared at the phone as he answered, "No, I'm sure that I hadn't talked to John in months, but maybe my brother had."

"So you're saying that maybe Ron had talked to John about killing George?" Doug asked.

"Hell, no. Just saying that he was closer to him, that's all. They talked every once in a while. Maybe even from my cell phone. Ron and I are often together, and sometimes he forgets his cell phone and uses mine. That would explain a call to John on my cell, if there is any," Rick said and again looked to his attorney for approval.

Doug was getting frustrated and thought the only way to get anywhere was to catch one of the brothers off guard. He wanted to focus on the original meeting with George. "You say you actually met George but don't remember where? That's pretty hard to believe. George was killed by someone left handed since the right side of his head was caved in. I can tell by the way you are drinking your water that you're left handed. You killed George Shannon, didn't you?"

Rick's attorney jumped in. "Since Mr. Sparks hasn't been charged, we feel that he has been more than cooperative here today, and you can either talk to Ron now or all three of us will be leaving."

As his attorney jousted with Doug, Rick's mind flashed to a vivid image of George from that day, standing in front of him, ready to absorb a fatal blow. Then, with the side of his head crushed just after Rick hit him, he remembered watching George grimly struggle to stay conscious, arms and feet buckling, with the emotionless look of a dying antelope in the crushing jaws of a lion. Maybe part of him wanted to live, but it looked clear to Rick that he was okay if he didn't. He then pictured George laying still for a second on the ground but being shocked and unnerved when he convulsed like a freshly caught fish flopping on a pier. Rick had replayed the images in his head each day since the murder.

"Before you go, can I say one more thing?" Rick asked.

His attorney nodded yes, knowing full well what was coming next.

"You see, one of your questions asked about my brother, and I don't want you thinking for a minute that I would roll over on him, even if he did something wrong. We are all each other has had through our whole lives. From baby daddies beating us, to juvie, jail, prison and every other stop along the way. I'd rather go back to prison than roll on my brother, and you can bet your life on that. And I'll bet my life that my brother would do the same for me." Rick finished and all except him left the room.

Ron gave a similar performance during his interview. He acknowledged his conversations with John, but he did not confess to knowing Mark. Unless they could find admissible evidence that the two had lied, Doug and Kyle had little hope of breaking either brother. Even if evidence pointed to one, the other would probably admit that they did it just to create reasonable doubt if it ever went to trial. Rick would likely say that Mark put them up to the murder, and Ron could potentially indicate it was John. On top of everything else, the attorney for the brothers handed the police in Whitefish a copy of the motion that they were filing to have the traffic cam footage and the ski tag scans thrown out as inadmissible because they were obtained without a warrant. Given the lengths that Kyle had gone to find the information, there was little doubt that the evidence would never see a courtroom.

Doug pushed himself away from the table, convinced that neither brother would ever flip on the other. It would be far more likely to get John or Mark to roll, but that was only if John lived. If he didn't, or wasn't involved, Mark would have little reason to cooperate and would likely soon know that key evidence against him would be inadmissible. Doug knew in his gut that Mark was somehow involved in George's death, or maybe even John's, but there was likely nothing that he could do to prove it.

51

Tommy was sure that all he and Pat needed to do to get out of this mess was to get out of the carbon business. He knew Doug wasn't going to pursue the murder charges, so all that remained for Tommy and Pat were Kyle and market charges. Mark couldn't afford to let that investigation linger. A second scandal was more than the market could handle. Mark had an industry and what now looked like hundreds of millions of dollars in McKinstry stock to protect. That was plenty of motivation and the resources to do just about anything to hold the market together and keep another scandal from surfacing. Pat would need to unwind the business and its holdings, but he was going to do that anyway. Easier for Kyle and others to put this behind them if Pat and Tommy weren't around. Mark would be on the phone in no time with Pat, working out a deal to buy all of the carbon offsets he owned. All Tommy needed to do was say the word.

If they were unlikely to get a conviction, Kyle and his bosses, along with Mark and everyone else involved in the carbon markets would want everything to be orderly. No need to spook or antagonize the market into large price swings. If all of this worked out, the industry would be indebted to Mark.

It irritated Tommy to think about that as the Hiawatha Amtrak headed north out of Chicago. Mark, the ultimate hero, even though he should be held accountable for whatever he had done wrong. It just didn't seem fair. Tommy thought about it some more as the Chicago urban sprawl faded and eventually turned to Milwaukee urban sprawl. Then again, what did he know for sure that Mark had done? Only that he facilitated a meeting that ended up with George dead. Getting the insurance money was the only way that George knew of to help his family and orchestrating the false trades was his way to get back at Tommy and John. Even if he told the police the story, there was no way he could prove it. And who would believe him anyway?

Tommy confused himself more with each passing mile. Maybe Mark killed John. John's money was already gone, and Mark had come out on top, but maybe he needed a scapegoat, or maybe John knew too much. If Mark was RD he couldn't afford to let John talk.

Tommy kept thinking back to the woman with John in Susan's law office who Susan had told Tommy about. He was paranoid at the time, and maybe rightfully. Was RD that woman? If so, Deb, Susan, and Barbara were the only women close to this whole ordeal to have been involved. Tommy didn't think Susan could be that vindictive. Deb wasn't involved enough in the business, nor did she have the resources to pull something like this off. Barbara had the resources but didn't need to get her hands dirty with this whole mess. However, she certainly could be manipulating Mark.

Tommy wasn't used to not having the answers, and he knew the truth was out there . . . somewhere. Thinking about it more, Tommy realized that if John died, Mark might be the only person left alive who knew who RD was, and he seemed truly afraid of something or someone when they were talking in the hospital. All of this was getting Tommy nowhere, and he knew that none of it would help the police.

Tommy knew that George had orchestrated the false trades and was probably working with RD. Presumably RD needed money to put the hedge in place, but why turn to John of all people? Maybe he was the only one who knew enough and had enough money to pull it off. It was all so bizarre. Tommy knew it would all finally make sense if he knew who the hell RD was.

It was shortly before the train arrived in Milwaukee when Tommy's phone buzzed with a text from Mark. It read, "John just died. Time to let go and move on with your life."

Tommy turned away from the text and was once again staring out the train window. Tommy believed Mark and thus had convinced himself that RD had killed John and was blackmailing Mark because of his involvement in George's death. Even if he was wrong, it didn't seem to matter anymore, and if he kept looking, he could end up dead, too. The danger was pervasive, and the worst part was that he didn't know where it was coming from.

By the time the train was wobbling down the last big turn in the tracks and into the station, Tommy knew he had no real choice. He had to let it go. Mark would have McKinstry buy all of Pat's credits and walk him through everything to get Pat his newfound wealth and get him out of the carbon markets forever. Tommy wouldn't end up in prison, and most importantly, he'd at least have a shot, he thought, with Jenny. He knew that if he went after Mark or RD, she would never forgive him.

Tommy headed out of the train station, walking east with the late afternoon sun warming the back of his neck and ears. As he walked, he dialed Mark's private cell number. After only one ring, Mark picked up.

"Have you decided? Are you moving on?" Mark said breathlessly without offering a 'hello' or waiting for a word from Tommy.

"Yes," was all Tommy said, and he hung up the phone.

Tommy texted Pat and simply said, *It's over. Mark will help cash you out.* Tommy figured it would be a couple of days before Mark and Pat wrapped up the details, and Pat would surely be back home as soon as he could, on his way to being the wealthiest man in a little town that was, in many other ways, already his—and Jenny's.

Tommy needed to go for a run, have a good meal, a restful night's sleep, hopefully, and Jenny needed some warning before he was back in town. It gave him time to think about what was next. From the time he saw Jenny in the upstairs bedroom at Pat and Mary's house, he had hoped for an opportunity to really show Jenny how he felt, especially now that he realized that he had buried his feelings for all of these years. That need was clear, but living in his little hometown for the rest of his life wasn't. Tommy was committed to finding a way to make it work with Jenny, and he thought that was all that really mattered.

Sleep eluded him again. If Mark was wrong, and John's death ended up being a suicide, that would hang over Tommy's head forever, and if Jenny had a role it in and found out, she would be devastated. In a perverse and selfish way, he almost hoped that it turned out to be murder. That would be easier to live with. Then he would only have to wrestle with the other aspects of what he did that directly or indirectly hurt other people, including John. Was it really fair to abuse his market ban for what he thought was right? The answers he was giving himself weren't helping. They lingered and festered in his mind like open blisters, oozing. And if losing all that money wasn't bad enough, he thought about all the other things that he could have done differently. He couldn't stop seeing John's face when he closed his eyes. He knew it might be a very, very long time before he got another good night's sleep.

Night forced a change in the weather that brought a glimpse of fall. Tommy knew he would have two perfect days to start the process of making things right with Jenny. He was surprised they even had a convertible at the rental counter, so when offered, he couldn't pass it up. Perhaps the wind would help clear the fog that a restless night's sleep had left behind. The dry air made it feel cooler than it was as Tommy headed north out of Milwaukee.

Jenny agreed to meet Tommy for a walk before lunch. She was about as anxious to see Tommy as he was to see her. They walked the beach north of town. Sandwiched between sixty-foot cliffs and the lake, they felt isolated, even though homes lurked above and just beyond their view.

Tommy started, "It's over Jenny. The whole mess is behind us. Pat's coming home a very rich man, and neither of us will be seeing the inside of a prison."

"I'm thrilled . . . and relieved!" Jenny said, "Now Mary and I won't need to kill you."

"I appreciate that," Tommy said.

"What about John and Mark?" Jenny asked.

"Mark has his work cut out for him to stay out of prison, but he's pretty resourceful." Tommy paused, "John on the other hand? I don't know quite how to say this other than bluntly. He's dead."

"Oh my god! What happened?" Jenny asked, her face contorting with fear.

"A car accident that, in all honesty, was probably murder," Tommy said.

"Who? How? Was it because of what I . . . what he did that day after we saw him in the park?" Jenny asked, fumbling her words, confusing Tommy.

"What did you do Jenny?" Tommy asked, remembering that neither he nor Pat saw her that night, and they knew she would do almost anything it took to help.

"Nothing. Just tell me why you think he got killed or who did it."

"Probably by his partner in Big Mountain Traders. It didn't have anything to do with that night, but do you want to tell me what happened?" Tommy asked.

Jenny looked relieved, and then said, "No. I don't want to talk about it. I will never want to talk about it. If you really love me, not knowing is something that you are going to have to accept."

Tommy wanted desperately to know what she did with John. Did she drug him or sleep with him? It took everything he had not to ask more, and he could tell that Jenny would not answer anyway. He changed the subject, "I love being by the water. I can't imagine living where I couldn't see it every day. It lets me know that I'm not surrounded by people."

"Not surprised," Jenny said, happy Tommy had let go, but struggling to regain her composure. "Remember when we used to sit out behind the Memorial Union in college, staring at the lake?"

"Yeah, we talked for hours. You and Pat are the only two people I have ever talked to for that long and at that level."

"In all these years, no one? Not once?" Jenny asked.

"Not even close. Not friends or girlfriends, not my mom, and certainly not my step dad," lamented Tommy.

"I feel bad for you."

"Don't. I really didn't miss it. I mean, I can't ever see doing it again with anyone other than the two of you."

Jenny was uncomfortable with where Tommy might try to take the conversation and tried to make light of his comment. "You probably only liked it because we were high half of the time we had those talks!"

Tommy laughed. "That may have helped me open up a bit, I've got to admit, but it's not like we got messed up very often."

"True," Jenny agreed, "but remember the time we hauled your entire living room out onto Bascom Hill and sat there watching TV?"

"Yeah, we thought we were like art, or a statement, or something," reminisced Tommy.

"Or something seems most accurate, looking back on it," Jenny said. "Do you remember what else happened that next day?"

Tommy thought for a bit, then his shoulders slumped. He remembered kissing Jenny goodbye as he was leaving for a month in Europe. Goodbye was supposed to be for that month, but it turned into many months, and then, years. Eventually, Tommy was too embarrassed to make contact, and Jenny was too proud.

"I'm so sorry I never came back," Tommy finally said.

They looked at each other with tear-welled eyes, both overwhelmed with thoughts about what they had missed. The two walked together comfortably, quietly, knowing that they didn't need to speak to share this moment.

When they got back to town they decided to have a sandwich at a local bar. Both ordered chicken sandwiches and iced tea and took their drinks to a small, circular table. "So, do you want to do something together this afternoon?" Tommy asked.

"Well, I would, but I have plans," Jenny said.

Not wanting to be presumptuous or demanding yet again, Tommy said, "Okay, I know that you need your space, but what can I do to prove that you are my priority? That I want to be with you, here, now?"

"You have to do more than say it, so there's nothing else you can do today. Let's just enjoy our lunch and talk. I'm free all tomorrow afternoon if you're interested," Jenny offered.

Tommy wanted to say, '*What the hell do I do in this town until then?*' but opted for, "That's great. I'll pick you up after lunch if that's okay."

"It's a date," Jenny smirked. She finished her sandwich, gave Tommy a kiss on the cheek and was off.

Tommy decided to visit Mary in the afternoon. He could tell she was relieved that things were over in Chicago, excited that Pat was coming home soon, but Tommy didn't think that she had much of an idea about how wealthy a woman she was. Or, then he realized, she probably just didn't care.

After seeing Mary, Tommy checked into a little bed and breakfast and prepaid for a week. He would take Jenny's advice and get to know the town. He turned in his rental car and bought a used moped from a guy two doors down from Mary and Pat. He spent the rest of the day motoring around town and in and out of just about every restaurant and coffee shop. He waved to the old man he had met on his first visit back to town and nodded to one of Pat's daughters and her other friends. He was always drawn to stop and talk to them but as had become his custom, fought off the urge, figuring the kids had no interest in talking to a weird guy who was putzing around town.

Mostly he talked to locals. Everyone seemed to know Jenny, Pat, or Tommy's parents. Most of the older ones wanted to know how his mom was doing. Tommy wanted to find out as much as he could about his hometown. He went to bed feeling good about how he had spent his day, but sleep didn't come easily again as thoughts of George, John, RD and Mark cycled through his head. He eventually drifted off to a restless sleep where he could no longer distinguish a dream from a thought.

Morning brought a spectacular day which Tommy greeted with a stop at the library and a moped ride to Jenny's. He parked on her front walk, rang the doorbell and attempted to mat down his windblown hair. Jenny opened the door and immediately noticed both the scooter and Tommy's unkempt hair and laughed. "That thing yours?" she snickered.

"Yep. Haven't owned a car in years. Thought maybe I needed to start small and work my way up," Tommy said.

"And you expect me to ride on that? We'll look silly. Plus, it's only built for one," Jenny said.

"Come on. It'll be fun. The cops in town must have something to do more important than bother us," Tommy said.

"Don't count on it."

"Probably true, but let's try it anyway," Tommy suggested.

"Is this just a ploy to get close to me?" Jenny asked sheepishly.

"No," Tommy said. "That's just an added benefit." They hopped on with Jenny questioning the integrity of the book rack on the back seat since it was holding up half her body weight. They took off with the overworked moped topping out at a whopping twenty miles per hour. Jenny didn't ask where they were headed and wasn't disappointed with a picnic table on the bluff overlooking the lake, town, and harbor. Tommy didn't know it, but this was one of her favorite places. He flipped open the seat to put his glasses in the storage compartment when Jenny noticed the book. *The Catcher in the Rye*, she said. "Why that book?"

"It's the only book I remember reading in high school. Thought maybe I should give it another read. Just trying to reconnect, I guess."

"Oh, really?" Jenny said.

"Yeah. I spent yesterday talking to people around town. I'm still trying to better understand this place."

"If you have to ask to know, maybe it's not right for you. Besides, are you seriously considering moving back here?"

"Why not? I don't assume *you're* leaving."

"Are you saying you would move back here for me?" Jenny asked.

Tommy grabbed both her hands, forced her to look him in the eye and simply said, "Yes."

Jenny pulled her hands away and said "You can't . . . not for me. You need to *want* to be here. Ahhh! That's way too much pressure. What if you and I don't work out?"

"Then, I'll move away. It's your town."

Jenny only needed a second to respond, having played out in her mind all of the possible scenarios of what Tommy would do next and her responses ahead of time. "Well, okay, then, I guess."

Tommy was caught off guard. "Okay, what?"

"Okay, you can move back here, and if it doesn't work out, you have to leave!" She said with a sly smile.

"That works for me."

"Three conditions. You get a job, a normal one, not breaking any laws."

"Okay, I need to do that anyway."

"Second, we need to stop whatever this relationship is, including sleeping together, for at least a few months," Jenny said.

Tommy reacted immediately. "Number two, I don't like!"

"You'll have to deal with it. I need time to figure this out, and you need time to decide what you are doing with yourself. I need to know you are staying because you want to be here," Jenny reasoned.

"Appears I have no choice. And what's number three?" Tommy asked.

"You can't just drop by my house. My dad is very sick, as you know, and he still hates you, as you may have guessed."

"I knew he didn't care for me, but didn't know it was that bad."

"Hate might be a bit strong now, but evidently a father doesn't forget when someone hurts their daughter."

"Even after nearly twenty years?"

"At least for my dad," Jenny said. "So, can you live with it?" Tommy reluctantly nodded in agreement. Jenny continued. "Let's go out and celebrate. Pat gets home tonight, and Mary is planning a welcome back party."

52

After spending the afternoon on his moped and walking around town, Tommy dropped Jenny back off at home and headed to the hotel to shower and change for the party. He got ready early and headed over to see if he could help with last-minute preparations. That was his excuse, at least, as he really wanted to talk to Pat before all the drinking, hugs, and back-slapping started.

Tommy knocked on the back screen door, and Pat saw him from across the room and yelled, "Tommyyy!" in a drawn out, low, frat boy kind of greeting. As soon as Tommy turned after closing the screen door, he was met with a bear hug that lifted him six inches off the floor.

Tommy squirmed out of his grip, "Okay, okay already!"

"Come on, what we did is pretty damn big," Pat said.

"What *you* did," Tommy reminded him.

"Come on. This wouldn't have happened without you letting go and moving on with your life, otherwise we'd still be battling with Mark. I'll make sure Jenny knows," Pat said. "And apparently you're no longer the number one suspect for anything in Chicago, which is great."

"So, you heard that from Mark?" Tommy asked.

"Yep, and Doug. He wanted me to pass along that he's retiring before they can fire him and try to take his pension. Thought maybe he would head to the suburbs to be closer to his kids and grandchildren. Before he retired, he convinced the CPD and feds to dedicate some resources to a small task force to investigate what happened to George and John. Looks like John's death was no accident, either, and they are investigating both Mark and RD Partners, but no one is completely convinced that charges will ever stick."

Tommy thought to himself that he needed to let Jenny know tonight that John was murdered. As bizarre as it sounded, it might ease her mind.

"So, did they figure out who RD Partners is?" Tommy asked.

"Yeah, I guess that Kyle tracked it down, but they sure weren't telling me. This kid is quite the wiz as it turns out. Got himself a promotion to a cyber security unit and is still going to help with the murder investigation," Pat said.

"Then why am I off the hook for both deaths, and why are both of us okay on the market related charges?" Tommy asked.

"Well, they had already figured that you didn't kill George, and it turns out that we were both under surveillance twenty-four seven when John died, which is a pretty good alibi," Pat said.

"Wow. Good to be watched, I guess, but doesn't that worry you about the market charges? If Kyle is as good as he seems, don't you think that he could make some charges stick to us?" Tommy asked.

"It would worry me except for all of the conversations with Mark and Kyle. I spent a fair amount of quality time with them over the last two days wrapping up all of the market positions the business had and closing things down. Mark said it wasn't that much different than the last time he had to clean up your mess two or three years ago when they had to sort through all the good and bad credits. This time around, McKinstry must have had at least fifteen people working on this full time for as many of the last forty-eight hours as they could stay awake. Wire transfers just kept coming into my accounts, and I just kept signing whatever they put in front of me. It was crazy."

"You sure? No chance this blows up? None?" asked Tommy.

"There were ten CFTC auditors and carbon market oversight people on this the whole time, too. So yes, I'm feeling pretty good. The whole thing was something to watch with Mark and Kyle working together, managing the two staffs. It was pretty complicated since many of John's positions were still open when he died, but they made sure the market was buttoned up tight," Pat said.

"Good. It makes sense. Look at all the money that was at stake. This market could go on for decades and be worth billions upon billions of dollars. Now that it's cleaned up, again, and stabilizing, no need for them to drag it through the mud anymore. Just like the first time with John and me, and the next time. Whether it's this market or a different one or a bank or whatever, greed prevails."

"That is pretty cynical, even for a guy like you." Pat hoped that Tommy wasn't completely jaded by all of this.

"Maybe, but it was also predictable. You were on the right side of a big squeeze bet because there were too many people out there who wouldn't let this market fail. This was a lot more than just Mark and McKinstry. Sometimes things are too big to fail, other times too important, and still others just too damn lucrative," Tommy said.

"Guess that's true. No other way to explain watching Kyle and Mark work together. They were working their asses off to get this cleaned up, and come next week, Kyle is going to be at work helping investigate Mark and others for murder," Pat said.

"Let them have at it, since things worked out for us."

"There's only one way left that I see this going to shit and that's if you can't keep your nose out of it," Pat said.

"No reason for me to go looking to do that," Tommy rationalized.

"Really? What if someday you find out who RD is? Do you think you can just let it go? Letting go isn't your strong suit."

"I learned my lesson. Whoever RD is, it's not someone I want to mess with."

"Well remember this conversation because I have a hundred million dollars, and neither of us is going to prison, *and* if you don't let it go you'll never have a chance with Jenny," Pat warned.

"I get it, and I'm so happy for you and your family. Have you stopped to think about what you have? You have everything—a wife and kids you love, a place where you are happy, and all the money generations of your family could ever need," Tommy said.

"I know. It's insane. This is all so surreal. Do you have any advice?" Pat asked.

"Yeah, don't fuck it up!" Tommy cracked Pat on the back, and then hugged him. He was genuinely happy for his lifelong friend.

"Exactly! That's all I can think about doing. I mean, not doing," Pat said.

"I know that this won't help, but not fucking up includes avoiding screwing up your kids and their kids, too, for that matter. Lots of responsibility there man."

"Right. And the responsibility to do something decent with this opportunity," Pat said.

"Hey, it's a bitch being rich."

"Plus, the guilt too . . ." Pat said.

"About me? Hell, take that off the list. I got what I deserved. Or is it about John? You didn't force him to come after you."

"But we did bait him into it," Pat said.

"That was on me, so let me lose sleep over that. Besides, whatever led to his murder wasn't our business. You should focus on the fact that all you did was help a friend, and it worked out well. You deserve it. You hung in there."

"Well, no one deserves this, but I'll take it," Pat said.

"Trust me, you deserve it if anyone does. Take good care of your family and Jenny."

"Aren't you going to be around to do that for Jenny?" asked Pat.

"I hope to be. Hell, if I end up being with Jenny out of this mess it will all be worth it." Tommy said.

"Will that really be enough for you? Pat asked.

"More than enough, my friend, way more than enough," Tommy

sighed and glanced beyond Pat. His life was out there, waiting for him. All he had to do was find it, and hope that it accepted him.

"Maybe you will get even more than you know. You know—me and Mary, the kids, this town, you know," Pat said.

"Is that really what you meant by 'even more?' I don't get it."

Pat panicked, knowing that Jenny would never forgive him for letting her secret slip. "Oh, that was a bit of an inside joke . . . with myself," Pat said and stared back at Tommy.

It wasn't close to the strangest thing Pat had ever said, so Tommy continued on, "Looks like I'll be around town for a while to find out. Jenny has me on probation, so I'll be settling down here, looking for a job," Tommy said.

"Great. How are you going about that?" Pat asked.

"I started with one of these software programs that are supposed to help me identify and nurture my strengths, and then find a job that fits."

"So, what did you learn?"

"Unfortunately, that I have no discernable job strengths," Tommy laughed a little. If he couldn't make fun of himself a little bit, he was definitely wound up too tight.

"Ouch, that is unfortunate."

"Yeah, evidently maniacal obsessions and a penchant for trying to control and manipulate people and situations aren't considered job strengths."

"How do you feel about being a delivery driver and warehouse manager? My old job is still open," Pat offered.

"Thanks, but I'm thinking that I could sell something. Anything."

"But you don't even like people. Are you sure that's a good idea?" Pat asked.

"For a while I could do it. We'll see. I've messed up so big and so badly that all I really want is a chance to make things right and to do better. That's all I need right now," Tommy said.

Pat listened and started to think about what the money and his new life meant to him, and how he and Tommy, in a way, had traded places. Giving it even more thought would have to wait as guests started to arrive, so they headed back inside.

As they mingled, the volume rose as one conversation escalated over the other. Pat was at the back of the family room when he saw Jenny enter the front door and survey the situation. When they caught each other's eye, Pat signaled her to go back outside, and they met up in the backyard.

"Well," Jenny said. "Welcome home. That was quite the ride from what Tommy told me. How does it feel to be the richest guy in town?"

"Not as good as I expected. I get all this money and you and Tommy get nothing," Pat said.

"We get each other if he wants."

"Yeah, what's this probation thing about? He'd stay if you just told him that you have a kid together," Pat stated.

"Hold on." Jenny got fairly close to Pat and glared at him. "I have a son who I raised. Tommy doesn't."

"Don't you think he deserves to know?"

"Oh, really? Why? Because we had sex one night?" Jenny's face darkened slightly as she spoke.

"Well, don't you think your son deserves to know who his father is?" Pat said, knowing that the few times they talked about this over the years he made inroads with this logic.

"He knows that his father is an old friend from college, and he knows someday, he'll get to meet him. That's been enough so far," Jenny said.

"Are you really willing to replay this again, just like after college?" Pat asked.

"Yes. Just like last time, he needs to decide he's staying for me, not because he thinks he has to stay. If he stays for me, he gets to be with his son now. If he doesn't, he'll get to meet him soon enough, when the timing is right," Jenny said.

"How long will you wait if Tommy leaves again?" Pat asked.

"Until my son is ready. Probably not long at all, but that will also be the day that it will finally be too late for me and Tommy," Jenny said.

"Too proud to ever give in?!" Pat said.

"Maybe, or maybe too naïve for wanting this to happen the right way . . . I am begging you, Pat, you can't tell Tommy."

"I haven't told him yet, although I almost slipped when Tommy and I were talking before the party," Pat said, "I'm not great at secrets or lying."

"Thank you. Just see if you can avoid the subject for a month or two, please. I suppose we should head into the party. You *are* the guest of honor," Jenny said.

As far as the crowd inside knew, Pat had made enough money to take a little time off and decide what he wanted to do next, and that he had done it to help an old friend. That's the way it needed to stay in a small town.

After about two hours and a few beers each, Jenny and Tommy finally ran into each other, literally, as they simultaneously turned away from separate conversations. "Hey, you want to get some fresh air?" Tommy asked. "This group is going to be going at it for a while yet."

"Sure," Jenny said, and the two walked out and sat at the picnic table where Pat and Jenny had talked earlier in the night.

Tommy started. "I was thinking about our conversation this afternoon. Why do we have to wait? Why should we waste more time not being together?"

"Let me ask you a question. Did you get what you wanted out of this whole crazy mess?" Jenny asked.

"Of course not. I never wanted to see John dead. I have to admit it, those few hours before the crash, when I knew he could lose everything, it didn't help. I finally realized all this time I was mad at him I should have been mad at me. Regardless of whatever he did, or George, or whoever, I fucked up," Tommy said.

"So, am I the consolation prize in all this?" Jenny asked.

"No, that's not what I said."

"Can you see why this can't happen now?" Jenny said, her shoulders slumping under the burden of her own words. As she stood up and grabbed Tommy's hands, pulling him up so they would be face-to-face. She locked her fingers behind his neck and pulled him close, their foreheads touching, and then they kissed. The intensity of the kiss startled both of them. Jenny broke it off and moved her hands down until both palms pressed against his chest. She pushed slightly to create enough separation to regain control of her emotions and looked Tommy in the eye.

"As I said before, if you still want to be here in a few months, come and find me. I can wait a bit longer, and if you have to leave, just say goodbye this time."

"I'm not going to leave," Tommy promised.

"We'll see," Jenny said, doubtful.

"How long is a few months exactly? Three?" Tommy asked.

"You'll know. Trust me," Jenny said, turning away from him. "Hey, I'll see you around town. I'll watch for the crazy guy on the moped. Tell Pat and Mary I said good night." With that, Jenny walked to her car, leaving Tommy unfulfilled.

53

Tommy walked out of a cold November wind, into a funeral home, and signed the book on the stand in the back hallway. This would be the first time in over two months that he had seen Jenny, and he spied her immediately. She was in a black dress standing with her sisters next to their dad's casket. James looked like every other dead person. He looked like George. He looked like John. He looked like his father. There was never enough makeup to cover the bluish-gray hue of death. His face was bloated from all the drugs pumped into his body over the last few months.

Tommy understood now why he and Jenny couldn't be together sooner. She needed time to be with her dad, and he now realized he needed the time to be with himself. Jenny caught Tommy's eye from across the room and she smiled slightly. The next thing Tommy knew, he was hugged from behind, although it felt more like he was choking and someone was giving him the Heimlich maneuver. Of course, it was Pat. Mary and the kids bustled up behind him.

"How's the job going, pal?!" Pat crooned.

"It's fine. Selling insurance isn't really my thing, but it's good for now because I need something, and I'm here to stay. I sold my condo in Chicago and rented a little house here in town. I've even been helping coach the high school football team, and I haven't popped a pill in over two months," Tommy said.

Pat glanced at Mary to get a nod of approval before he spoke. "Say, now that you are a permanent and upstanding member of the community, are you interested in a new job?"

"Pat, remember, we're playing by the rules here. I can't take any money or a job from you."

"Absolutely. So, I was hoping you would work with me at this new, non-profit foundation that Mary and I started. You can handle all the investments and finances, and I get to pick the organizations we work with," Pat explained.

"Pat . . . what did you do?" Tommy asked.

"We gave away the money. Put it into a non-profit foundation. All perfectly legal with a board of directors and all. I couldn't see paying taxes on all that money. Plus, it probably would have gone to my head, screwed up the kids and their kids. It would have gotten ugly. Remember our conversation?"

"You didn't give it *all* away, did you?" Tommy asked, baffled by this unexpected turn of events.

"No, we kept enough so that Mary, me, and the kids are set. The rest is in the charitable foundation. We can do some good things with it and take decent salaries. Nothing obscene. All legitimate."

Tommy smiled at the genius and the generosity of it. "I would like to do that. Thanks," Tommy said, and for the first time ever, initiated a big bear hug with Pat.

"Great. We'll work out the details, but I'm sure the board will insist on flexible hours so you can keep coaching and pursuing other interests," Pat said.

"Thank you," was all that Tommy needed to say. Then he noticed Jenny was taking a little break in the back room reserved for family. "I would like to pursue such an interest now, if you'll excuse me."

"Ha. Good luck," Pat said and slapped Tommy on the back, as usual, slightly too hard.

Tommy knocked lightly on the open door and waited for Jenny's permission to enter. "Come in and close the door," she said.

"I am so sorry to hear about your dad. How are you doing?"

"I'm okay. We had a long time to say goodbye. A long time to make sure everything between us was good. We even talked about you and what might happen in the future. The whole family had time. Today is more about closure for everyone else."

James had approached death coolly and calmly, knowing how he handled it was the last gift he could give his daughters. It gave them peace and strength to move on.

"I guess you knew back at Pat's party, didn't you?" Tommy asked.

"Yes, and thanks for respecting my wishes," she said.

"It wasn't easy. I wanted to see you every day, but you were right, I needed the time, too," he said. "And I know now isn't the right time . . ."

"Now is actually good because if it's bad news, I'm already in the mood," Jenny said, expecting the worst. "Are you coming to say goodbye?"

Tommy smiled. "Come on. You know that's not what I *want* to say."

"What *do* you want, Tommy?"

"I want you. I love you. Jenny, you're the only one in the entire world who makes me want to be a better person. I'm trying so hard to be that better person that you deserve. There's no place I would rather be than with you, right here, right now," Tommy said, and then smiled awkwardly as he thought about where they were.

Jenny could read Tommy so well she knew what he was thinking, "So you want to be at my dad's funeral?"

"You know what I mean. My god, your dad is probably really enjoying watching me struggle."

Jenny paused, looking a bit uncomfortable and said, "Tommy, I loved you then, and yes, as stupid as it is, I still love you now." The tears from both their eyes turned a long kiss salty.

"So, would your dad approve? Did he ever forgive me? Did he know before he died that we would be together?"

"He didn't forgive you until years after I did."

"So, you *do* forgive me?" Tommy asked.

"I forgave you as soon as I saw the son you gave me."

Tommy stared in shock at Jenny before slumping into a chair, struggling to comprehend what he just heard. Tommy sat in a daze and didn't notice Jenny going to the door, signaling her son to come in. Tommy regained some level of control and looked up at the boy, *his* boy, but still couldn't stand. He realized that it was the young man he had seen at the breakwater, the one with whom he shared a favorite quiet spot on the water, the bushy-haired kid who was a friend of Pat and Mary's kids.

Tommy finally stood up and faced him and said, "It's my honor to meet you."

"Likewise. I'm Jim." His calmness made it clear that Tommy was the only one who was really surprised.

"How long have you known?" Tommy asked Jim.

"Well, I always knew my father was an old friend of my mom's, so I kind of suspected for a while, but mom and I talked about it a few weeks ago with my grandpa."

Tommy turned to Jenny. "So, your dad knew, and he forgave me?"

"He said he was okay with it as long as you stick around this time. Otherwise, he thought he might still be able to 'reach out,' if you know what I mean," Jenny said.

"Who else knew?" Tommy asked.

"Well, Pat and Mary . . . since before Jim was born. That's pretty much it."

"And you were going to let me leave again? Without telling me?" Tommy was stunned that she'd let him go . . . just like that.

"Yeah. So, this is where I ask for your forgiveness. I am so sorry for not telling you. I took your opportunity to watch him grow up away from you, and that's not fair, but I knew that as soon as you found out about Jim, we could never be together."

Tommy turned away from both Jim and Jenny, his eyes darting randomly as he absorbed it all. Jenny looked pale and sick as she waited for Tommy to respond. He pivoted back, starting with no more than a shallow whisper, but his voice grew stronger as he continued. "I didn't deserve to know. I was too selfish, and if I did, who knows what might have happened. This is hard. I missed everything you two ever did or thought . . . I missed so much."

Jenny still looked scared. "Do you need more time?" she said.

"No," Tommy said. "You have given me so much more than I have lost. Now there are two people who I want to make proud of me, two people for whom I want to be a better person. I had no one before."

Suddenly, Pat burst into the room, looking like an excited kid on Christmas morning. He looked at Jenny and blurted out, "Does he know?"

"Well, it would certainly be awkward now if he didn't," Jenny said.

"True that!" Pat said playfully and turned to Tommy. "Dude, I'm so sorry for keeping this a secret. Jenny and Mary made me. No hard feelings, right?"

Tommy smiled and said, "I know it was them. No hard feelings. Hey, I have a son!"

"Yeah, and keep him away from my daughters! No offense, Jim, but I've been waiting a long time to say that," Pat said as he joined Jim, Tommy and Jenny. Tommy and Jim stared at each other briefly and hugged awkwardly. Jim walked back out in the main room sensing that the other three wanted some time to talk. As they chatted Mary entered the room and joined them and the four talked some more, enjoying their first moment united as parents.

Then there was an awkward pause as the reality of the funeral started to creep back into their minds and Jenny said, "I should get back out front. I suppose there are people wondering where I am."

Mary jumped in, "Yeah. It's actually a little weird out there. Some woman came in. Never saw her before. Looks like she has a bodyguard. Not local, so people were whispering."

Tommy looked at Jenny. "Maybe a friend of yours?"

"I doubt it," said Jenny.

Mary added, "No one I've ever seen around here, and who wears a bright red dress to a funeral, right?"

Tommy and Pat instantly locked on each other's surprised eyes and sprinted out into the funeral home's main gathering area, scanning the crowd. However, they didn't see anyone. Tommy bolted through the foyer, past friends, family, and strangers, almost knocking over a vase of sympathy flowers. In the parking lot, his eyes looked desperately for any sign of movement. There had to be something, somewhere. Then he saw it. A man driving a Mercedes. The man slammed on the brakes near the exit, just a stone's throw from Tommy. The person in the back seat rolled down the heavily-tinted window a few inches. She stared at Tommy with a cold, calculating glare, and he stared back in disbelief. It was Deb. *My god, it couldn't be,* he thought. The window closed and the car eased around the corner.

Made in the USA
Middletown, DE
20 July 2019